BLINDED

ALSO BY STEPHEN WHITE

STEPHEN WHITE

BLINDED

DELACORTE PRESS

BLINDED
A Delacorte Book / February 2004

Published by
Bantam Dell
A Division of Random House, Inc.
New York, New York

Book design by Glen Edelstein

Delacorte Press is a registered trademark of Random House,
Inc., and the colophon is a trademark of Random House,
Inc.

ISBN 0-385-33620-9

Manufactured in the United States of America

to Kate Miciak
for your vision, and your friendship

Every love's the love before
in a duller dress

—Dorothy Parker

PROLOGUE

SAM

Every cop knows the taste and the odor that assault the senses when tenderness collides with evil. It's a baby coddled in a bassinet in a fume-filled meth shack. It's the fractured face of someone's grandma after a purse-snatcher has done his thing. It's a pregnant woman bloodied and dead on the floor.

I'd been a cop a long time. I knew the aroma. And I knew the taste.

I did.

It may sound goofy, but I also believed that on good days I could smell the spark before I smelled the fire and I could taste the poison before it reached my lips. On good days I could stand firm between tenderness and evil. On good days I could make a difference.

*   *   *

What the heck is it about a woman sleeping? Okay, a woman who isn't your wife of double-digit years.

A woman was sleeping right beside me, no more than half a foot away. The spice of her perfume tickled the back of my throat, and the fire from inside her radiated right through my clothes. Yeah, I was paying attention to a thousand things I should have been ignoring. The intimacy of her breathing. The edginess of her eyes darting below their lids. The pure power of the rise and fall of her chest. The vulnerability of her slightly parted legs. They were all way too distracting to me.

Guilt about it all? A little maybe. Not that much. Not given what had happened already.

Still, I should have been looking in the other direction, out the window. I should have been watching for signs of the inevitable collision—for the arrival of the evil—because I knew that it was coming. I did. I could taste it in one tiny spot on the back of my tongue. Left side, all the way back where an oral surgeon having a very bad day had once hacked out one of my wisdom teeth.

I allowed myself a last greedy inhale of her tenderness—just one more taste—before I forced my attention outside. Had I missed something? Didn't look like it, no. But when I cracked open the window, I instantly detected tenderness in the air out there, too. Outside right on in, the tenderness was being swept along on the glorious aroma of a roasting Thanksgiving turkey.

I even thought I knew the bird. It was a big tom, twenty-two pounds. Traditional stuffing like my mom used to make.

Tenderness in here. Tenderness out there.

So where was the evil?

Where?

I could taste the turkey as though it were already on my lips, and I could taste her spice as though her sleepy head were resting on my chest. But I could also taste that tiny spot of evil on the back of my tongue.

She moaned just a little.

Inside, I did, too.

ONE

ALAN

Nine-fifteen on Monday morning. My second patient of the day.

Gibbs Storey hadn't changed much in the ten years since I'd last seen her. If anything, she appeared to be even more of a model of physical perfection than she'd been in the mid-nineties. I guessed yoga, maybe Pilates. Her impeccable complexion hadn't suddenly become pocked with acne or ravaged by psoriasis, nor had her high cheekbones dropped to mortal levels. Her blond hair was shorter but no less radiant, and her eyes were the same sky blue I remembered. The absence of any wrinkles radiating around them caused me to wonder about a recent Botox poke, but I quickly surmised that Gibbs's fair skin would probably never be susceptible to the tracks of age. She'd be in possession of some magic gene, and she'd be immune.

She'd always had beauty karma. Along with popularity karma. And the ever-elusive charm karma.

She didn't have marriage karma, though.

I'd first met Gibbs and her husband, Sterling, when they came to see my clinical psychology partner, Diane Estevez, and me for therapy for their troubled relationship. Diane and I saw them conjointly—a quaint, almost anachronistic therapeutic modality that involved pairing a couple of patients with a couple of therapists in the same room at the same time—for only three sessions. Ironically, with therapy fees being what they are and managed care being what it is, Diane and I hadn't done a conjoint case together since that final session with Gibbs and Sterling Storey.

After they'd abruptly canceled their fourth session and departed Boulder—"Dr. Gregory, Sterling got that job he wanted in L.A.! Isn't that wonderful!" Gibbs informed me breathlessly in the voicemail she'd left along with her profound thanks for how helpful we'd been—neither Diane nor I had heard a word from either of them. That was true, at least, until Gibbs called, said she was back in town, and asked me for an individual appointment.

Gibbs's call requesting the individual appointment had come ten days before, on a Friday. My few free slots the following week didn't meet any of her needs, so we'd settled on the Monday morning time. At the time she had accepted the week-and-a-half delay graciously.

In the interim between her call and her first appointment, I'd pulled her thin file from a box in the storage area that was stuffed with the records of old, inactive cases and examined my sparse notes. The few lines of intake and progress reports that I'd scrawled after the conjoint sessions told me less than did my memory, but I didn't need copious notes to remind me that Diane and I hadn't been all that helpful to Gibbs and Sterling.

Couples therapy is not individual therapy with two people. It is a whole different animal, more closely akin to group therapy with a radioactive dyad. Issues within couples aren't subjected to the simple arithmetic of doubling; problems seem to be susceptible to the more severe forces of logarithmic multiplication. Therapeutic resistance in couples work, especially conjoint couples work, isn't just the familiar dance between therapist and patient. Instead, a well-choreographed routine between husband and wife takes place alongside every interaction between either client and either therapist. Each marital partner knows his or her steps like an experienced member of a ballroom dancing pair. She retreats as he aggresses. He surely demurs as she swoons.

A couples therapist needs to learn everyone's moves before he or she can be maximally effective.

My memory of the Storeys' conjoint treatment was that Diane and I had only just begun to recognize their peculiar tango when they terminated the therapy and moved to California.

The first conjoint session had been a typical "what brings you in for help" introductory. "Communication" was the buzzword of the day in the care and feeding of relationships, and that's the culprit the Storeys identified as the reason they had entered into our care. Each maintained that they desired assistance "communicating" more effectively with the other. He was, perhaps, a little less certain than she of his motivation.

Neither Diane nor I had believed either of them. No, we didn't entertain the possibility that they were out-and-out lying to us—at least I didn't; I could never be a hundred percent certain about Diane—but rather we were waiting for them to approach the revelation that they might be lying to themselves, or to each other, about their reason for being in our offices. "Communication problems" was a socially acceptable entree to treatment—an acceptable thing to tell their friends.

But Diane and I weren't at all convinced at the time that it was the reason we were seeing the Storeys.

"Hi, Dr. Gregory," Gibbs said as she settled on the chair in my office for her first individual appointment. Her greeting wasn't coy exactly, but it wasn't not-coy exactly, either. "Long time," she added.

Her fine hair was pulled back into a petite ponytail. She smiled in a way that almost dared me not to notice how together she looked.

I nodded noncommittally. My practiced chin dip could have been measured in millimeters.

"I'm sure you're wondering why I'm here," she said.

Another microscopic nod on my part. Most days while doing my work as a psychologist, if I were paid by the word I'd go home a pauper. But Gibbs was right, I was wondering why she'd come back to see me after so many years. I had a guess—I was wagering that she'd divorced Sterling and had moved back to Boulder to start a new life. It was a scary journey for most people. Me? I was going to be the tour guide.

That was my guess.

"You remember Sterling? My husband?"

Husband? Okay, I was wrong. The Storeys were separated then, not divorced.

I spoke, but since it was Monday morning I failed to assemble a complete sentence. "Yes, of course" was all I said.

Gibbs raised her fingertips to her lips and leaned forward as though she were whispering a profanity and was afraid her grandmother would overhear. She said, "I think he murdered a friend of ours in Laguna Beach."

Okay, I was wrong twice.

TWO

The previous weekend.

I decided that I couldn't stand watching her struggle with the damn halo.

It just wasn't natural.

She hated it. And even for something as unearthly as a halo, it didn't look right on her. Maybe it was the size—did the thing really have to be that big?—or maybe it was the way it seemed to block her off from the world. Was that the intent? And tight spaces? No way. If she could squeeze through a narrow pathway headfirst at all, she ended up making enough of a clanging racket that she emerged hanging her haloed head in shame. I wasn't sure exactly what she hated most about wearing the damn thing, but I was absolutely sure that she hated it.

Still, I'm a psychologist not only by training but also by demeanor, and I was determined to help her live with the halo. Taking it off wasn't an option.

We had our orders.

I wondered, why not transparent material instead of opaque? Wouldn't that be an improvement? Maybe a rearview mirror would be nice. Or . . . wouldn't the plastic cone be more tolerable if it were just smaller?

And there was always duct tape. Couldn't I create some alternative with duct tape?

The ultimate solution hit me at a quarter to three in the morning in the utter darkness that divides Saturday from Sunday as I was soothing my year-old daughter back to sleep on the upholstered rocker in her room.

A paw umbrella.

I had to figure out a way to make Emily a paw umbrella. If I could shield her paw from her mouth, then she wouldn't have to wear a bizarre plastic Elizabethan collar to shield her mouth from her paw. A little over a week before, her veterinarian had excised a basal cell carcinoma from the top of her front left paw. Now the dressing was off so that the excision could be exposed to the air. Emily's only job was to let the wound heal without the aid of her big tongue and her copious saliva, a state of affairs absolutely in contradiction to a Bouvier's instincts, which dictated that her drool was the finest salve on the planet.

The halo effectively prohibited her from licking the wound. But the bizarre collar was making our dog morose. A paw umbrella was the obvious alternative. How hard could that be?

I explained my project to my friend Sam Purdy, who'd come over for a late-morning bike ride. We were sitting at the kitchen table in my Spanish Hills home. The Thanksgiving decorations embellishing all the stores in Boulder and the naked trees below us in the valley at the foot of the Rockies screamed late autumn, but the day promised to read more like late spring. Bright sun, clear skies, gentle breezes, and the guarantee of an afternoon in the seventies.

"I decided—I think it was sometime around four o'clock this morning—that I needed to use rigid foam to make the doughnut piece," I said. Sam didn't answer me. I thought he was trying to swallow a belch. The surprising part was that he was trying to swallow it;

Sam didn't usually allow social decorum to interfere in his digestive processes.

I proceeded to trace a circle about five inches in diameter and then began cutting a hole in the gardener's kneeling pad that I'd swiped from my neighbor's barn. "It has to hold its shape," I explained. "This foam will be perfect."

"Lauren won't care that you're cutting up her stuff?" Sam knew me well enough to know that if it had to do with gardening, it couldn't belong to me.

"It's not Lauren's. I stole it from Adrienne's shed. But even if it were Lauren's, she wouldn't care. It's for a good cause." Sam was a Boulder police detective, so I was demonstrating a modicum of trust by copping to a misdemeanor before lunch.

Adrienne was my urologist neighbor and the keeper of a sizable vegetable garden. Our unofficial deal was this: For the right to steal goodies from her plot at will, each August, using her tomatoes, I made a year's supply of fresh tomato sauce and roasted tomato salsa for her freezer.

Her tomatoes and basil and chiles, my kitchen labor. Communal living at its purest. I figured that the foam rubber I'd swiped would somehow become part of the annual accounting.

I cut a Bouvier-ankle-sized hole in the center of the disk of foam and then sliced from the center to the outside so I could close the contraption around Emily's lower leg like a handcuff or, more accurately, pawcuff. The thing I'd created was the size of a DVD, more or less, but the hole in the center was larger, more like the circle in the middle of an old 45 rpm record.

"Is Adrienne home?" Sam asked.

I was so distracted by my veterinary appliance manufacturing that I almost failed to notice his fingers pressing up under his rib cage. Almost.

"Why?" I asked. Adrienne was a good neighbor—she lived with her son in a big house across the dirt lane—and a great friend, but what I suspected was more germane to this discussion was the fact that she was also a fine urologist who had once treated Sam for a kidney stone.

"Nothing," he said. "I was just wondering."

I began laying out some rigid plastic craft strips that I'd swiped from Lauren's craft cupboard. Lauren wasn't particularly craft-y; supplies tended to age indefinitely once they made it into crafts storage. There was some Elmer's glue in there that I suspected dated back to Jimmy Carter's administration.

The plastic strips I chose were about two inches by four. To accomplish my design, I'd figured I would need to cover about 270 degrees of the foam circle with the plastic strips. With a pair of kitchen shears I began to turn my circle into a rough octagon to accommodate the attachment of the flat strips.

Sam rotated his neck. Up. Side to side. Back. His fingertips disappeared below his ribs again.

"Nothing?" I asked. "You sure?"

"I'm thinking I may be developing another damn stone."

I tried not to act obvious as I began using filament tape to attach the plastic strips to the octagon of foam, but I was watching Sam, too. Sam was usually stressed out, he was chronically overweight, he frequently ignored the diet that Adrienne had recommended after his first stone, and he didn't get enough exercise unless I dragged him along on an occasional bike ride somewhere. All in all, he was a prime candidate for a return trip down the river of agony that carried sharp little stones from the kidneys to the hellish port of *Oh my God!*

"I'm sorry. Does it feel like the last one?" I asked. I'm quite adept at keeping alarm out of my voice. I think I kept the alarm out of my voice.

"Not exactly. But then I've worked hard to repress the memory of the last one. Who knows?"

"Suppress. Not repress. If you have to work hard at it, you're suppressing. Repression is an unconscious act."

He snorted at me and shook his head. "Work on your damn paw umbrella. Don't insult me with your psychobabble."

I used a totally benign please-pass-the-salt voice to inquire, "How is it different this time?"

"I don't know."

He stood up but didn't go anywhere. He craned his chin upward, then side to side.

"Is your neck stiff?"

His face said it was. He added, "I must have slept on it funny."

"Adrienne's already gone for the day. She and Lauren took Jonas and Grace to the zoo in Denver. But I can probably reach her on her cell. Do you want me to give her a call?"

"Nah. I'll be fine. You almost done with that thing?"

I was taping the plastic strips together, sealing the gaps between them with filament tape. I figured any slender gap was a potential escape route for Emily's wily Houdini of a tongue. "Why don't you sit, Sam?"

To my surprise, he did. I noticed beads of sweat dotting his wide forehead like drizzle on a car windshield.

"You don't look too good. Let's bag the bike ride. Why don't I— I don't know, take you somewhere? Go see a doctor. If you're passing a stone, you're going to need some drugs. Given how bad you felt last time, some serious drugs."

"I'll be okay. If it doesn't go away in a minute, I'll take some Tylenol or something."

Yeah, that should help. And when you're done, I thought, *why don't you go put out a forest fire by pissing on it?*

He grimaced and twisted his neck some more. "Put that thing on her. I want to see how it works."

Taping the device to Emily's left front paw proved more challenging than manufacturing it had been. She didn't fight me; the halo was so humiliating to her that a multicolored Clydesdale-hoof-shaped paw umbrella was little additional insult to her doggie fashion sensibilities. I needed two different adhesive tapes from the first-aid kit and then had to reinforce the harness with an astonishing quantity of filament tape. But the thing ultimately held together and stayed where it was supposed to stay on her lower leg.

I told Emily to stand.

She didn't. She sighed.

I took the damn plastic halo off her collar and told her to stand.

She stood.

The umbrella hung over her wounded paw. The plastic strips stopped half an inch above the floor. Without delay her instincts emerged, and she leaned over to lick her open wound.

She couldn't.

She lay back down to lick her wound.

She couldn't.

She got back up and took a few tentative steps, offering a quick disciplinary nip at our other dog, a miniature poodle named Anvil. Anvil hadn't done anything to warrant the discipline. Emily attempted to discipline him at irregular intervals because she could and, she believed, she should.

Anvil, as always, was unfazed. I'd realized long ago that he didn't recognize discipline in any form.

"You know Jonas? Adrienne's son?" I asked.

Sam grunted in reply.

"He has trouble saying Anvil, so he renamed him, calls him Midgeto. I think it fits, don't you?"

Sam's eyes were shut tight. Apparently so were his ears.

Emily returned her attention to the multicolored umbrella on her paw. She walked in a circle as though she were trying to determine if the thing was really going to stay with her.

After a careful appraisal from multiple angles she stared at me, gave a little flip of her bearded head, and uttered a familiar, guttural, all-purpose murmur of approval. To the untrained ear, the noise probably sounded like an insincere growl. But since I spoke a little Bouvier, I knew differently.

Rarely in history have members of two different species been so enamored of the same invention. I loved the paw umbrella. Emily, our big Bouvier des Flandres, loved her paw umbrella.

Sam's opinion of the paw umbrella was more difficult to discern.

When I turned back to him to share our joy, I finally realized that he was having a heart attack.

THREE

Not wanting to alarm Sam unnecessarily with my
amateur diagnostic assessment, I excused myself,
walked then ran to the bedroom phone, and called
911. When I got back to the kitchen, Sam said,
"I'm a little better, I think."

I handed him a small handful of baby aspirin.
"Chew these, and come lie down on the couch in
the living room."

"What are they?"

"For once don't argue with me."

He chewed the aspirin and followed me the
short distance from the kitchen table to the sofa
in the living room. The hand that had been poking below his rib cage was now pressing firmly at
his sternum.

"You called for an ambulance, didn't you?"

I considered lying. But I didn't. I simply
nodded.

Anvil—Midgeto—jumped up on the couch
and snaked under Sam's arm to spread his lithe

body across Sam's lower abdomen. It appeared as though he was determined to be a little canine heating pad.

Emily rested her big head on Sam's thigh.

Sam absently stroked the dogs' fur and said, "You have good
dogs."

Sam and I rarely agreed on anything. But we agreed on that.

"Am I having a heart attack?"

"I don't know. I'm afraid you are."

"I don't want to die, Alan."

We agreed on that, too. I didn't want him to die, either.

FOUR

"I think he murdered a friend of ours in Laguna Beach."

I kept my gaze locked on Gibbs. Her words were as provocative as anything I'd heard in a therapy session in quite some time, but I was having a hard time not thinking about Sam.

Less than twenty-four hours earlier the ambulance had taken him to Avista Hospital, which was closest to my house in the hills on the eastern side of the Boulder Valley, not Community Hospital, which was only blocks from his house in the shadow of the Rockies on Boulder's west side. The cardiologist who worked him up in the ER and busted his clot with some cardiac Drano had scheduled an angiogram for the precise hour on Monday morning that I was seeing Gibbs Storey. At the moment when Gibbs told me she suspected her husband of murder, Sam probably already had a puncture hole in his groin and a long catheter snaking up an artery to his heart.

What would Sam, an experienced homicide

detective, do in response to Gibbs's revelation, were he sitting here with Gibbs and me? I wasn't sure. If I could have channeled his presence to assist in this interview, I certainly would have.

I could have said, *"Holy shit!"* in response to Gibbs's accusation of her husband, but I didn't.

Or I could've said, *"That doesn't really surprise me,"* because it didn't. Not totally, anyway. Sterling Storey was, like his wife, not only charmed but a charmer. I also suspected that he was a bully. Or more accurately, an intimidator. I'd seen his act up close and personal during one of our conjoint psychotherapy sessions.

As I exhaled, I reminded myself that the fact that Sterling had taken a few cheap verbal shots at Gibbs a decade before didn't mean he was capable of murder.

But I also recalled the razor edge of his glare. The fact that I remembered it at all told me something that I was certain was relevant. I'd witnessed the glare, I think, during the second of our three sessions. Gibbs had said something about . . . God, I couldn't remember what Gibbs had said something about, and Sterling had touched her knee to get her attention and had then frozen her with a look so menacing that I remembered it as though it had happened only yesterday.

Gibbs had backed down like a good hound ordered to heel.

And then she'd changed the subject.

What had the subject been?

I couldn't recall.

In reply to her accusation about Sterling, I could have asked Gibbs, *"Why are you telling me this? Why aren't you at the police station with this information?"* But I knew there would be a reason. Maybe not a good reason, one that might sway me. But there would be a reason, one that would teach me something important about the woman who sat across from me.

I bought time. I crossed my left leg over the right and said, "Why don't you tell me exactly what you're concerned about."

Announcing her suspicion of her husband hadn't robbed Gibbs of any of her composure. Her feet stayed side by side in their fashionable slides, and the smooth inner surfaces of her knees still touched as though she were intent on keeping a slip of paper clenched between them without dimpling it. Her shoulders were straight enough to please a Marine drill sergeant, and her spine erect enough to parallel a flagpole. She held her hands as though she were waiting for a photographer to finish snapping a glamour shot of her God-knows-how-many-carat engagement ring.

"I don't really even know how to talk about this." She adjusted those lovely hands, moving them to a position as if in prayer, but her fingertips were pointed toward me, not the heavens. "Louise was our friend in California. In Laguna Beach. But . . . it's not just Louise."

It's not just Louise?

"Louise is the one who was murdered?"

"Yes, in 1997. While we were living in Corona Del Mar. She was killed at her apartment on Crescent Bay on Thanksgiving Day. Or nearby, anyway. We'd just finished redoing our cottage. Right from the start the police suspected that her assailant wasn't close to her. They thought the guy who killed her might have known her, you know, casually, but wasn't close to her. She wasn't from there; she was British. But no one has ever been arrested."

We'd just finished redoing our cottage?

"And you think Sterling was involved?"

"Involved? That's a funny word. Well, I think Sterling did it. Who am I kidding? Although I don't want to believe it, I guess I know he did. He had a thing . . . going with her."

"A sexual thing? An affair?"

"Of course."

The string of her earlier words that had initially caught my attention was still bouncing around my head like a Miller moth trapped behind a miniblind. I repeated the words aloud. "Gibbs, what did you mean when you said before, 'It's not just Louise'?"

"This is weird," she said.

Tell me about it, I thought.

"What did that mean, Gibbs? 'It's not just Louise.' What did you mean by that?"

"I don't even know why I said it."

My mind raced ahead of her, but I tried to keep my focus. I decided not to say what was on my mind. Why? What was on my mind was that I didn't believe her most recent denial. Inconsequential to the therapy perhaps, but an important point considering the circumstances.

Things that are unimportant to the progression of therapy may be crucial to the prosecution of a murder.

She clenched her teeth and tried to smile. Maybe she was fighting tears, but as incongruous as it was, I thought she was actually trying to smile.

She raised her hands to her face to cover her mouth, then took them down again before she said, "You know Sterling, Dr. Gregory. I mean, yes, yes, yes, he has a temper. But could I really be married to a murderer? Or am I nuts?"

Two different questions, I thought.

Two different questions.

Before I conjured up a response, I remembered what it was that Gibbs had said a decade before that had earned her the memorable glare from Sterling.

Sex.

Gibbs had said something about sex.

FIVE

Louise had walked down the path to Crescent Bay from her flat on the cliff above the beach a hundred times. A thousand. She could have dodged the fat ropes of seaweed on the sand in her sleep. From where the shoreline started at the foot of the trail to the beginning of the rough rocks on the north end of the horseshoe cove wasn't more than a few dozen steps. Carrying her old trainers in her hands, she crossed the area in seconds, careful to stay above the high-tide line. The beach had already yielded the day's heat, and the sand that crept up between her toes was cool and dry.

She wondered what he had planned.

Something imaginative, she hoped. God, she needed a man to show some imagination.

That lad in Paris? The Australian? He hadn't been bad. But it was all about the shot for him, not about the setup.

She needed someone to care about the setup, too. The match wasn't just about the goal.

She'd checked her watch before she left her flat. He'd said seven-thirty. She hadn't walked out her door until a quarter to eight. She knew she was worth waiting for. Whatever he had planned, she was worth waiting for.

And she was game.

She checked the Walkman in her hand and adjusted the head-phones on her ears, waiting for his next words. His first words had been "Leave it running, now. The silence is part of the mystery. Follow my commands. And trust me. Do what I say."

At the foot of the rocks she brushed the sand off her feet and pulled on her shoes, then scampered up the rocks toward the tide pools. Her favorite pool, the big one that was shaped like Maui, would be covered by the encroaching tide already. She hoped that in the re-cession between waves—she thought of it as the ocean's inhale—she could maybe steal a quick glance at the cluster of urchins in the south-east corner of the pool.

She loved those urchins, though she couldn't have said why.

"Up toward the pools. Do it without a flashlight, now. No peek-ing. Let yourself be surprised." The voice in her ears, electronically distorted, made her smile. It was a nice touch.

She wasn't carrying a torch; she didn't need one here any more than she'd need one to find the loo in her flat in the dark. The night wasn't totally black, but even if it were, she knew these rock paths like she knew the cabin of a 747. She could wander these cliffs at any tidal level without a map. She knew the path all the way from Crescent Bay to Emerald Bay. She could do it in a storm if she had to.

"Keep going, my lady. Don't be impatient. You'll find your re-ward. Soon, soon, soon." The voice prodded her. "Look up. Look down. Look, look, look."

Finally, she spotted a basket. An old-fashioned picnic basket. High up on a rock shelf, almost above her reach.

She pulled it down, flipped open the lid, and her heart soared just a little.

Meursault. God, she loved Meursault. Fresh gherkins. Pâté. Well, she thought, I'm not a vegan tonight.

She was late. But where is he?

She removed the cork from the bottle, poured herself a glass of wine, and nibbled on a gherkin as she watched the fluorescence of the nighttime waves crash higher and higher on the rocks above the pools, closer and closer to her perch.

"Lovely," she said aloud. "Lovely."

"The night will surprise you. Prepare," the recorded voice murmured into her ears.

"It's a good start," she admitted out loud.

Sitting on the sharp edges of the jagged rocks was less than comfortable. She moved to a squatting position and began to wonder how on earth the goal was going to be scored without scarring one of them forever on the rock faces.

She smiled. It will be fun to find out.

"Open your blouse. Now!"

Ooooh. Urgency.

Okay, okay. *Button by button, she did.*

"Don't turn around."

Her chest pounded. She was having trouble catching her breath.

Less than a second later her feet were out from beneath her and something sharp and hard was surrounding her neck and her attempts at breathing were thwarted. Totally thwarted.

She struggled at the ligature. It didn't help.

Moments later she didn't even feel the cold chill of the Pacific as she spilled forward into the darkness.

SIX

Patients returning to see me after an extended absence from treatment, like Gibbs Storey, tend to labor under the suspicion that a decade does nothing to alter my recall of the facts of their lives. The truth is that that is not the truth. Since Gibbs and Sterling last left my office on their way to Capistrano or Corona or Laguna or Newport Beach or wherever they ended up, a few hundred new patients had crossed my threshold and told me their tales. That's too many stories for my brain to juggle. Way too many. Scores too many. Sometimes I got the details confused. I would assign faulty facts to a patient or misremember who had died in what year, who had what illness, and who had slept with whom.

So why didn't I just go back to my patient files and refresh my memory?

Because as a general rule I put few facts in my case notes. The more potentially private the fact, the less likely I was to put it on paper. Why? Because doctor-patient confidentiality is not a brick wall that forever separates my knowledge of my patient from the gaze of the judicial system. Confidentiality is actually a brick wall with a few conveniently spaced locked gates. And the courts, not I, hold the keys to those gates. Whatever I wrote down might therefore someday become public. In all my years in clinical practice I hadn't discovered a single reason to volunteer to be a conduit to making the private public.

Consequently, I didn't write much down.

I caught Diane Estevez in our little kitchen about an hour after Gibbs left my office. Diane would remember everything that I'd forgotten about our ancient conjoint treatment of the Storeys. I suspected sometimes when I queried her about such things that Diane made up whatever she didn't actually remember, but in any event, her recall would appear seamless and complete.

"Hey, Alan, how's Sam?"

Although I hadn't had a chance to tell her about Sam's heart attack, I wasn't surprised that she already knew. Diane had sources everywhere. If gossip was an art form, she was the Picasso of our generation.

"He had an angiogram this morning. I'll know more later today when I go visit him."

"Angioplasty, too? Stent?"

"I'm still waiting to hear."

"But it was an MI?"

"Enzymes say yes. They used clot busters."

"Keep me informed."

"Of course, but we both know that you'll probably know his prognosis before his cardiologist does. Guess who I saw this morning?"

Diane was scooping ground coffee into a filter basket. My question caused her to lose count of her tablespoons. She said, "Shit. Tell me."

Dr. Estevez and I had been friends since we'd interned together many years before. Although our practices were independent businesses, we shared the first floor, and the ownership, of a small century-plus-old Victorian that housed our clinical offices on Walnut Street on the edge of downtown Boulder.

"Guess."

"D. B. Cooper?"

An inside joke. "Close," I said. "How about Gibbs Storey?"

She looked at me. "The Dancing Queen?"

Diane had always called Gibbs "the Dancing Queen." I thought the moniker was some obscure reference to the old ABBA song, but I wasn't absolutely certain what the allusion was. I did know that Diane had never been fond of Gibbs. And I'd never been fond of ABBA. Not before the Broadway play.

Not since.

"That's the one."

"Where'd you see her? In town someplace?"

"No, right here. In my office."

She placed the carafe full of water in the sink and faced me.

"For therapy?"

"It's what I do."

"Why are you telling me this?" Diane wasn't being argumentative— although she was quite capable of it. She was querying me as to why I was breaching Gibbs's confidentiality so cavalierly.

"Because I have a signed release to talk to you." Before she'd left my office at the conclusion of her session, I'd asked Gibbs if I could consult with Diane, and she'd said I could.

"I'm not going to like this, am I?" Diane asked.

"Probably not."

"Is she still with Platinum? Or did she leave him? If she's still with him, don't even ask because I'm not doing conjoint again. Especially with them. With her. Count me out. I mean it."

"Platinum" was Diane's nickname for Sterling. Although I was never quite sure, I'd always operated under the assumption that she wasn't particularly fond of him, either. Regardless, I knew she'd liked him more than she'd liked Gibbs.

Hell, she liked bad cheese more than she liked Gibbs.

"She's still with him. At least temporarily. She doesn't feel she can leave him without him resorting to stalking her, or something worse."

Diane shot me an I-told-you-so glance. "Every battered woman feels that way. That's why God invented safe houses and restraining orders. The Dancing Queen will need a good kick in the butt to get out of that marriage. God knows Sterling will never leave her."

"Why's that?"

" 'Cause she's such a little dreamboat. You ever notice her fingers? She has perfect little fingers."

I didn't admit to Diane that I had, in fact, just noticed Gibbs's fingers. Instead, I said, "Anybody ever tell you that you have a propensity for sarcasm?"

"Don't worry; the tendency is soluble in caffeine. Let me finish making myself some coffee, and I'll be much nicer. I'm glad it's your job to help the Dancing Queen, not mine. Don't even think of recruiting me for this one. I'm out, Alan. Out. Out, out, out."

Diane was better at acting definitive than she was at being definitive. Despite her best efforts, compassion softened her steely heart. Still, I knew I had to get her on board before she convinced herself that she really was a taciturn bitch. I said, "Gibbs thinks Sterling murdered someone a few years ago."

Without missing a beat, Diane said, "Sometimes I pretend Raoul's on the FBI's most-wanted list. I play the special agent making the bust. If we don't run it into the ground, it's always kind of fun."

Diane's husband was an irascible Spaniard named Raoul Estevez. I knew nothing about their sex life and preferred it that way.

"I'm not kidding, Diane. Gibbs thinks he may have killed a friend of theirs. A woman he was involved with."

The pause that followed permitted Diane sufficient time to convince herself that the calendar indicated November, not April first.

"And you believe her?"

"A hundred percent? No, not that he did it. Not yet. But yes, I do believe that she believes what she told me."

"How does she know? What's her evidence against him?"

"It's a mix of things. Things he did. Things he said. Part circumstantial, part supposition, part confession."

"If Lauren heard it, would she be swayed?" Lauren, my wife, was a deputy district attorney for Boulder County. Where prosecutorial conclusions were concerned, she was a stickler for, well, facts.

I shrugged. "I asked myself the same question and decided Lauren would be interested in what Gibbs has to say."

"But Sterling confessed?"

"So Gibbs says. Not an 'I did it' confession exactly, but he told her things that she thinks only the murderer would know."

"If—a big 'if'—what she says is real," Diane reminded me before she shifted her focus from the forensic to the psychological, "why now? Why is she talking about this now? The murder of the friend was when?"

"Nineteen ninety-seven. It's a good question, and I'm not sure about the answer. I assume it has something to do with them being back in Boulder. But that's a guess on my part. I asked, of course, but she didn't have an answer."

"Why you?"

The subtext was *Why not me?*

"I wish I knew the answer to that one, too. Maybe she's aware of your, um, countertransference issues."

I was certain Diane was going to argue that she didn't have any negative feelings about Gibbs. But she didn't go down that road.

"Other than murder, did you and Gibbs talk about anything else that was important during your . . . session?"

I explained that Gibbs wanted me to make a call to the police about the murder. Diane narrowed her eyes upon hearing that news. I continued. "And we talked about you, and what help you could be. I'd like your consultation about all this, and specifically your help setting up a meeting with Celeste what's-her-face over at Safe House. Make sure she's okay with this situation. Gibbs will need Safe House's services when the shit hits the fan."

"Clayton. Celeste Clayton. When?"

"Later today, if possible. I'm seeing Gibbs again tomorrow morning. I'd like to be confident that Safe House is comfortable having her by then so I can assure her it's safe to go to the police with what she knows about Sterling."

"She should be in Safe House right now, Alan. Not tomorrow."

"I know. I suggested. She refused. I strongly encouraged her to reconsider. She refused."

"Can I come to the meeting with Celeste? I'd really hate to miss this."

"I was hoping you would. The release lets me tell you whatever I think is appropriate."

"And Gibbs signed one for Safe House, too?"

"She did."

"She didn't argue with you?"

"No. She's not the arguing type. You know that. Maybe that's the source of your countertransference."

Diane considered my words for a heartbeat before she said, "I treat lots of wimpy women. That's not it. Do you find it odd that she dumped all this in your lap? The old murder, making the call."

"I find this whole thing odd."

"I know you don't want to hear it, but this isn't just about *my* countertransference, you know?" Her voice was now at least a half-octave lower. The change was intended to draw my attention.

I bit. "What do you mean?"

"Are you going to call the police for her?"

"I don't know. I guess."

"This is your countertransference, too, Alan. What you're doing for Gibbs you wouldn't do for a lot of patients. Making all these arrangements, making all these calls. She's pushing some button for you, too. Call me cynical, but I suspect it has something to do with the blond hair and the pert breasts."

Pert breasts? "I don't think so. The circumstances are unusual. If they were repeated with anyone else, I'd do the same thing."

"You would call the police in another state and report an old crime for any patient who asked?"

"Yes."

"Any old patient who wasn't cute and blond?"

I was grateful that the pert breasts had disappeared from the equation. I said, "Yes."

"Sure you would." Diane returned her attention to finishing the coffee-making process. With her back to me, she said, "Alan, why is it you who always gets cases like this? You have more dead bodies in your practice than a small-town undertaker. Do you ever think about that?"

I could have confessed that I thought about it all the time, but I didn't want to give her the satisfaction.

"I promise to think about it if you'll think about something for me, too. Way back, Gibbs brought up something during conjoint therapy. When she mentioned whatever it was, Sterling doused it like a Boy Scout putting out a campfire. Do you remember what it was? He glared at her. Really glared at her. That's what I remember most clearly. The glare."

"I don't have to think about it at all. I know what it was. I know exactly the incident that you're talking about."

"Yes?"

"Gibbs was saying that at some point she wanted to talk with us about their sex life."

"Yes, yes, okay," I agreed. "Maybe that was it. I remembered that, too, that it was something about sex."

Sort of.

Diane said, "Don't patronize me. That was it. And what she was about to tell us was that she and Sterling were swingers, or he was a cross-dresser, or something good and juicy like that. For a while I thought it might be bondage, but try as I might, I could never quite see the Dancing Queen in a black leather G-string and a studded bra. The whip? Maybe."

The mental image that Diane was painting was a little distracting to me. "And you think she wanted to talk about it?" I asked.

"Exactly. Something about their weird little sex life was starting to give her the heebie-jeebies. And Sterling didn't want her to let the cat out of the bag. He let her know he didn't want her to talk about it. That's what the look was about. You can take it to the bank."

"Come on, Diane. Seriously. Bondage? Cross-dressing?"

She stared me down. The glare was only minimally less effective than Sterling's glower at Gibbs had been.

"I am serious. But I told you, I ruled out bondage and S&M early on. My vote? I think they were swingers. Probably still are swingers. Gibbs wanted to talk about it with us; Sterling didn't. I'd guess he was pushing her to try something she didn't want to do, and he didn't want our votes counted."

"Swingers swingers? Like . . . you know?"

"Yeah, like having sex with other couples on a regular basis. That kind of swingers. Do you know another kind?" She giggled to herself. I assumed it was at the thought that I might possess more esoteric deviant sexual knowledge than she did.

I didn't admit that I had been actively considering the country-and-western dancing connotations of the word "swinger."

"Gibbs and Sterling, swingers? How exactly did you come to this conclusion? She never actually said anything about that, did she? Did she say something to you in private? God, you'd think I'd remember if she'd implied they were swingers."

"I just knew where she was going. You could tell."

"How come I didn't know where she was going?"

"What we do? Psychotherapy? People sometimes think we read minds. But what we do is more like seeing in the dark, you know? I knew where Gibbs was going. Sterling knew where she was going. You, sweetheart? You're such a prude. You don't like to go places like that. You're a very good therapist, but where sex is concerned, you can't see too well in the dark. Honestly, it's one of the things I love about you."

"You love that I'm a prude?"

She placed a mug beneath the dripping brew to catch the first, strongest cup of coffee. "I have to pick something to love, don't I?"

SEVEN

Sam's heart attack wasn't awful by heart attack standards. The cardiologist didn't think he'd suffered significant muscle damage.

During my visit to the hospital early Monday afternoon, Sam pointed out the location of the narrowing they'd discovered on a plastic model of the human heart that was about the size of a grapefruit. I'd had to hand him the model; he was flat on his back with some strange device that looked like a single-span suspension bridge straddling his groin. He'd explained that it was pressing on the incision in his artery with approximately the force that nature used to turn coal into diamonds.

All in all, not the precise degree of pressure that most men preferred in the vicinity of their groin.

"The one that got blocked up is called the diagonal artery. It's that one there." He pointed at a little red line on the model. "They put a stent in it to hold it open. You know what that is?"

I nodded. I rested my fingertip on the diagonal artery on the model in my hands and tried to visualize the blockage in Sam's heart and the small wire-mesh pipe propping open his fragile blood vessel.

"Doctor said it could've been much worse. My other arteries are open. Not wide open. But enough open."

"That's good news, right?"

"It's not bad news. But best case is you want them all wide open."

"Where's Sherry?" I asked. I sat and held the model heart in my hands. It seemed inappropriate to set it back down. Even though it was plastic, I felt like I should be extra careful with it.

"She's been here most of the day. Right now she's taking a walk or something. Getting some tea, I don't know. She said she needed a break from all this." He waved at the voluminous paraphernalia of the cardiac care unit. Monitors, pumps. Lots of plastic tubes and two- and three-digit LEDs telling those intelligent enough to understand them important things about Sam's condition. "It's okay."

I knew Sam's wife pretty well. I thought I knew her well enough to guess that her sympathy for her husband's condition would erode at some point and that her anger that Sam didn't do shit to take care of himself would emerge in a form that would cause him to cringe.

"Is she mad already?" I asked.

Sam nodded. "I fucked up. She told me this was coming. The heart attack. My father had one, you know. Same age I am right now. She's been bugging me to work out with her, eat better. Shit."

I couldn't see how regret and remorse were going to aid Sam's short-term recovery. I said, "That's neither here nor there. It's what you do from now on that matters, right?"

He snorted. "God, that's an intelligent thing to say, Alan. If I had my checkbook, I'd write you a check for your wisdom this very second. What is it these days, a hundred and something for fifty minutes? What a bargain! But they took my pants when the ambulance brought me in, sorry. My wallet was in it."

Sam fenced with me constantly about my profession; it was part of the fabric of our friendship. This particular jab was halfhearted at best. After dealing with Diane—who had been at the top of her game during our morning joust—I had no trouble absorbing Sam's feeble sarcasm. "Forty-five minutes, actually. You scared, Sam?"

He looked away from me before he nodded. "I'm glad I was with you yesterday. I never would have called for an ambulance if I was by myself. I would have convinced myself that it was a kidney stone. Or two stones. I'd probably be dead because I'm stubborn."

"I'm glad I guessed what was going on. It was lucky."

"How did you know?"

"I didn't know. The neck thing got me worried, though. Didn't see what it could have to do with your kidneys."

He sighed, or groaned. I wasn't sure.

"The doctor told me I need to develop some collaterals, whatever that means. In case there's a next time."

"Collateral what?"

"Blood vessels. Blood supply."

"How are you supposed to do that?"

"Exercise, apparently."

He spoke the word with an inflection usually reserved for a phrase like "root canal" or "prostate exam."

"I'll help," I said. "We'll start off walking, then we'll bicycle or run. Whatever they recommend."

"Thanks," he said. He hadn't wanted to ask for my help, but he'd hoped that I'd offer. "Want to know what's ironic?"

"Sure."

"Krispy Kreme is finally coming to Boulder. That's what I heard. I'm probably never going to get to eat another doughnut in my life, and the Taj Mahal of doughnut shops is finally coming to my town."

"There are worse things."

"Name three."

"I thought your cholesterol was okay."

"It's been going up for a while. It's kind of high. The truth is, I eat a lot of crap. So I've been wondering, how did that thing work on Emily's paw? The umbrella thing you were making?"

"It's working great; she loves it. Lauren thinks I should quit my job, patent it, and get rich."

"You don't want to be rich."

"I don't?"

He shook his head, but he didn't elaborate. In other circumstances I would have pressed him, but my mind had already darted back to the conundrum of the Dancing Queen and her husband the murderer.

I opened my mouth to ask Sam for advice about Gibbs and Sterling, but as my eyes flitted from one of the unpleasant accoutrements of acute cardiac care that were surrounding him to another, I kept quiet. I admit that I briefly entertained the notion that Sam would find my unsolved homicide problem a pleasant distraction from his health and family problems, but that rationalization left an immediate sour taste.

Discretion ruled. I decided that I would struggle with the Dancing Queen on my own.

A nurse bustled through the door to Sam's room as though she'd had a running start. She was all business, and her fresh white Reeboks told me she had a sprinter's soul. She checked me out while her eyes took in the readings on Sam's various monitors. She adjusted the pump on his IV and flicked at the spaghetti of plastic tubing leading to his forearm as though she were sending a malarial mosquito on its way to the afterlife.

"How's your pain, Detective?" For some reason she was touching his toes as she inquired.

"Hey, Snoopy," Sam said, as though he'd just recognized she was in the room. "It's still there. It's hard to stay in this position for so long, you know. I feel like Ray Bourque kicked me in the kidneys and he's been standing on my groin for most of the third period."

"Yeah, that's exactly what I hear it's like," she replied.

I stole a glance at the hospital ID hanging around her neck. It indeed read "Snoopy." Snoopy Lipner, R.N. I could tell she didn't have a clue who Ray Bourque was and was more than content to go to her grave without learning why Sam Purdy would have an image of the man standing on his groin. I could've explained to her about hockey's place in Sam's universe and his peculiar love of traditional defensemen, but I didn't think Snoopy really wanted to know that, either. I was tempted to ask her about her first name, but was guessing that just about everyone did and that she'd grown weary of the inquiries a long time before.

She pulled a syringe from the front pocket of her tunic, uncapped it with her teeth, and had the needle in a port in Sam's IV tube faster than Wyatt Earp could draw his six-shooter. She depressed the plunger and disposed of the empty in a sharps container in another blink of the eye. "This'll make it easier for you. Just another hour or

so, and we can take that thing off your groin. Hang in there, and I'll
be back to check on you soon."

"Can I have some more of those ice chips before you go?"

She lifted a paper cup off the table and placed the edge against his
lips.

Sam tilted the cup and spilled a few slivers of ice into his mouth.
Afterward he seemed to exhale for ten seconds as the medication from
the syringe entered his bloodstream and the molecules started mating
with the appropriate receptors in his brain.

"What did you give him?" I asked.

"Water, in the form of ice chips. Who are you?" Snoopy asked.

"A friend."

"He's the one who brought me in," Sam said. "He's a good guy, a
doctor. Not a real doctor. You know, a Ph.D., a psychologist."

She eyed me as though she'd finally decided that she'd let me stay.
She lofted the IV tubing. "That was fentanyl. For the pain. That position he's in is a killer." She returned Sam's water glass to the bedside
table. "You did good work yesterday," she told me. "We got him
early enough that we were able to bust his clot in the ER. Because of
that he's going to walk out of here with most of the heart he came in
with."

She was gone in a flash.

Sam mumbled, "Nurses are nice to cops. Don't know why that
is."

Gingerly, I placed the plastic heart on his rolling bedside tray and
watched his eyelids grow heavy as the fentanyl continued its work
and the inevitable sedation went along for the ride.

His eyes suddenly popped open, and he said, "Marriage is a funny
thing. Love isn't enough, you know? People think it is, but it isn't.
Other things happen sometimes. They do."

"What do you mean?" I asked, honestly curious.

He didn't respond.

I sat beside him for a few moments more and watched his breathing get into the uniform rhythm of narcotic semisleep.

I was aware of an impulse to run home and make Sam an umbrella for his heart. Rigid foam rubber, plastic strips, some filament
tape. That should do it. Something to shield his heart from whatever

out there might want to bruise it. And to protect it from whatever he might be inclined to do to it, too.

I whispered, "Nurses are nice to cops because most of the time the cops deserve it, Sam. That's why."

I sat beside him for a few more minutes, silently rehashing what Gibbs Storey had told me that morning. In my mind I asked Sam what a cop like him would say to a story like hers. I asked him what the Boulder police were likely to do after the police in California informed them that they had a killer in their town.

Sam slept through it all.

EIGHT

In the dozen-plus years I'd been in practice in Boulder, I'd referred at least a dozen women—and one man—to Boulder Safe House. I helped Safe House raise money each year. I was an advocate for all they did.

But I didn't know where the actual sanctuary was located. None of my patients who used the services had ever told me. None of the Safe House staff had ever told me. My wife, the DA, had never told me.

Why? The more people who knew the location of the building, the less safe Safe House was.

So I wasn't surprised when Diane's message informed me that the five-thirty meeting with the Safe House director to discuss Gibbs Storey's situation would be at our offices on Walnut Street, not at Safe House.

Celeste Clayton—CeeCee to her friends—was a contemporary urban *balabosta*. She was all smiles and hugs, competence and compassion. If she couldn't tuck you in, feed you, or wipe away

a tear, her day was ruined. Ten minutes late for our meeting, she bustled into my office with a big smile and with her arms spread wide to
engulf Diane in an embrace.

My turn was next. I'd been perfunctorily introduced to Celeste at
a couple of fund-raisers and had spoken with her on the phone a few
times about mutual clients. Still, the hug she gave me was every bit as
robust as the one she gave Diane.

She plopped onto the chair across from me, looked around my office, and said, "Nice digs."

Diane said, "Don't be fooled. The decorating panache is mine. He
just wrote the checks."

It wasn't completely true, but Diane knew that I wouldn't contradict her in front of company. I said, "Celeste, thanks for doing this on
such short notice."

" 'Notice' is a foreign concept in my business. People don't usually anticipate when they will need emergency shelter from abusers. So
what's up? Diane said this one would raise my eyebrows. That'll take
some doing. I've been in the battered spouse business for so many
years that I know most of the stories before anybody tells me word
one."

I handed Celeste a signed release from Gibbs Storey. She glanced
at it and proceeded to stick it into a fat Day-Timer that screamed
"black hole." I was confident there were papers stuffed in that book
that were older than my Social Security card.

"Years ago, ten or so, Diane and I briefly treated a married couple. The wife's name is Gibbs Storey. They left—"

"Gibbs. That's b-s?"

Diane laughed. I said, "Yes. Well, two bs and an s."

"Go on."

"The Storeys left town after what, Diane, three or four sessions?"
Diane nodded. "Neither of us heard from them again until ten days
ago when Gibbs called me for an appointment that took place this
morning. She told me they'd moved back to town a few months ago.
Within a few minutes she went on to implicate her husband in an unsolved murder in California."

"Implicate?" Celeste asked.

"She accused him of murdering a friend of theirs with whom he
was having an extramarital affair."

"Wow." My impression was that Celeste wasn't registering amazement at the facts. She was registering amazement that she was really hearing a new battered woman story.

"Gibbs feels that she will be in significant physical danger from her husband once he discovers that she has spoken with the police. I don't have any valid reason to question her conclusion."

"Is there a history of battering?"

Diane spoke up. "We're in a difficult position with you on that, CeeCee. Alan and I saw the Storeys as a couple. Virtually all of what we know about him comes from that couples treatment. That therapy is confidential—we can't talk about it without his permission."

"Even if she's in danger?"

"Danger's not enough," Diane replied. "He would have had to make a threat against her for us to breach privilege. Sterling"—she cleared her throat—"hasn't done that. At least not in our presence. Absent the overt threat, we can't talk about him without a release."

Celeste said, "Something tells me he's unlikely to grant the release, isn't he? How about I just assume that I wouldn't be here if his history in the bully department was untarnished? Is that an assumption that we all can live with?"

Neither Diane nor I contradicted her.

I thought, *And that is how the high hurdles of confidentiality are effortlessly cleared.*

"Well, good. Where is Ms. Storey right now?"

I said, "She went home after our session this morning. She feels certain that her husband doesn't suspect anything. She insists she'll be safe until the police show up to talk with him."

Celeste smiled ruefully. "I can name this song in three notes. In case you're wondering, it's a very sad song."

"I did my best to keep her from going home." I don't know why I felt the need to protest my innocence, but I did.

"I know how it goes. I've beaten my head on that wall a few hundred times myself, Alan. Kids? Please tell me there are no kids."

"None, thankfully."

"You'll talk to her again when?"

"Tomorrow morning. At that point I hope to get her permission to contact the police in Laguna Beach and pass along her suspicions about her husband. She prefers not to do it herself. Obviously, the moment that occurs—should they believe her—she'll need protection."

Celeste said, "Her suite at the palace is ready."

Diane said, "This could be high profile, CeeCee. You sure you're ready for the publicity?"

"There's no reason for anyone to know she's at Safe House. If someone does connect the dots and is irresponsible enough to go public with the information, we'll deal with it. That's what we do. We're here to protect women at risk. This sounds like a woman at risk."

"You're sure?" Diane asked. "The press will be all over this."

Celeste took a moment to move her gaze between Diane and me, then back to Diane.

"What don't you like about her?"

"Me?" Diane asked. "What do you mean?"

"Don't play with me, Diane. What is it about this woman you don't like? Something's bugging you."

Diane uncrossed her arms and crossed her legs instead. She started to speak and stopped. When she started again, her words came out as though she'd floored her tongue and her transmission was locked in first gear. "Gibbs Storey is an alpha bitch, CeeCee. She's everything I—I—I hate about every *über*-popular girl wrapped up into one too-cute, too-thin, too-precious, too"—Diane actually growled at this juncture—"too-perfect little package."

Without the slightest alteration in her tone, Celeste said, "You know I love you, right, Diane? Good. Then please take this the way I intend it: It's obvious your high school years left you with some unresolved issues, dear." She paused. "I suggest you get over them. I'm happy to refer you to someone who will be delighted to help you exorcise those demons."

Celeste's hand disappeared into the Day-Timer and miraculously emerged with a business card. She handed it to me. "That's my cell number. Call me when your lady's ready for our services. I'll have someone come over here and get her. I don't want her followed to the shelter. Anything else? You guys know about the Christmas benefit? Good, I thought so. I'll see you there. Be sure to bring your checkbooks."

And she was gone.

I looked at Diane and said, "*Über*-popular alpha bitch?"

NINE

I was late getting home.

After the meeting with CeeCee ended I squeezed in a few minutes of decompression with Diane before I drove out to Louisville to visit Sam again. The torture contraption had been removed from his groin, and he'd been turfed from the coronary care facility to a telemetry unit. I found him propped up in bed staring at a muted TV screen. He'd already trashed the hospital gown and was wearing nothing but a pair of running shorts and a tangle of wires that snaked to an array of sensors plastered to shaved rectangles in the thick mat of hair on his chest.

Sherry plodded into the room a minute or two after I arrived. We hugged. I explained that Sam had just asked me a poignant question about his son Simon's reaction to the heart attack. Sherry stood with her arms folded across her chest while I finished telling Sam what I thought he might expect to see.

Sam's wife had lost weight since I'd last seen

her. Her face was thin, almost gaunt. I wasn't totally convinced that the gauntness wasn't a side effect of the makeup that was liberally applied around her eyes. Saturday night makeup in the middle of the day, I wondered. *Stress,* I thought. *What's that about? Sam's health, probably.*

I excused myself moments later, kissing Sherry on the cheek. I implored her to call if she needed anything from Lauren or me. Anything. I told Sam I'd see him the next day.

Before I made it to the door he said, "Alan?"

I turned back toward him. He pinched a thick roll of skin at his waist—the roll of flesh had the heft of a healthy brisket—and asked me if I thought he was fat, adding, "I think my cardiologist thinks I'm fat. He hasn't said so exactly, but that's what he thinks."

I glanced at Sherry before I looked my friend in the eye and said, "Yes, Sam, I think you're kind of fat."

For a split second he looked injured, then he said, "Yeah, me too."

My laugh echoed in the room.

It sounded like a fart at the opera. The tension between Sam and his wife was as thick as plasma.

Ten minutes later I was home.

Grace was sick. Lauren had her hands full with a work problem that had followed her home from the office. She was short-tempered and fearful that our daughter had croup. I was determined not to join in the chorus of catastrophizing—rare things happen rarely, after all, and common things happen commonly—and I decided that I would act as though my daughter had a cold until her symptoms insisted otherwise. But it was clear that both of my girls required some immediate attention.

The dogs hadn't been out all day, and Emily in particular was restless. Her paw umbrella had fallen like a forty-year-old's butt so that it *clack-clacked* on the wood floors with every step she took. The noise, coupled with whatever was going on at work, was driving Lauren closer and closer to distraction, or worse.

"Do that first," she directed me as I went to relieve her of Grace. She was pointing at Emily's paw. "Fix that thing, please."

I did what I was told. It took me fifteen minutes to check Emily's paw wound—it looked terrific—to dress it with antiseptic, to retape the plastic umbrella into place, and to walk both the dogs down the lane and back.

Lauren tucked the portable phone between her ear and shoulder and carried Grace to the nursery while I threw together some pasta and bean soup. Experience told me that if I hurried I could make a passable version in twenty-five minutes.

During the half hour or so until I had dinner on the table, Grace finally fell asleep. Lauren came into the kitchen for dinner with her hair wet. She appeared much less harried after her quick shower, and with a smile she told me that the work problem was solved.

I poured her a glass of wine and filled her in on developments with Sam and Sherry.

She asked a few questions. I answered as best I could.

"Has Sherry said anything to you, Lauren? Is there any trouble brewing between them? She seems really angry at him."

"I haven't talked to her in a while, and the last couple of times we did talk she wasn't very open with me. But you know that Sam was a heart-attack-in-waiting. His weight, his stress, his diet. His family history. I'm not surprised she's furious. He should have been taking care of himself."

Not the level of compassion I'd expected to hear from her. "Tough day?" I finally asked. "You feeling all right?"

The second question was a back-door way of wondering out loud about the current status of her struggle with multiple sclerosis. New symptoms? Aggravated fatigue? Anything?

I hated asking. She hated answering. I think I hated asking because of how much she hated answering. She hated answering because she believed that her chronic illness and its myriad symptoms constituted the most grievously tedious subjects in the world.

"I just realized what I said about Sam and Sherry. Do you get angry with me, Alan? Because I'm sick? Do you think it's my fault when I'm not feeling well? That I do something to . . . or I don't do something that . . ."

I sat back. "I get angry that you're sick. But no, I don't get angry at you for having MS."

"I do," she said. "I get angry at me. I think it's okay if you do, too."

No, it's not, I thought. *It's not. You would like it to be okay, I know you would. But it's not.*

Lauren sipped some wine. "Grace isn't going to let us sleep tonight," she warned, having successfully ignored my question regarding the current state of her health. "We can't let her stay down too long."

"Let's leave her down long enough to have dinner. We'll get her up after. Maybe she'll be in a better mood."

Lauren lifted a spoonful of soup. "Yeah, that's likely to happen. So, is there anything new at the office?" she asked in a playful, I'll-go-along-someplace-else-with-you voice.

I surprised her. I said, "Actually, there is something that came up. I could use your advice."

Without using any names or revealing in what state, let alone in what city, the events had taken place, I gave Lauren the broad outlines of the tale of Gibbs and Sterling Storey. I included my suspicions about the psychological and likely physical abuse that were part of the fabric of their relationship.

My indiscretion with Lauren was a gray area in confidentiality that I usually tried to avoid. These "I have a patient who . . ." conversations happen all too frequently between psychotherapists and colleagues or laypeople. Most mental health professionals engage in them with a rationalization that if they do not reveal sufficient details to allow the listener to identify the patient in question, then the letter of the patient's confidentiality has not been violated.

Lauren's soup bowl was empty when I completed my exposition. I ladled her some more.

"So what are you going to do?" she asked me.

"Exactly what she wants me to do, I guess. As soon as I'm sure she has a safe place to stay, I'll call the police in the town where she was living and tell them what she told me."

"Yeah?"

"What do you think will happen when I do?" I asked.

"Depends on whether or not the cops believe you."

"And what does that depend on?"

"On whether she's given you any information that coincides with what the local cops already know about the crime. If your client knows something that isn't in the public record, I would predict that they would take you quite seriously."

"And then what?"

"I'm speculating, okay? If they believe her story, they would either ask her to travel back there so they could talk to her, or they would send somebody out here to interview her. Maybe him, too—her husband—if he's stupid enough to be accommodating. It all depends on what they've been able to develop at their end and how it matches up with what she knows. But it's hard to predict. You know what these cold cases are like. Detectives lose interest. Evidence gets lost. Witnesses die or move away. People forget."

"She said she'd testify against him."

"Sorry," Lauren said. "It's not that simple."

"I don't understand."

"Spousal privilege."

"So?"

"Spousal privilege is a trickier thing than most people realize. Each spouse has a privilege not to disclose marital communications, and—this is the part that people don't know—they also have a privilege to prevent their spouse from disclosing marital communications."

"Really? I thought spousal privilege meant that spouses couldn't be compelled to testify against each other. Well, she's willing to testify. Eager even. Her testimony would be voluntary."

"Like I said, it's not that simple. He could assert his privilege and prevent her from testifying. But there are some circumstances that would allow his privilege to be overridden."

"Teach me."

"There are statutory exceptions to the spousal privilege evidence rules. Every state I'm aware of has a battering and child-abuse exception. If one spouse batters the other or injures a child, the injured spouse is free to testify about that against the batterer. But the case you're describing is the murder of a third party, not domestic violence. Take Colorado. If the homicide you're talking about had happened in Colorado, spousal privilege wouldn't apply at all, because the case that's in question involves a serious felony and in Colorado all spousal privilege is waived for serious felonies. Other states have different spousal privilege statutes, with different exceptions. Some have felony exceptions, like Colorado, some don't. Ultimately, a lot is going to depend on what state this homicide of yours happened in."

"Please go on."

"In many states, including ours, spouses can't testify against each other without the consent of the other spouse. But in some states there's no felony exception to that rule. If your client is from one of those states, unless her husband granted his consent—which I think we can agree is unlikely if she's about to accuse him of murder—she wouldn't be allowed to testify against him, even for an alleged homicide."

Emily walked over, wanting her ears scratched. I obliged. "Do you know how the law works in any other states?"

"Any one in particular?" Lauren teased.

"Sorry, I can't tell you which state this is about. I wish I could. What other ones do you know?"

"I passed the California bar, remember?"

Lauren and I were both on our second marriages. Her first had taken her briefly to California. We didn't talk about our exes much, so her reference to her time in California hung in the air like the scent of burnt garlic.

"Okay, what's California's spousal privilege statute? Do you remember that kind of detail?"

"It was a lot of years ago, but my memory is that it's one of the more conservative laws, or liberal laws, depending, I guess, on whether you're a prosecutor or a defense attorney. I think there's a mutual consent rule in California, but I don't believe that there's a felony exception."

"Which means that, hypothetically, if this old murder took place in California, my client couldn't testify against her husband without his consent."

"If I'm right, that's exactly what it means."

I figured she was right; my experience was that Lauren was usually correct about matters of the law. I thought about the complications that her facts presented and explained, "I was going to run it by Sam today. To see what this would be like from a police point of view—you know, to get a call like the one I'm about to make. But I decided that it wasn't a good idea."

"No, it wouldn't be a good idea for him. Not now, given his condition. I'm not sure it's even a good idea for you. You may not want to be in the middle of this, Alan. Think it through carefully."

"Why? What do you mean?"

"Let's say it turns out that your client is right about . . . everything that she believes her husband did. If that's the case, then you know three things about her husband. One, that he's a killer. Two, that he's a batterer."

She raised her spoon to her mouth.

"And number three?" I asked.

Lauren swallowed, sat back, and sipped some Riesling before she answered. "That he's not going to be happy with you for turning him in to the police." She reached across the table and took my hand. "And Emily and Grace and I don't know what we'd do without you."

"Anvil too," I said.

"Yeah, Anvil too."

"Why don't you rest a little bit? I'll go wake Grace."

Lauren stood up. She probably didn't know that I was checking her balance when she did. She probably didn't know that I would be examining her gait as she left the room.

I stopped her before she cleared the doorway. "Does spousal privilege restrict the police in any way? Does the mutual consent part of the spousal privilege law apply to their investigation? If she tells the police things now without her husband's consent, could it taint future evidence?"

"Why would you think that's a problem?"

"Fruit from a poisonous tree?"

"Doesn't apply. Spousal privilege is limited to testimony in court. During the investigation, the police can find out whatever they can find out. They can talk to either spouse about the other. But . . . keep in mind that I haven't reviewed the case law or the precedents recently. You might want to talk to a defense attorney—someone like Cozy or Casey—before you decide what to do next."

Cozy Maitlin and Casey Sparrow were criminal defense attorneys whom Lauren and I knew well. Professionally speaking, too well.

"I thought I just did talk with an attorney."

"I told you the legal issues involved, Alan. I didn't give you any advice."

"Well, may I have some advice?"

She thrust out a hip. The move was erotically provocative, all in all very unlawyerlike. "A little more salt in the soup next time. But the Riesling"—she blew me a kiss—"was perfect."

"Thanks," I said.

Lauren smiled warmly. "This all happened in California, didn't it?"

I smiled back. My smile was kind of sick.

As if on cue, our daughter's throaty wail pierced the quiet.

Lauren was right in her prediction. Neither of us got much sleep that night.

TEN

The whole country had seen a single, grainy, black-and-white security photograph of my Tuesday eight o'clock. Her likeness had been on TV, in the newspapers, in magazines, on the Internet—anywhere a picture could be plastered. But as far as I knew, I was the only person who could actually put a name to the infamous photo.

Who was she? My first patient was an over-stressed sales executive named Sharon Lewis who worked out the Diagonal at a company called Micro Motion. A fortnight plus one day before, at almost the exact same hour when she and I were sitting down for her second psychotherapy session, Sharon had been hustling to recover from a blown tire on the Boulder Turnpike that had caused her to arrive much too late for her flight at Denver International Airport. Her tardy arrival meant that she had exactly thirty-three minutes to get from her car in the parking garage to the B Concourse to catch her plane to Houston for a sales meeting that she absolutely couldn't miss.

Denver's airport was always a mob scene on Monday mornings, and Sharon jogged into the terminal to discover that the post–9/11 security station was already jammed with an army of impatient briefcase warriors charging out on their weekly business patrols.

Sharon was schlepping her rolling suitcase on board the plane and wasn't surprised that she was immediately jostled by federal security personnel into a cutback queue that was moving like the blood of a glutton after a meal at Morton's.

When she finally arrived at the front of that line, she was directed toward a shorter line at an X-ray machine, where she was once again forced to cool her heels. She found herself behind a family of six who were behaving as though they'd never confronted a magnetometer in their entire lives. Each of them had more metal secreted on their bodies than Edward Scissorhands at a piercing convention.

After a lifetime's worth of sighs and rolled eyes, Sharon finally cleared herself through the metal detector where she was—no surprise—selected for a secondary security screening by a large, taciturn woman armed with an electronic wand and an attitude.

By her own admission Sharon Lewis was the type of person who tailgated mercilessly, who counted items in the baskets of those in front of her in the supermarket express lane, and whose idea of a vacation was an uninterrupted bath. Her friends—and there were precious few of those—would call her intolerant.

While waiting impatiently for her turn to be wanded by the uniformed woman she was certain was an ex-Marine, Sharon saw from a fleeting glance at her watch that she had nine minutes remaining to get to her gate to catch her flight to Houston. That meant she had only nine minutes to accomplish all of the following: to get past this grizzly bear of a security officer, to hustle downstairs to board the train, to make it down the track two stops to B Concourse, and then to run like hell all the way to Gate 19, which, of course, was almost the farthest possible gate location from the concourse train station.

It was then—at the crucial moment of her morning endurance trial when she looked at her watch and did the calculations—that Sharon Lewis made a memorably bad decision.

*   *   *

The infamous photograph of her—that grainy one that just about everyone had seen and that anyone who had ever been inconvenienced at any airport anywhere in the world had cursed—had run in that week's *Time* magazine with the telling caption: THE MOST SELFISH WOMAN IN AMERICA.

How had Sharon earned the title?

Sharon had gazed around the bustling security area and concluded that no one was paying any particular attention to her, especially not the gruff woman with the wand, who at that moment was busy assisting an elderly Asian gentleman with an aluminum cane remove his wingtips. The fact that Sharon was being totally ignored not only infuriated her but also permitted her an odd sense of freedom. She was tired of waiting for her turn to be wanded. She was tired of things going wrong that morning. She was, as she put it to me later, "tired of counting idiots."

Her flight to Houston was minutes away from leaving Denver without her.

What did Sharon do? She took things into her own hands. She proceeded to lift the black nylon band from the security corral in which she was penned, casually slipped through to the other side, replaced the band into its track, grabbed her rolling suitcase off the stainless steel table where it awaited her post-X ray, and strutted—unimpeded—toward the escalators.

Less than a minute later she pushed her way in front of yet another old man—this one was in a wheelchair—to squeeze onto a departing train that carried passengers from the terminal to the distant concourses.

News reports revealed that eight minutes passed after Sharon removed herself from the secondary screening queue before the security force in the terminal—tipped off by a passenger who had been waiting behind Sharon—ascertained that their security perimeter had been intentionally breached. Within two minutes all the airport's security checkpoints were closed. Four minutes after that the trains to the concourses were shut down. And a couple of minutes after that, planes at the gates were directed to stop boarding, planes that were taxiing were ordered to return to their gates, and procedures were initiated to sanitize the concourses and return everyone to the main terminal to once again pass through the interminable maze of security.

Later, when supervisors reviewed the security tape of the incident, the authorities were able to isolate a terribly grainy picture of Sharon Lewis strolling unhindered around the boundary of the secondary security screening area, her suitcase trailing behind her.

But the security personnel didn't know it was Sharon Lewis who had caused the entire system to grind to a halt. They didn't know that the person who was responsible for costing tens of thousands of passengers precious hours and the airline industry millions of dollars in delayed and canceled flights all across the nation was a Boulder business executive. All they knew was that the culprit was a thin woman with dirty blond hair, about five six or five seven, wearing a black suit with a white blouse and tugging a rolling suitcase.

Sharon? She didn't know what the fuss was all about because by the time DIA was shut down, her United Airlines flight to Houston had just gone nose up. She only learned about the repercussions of the incident later that day. The buyer from the company she was visiting in Texas told her the entire story, describing the woman who had skirted security as "that self-centered bitch who shut down DIA."

She'd smiled wanly at him through her nausea. But, she assured me later, she'd closed the sale.

For the two weeks since the breach at DIA federal law enforcement authorities had been searching desperately for the woman in the grainy security photograph. They wanted to arrest her, convict her, fine her, and imprison her, though not necessarily in that order. From the tone of the public discourse that followed the incident, drawing and quartering didn't seem to have been totally ruled out as a punitive option, either.

But no one knew who she was, or where she was.

Except for me. And my lips were sealed.

ELEVEN

After Sharon's visit at eight o'clock I had another patient at eight forty-five. And another at nine-thirty. Yet another at ten-fifteen. A scheduled break at eleven o'clock to catch my breath—and cram in a visit to the toilet—was sacrificed for a follow-up session with Gibbs. My bladder wasn't happy.

"Sterling thinks I'm at that mall in Broomfield. He thinks all I do is shop," she announced as she settled onto the sofa.

I waited for her to go on. With that opening, all she had told me was that she considered me to be her coconspirator. But I already knew that. Apparently, I'd volunteered for the role during the previous morning's session.

Admittedly, I was having second thoughts about how quickly I'd raised my hand to enlist.

"If he knew I was here talking to you, he'd kill me."

"Kill you?"

"You know."

"No, I don't know."

"He wouldn't be happy. Let's leave it at that."

Right, I'll leave it at that. That sounds like a great idea.

The high-pressure ridge responsible for the warm air that had enveloped the Front Range since the morning of Sam's heart attack remained firmly in place, and this mid-November day had broken from the gate fair and mild. I'd led Gibbs from the waiting room at one minute past eleven o'clock, and a glance out the window suggested that a day that had started gloriously had only gotten better. A month-plus before Christmas, a mile high, and eighty degrees wasn't out of the question.

Gibbs was dressed as though she had stayed up the night before in order to catch the late weather report and plan her outfit accordingly. She wore capris that were almost too pink and that hugged her slender legs almost too snugly. Almost. Her shoes, as always, looked fresh from the box. Actually, my shoes never looked that good, even straight from the box. Her champagne sweater set—I was guessing silk but allowing for cashmere—displayed a wide swath of her smooth chest but only the barest hint of cleavage. I tried to conjure the image of another one of my female patients who would have dressed the same way Gibbs was dressed for a similar morning session. I couldn't.

But on Gibbs the look worked.

Diane, I figured, would have argued that Gibbs looked slutty.

Über-*popular alpha bitch* slutty.

As far as nicknames went, I'd already decided that I preferred "the Dancing Queen."

My impression of Gibbs during the earlier treatment had always been that she liked to live her life near the line where classic style and fashionable trends collide, but that she rarely wandered across it. Her outfit was a good metaphor for all that.

Accusing her husband of murder, though—that had definitely taken her across the line.

"Did you talk to those people you were going to talk to?" she asked.

"Yes, I did. I spoke with Dr. Estevez, and then she and I met with the director of Safe House on your behalf. The admissions people at Safe House are waiting for your phone call. They are more than happy to provide you with a safe place to stay. As soon as you're ready, they will send somebody over here to pick you up. They want to be certain that you're not followed on your way to the residence."

She crossed her legs, flinched a little bit with her eyes, and said, "I don't think I want to go there after all. I've changed my mind." With the slightest shrug of her shoulders, she added, "Don't be mad at me."

Perhaps there had been a time in my career when I might have found her display of world-class denial the slightest bit endearing, but if there had been, I was definitely past it.

"Yes?" I said.

That's what I said out loud, anyway. Inside, I was screaming things like *"What the hell are you talking about? Are you crazy? You just said the man would kill you!"*

But was I surprised at her change of heart?

Hardly. A colleague who spent much of her time treating abused spouses once told me that battered women had to leave their husbands five times before they stopped being drawn back. In her world, the sixth separation was the magic one.

Usually, anyway. She'd reminded me that she'd once treated a woman who went back eleven times.

Eleven. And anyone who'd been in practice doing psychotherapy for a while had treated abused women who never considered leaving even once.

As far as I knew, Gibbs was one of those. She hadn't left Sterling even once. This morning's short trip to Boulder's Safe House was going to be their virgin marital separation.

"You're concerned that I'll be angry with you?" I kept my voice as mild as the shampoo that I used to bathe my daughter's silky hair. I was already past my reactive anger and back in the shallows of the sea of compassion for the constellation of psychology and circumstances that caused abused women like Gibbs to make decisions that would seem muddled even for a four-year-old faced with a decision about whether to be friends with a bully.

"You went to a lot of trouble for me. And I don't like to appear ungrateful. That was nice, what you did."

Nice?

"You're concerned about my reaction?"

"Yes."

"Does that tell you anything?" Experienced therapy patients ask questions like that one on their own, without prompting. I didn't expect that Gibbs was even close to being able to do it.

"That I don't like to disappoint people?" She was guessing at the answer. I had sat next to a kid in high school algebra who'd answered every question with that exact same inflection. For an entire year.

"Or . . . maybe . . . you feel the same way with me that you feel sometimes with Sterling."

"I don't know what you mean."

"You make your decisions based on fear of disappointing people, or concern about making them angry. If you're worried about making me angry, I can only guess how concerned you might be about Sterling's reaction to finding out what you've told me, or about his discovering that you've left him."

"I don't think that's it," she said.

How much consideration had she given it? Less than a second. Apparently we weren't at a point in the therapy where I was being granted any wisdom transference.

I punted. "So you've changed your mind?"

"Not about the murder thing. No, no. About not feeling safe at home. That's what I changed my mind about."

Had she just said "the murder thing"? She had.

"You no longer think your husband will be angry that you're turning him in to the police for murder?" There is a yearlong seminar in clinical psychology graduate school on how to ask obvious questions with a straight face.

I'd aced it.

"Sterling really loves me. I think he'd want me to stay with him while this works out."

"Works out? And how is this going to work out?"

"I think he'll get arrested. That will solve my problems for a while. At least about the murder thing. After that I just don't know. With a good lawyer these days, anything is possible."

Gibbs's musings were at once both rational and incredibly naïve. Although I knew what I wanted to say next, I paused through a couple of breathing cycles before I said it. I would have preferred for her to respond to the echoes of her own words, but she didn't.

"When you started today's session, you said that Sterling was going to kill you. Now you would like me to believe that you're convinced that you are safe living with him even though you're about to turn him in to the police for murdering your mutual friend?"

Her face brightened inexplicably. She blurted, "That's so great! I think that's almost exactly what Dr. Phil would say."

"Excuse me?"

"Dr. Phil—you know, on the—oh, you don't know, do you? The guy on TV?"

She could tell I was befuddled.

She quickly added, "Don't worry, it's not *that* important that you know who . . ." Her voice trailed away.

I actually had a vague idea who Dr. Phil was. What I was befuddled about was the question of whether it was a good thing or a potentially embarrassing thing that I was beginning to sound like a psychologist who plied his trade on daytime television.

I made a mental note to ask Diane how humiliated I should be. She had her finger on the pulse of things like that.

"Yesterday," I said, "you were frightened enough of Sterling that you asked me to solicit help for you from Safe House. Today you've convinced yourself that the danger isn't real. Which am I supposed to believe?"

"Sterling doesn't want to hurt me."

I thought it was an interesting statement. Wishful, but interesting.

"Can you hear your own confusion?" I asked her.

"I'm not confused. I changed my mind. People do that. People react impulsively sometimes."

Softly, I probed, "Gibbs, has Sterling not wanting to hurt you kept him from hurting you in the past?"

She sighed, gave me a little half-smile. I took it to mean that I'd asked another Dr. Phil question.

"If he hurt me now, wouldn't that be like proof of what he did to Louise? He wouldn't risk that. Sterling isn't stupid."

"And you are willing to run that risk? You're willing to believe that, despite his threats, despite his past behavior, despite the fact that you're accusing him of murdering a friend of yours, he won't hurt you now?" I allowed a tincture of incredulity to enter my voice.

"Yes, I am," she said definitively. "I am. I don't want to go to Safe

House. I want to go back home. Will you call the police in California now? Right now? I want to get that over with."

"Why me? Why don't you make the call yourself, Gibbs?"

"I can't. Betraying Sterling to you is as far as I can go. It's been hard even going this far."

I sat silently, urging her to say more. She didn't. The quiet stretched over two minutes or more.

Finally, I said, "But you'll cooperate with the police and testify about what you know?"

"If they arrest him? Yes, I'll testify. And if the police ask to talk with me before that, I will talk with them. I already told you that. I'm trying to do the right thing, Dr. Gregory."

I recalled Lauren's caution about spousal immunity. I wondered if Gibbs knew what I knew on that topic, that she couldn't testify against Sterling in California, which meant that the police would have to develop substantial evidence on their own to support her allegations.

"If the police ask to talk with you right now? While I'm on the phone?"

"No. Not right now."

I considered the fact that I had an out. Gibbs wasn't keeping her end of the bargain we'd made the previous morning—seeking shelter at Safe House. I concluded that her change of heart abrogated my responsibility to keep my end of the bargain—calling the homicide detective in California.

In my own heart, however, I knew that I was still inclined to make the call to California, not solely because I'd told Gibbs that I would, or because of some absurd sense of responsibility I was feeling because of a hypothetical bargain I'd made with her.

I was inclined to make the call because it was the right thing to do. Why? Because of the murder thing. I could spend some unpredictable amount of time in therapy trying to influence her to make the phone call herself, but with an unsolved homicide hanging in the balance, it didn't seem like a prudent plan.

I had received information about an unsolved murder; I was in a position to help the police close the case and put the responsible party behind bars. That was a novel state of affairs for me. But what made things even more unique in my experience was the fact that the screwy circumstances allowed me a rare ethical sanctuary: I actually had my patient's permission to share information in my possession with the police.

That doesn't happen very often in my business. I couldn't think of another time it had happened in my career.

But sitting across from Gibbs, I wasn't feeling free to act. What I was feeling was hesitant. Maybe I should have heeded the caution I was feeling right then. The caution was saying: *Reconsider.*

But I didn't. Instead I stood, walked over to my desk phone, and lifted the receiver.

"I brought the number with me," Gibbs said.

I placed the receiver back down. "I'm not as comfortable proceeding with the call as I would be if you weren't planning to return to your home."

Her shoulders sank a little. "Sterling is what he is whether or not you make the call."

"True. And I'm afraid he's someone who may hurt you."

"I don't think so. He's protective of me. I'm not saying it's normal protectiveness, Dr. Gregory, whatever that is, but he's protective of me."

"Protective?"

"Yes. Very. Sterling is controlling. Very controlling. But he's only touched me once. In anger, I mean, and that was . . . years ago. Many years ago. Are you going to make the call?"

"I don't know." I didn't.

Gibbs shifted on her chair. She sat back, crossed one leg over the other, and rested one forearm on the other. Each hand grasped the opposing biceps. "Remember I said yesterday that it wasn't only Louise?"

"Yes." Goose bumps shot up my spine.

She looked away from me. "You can't tell this to the police, okay? What I'm about to tell you."

"Actually that's not my call to make, Gibbs. It's yours. You decide what leaves this room."

"Then what I tell you from now on doesn't leave the room. You can't tell this to Dr. Estevez or to the California police."

"Would you like to rescind your previous release in writing?"

I immediately wondered why I'd asked her that. I couldn't re-member ever making that offer to a patient before.

She made eye contact again. "No, that's not necessary. I trust you."

Somehow her assurance that she trusted me wasn't the most com-forting of news. I didn't say "okay" or "fine." I waited silently for what was going to come next.

It turned out that Gibbs didn't need much time to hurdle what-ever obstacles she faced about continuing.

"It's not just about Louise. I wish it were. Although I think she was the first, it's not just about Louise. My husband has killed a num-ber of women. All over the country."

With false confidence I'd set down the cards of my two-pair hand, and Gibbs had trumped me with the old serial killer royal flush.

TWELVE

Good advice.

"Do not wander from designated paths and trails." That's what the first sign said. It was a hundred yards back, where there was still some light from the visitors' center.

"Do not go near any water." That order was posted ten yards farther along the trail.

Now here she was breaking all the rules. She was off the trail. She was near the water. Beneath her bare feet she could feel the muddy ground begin to turn into something that was the consistency of wet, putrefied hay. The stench was sour. In the darkness the odor screamed at her.

Gritty moisture squished up between her toes.

She bathed twice a day. Every day. Morning and night. She detested filth.

And decay? Please! Shivers shot up her spine.

The night was moonless. Her eyes found streaks to focus on, but the streaks disappeared as soon as she tried to reel them in. She couldn't see. It was the smell, and the feel of the rotting

*life between her toes, that convinced her that the swamp water was
near.*

*And there had been one more sign. It had read, "Do not smoke or
litter."*

*She wasn't breaking that rule. Five minutes ago, maybe. No, it
had only been two or three. She'd been breaking that rule, sitting
there in the car. Smoking, yes; not littering. Fantasizing. Had everything changed so much in two minutes?*

Yes. Everything had changed.

She shivered. And why am I naked?

Oh, yeah.

Sterling.

Damn Sterling.

*Five minutes ago she was still loving it. Every bit of it. The head-
phones, the tape, the music, the voice, the whole thing. Disrobing in
the car. Waiting for him there, naked. Waiting for him to . . .*

She tried to think.

*Truth? She was more frightened of the swamp than she was of the
gun. She'd grown up around guns in Virginia, was a pretty good shot
herself. She didn't have the gun this time, though. It was pointed at
her. That was hard to ignore.*

But not as hard to ignore as the swamp.

*She hated swamps and everything that lived in them. She hated
snakes. She hated alligators. She hated frogs. She even hated the damn
harmless dragonflies. When she was thirteen, one had become tangled
in her hair at school. She'd been so frightened by the flapping that
she'd pulled the hallway fire alarm to get some help.*

Her friends had never let her forget it.

*She told herself not to panic in the swamp. There was a way out.
She had to find the way out.*

*The voice from the Walkman had instructed her to duct-tape her
mouth. Let that awful stuff even touch her hair? Yeah, right. She'd
thought he was kidding. He wasn't. She'd done it. Now the tape
across her lips limited her to whimpers.*

*Her wrists were bound in front of her with the same awful gray
tape. The instructions had made sense at the time is what she told herself.*

What was I thinking?

On an exhale, she thought of blue herons. Herons liked swamps. She'd loved watching them on that boat tour she'd taken that time in the Everglades. She liked herons. Okay, she didn't love them. Birds made her nervous. But she tried to imagine walking into a flock of blue herons. That would be okay. She could survive that.

She stopped.

Behind her the voice said, "Keep going." It was a hoarse whisper. The same strange voice that was on the Walkman. "Don't turn."

The voice said keep going. She kept going.

Her next step took her ankle-deep into the dank water. Two more steps, and her kneecaps sank below the surface.

She'd lived in Augusta for four years. During that time she'd never visited the Phinizy Swamp Nature Park. Not once. She hated swamps. A girlfriend had once said something about there being bobcats out here.

Bobcats? She shivered.

She preferred golf courses. That was all the nature she needed: the back nine at Augusta, across town. Midnight on the thirteenth green again? She didn't need to be a member for that round, did she? That night was . . . perfection.

She had no idea what was spread out in front of her. A pond-size swamp? An Everglades-size swamp? Are swamps deep? Shallow?

She heard a splash, then realized that she had made the noise herself. How far behind her was the gun? She didn't know, but she couldn't wait. She had to move. She decided to run. In her head she flipped a coin. Tails.

She would run right.

Before her first step, she heard another splash. She knew she hadn't made that one. She screamed into her gag.

"Keep going." The gun hadn't moved with her. "Don't turn." The gun was farther away, back a few steps. The odds said now.

Now!

She lifted her knees high and sprinted to her right, hoping, praying that her next few steps wouldn't be her last few steps.

She splashed. Can't run in knee-deep water without splashing.

Please don't shoot, please don't shoot.

She thought she spotted the glooming outline of a tree. Someplace to hide. Something to provide cover. How far away was it?

She heard more splashing. Her own? She didn't know. She tripped on something solid below the surface of the swamp and slipped right down as though she'd been slapped. Muck seeped into her nose and ears. She tasted decay as she tried to scream, "I'm sorry, Daddy," but despite the tape her mouth was full of the effluent of the Phinizy Swamp.

Have to get up. *She tried to stand.*

She felt a tug on her thigh.

It was insistent. And then it was crushing.

Suddenly, she was swimming backward involuntarily. Her last thought was I hate alligators.

THIRTEEN

"A serial killer?"

"I don't want to say any more than what I said, Dr. Gregory. I just needed you to realize what is at stake here."

"Sterling has killed women all over the country?"

"Yes. Please call the police. He needs to be behind bars. We can't wait."

We?

I digested the implications.

"Is anyone else in danger?" If Gibbs identified a future potential victim, it would launch me into a gray stratosphere where I might be required to breach her confidentiality.

"Not that I know of," she said.

Silently I counted to five. I spent the seconds trying to decide whether or not I believed her.

FOURTEEN

I had only fifteen minutes to begin to digest what I'd just learned.

The lunchtime appointment that followed my Tuesday morning session with Gibbs belonged to a member of the local bar. Jim Zebid was a defense attorney, a litigator who also did occasional plaintiff's work on malpractice claims. He had an interesting background, having been around the Boulder County criminal justice system working as a private investigator while putting himself through law school.

I'd been seeing him for a few months during the same Tuesday slot, and the therapeutic relationship continued to fascinate me. At times he was eager to spar with me over seeming inconsequentials; at other times I felt he would be content to curl up in my lap in parody of my foster poodle, Anvil. Not having a solid handle on one of my patients' psychological profiles was nothing novel for me, but I found Jim Zebid a particularly interesting and perplexing man.

Since our first session I'd been working under the assumption that Jim chose me as a psychotherapist because I was married to a prosecutor whom he knew. His underlying motivation for making that choice? I wasn't sure, but I felt confident that he and I would come around to it before too long. I suspected that it had to do with competition, or with secrets, or with some curious transference that would follow a serpentine trail back to his mother and his father.

Or maybe it had to do with all of the above.

Jim's presenting problem was anxiety. His anxiety manifested itself in traditional ways: through nervousness, irritability, trouble sleeping, rumination, and occasional self-medication with alcohol and marijuana. By history, the present symptoms weren't novel for him. Although only thirty-one, he'd suffered from anxiety problems since his days as an undergraduate at UCLA. Later, when the symptoms had aggravated during law school, he'd rationalized away the problems as stress-related. But the symptoms continued unabated, and Jim had recently, albeit reluctantly, come to the conclusion that something more intrinsic might be responsible for his chronic misery.

Early on I referred him to a psychiatrist for a medication consultation. The Xanax Jim was prescribed had succeeded not only in taking the edge off his symptoms but in making him more psychologically available for the insight work that he insisted he wanted to do with me. Occasionally, though, I thought that his anxiety still proved an impediment to psychotherapy, and I wasn't quite sure about the ultimate efficacy of the Xanax.

For a few weeks I'd been weighing asking the prescribing psychiatrist to consider an anxiolytic antidepressant instead.

The session after Gibbs's second individual appointment was one of those days when I wasn't so sure about Jim Zebid's desire to work.

I admit that he didn't have one hundred percent of my attention. Although most days I prided myself on my ability to move from one patient to the next with the clarity of flipping channels on a TV remote, Gibbs's most recent revelations were still clouding my focus that morning. I was making a conscious effort to fight through the static of Gibbs's serial killer accusation so that I could make certain that Jim had a sufficient quantity of my concentration.

"Anyway, my client says he sold half an ounce of blow to Judge Heller's husband. My guy is only up for an aggravated burglary, and I'm not sure I want to complicate things by revealing he's dealing, so I'm not sure what the hell I'm going to do with the information. But you have to admit it's something. Too bad it's not Judge Heller's case."

Jara Heller was the youngest judge on the District Court bench. I knew her socially—in the sense that I could have picked her out in a crowded room. I wasn't sure I could say the same about her husband, although I felt it was likely that I had met him at some legal affair or reception or cocktail party over the years. For all I knew he and I may have commiserated or shared a look of mutually felt angst while fulfilling our spousal obligations by our attendance.

"Still . . ." Jim said, apparently continuing to muse over the illusion of leverage that came with knowing that a young judge's husband used cocaine and purchased it in quantities large enough to suggest that he sold some, too.

The look on Jim's face reminded me of a guy who'd just witnessed a wallet crammed with bills spill from a woman's purse and was wondering how he could rationalize clipping a few fifties before he handed the billfold back to its owner.

Most days I don't hear a single fact during psychotherapy that would be meaningful to anyone other than my patient, me, and a limited circle of people who happen to share my patient's plot in the universe. But that day? I'd already heard an update from a wanted woman, a report about a serial killer, and news about a judge's husband possibly selling cocaine, and I hadn't even given a thought to my midday meal.

FIFTEEN

Gibbs's revelation that she feared her husband was a serial killer, and not merely a killer, had changed things for me. The shocking news that he'd left a string of victims across the country not only cemented my decision to make the call to the detectives in California but also subtly altered my resolve. As I drove across town to visit Sam after Jim Zebid's session, I turned down the radio and pondered the philosophical underpinnings of it all, ultimately concluding that John Donne wouldn't be pleased by the metamorphosis of my attitude. One death should have been as consequential as many. One death should have been sufficient.

Sam had one additional "should" for me: "You should've talked to me as soon as you knew" was how Sam admonished me after I gave him the headline about the California murder.

He was feeling better. Although he was still in the telemetry unit when I was with him during my late lunch break, he and his cardiologist had radically different opinions on how long he should remain tethered to heart-monitoring equipment.

"You've had a few other things to deal with," I said.

The automated blood pressure cuff encircling Sam's biceps chose that moment to inflate. Sam jumped. "Damn thing scares me so much that it probably sends my blood pressure right through the roof. Hey, maybe you can convince my cardiologist that my mental health requires that I return home immediately."

"Good one, Sam. But I don't think you really want me to go on record commenting on your mental health."

"Point."

After I'd heard the multiple murder accusation, I negotiated one final rider to my bargain with Gibbs Storey. I would go ahead and make the call to the homicide detectives in California only if she would permit me to consult with a friend of mine who was a local detective regarding the Louise/Sterling situation, and with an attorney, if I chose. I told her I wouldn't need to use any names, just the facts of her accusation. Gibbs had agreed to my request without protest.

Actually, what she said was "The whole world is going to know my family's dirty secrets in a few days, Dr. Gregory. What's to be lost by giving this detective friend of yours a head start? If it will help you better understand the legal process that's about to happen, please go right ahead. Talk to a lawyer, too. I don't care. But just about Louise. And no names until it's in the press."

I'd had her sign a release.

Once I'd explained the broad outlines of the Louise/Sterling situation to Sam, he asked me to clarify some facts about Gibbs's accusation before he said, "So when you called the detective in this other state, this mystery state? Did he hang up on you, or what?"

"She came close. It actually didn't come down the way I thought it would. When I called, there was nobody there who could talk to me. I left a message. Eventually a Detective Reynoso called back. We didn't stop playing phone tag until about an hour ago."

"Well? Is your lady's story for real?"

"Reynoso seemed interested enough in what I had to tell her, but

she didn't reveal much to me. It was kind of like trying to get information out of you."

"Be nice. I just had a heart attack."

"What's going to happen next, Sam?"

"Hard to say without knowing how closely your client's story
meshes with what the cops already know. That's the gold standard."

"If it meshes, then what?"

"If it were my case and I got the call? I'd go to my superiors and
make a case that I should fly to wherever the woman is and interview
her. Maybe talk with her husband, too."

"Would you make an appointment with her or just show up?"

"I'm a big proponent of just showing up."

"Why?"

"In my business, when you make appointments, you almost always end up talking with lawyers. As much as I adore your wife, she's
a rare exception to the breed, you know? I'm trying to arrange my life
so that I interact with as few lawyers as possible. It's a good stress-
reduction strategy—you know, for my heart."

"So you show up. When you get to town, do you have to call the
local cops?"

"Absolutely. My guess is that one of my colleagues has already
spoken with your detective—what's her name?"

"Reynoso. Carmen Reynoso. Can you find out who?"

"Can I find out, or will I tell you? What's the question here?"

"Will you tell me?"

"No."

"Didn't think so. So this Detective Reynoso talks to one of you
guys at the police department, and you do what?"

"We listen to her story, weigh what she wants to do, and decide
whether we want to cooperate. Odds are that her requests are somewhere close to reasonable. We consent, maybe we tag along on the
interviews, whatever."

"How long could all this take?"

"Depends how hot it all seems. Reynoso could get on a plane today if she wanted to. Politics might be tough on her end and that
might slow her down, or she could spend a couple of weeks, maybe
even longer, getting her ducks in a row before she comes out."

"And the whole time a murderer is just wandering around doing his thing."

Sam made a dismissive face. "Perps are like snakes, Alan. They're always out there, living in holes. They're always close by, doing their snake thing, whether you see them or not. The ones that end up scaring the shit out of us are the ones that slither across our backyard during a barbecue. Well, this one—this lady's husband—just slithered right across your yard. But the truth is he was out there for years before you knew about him. And he may be out there for years longer before anybody does anything about him. Fact is, he's just another sick snake."

Over my first cup of coffee early that morning, I would probably have been placated by Sam's assertion that Sterling was just another sick snake. But no longer. If Gibbs was right about Sterling, I knew he wasn't just another sick snake. He was a cobra with blood from some undetermined number of women dripping from his needlelike fangs.

I reminded myself that Gibbs hadn't given me permission to talk with Sam about the other women she believed her husband had killed, only about Louise. "Some guys are . . . more dangerous than others, Sam. Right?" was all I could think of to say.

"You mean this guy? I don't know. From what little you've told me, I'm thinking the murder was a heat-of-passion thing. What are the odds of a repeat? Higher than you and me—or at least me, anyway—but statistically not that high. Contrary to public opinion, most people don't develop a taste for it. For murder, I mean. What does he do, anyway? For a living?"

I wondered whether I could reveal that information based on the limited release I had from Gibbs. I decided I could. "He's involved in the production of sporting events for a national cable TV channel."

"ESPN? Does he do hockey?"

"I'm not going to tell you any more than I've told you."

"Have I heard of him?"

"I doubt it. Maybe if you read credits." If Sam read credits, I'd eat a hockey puck.

"It's not like . . . Barry Melrose or Don Cherry, is it?"

I didn't know who Barry Melrose was. Don Cherry? I knew I'd heard of him, but I couldn't have guessed who he was, either. Given that Sam was asking, I assumed that both of them had something to do with hockey, and neither was in the production end of the game.

I said, "Production, not talent."

"Cherry has a temper. Impulse problems, you know?"

"And that's unusual among hockey players?" I asked innocently.

"It's all relative."

"Don't worry; it's not Don Cherry, Sam."

He sipped water out of a cup with a straw. "She's going to stop by to see you, too, you know."

"Who is?"

He burped and lifted his hand to the center of his chest.

I almost screamed for a nurse.

"Reynoso. She won't make an appointment, or ask you to Starbucks for a latte. But she's going to show up to talk to you, too."

"That's okay. I'll tell her exactly what I told you. That's all I have permission to tell her."

He stuck the tip of his finger so far into his ear canal that I wondered whether he was missing some essential part of his aural anatomy. "That might not satisfy her. Some cops aren't as easygoing as I am."

"Now there's a scary thought."

"You know more, don't you? Your client didn't give you permission to tell me everything, did she?"

"I can't answer that, Sam. Confidentiality. I'm sorry."

He nodded. "I may get out of here today. Doc's coming by later. Says he may let me go home and get into an outpatient rehab program. You know: exercise, diet, stress reduction."

"That's great," I said. "Maybe Adrienne can get you doing some yoga. It'd be great for your stress."

"You're kidding, right?"

"Hockey players do yoga."

"Now you're giving me chest pain."

"Don't joke about that, Sam. What about work?"

"My captain came by, made reassuring noises about me going back. He says they want to make sure I'm in the best possible shape before I'm back on the job. A million docs will have to clear me. He said I shouldn't even think about working until after New Year's."

"A six-week vacation will do you good. Give you a chance to break in your new healthy lifestyle."

"Six weeks at home right now is not exactly my idea of a stress-reduction prescription. Sherry's already making noises about having to roast tofu instead of turkey next week. She's not going to be happy having me moping around the house until after New Year's."

I knew I didn't want to ask Sam what was going on in his marriage. I sensed he didn't want me to ask, either. I played along with his denial. I didn't feel good about it, but that's what I did.

"You'll have a great time with Simon, Sam."

"He's in school during the week, takes the bus up to the mountains to snowboard with his friends every weekend. Copper Choppers, you know about it? When Grace gets older, you will. Anyway, I don't think my cardiologist is going to endorse me doing a whole lot of snowboarding this winter." Sam asked, "Why did she stay with him so long? Your client? She's known he was a murderer for a while. Why did she stay with him for so long?"

"Fear. Loyalty. Denial. That's a tough question, Sam. Why do women stay in unhealthy marriages? We both see it all the time."

He turned away from me and from my question. He moved a tissue box on his bedside tray. "Why is she turning him in now?"

"Another tough question."

Sam picked that moment to adjust his bed. Once he had it right he said, "If it happens—if I get released from this place—would you maybe be around later to give me a ride home?"

I almost asked, "What about Sherry?" But I didn't. I said, "Of course."

SIXTEEN

"Although I don't really want to," Gibbs began, "I think maybe we should talk about sex."

I almost said what I was thinking. What I was thinking was that Gibbs and I should be talking about serial murder. Sex could wait.

Instead I stifled a yawn.

At my insistence Gibbs had come back in for a session on Thursday. My only free time was seven-fifteen. In the morning. As good a time as any to talk about sex, right?

There was a brief time in my career when a preamble like the one Gibbs offered would have caused my ears to perk up just a little. Part of the arousal of interest I'd have felt would have been prurient or voyeuristic, I'm sure, but mostly the increased interest on my part would have had to do with inexperience.

I would have mistaken an introduction like hers for a promise that I'd hear the titillating prelude to something new, something different, something intrinsically interesting.

But just as my first visit to a nude beach had taught me that most people are more attractive—much more attractive—with their clothes on, my experience doing psychotherapy had taught me that most people's sex lives weren't particularly fascinating, and that the more details I knew, the less fascinating they turned out to be.

Where sex was concerned, a little mystery did indeed go a long way.

After well over a decade of clinical practice I tended to listen to tales of erotic encounters, or supposed erotic encounters, with the same detachment that I listened to the details of marital arrangements over housecleaning or the choice between individual and joint checking accounts.

"Just grist for the mill," one of my old supervisors would have said about sexual topics in psychotherapy. "It's all just grist for the mill." I would nod knowingly to her in response to her maxim, but the truth was that I didn't even know what grist meant. Still don't.

I found that I looked back and contemplated the professional road I had traveled more and more as the years passed. Maybe it was a function of age, maybe it was just the fact that I had a growing list of things to look back on. In graduate school I knew a guy who insisted that he never looked back and didn't even use his mirrors while driving. "Everything I need to see is out in front of me," he claimed.

Me? I lived believing that whatever I didn't spot creeping up behind me was likely to take a good-sized chunk out of my ass.

One of the items in my rearview mirror that early Thursday morning exactly a week before Thanksgiving was Diane's contention that during the prior conjoint therapy I'd suffered from night blindness and totally missed the sexual fuel that was simmering in Gibbs and Sterling Storey's relationship. I was determined not to make the same mistake twice.

Gibbs and I would talk about sex first.

Then serial murder.

"Okay," I said to Gibbs. *Let's talk about sex. Swinging, right?* "But first I'd like to take a moment to check on your safety. Are you all right, Gibbs?"

"Yes."

I waited for her to elaborate.

"I am," she insisted.

"You haven't told Sterling, though?"

"No. And I don't plan to until I have to."

"And the California police haven't contacted you?"

"No, they haven't."

"What if they suddenly show up at your door? And what if Sterling answers?"

"That will change things, won't it?"

"Are you as cavalier about this as you sound?"

"I'm really not. I'm serious about what I'm doing."

"Then I strongly recommend you reconsider your decision not to go to Safe House."

"I understand why you're concerned about me, but I don't think I can move out. I'm going to stay at home." She gazed down at her hands and said, "Now do you think we can we talk about sex?"

Seven-twenty, and Gibbs looked like she'd been up for a couple of hours and had spent the time getting herself prepped for tea with some friends she was trying to impress. Her hair—perfect. Makeup—ditto. Outfit? A little too . . . something.

"Slutty," Diane would say, of course. But Gibbs's ensemble wasn't really slutty, just a shadow or two sexier than almost any other woman would assemble for an early-morning meeting to discuss her sex life with her therapist.

"Sex," she said, her voice suddenly crusty in a sultry Peggy Lee kind of way. "It's not just for procreation anymore."

Was it ever? Instantly, I was wide awake. Even at that hour I had the presence of mind to know that my sudden vigilance wasn't entirely a good thing.

"Sterling and I met in St. Tropez. Did we ever tell you that?"

I thought it was the kind of fact I'd have remembered from the earlier therapy. But I didn't recall previously musing with Gibbs, or any other patient for that matter, about any of the playgrounds of the privileged in the South of France. It was one of those things that didn't come up regularly in psychotherapy in Boulder, Colorado.

"I don't think so," I said.

"Sterling was working as crew on some rich guy's yacht—a big boat—and I was doing a summer-in-France-learn-a-language thing with a girlfriend after my freshman year in college. We all met at this big Saturday morning market in town in St. Tropez—Oh, you should go! The market was so much fun!—and he and his friends invited us onto the boat for a party later that day. It started with everybody swimming in the afternoon. We were anchored within sight of the beach, and Sterling put on this diving exhibition off the bow. He was really good. Flips and pikes and God knows what else he was doing. He was the center of everybody's attention. I admit that I couldn't take my eyes off him.

"We hit it off; I mean, I really liked him right from the start. But you know, the party was going to be it as far as seeing him went; the yacht was sailing the next morning to Greece or Yugoslavia or some-where. When my girlfriend and I left at the end of the evening— actually it was more like the middle of the night—I told Sterling where he could look me up in Palos Verdes if he wanted, but I never thought I'd see him again after that.

"Those summer things, they tug and tug, don't they? Did you ever have one, Dr. Gregory?"

Gibbs's breathing seemed to have grown deeper. Recalling her youthful memories had softened her persona just a little. My judg-ment was that she didn't really care whether or not I'd ever had a summer thing, but nonetheless my focus wavered for half a heartbeat with lusty reminiscences of an ancient August week with Nancy Lind when our families were both—

"Have you ever been to St. Tropez?" she asked, yanking me back to *her* summer thing.

I knew she didn't really want to know that, either. It was merely a way of stressing that *she* had.

"No," I said.

"It's not what you think. As a town, I mean. Well, it is, but then, you know, it isn't. It's not just the stereotype."

I was wondering why it was important what I thought of St. Tropez, a topic about which I never expected to have an opinion, let alone one firm enough to degrade into a stereotype. Asking her why it was important to her what I thought, I decided, would risk interfering with the direction of a journey I knew next to nothing about.

All I knew was that it was, directly or indirectly, about sex.

She didn't wait long to learn what misconceptions I might harbor about St. Tropez. "We didn't have sex that night," Gibbs said. "Other people did, almost everybody did. You know, it was that kind of party, but Sterling and I didn't do anything."

"Sex. It's not just for procreation anymore."

I started thinking that I'd never been to that kind of party. The kind of party where young beautiful people gather on a rich guy's yacht in St. Tropez and everybody has sex under the stars. A lost opportunity of my youth, perhaps. I didn't even recall the fork in the road with the sign marked WANTON SEX IN ST. TROPEZ, THIS WAY.

"We wanted to—I did anyway. I was a prude, and I wanted to, so I'm sure he did. For me, it was the most romantic night of my life. And not just romantic, but . . . erotic, sensual, you know? The Mediterranean, the yacht, the sky, the music, the wine, and these gorgeous people from all over the world. Sex was in the air. When you breathed, you inhaled it. It filled your nose like the flowers at the market that morning. You sipped some wine, and you could taste it. The sex, I mean. It was everywhere. Do you know what I'm talking about?"

Hardly. But I didn't say anything. I thought she had enough momentum to continue on her own.

"I'd never been to a party like that before. With people so . . . uninhibited. Brazen. I mean, bold. And with strangers . . . So many languages . . . So much . . ." The final thought drifted away.

I admit that I was curious how her sentence would end, but any words on my part would have been distracting. I waited some more.

When she started up again, it was as though she were answering a question that I had never asked. Silence does that sometimes.

"What was it like to be there? I wanted to fall in love that night. I wanted to fall in love that night, and Sterling was there. He was handsome. He was charming. Oh, Sterling's not really tall enough to be my dream man, and I'd always fantasized that I'd end up with a guy with darker hair, but . . . that night he let me be there, but not be there. He let me dip a toe in the water—of, of that world—but he didn't throw me in the pool. He stayed with me almost the entire night while I tried to find out exactly where I might fit.

"That's not easy when you're nineteen and you're on a yacht in St. Tropez, right? Knowing where you fit?"

She found some affirmation somewhere in my impassive face, and she went on.

"There were other . . . you know, people for him on the boat. Plenty of them. Prettier than me. More adventurous than me, that's for sure. But . . . he didn't . . . go with them. He stayed with me. We danced. We kissed a little. Okay, we kissed a lot. And . . . you know. We watched a . . . little. But we didn't . . . So I guess that's why he was the one I . . ."

I was aware of the disconnect I was feeling. Despite the hour, despite my aversion to true sex adventures, the erotic escapade that Gibbs was spinning was actually interesting to me. I pushed myself hard against the cushion of my chair. It was a way of telling myself to take a step back. A way of reminding myself that whatever it was that was happening right then in my office, it was about Gibbs, not about her interlude in St. Tropez with Sterling.

My job was to ignore the fireworks and focus on the night sky.

To use my night vision. Not to be blinded.

"Anyway, he did call," she went on. "He actually called my parents' house the following Christmas Eve. I was home from school for the holidays. He came over, and we stayed out almost that whole night, just talking."

Instinctively, I guessed what was next. *No sex,* I thought. *He played it cool. It was just like St. Tropez, sans the yacht and the Mediterranean.*

"We didn't have sex then," she confirmed. "We just talked. But the whole night I felt like I was back on that yacht with him. It was that sensuous, that romantic, you know? I felt an anticipation, a sense of I-can't-wait, I-can't-wait, that I hadn't felt on Christmas Eve since I was eight years old. But of course it was different. And that's the charge I feel—still feel—when I see Sterling."

Mental note: She said "feel," not "felt."

The slope Gibbs was on suddenly changed. I experienced it as a physical sensation. Her momentum slowed as the gravitational forces eased. She pulled into herself, squeezing her biceps against her upper body. The effect was to force her breasts together, accentuating her previously modest cleavage.

Was that her intent? And was it conscious or unconscious? That was my call to make. It was why I was paid the big bucks.

But I didn't know.

"We had sex the first time a week later, on New Year's Eve," she said. "We were at a party, at a high-rise apartment on Wilshire Boulevard. You know, in L.A.? Some friends of his lived there. We ended up doing it on the balcony. The night wasn't that different from the party in St. Tropez. People were having sex all over the place. I could see another couple going at it in the bedroom next door while we were doing it outside."

She flicked a glance at me. If she could have read my mind, she would have known that I was musing that she and I had certainly spent our youths being invited to different parties.

What was she hoping? That I'd find her tale titillating? Scandalous? Mundane? I couldn't guess. I didn't like that I couldn't guess.

"That was the first time he said 'catch me.' "

" 'Catch me'?" I said.

"Yes," she said. " 'Catch me.' He said it again last night. It brought me back, reminded me."

I adopted a studied silence, waiting, wondering where Gibbs was going to go with her story of erotic adventure. It was clear that she wanted me to know that she'd made love to her husband the night before.

Was that it? Was that all?

What did the *catch me* story mean?

She matched my quiet. I set my sensors for defiance but wasn't sure exactly what I was detecting.

During the ensuing interim of silence I had a revelation—a slap-across-the-face kind of revelation.

My insight permitted me—hell, it compelled me—to finally ask the question I should have asked three days before, when Gibbs had first waltzed into my office and revealed that she believed her husband, Sterling, was a killer.

"Why did you come to see me, Gibbs?"

"What do you mean? We had an appointment."

My question had ambushed her, and her reply was more concrete than an interstate highway.

"Not this morning. I'm wondering why you came back into therapy with me."

She blinked twice in rapid succession. She parted her lips. But she didn't respond.

Finally I felt I knew something. Suddenly the therapy wasn't as amorphous as it had been.

What is it that I know?

I knew I had asked the right question. It wasn't much, but at that moment it felt pretty darn good.

So why had she come to see me?

SEVENTEEN

Twenty long seconds passed.

"I don't know what you mean. Why did I come to see you? I need your help to . . . get the situation with Sterling taken care of."

"Really?" I said. Her defenses had stiffened and become awkward as she tried to parry my thrust. My compassion for her swelled. With my simple question I was trying to sound dubious. It wasn't too difficult.

She dissembled. "What else could it be?" Gibbs asked. "I can't live with—what he's done. What else could it be?"

A tough question, one I was not prepared to answer.

I knew she wasn't, either.

I asked myself another tough question: *Well, Doctor, if this isn't all about sex and murder, what is it about?*

Something else.

Deep in my gut I believed that Gibbs Storey was distracting me. First with her tale of murder.

Then with the suggestion of serial murder. And now with sex in St. Tropez. I had to give her credit. As distractions, those were good hooks. Major league hooks. And yet I'd taken the bait for only three days.

Not too bad. For me, anyway. Skilled sociopaths had been known to suck me in and drag me along in their off-Broadway dramatics for months at a time. Diane liked to say that when sociopaths had me for lunch, they didn't spit out the bones until bedtime.

Diagnostically I didn't think Gibbs was a sociopath, but her diversion ammunition was as high quality as anything I'd run across recently.

The fact that I thought Gibbs was setting up psychological screens with me didn't mean I no longer believed her contention that Sterling was a murderer. And it didn't mean I no longer believed her tale about the summer thing on the yacht in St. Tropez. Nor did it mean I felt her efforts to dissemble were consciously driven.

My conclusion about her psychological deke—that's one of Sam's hockey words—wasn't even a hundred percent firm. From a therapy perspective, I wasn't prepared to put it to her in the form of an interpretation, or a confrontation. But it was my new working hypothesis: Gibbs was talking about murder and sex as a way of distracting me— and yes, possibly herself—from something that felt even more psychologically dangerous to her.

So what was more dangerous than extramarital sex and a husband who was a murderer?

Her final words of the session surprised me. She said, "It's as though you can read my mind."

I left her thought there, hanging. The truth was, I couldn't read minds.

On good days I could see a short ways into the dark, but that's as far as it ever went.

EIGHTEEN

I should have predicted it, of course, but I wasn't prepared for Sam's vulnerability. He had always been the tough guy. But that day, despite his size, he seemed frail and more than a little frightened.

A few hours after my appointment with Gibbs, Sam and I walked from his home near Community Hospital over to North Boulder Park. He met me outside by the curb. He was carrying a pedometer that he didn't understand how to use, and he futzed with it continually for a couple of blocks before he cursed at it and stuck it into the pocket of his sweatpants. It was apparent that he had about as much faith in the operation of the thing as he did in the diameter of the opening of his coronary arteries.

I was lugging lunch in a shopping bag that had originally been used to cart home a toaster from Peppercorn on the Mall. Lauren had packed hummus and roasted vegetable sandwiches on flatbread for Sam and me. Dessert was first-of-the-season Clementine tangerines. The beverage was caffeine-free green tea. I considered the homemade meal a special treat. Sam, I was afraid, would consider it evidence of all that was wrong with Boulder.

We did a lap around the park before we chose a place to sit and eat. Boulder was getting one of the latest extended Indian summer sojourns I could recall. The day was glorious.

Once we were seated, Sam didn't jump to unwrap his sandwich. He had two fingers on the underside of his wrist and his eyes on his wristwatch. "I think I'm okay," he said.

"That was convincing."

He chuckled, just a little. What was more interesting to me was that he started downing the hummus and vegetables without complaining about the absence of animal flesh in his meal.

"That Laguna Beach detective has been in touch with the department," he said between bites.

"What?"

"You know, that Carmen . . . something. The one you talked to. She reached out to us."

"And?"

"And nothing. I asked Lucy if any of the detectives had heard anything, she told me somebody had gotten the call. Maybe Danny, she thought. But that's all I know. I'm a little out of the loop."

Lucy was Sam's partner. I didn't know any detectives named Danny.

"So you don't know the next step for Detective Reynoso? If she's coming out here?"

"I don't know anything. I know less than nothing." He took another bite of his sandwich. "You make this? It's pretty good. There's no cheese in it, right? I'm trying to cut back on cheese. I used to eat a lot of cheese. The French eat a lot of cheese; they're not fat. I eat a lot of cheese, and I'm fat. I don't get it. One of life's mysteries, I guess. And how come so many of life's mysteries involve the French? Why is that?"

I didn't have an answer for his French puzzle. "You can thank Lauren for lunch. And no, no cheese. You want to know what's in it?" He didn't answer. I started to tell him anyway. "Garbanzo beans, tahini, a lot of garlic—"

"Did I tell you yes? Did I? I don't want to know what's in it. It

tastes okay, that's all I care about right now. Tahini? Jeez. I can't believe I'm eating something called tahini."

"I'll tell Lauren you liked it."

"I'm ready to go back to work," he proclaimed.

"Yeah?"

"It's going to be a long time until January. I'm going to go stir-
crazy. You know, I won't even be done with this stupid rehab program
until Christmas. I only go for a couple of hours three times a week.
Why don't they just let me go straight through for a couple of days,
and then I'll be done with it? Wouldn't that be more efficient, less
stressful? Isn't that the whole idea, to reduce my stress?"

"They give you any handouts on type A personality, Sam? If they
did, you might want to take a minute and read them."

He grumbled.

I went on. "Attitude is half the battle. Give rehab a chance. And
you can use your free time to get into the holidays this year. Make it
fun. Decorate the house. Sing Christmas carols."

"Holidays mean food. Ham and prime rib and pumpkin pie and
Christmas cookies and all sorts of stuff I'm not supposed to eat anymore. I can't even sit around and watch Bowl games and eat crap in
front of the TV."

"There are other things you can do." I finished peeling a tanger-
ine and tossed it to him.

He missed it.

"You this banal when you're seeing people in your office, or you
save most of your trite shit for your friends?"

I glanced at my watch. "I need to get back to the office. Come on,
I'll walk you home."

"Maybe I'll stay here for a while."

I stood up before I asked, "Things tough with Sherry, Sam?"

"We've been here before. We'll muddle through." He stopped for
a long pause and picked at some dead grass. Colorado's prolonged
drought meant that there was a lot of dead grass to choose from. "She
feels, I don't know, unfulfilled with me sometimes. I think I understand, kind of."

"It's not just the heart thing, though?"

"I don't know what it is."

"How do you feel? About things with Sherry?"

He didn't answer. He pulled himself slowly to his feet and walked beside me as I crossed the park. I matched his pace, wondering whether it was his wounded heart, literally, or his wounded heart, figuratively, that was slowing his progress across the wide lawn.

We spoke little until we got to his door. I went inside with him to use his bathroom before I drove the short way back to my office.

When I'd finished washing my hands, I stepped into his tiny kitchen to say good-bye. He was slumped over at the counter with his head in his hands.

"Sam? You okay?"

He didn't look up. With his elbow he slid a single sheet of floral paper in my direction. I could see it was covered in a tiny, neat script.

He said, "It looks like Sherry's gone. She took Simon to see his grandparents."

"For Thanksgiving? In Minnesota?"

He looked up, finally. His eyes were red. "I guess. I imagine I'll be alone for the holidays."

"What does it say? You guys haven't talked about this?"

"Talking's overrated. I think she's taking a break from me."

"Sherry's leaving you?"

He picked up the paper and shoved it into his pocket. "I don't know. Maybe."

The shock I felt was seismic. I couldn't imagine the effect of the quake on Sam's recovery.

"She loves me. That's not it, Alan. I'm not a hundred percent sure what it is, but it isn't that."

"Sam, I—"

"Go back to work. I think I want to be by myself for a while," he said.

My feet were stuck to the linoleum.

"Go on. I need the practice," he said.

He meant practice being by himself.

NINETEEN

I don't work most Fridays. No, that doesn't mean I
do a short week. Even though I pack forty-plus
hours into my four-day calendar, Puritan guilt occasionally interferes with my enjoyment of the
break that I schedule every week. Still, most Fridays I treasure the extra hours I have to spend
with Grace, or to do an uninterrupted bike ride
on relatively uncongested roads.

That Friday wasn't destined to be one of the
days off that I treasured, however.

I packed up Grace along with all her voluminous paraphernalia—once in college I went to
Europe for a month with less stuff than Grace
needed to go across town—and together we headed
out of the house a few minutes after nine. We were
going to do some errands. Not routine errands.
Grace and I were skilled professionals at the gro-
cery store and the dry cleaner. Returning videos?
Getting gas? No problem. We could have a great
time strolling the aisles at McGuckin Hardware
or picking out a new pair of miniature tennis shoes

at a shoe store. But the errands we had to do that Friday were errands I'd been putting off for weeks because they involved—gulp—public agencies and public utilities.

If doing errands was purgatory, doing that type of errand was hell.

Our first stop was the office that issues drivers' licenses for the state of Colorado. I was due for a renewal. Technically, because I hadn't been apprehended any of the times that I'd bent Colorado's traffic laws, the statute said that all that the renewal required was my right index fingerprint, my digital photograph, a few brief written questions, and fifteen dollars and sixty cents of my money. How long could that take?

How long?

Sixty-four minutes. I counted every one of them.

Next stop: the United States Postal Service. I had to mail a small package to Italy. Once the customs forms were filled out, Grace and I got in line. Maybe twenty people were ahead of us. Three clerks at the counter. I did the math and told Grace, "Fifteen minutes tops, baby."

Moments later, one by one, two of the clerks mysteriously closed their windows and disappeared into the back of the building. Someone asked, "What kind of business closes cashiers when they have this many customers?"

Nobody bothered to answer. The question was not only rhetorical, it was also supremely cynical. All of us in United States Postal Service suspended animation already knew we weren't in Kansas anymore.

There were still fifteen people in front of Grace and me in line. And at least that many had piled into the building behind us. Grace asked me how much longer. She did this by squealing and pulling at my ear.

"Another half hour, Boo," I explained. She asked again, and again.

How wrong was I? The total wait at the post office to mail our package turned out to be seventy-seven minutes.

On to Boulder's cable TV franchisee. The remote control to our cable box had died. I was on a simple mission to trade it in for a working model. In the parking lot of the cable company, I told Grace, "This is corporate America. This will be quick. Ten minutes, tops."

Times five, maybe. Fifty-three minutes later I had a fresh remote control unit and a splitting headache. Grace's patience, never exemplary, had evaporated totally.

My watch said ten minutes after one. Viv—our lovely, indispensable child-care-worker-nanny-person—had been waiting for us at the house since twelve-thirty.

I drove home, handed Grace off to Viv, downed an energy bar and a big glass of water, and went to change my clothes for a bike ride.

I'd finished stripping naked and was fishing in my closet for my cycling clothes when my pager started vibrating on the shelf.

I checked the screen.

It read "911" beside a Boulder phone number.

Before I had a chance to return the call, the phone rang. I jogged a few steps to the bedroom and answered. To my surprise, I heard Sam's voice.

"The shit came down," he said.

I thought he was talking about Sherry. I guessed he'd been served with dissolution papers or something similarly awful.

"God, I'm sorry, Sam. What happened?"

"They're executing a search warrant as we speak. Understand, you didn't hear it from me."

Why would they want a search warrant for Sam's house? And who else would I hear it from?

"What for? Who's searching your house?"

"Not here, you doofus. Don't be a jerk. At your client's house. That detective from California? The old murder? Getting warm yet? Need any more clues?"

"A search warrant? They haven't even talked to anyone. I didn't even know they were in town."

"I'm so sorry you didn't get copied on the memo. I promise to have someone look into that; it's inexcusable. Anyway, Lucy says Reynoso came into town with another detective, they met with the brass, and in no time they got a warrant from Judge Heller. They sure didn't waste any time exercising the thing. She said they have their game faces on. This one's serious, Alan. I gotta go."

He hung up.

My pager began to dance on the shelf again.

Same message as the previous one: "911" and the same local phone number that I didn't recognize.

I dialed the number and said, "This is Dr. Gregory returning a page."

"Can you come over?" Gibbs begged. "Please? They're searching our house. They're going through everything. They have our computers. They're even taking Sterling's *shoes.*"

I was tongue-tied. Partly I was wondering why it was such an affront to Gibbs that the police were taking her husband's shoes. But mostly I was considering the curious strategy that Detective Carmen Reynoso had adopted for dealing with the accusation against Sterling Storey.

No talk, just action.

"Please?" Gibbs repeated.

"Give me your address, please, Gibbs. I don't recall where you live." She gave me directions to a new neighborhood I was almost totally unfamiliar with, somewhere west of Broadway and north of downtown. "Did you ever get in touch with a local lawyer?" I asked.

"Kind of."

Whatever that means, I wondered.

"Well, I suggest you give that person a call. I'll be over in a little while, although I'm not sure what I can do given the circumstances."

As I pulled on some boxer shorts and gazed longingly at my Lycra, I said aloud to myself, "I don't know why I'm coming over. But I'm coming over."

Sam had said that they "had their game faces on." That they were "serious." Which to me meant one thing: Detective Carmen Reynoso believed some aspect of Gibbs's story.

Suddenly Diane's caution about my therapeutic behavior flowed into my head the way water emerges from a cracked pipe: loudly, and with great insistence.

"What you're doing for Gibbs you wouldn't do for a lot of patients."

I stopped with one foot hovering above my trousers.

Diane was right.

Now what the hell had I gotten myself into?

TWENTY

Gibbs and Sterling lived in one of those big faux Victorians that had been all the rage in the build-out of the northwest and eastern expanses of Boulder in the 1980s when developers were finally beginning to believe that the city was serious about growth control. The architects had, I'm sure, been trying to pay respectful homage to the original Victorian heritage of the city's housing base in the 1880s, but the end result turned out more like Main Street in Disneyland than like Mapleton Hill in Boulder.

The Storeys' three-story house had to be five thousand square feet in size. As I approached the home from the corner—it was easy to tell which one it was by the convention of marked and un-marked police department vehicles clustered out front—I wondered what the Storeys did in there by themselves. A two-person game of hide-and-seek could go on for weeks without resolution.

Gibbs was sitting by herself in the driver's seat of a monstrous gold-colored SUV, the kind of motoring behemoth that I hated driving behind, next to, in front of, or on the same road with. It wasn't just that the latest-generation SUVs were big, it was that they tried so hard to be big. It was as though they thrust out their chests and puffed out their cheeks. Gibbs's colossus was a Cadillac. She was swallowed up behind the steering wheel of the thing like a five-year-old pretending to drive a fire truck. She was startled when I knocked on the passenger-side window, but waved me in after a moment.

She wasn't effervescent.

"Thanks for coming. I don't even know why I called."

I could have admitted that I didn't, either, but if I had, then I probably would also have had to consider aloud why I had responded by driving across town to be with her, and I wasn't eager to do that.

"What's going on?"

"They just showed up, shoved some papers in my face, and started rummaging through my house. God knows what they're doing in there. There are five of them."

"Are they from California? The ones I called for you?" I already knew the answer to the question, but I wasn't going to learn much about Gibbs if I didn't keep her talking.

"Yeah, um, yes. At least one of them is. Maybe two. There's a woman. She's really tall. She told me she's from Laguna. She said she was the one you spoke with on the phone."

"Detective Reynoso."

Gibbs shrugged.

"Any detectives from Boulder?"

"Yes."

"Did you get a name?"

"I've forgotten it already."

"Sterling? Is he here?"

"He left yesterday for Florida. The Seminoles, the Gators, the Hurricanes—I don't know. He's doing some game, a Florida team against some team not from Florida. Georgia, maybe. Or Alabama. Auburn? Where's Auburn? I'm sorry. I've tried and tried and tried, and I can't tell them all apart. I know it's important to some people, but for the life of me I can't tell them apart."

She actually seemed ready to break into tears over her college football dyslexia. In a more conventional psychotherapy, I would

have figured that the marital repercussions of her gridiron ignorance—
and her feelings about the same—were a topic we would get around
to talking about in some more detail.

But now wasn't the time. "What city is he in?"

"Tallahassee."

"Have you tried to reach him?" I was aware that I was asking a
lot of questions, not typical for me in psychotherapy and usually not
a sign that things were going well. My database of therapy sessions in
the front seats of Cadillac Escalades was, however, limited.

Gibbs lifted a cell phone from her lap. "He's not answering. He's
always busy when he's setting up these broadcasts. Deadlines, deadlines. I left him a message."

"And your attorney?"

"There really isn't one."

"And you implied that there was one because . . ."

I allowed the thought to settle close by her like an unfriendly dog
to see if she'd respond to it. I thought I noticed her jaw clenching, but
that was the only reaction she displayed.

I finished my own sentence. ". . . because you thought I'd be angry or disappointed if you didn't have a lawyer."

She nodded. She wasn't looking at me. She was watching a very
blond, very strong police officer carry an iMac out of her house.
"That's not even Sterling's, it's mine. He hates Macs."

The strong blond officer placed the computer in the back of a gray
Chevy Suburban.

"You didn't want to—what? Make me angry?"

She huffed. Just a little huff, but a huff nonetheless. "I don't like
expectations in relationships."

Noted. "And you think that I had an expectation about you having
a lawyer?"

Her nostrils flared. "From the beginning you've had an expectation about my doing this your way."

I reminded myself that my relationship with Gibbs was psychotherapy, a form of human interaction that often appears to have little
in common with reality.

"My way?" is all I said, and I managed to say it in a measured
voice, as though I were curious and not incredulous. I knew I could

have pounced. Fortunately, I was also aware at some level that I wanted to pounce.

My way would have included Gibbs staying in Safe House, not sharing a bed with the man she was accusing of murder. My way would have included Gibbs calling the Laguna Beach Police Department on her own, not having me do it in her stead. My way would not, ever, ever have included my sitting in the front seat of a Cadillac Escalade while a search warrant was being carried out.

But Gibbs wasn't talking about reality, she was talking about reality as she experienced it. Her real world. Not *the* real world. She was talking, especially, about the role that men assumed in her real world. My job was to help her make some sense out of that experience and perhaps ultimately help her see the extent of the divergence that existed between her real world and the place where most of us hung out, that universal theme park called "reality."

Just then a parade of three peace officers marched out the garage door of Gibbs's home. Each of the cops was carrying two large brown-paper bags that were folded once at the top. A tag was stapled at the fold of each bag.

Gibbs said, "I wonder what they're stealing. I have some nice things."

A little reality testing was in order. "I think they're trying to solve a murder, Gibbs. Your friend Louise? You called them, right? That's why they're here, isn't it?"

"I know," she said.

But she was much more annoyed than sympathetic.

"That's her," Gibbs said.

Carmen Reynoso *was* tall. From the distance where we were sitting, I guessed six feet tall. Like many visitors to our fine state, she was also unaccustomed to the vagaries of Colorado weather. The calendar said November, and many if not most outsiders figure that means blizzards followed by subzero temperatures followed by snowplows followed by commuters getting to work on cross-country skis until the mud season starts in May.

Reynoso was dressed perfectly according to the common lore. She was decked out in good leather boots, wool pants, and a thick turtleneck sweater that would have left me begging for a place to change into something more temperate. She carried a heavy navy jacket draped over her left arm.

The tail end of a little cold front had come through overnight, clipping the Front Range and dropping us from the high seventies into the mid-sixties. The sun was sharp, though—its rays filtered only by the thinnest ribbons of high clouds—and I thought I was a bit over-dressed in cords and a cotton sweater.

"Nice boots," Gibbs said. "Though I wouldn't wear them with that coat. Nope."

Nice boots?

Detective Reynoso took two long strides down the serpentine herringbone brick walkway before she pirouetted to the sound of her name being called from inside the house and returned to the shadows.

"Did Detective Reynoso say anything to you about when she'd like to speak with you?" I asked.

"She asked me to stick around during the search. I assumed that meant she wanted to see me after."

"You should have an attorney present, Gibbs. For your protec-tion." My wife had drilled into me that I should have an attorney pres-ent whenever anybody from law enforcement wanted to talk to me about anything. Yes, she would admit that there were exceptions, but she would insist that I first run them past my attorney.

Exasperated, Gibbs said, "I'm the one who called. I don't *need* protection. Don't you get that?"

I swallowed involuntarily. I didn't correct her and remind her that technically it had been I who had called.

"Not from you, not from an attorney, not from Safe House, and not from *her*." Gibbs pointed in the general direction of Carmen Reynoso. "Got it?"

TWENTY-ONE

The last thing I did before I left Gibbs alone in her Escalade was set an appointment with her for the following Monday morning. Early. Seven A.M. early. It's all I had free.

I zipped down Ninth and stopped by my office to get some material for a report I planned to write over the weekend, then decided to run a couple of errands downtown.

I regret sometimes that the Downtown Boulder Mall is no longer a place where I can buy some brass Phillips-head screws or have a prescription refilled. Before the Mall was built—transforming a few blocks of Boulder's "Main" Street into an alluring brick and tree-lined promenade—downtown Boulder was like a thousand other Great Plains downtowns: a two-lane thoroughfare with a coffee shop, a hardware store, a drugstore, and maybe even a five-and-dime.

My old landlady—the kind woman who had

given me a lovely place to live during graduate school and had ultimately sold me the house that Lauren and I now live in—had regaled
me over endless cups of jasmine tea and plates of fresh-baked cat's
tongues about the Boulder she'd fallen in love with, the Boulder that
existed before the gentrification of downtown in the seventies and
eighties.

Lois had been a good friend of Fred, who'd owned Fred's Restaurant, and of Virginia, the matriarch behind the Printed Page. Lois didn't
live much in the past, but she'd occasionally allowed herself some in-
tense longing for a piece of Fred's apple pie, or for a copy of some un-
heralded book that Virginia would insist she just had to read. Neither
the pie nor the literary recommendations had, apparently, ever disappointed Lois. Although she loved walking the new mall right up until
the time she repatriated to Scandinavia, Lois never lost her affection
for what Boulder had been for most of the century before.

Now? Fred's is gone. So is Fred. The Printed Page has moved
away, and the Downtown Boulder Mall is lined with shops, not
stores. There are lots of places to buy crafts. National chain stores
seem to outnumber local retailers.

I was thinking about those kinds of changes as I rushed down
Pearl Street in search of a DVD that Lauren wanted me to pick up for
Grace. My daughter had developed an inexplicable fascination with
trucks, and apparently there was no shortage of videos on the subject
that were specifically intended for the toddler set. I had a list of acceptable titles from Lauren. What I didn't have was any confidence
that the Downtown Boulder Mall contained a store that sold toddler-
oriented DVDs about eighteen-wheelers and hooks and ladders.

I was approaching the pedestrian light at Broadway when I heard,
"My God, would you slow down a little? Whose idea was it to put
bricks down here, anyway? And whose idea was high heels? And is it
'was high heels' or 'were high heels'? I want to know that."

The fancy digital walk signal on the far side of Broadway counted
down from six to zero while I waited for Diane to catch up. Traffic began to zoom by before she huffed up beside me. "You can probably
find the answer to all your questions on the Internet," I said.

"Want to know the last thing I found out on the Internet? You'll
love this. I decided that I wanted to be able to say 'My God' to my
husband in Spanish—you know, so I could say 'My God, Raoul,

aren't you lucky to be married to me?' in his native tongue—so I typed 'My God' and 'Spanish' into Google. What do you think I got? I got a website that told me how to say 'Oh my God, there's an axe in my head!' in one hundred and two different languages."

"Was one of them Spanish?"

"Yeah."

"There you go, then."

"*¡Dios mío, hay un hacha en mi cabeza!*"

"That will come in handy someday, I'm sure. How are you doing, Diane?"

"Good. My practice is full, my patients think I have a healing touch, my husband's a dream, I have money in the bank, and I don't have a *hacha* in my *cabeza*. What more can one ask? Oh, I know: What are you doing down here on Friday, and why the hell are you in such a hurry?"

"I'm on a mission." I explained about the DVD. I didn't explain about my front-row seat at the execution of the search warrant at Gibbs's house.

"Mind if I jog alongside? I have something important I've been meaning to ask you."

"I'd love some company. What do you want to know?"

The walk signal changed to green. The digital scoreboard said we had twenty seconds to cross Broadway. It seemed like a long enough time, in theory, but the numbers were descending so rapidly that I wanted to hurry even more.

"Were you popular in high school?" Diane asked.

"Excuse me?" I said, though I did not miss the irony that she had asked the question as we were approaching the display windows of the teenage clothing mecca, Abercrombie & Fitch.

"In high school, what group did you hang with? The geeks? The nerds? The jocks?" She took a moment to laugh at the thought of me hanging with the jocks. "Come on," she prodded. "What group? I'm testing a theory here. I won't tell anybody."

"I wasn't one of the popular kids, if that's what you're asking."

"Aha! I bet you were in the Freud Club or something."

"Your school had a Freud Club?"

"Never mind. Next question. This one's important. Did you ever have the hots for any of the popular girls?"

Oh. I watched the pieces begin to fall into place. "You mean the *über*-popular alpha bitches?"

"Just answer me."

"Where is this going?"

"I'm trying to understand why you're being so precious with Gibbs. Like I said, I have a theory."

"And you've decided it has to do with some high school time warp I'm locked in to?"

"Just tell me, did you ever have a thing for any of the popular girls? You know who I'm talking about. *Them.* The ones who sat at *that* table at lunch, the ones who never said anything in a normal voice. The ones who were always whispering to each other or saying things loudly enough that the whole world knew what they were thinking."

Several steps passed before she repeated, "*Them.* You know exactly who they were."

"No," I said. But I immediately had a 70mm Technicolor image of Teri Reginelli flash onto the wide screen in my brain. Wavy hair, brown eyes, and a smile that could plaster me to Teflon.

"You're sure?"

"Yes."

"No, you're not. Be honest—who are you thinking about right now? Give her a name, come on."

I sighed. "Teri Reginelli."

"Cheerleader? Prom queen?"

"Neither. Mere goddess."

"She was above you socially?"

"It was crowded territory."

She punched me and said, "Still is." Her tone softened. "Isn't it strange how being an adolescent never really stops? Isn't it? Show me what someone was like during their high school psychosis, and I'll put together a damn good road map into their romantic future."

I didn't want to argue with her. Mostly because I knew that there was plenty of truth in her words. To deflect attention from myself I asked, "What was high school like for you?"

"I was fully occupied thinking up ways to kill the Teri Reginellis of the world. And *that* is the source of my transference to the Dancing Queen." She admitted her introspective success triumphantly.

"A question," I said. "Did you ever think about whacking a *hacha* into the *cabeza* of a Teri Reginelli or three at your school?"

"I was taking French—*Mon dieu, il y a une hache dans ma tête!* Otherwise, I'm sure I would have gotten there eventually. So, at what store down here do you think you're going to find your daughter a DVD about trucks?"

"I don't know." I'd totally forgotten about the DVD. Teri Reginelli had that effect on me.

We crossed Thirteenth. Diane leaned close to me, tugged my head down so my ear was closer to her level, and whispered, "It's called transference, Alan. It sneaks up on all of us. Don't ignore it just because I'm the one who brought it up."

Before I could reply, Diane peeled away from me like an F-18 dropping out of formation. She was making a beeline for the bank down Thirteenth, one of her favorite places downtown.

"*Dios mío,*" she said over her shoulder. "*Adiós.*"

Transference: treating, responding to, and/or having feelings about someone in the present as though they were someone important from the past.

Teri Reginelli.

Gibbs Storey.

Me.

Help.

TWENTY-TWO

DVD procured, the drive east was uneventful. I parked my car in the garage, got out, and took a moment to linger near my dark blue not-too-old Trek road bike. The bicycle was hanging securely on its pulley system from the rafters in the garage. I glanced outside even though I knew it was already too dark to make up for the ride that I hadn't taken that afternoon.

Lauren kissed me, Grace squealed, and the dogs seemed happy to have me home. Lauren got the DVD going for Grace while I made a couple of adjustments to Emily's paw umbrella. The thing was protecting the wound on her paw marvelously, but it required an abnormal amount of maintenance. I was no longer certain that a trip to the patent office and instant wealth were on the horizon for me.

Once we moved to the kitchen, Lauren sat down across from me while I sorted through a seriously uninspiring pile of mail. Neither of us had any fresh news to report from either Sam or Sherry.

I filled her in on the morning adventures with the cable company, the post office, and the drivers' license office. Unmoved by my tales of institutional indolence, she moved into the business part of the kitchen to attend to the meal she'd been preparing.

Once she had her back turned to the stove, she said, "That's interesting. So who's Teri Reginelli?"

My breath caught in my throat.

Instinctively, I knew that my wife was facing away from me so that I couldn't see the I'm-sitting-in-the-catbird-seat grin that she had plastered across her cute mug. I said, "Oh God. I bet Diane called you right from the bank, didn't she? She was going straight to the bank."

"I heard the whole story while she was standing in the teller line. She said she left you befuddled on the Mall."

"Figures."

"Were you?"

"Was I what?"

"Befuddled on the Mall?"

"Most of the women in my life leave me feeling befuddled. I'm beginning to feel befuddled right now, for instance. Teri Reginelli was not an exception. Believe me, she was not an exception."

"So who was this mystery girl I've never even heard about? High school, right? Should I be worried?"

Lauren's tone was ninety-nine percent tease. "No," I said. "But Diane should be."

"Is this going to end up being like that Sawyer thing a few years ago? Is Teri Reginelli about to show up at our door with a suitcase and a few verses about how her life isn't complete without you? God, I hope not. I didn't like the Sawyer thing much at all."

"The Sawyer thing" was the one percent in Lauren's tone that wasn't tease. She wasn't kidding; she hadn't liked the Sawyer thing at all.

"I swear that Teri Reginelli wouldn't be able to tell you who I was if you held a gun to her head. Actually, get Diane to hold the gun to her head. Or a *hacha* to her *cabeza*. She'd relish the opportunity."

"What? What language are you speaking?"

"It's not important."

"Teri Reginelli is. At least to me. Go on. I want the details. Pretend you're talking to your therapist."

"Teri Reginelli was a high school crush I had. I never even went out with her. Not once."

"Then why are we talking about her?"

"Ask Diane."

"I did. She said you had the hots for her. For Teri, that is. She said after all these years Teri's still changing your oil. She told me to mention Teri's name, sit back, and watch you dance like your toes were on fire."

"That's Diane's phrase, isn't it? 'Changing your oil'? Diane said that, right? Am I right? Diane thinks I'm a prude. Do you know that? Do you think I'm a prude? A serious prude?"

"Don't change the subject."

"Part of it's true, I guess. In the high school era of my life Teri was the neighbor's wife whom I coveted."

Lauren looked puzzled.

"Figuratively speaking. Teri Reginelli was the head of the pack in high school. You know, the leader of the popular girls. The alpha chick? Senior year she dated a guy who slummed with me and my friends sometimes."

"Was he a hottie?"

"Yeah, Sean was a hottie."

"And?"

"This guy Sean treated her like shit. She would talk to me about it, ask me about things he did with other girls, what he said about her. You know how girls are when they're seventeen. She wanted to know what made him tick. I was a good listener—"

"Even then?"

"Yes, even then."

"And you fell in love with her, and she never even knew it. Right? It was unrequited love?"

I sighed. What had felt like a monumental event in my life was suddenly sounding like a carefully carved monument to banality. "Right, something like that."

Lauren was really getting into it. Me? I was losing interest, fast.

"She signed your yearbook 'Alan, you're the best!' or 'What a great friend!' or something like that, I bet. Yes? The 'XXX' was the closest you ever came to kissing her. Am I right?"

I sighed once more.

Lauren asked, "So what does all this have to do with Diane?"

"It has absolutely nothing to do with Diane. She's teasing me about an old conjoint case we did together."

I watched Lauren make connections, all the wrong ones.

"No, we didn't treat Teri Reginelli and her significant other. I don't even know where she's living, and I don't have a clue what guy is stuck with her. Teri Reginelli is just a metaphor for a point Diane was trying to make. Can we talk about something else? Please."

"Of course," she said.

Lauren leaned over to check something in the oven. I inhaled deeply but couldn't figure out what she was cooking in there. I was thinking chicken. I thought I captured the aroma of balsamic vinegar, too.

Her willingness to change the subject concerned me. It didn't take long for me to discover that I had good reason to be concerned.

She said, "There was an interesting thing at work today. Mitchell got called to oversee the execution of a search warrant on the home of a guy in town who's apparently become a fresh suspect in an old murder in southern California. A couple of detectives flew in from Laguna Beach and requested our assistance. The Boulder detective thought it would be better if somebody from our office was involved as an observer to the search."

I don't know whether I said "shit"—if I did, it certainly qualified as a mumbled profanity—or whether I merely thought *shit*.

Lauren said, "The whole case—a husband suspected of murder in another state, a loving wife who knows a little something—it reminded me of that question you asked me earlier in the week. Do you remember? The one about exclusions to the spousal privilege statute? Felony exceptions? Even as they might apply in some other state? Like California?"

"Yes," I said. "I remember."

She left the oven, walked over, and kissed me full on the mouth, tracing the outline of my lower lip with the tip of her tongue.

"Sometimes I love to watch you squirm. Mitchell saw you over at the house where they served the warrant today. So I think I know what spouse might be trying to exclude what testimony, and I think I know who the reincarnation of Teri Reginelli is, too."

She kissed me again. No tongue the second time.

There were days I had doubts that Boulder, Colorado, was still a small town.

Well, that day I had no doubts.

TWENTY-THREE

Saturday broke from the gates like a day that was intent on setting a new standard for late November. The morning was glorious. The air was crisp, clear, and dry, and the sunrise lit up the eastern horizon in shades of vaporizing gold.

I knew all about the beauty of the sunrise because I was heading east at the moment when the sun completed cresting the earth, my head up, my jersey zipped all the way to my Adam's apple, my spin well above a hundred, my padded butt barely on the saddle, my bike weightless between my legs. The back roads in Boulder County belonged to me alone.

I covered fifty miles of asphalt at a brisk pace and was back home sipping juice on my deck by nine o'clock.

The phone rang. Sam.

"You been outside yet?" he asked.

"I've done fifty miles already."

"Me, too," he countered. "Actually more like fifty yards. I walked out to get the paper. Who am

I kidding? Given the size of my lot, that's more like fifty feet, isn't it? Astonishing day, huh?"

"Couldn't be better."

"We're going to get blasted, you know."

My living room deck faced the mountains. There wasn't a cloud in sight between my house and the Continental Divide, or from Pikes Peak down south to whatever peak that was past Longs Peak way up north. "Really? You think?" I said.

"It always happens. You get a run of unseasonably good weather like we've had lately, and then you get a day that's like, I don't know . . . perfect—like this one—and then five minutes later you're walking someplace and the wind is blowing hard enough to send you to Nebraska, and then five minutes after that you've got snow in your flip-flops."

He was right. That's just the way it usually happened. While I considered the image of Sam in flip-flops I took another glance toward the Divide.

Not a cloud. Not today—maybe tomorrow we'd get blasted.

I said, "How are you doing, Sam?"

He didn't exactly respond. He said, "There's somebody I have to talk to in Gold Hill. Want to come with? Bet it's pretty up there."

Lauren and Grace were at some weekly mother-child yoga event that Adrienne thought was the greatest thing going. I was tempted to go some Saturday morning just to watch. Grace had the not-so-svelte physique of a well-fed, chunky baby. My daughter could no more do yoga than I could fly. I left them a note about my plans and headed to Sam's house.

Depending on the weather, on a typical weekend before Thanksgiving the ten-mile drive from Sam's house on the west side of Boulder up the Front Range to Gold Hill can take as little as twenty-five minutes or as long as—well, a long, long time. The road that curls up Sunshine Canyon into the mountains was paved for a while and then it isn't paved for a much longer while. In some places the dirt and gravel portion of the track is particularly steep and curvy, and in winter, with the sun low in the sky, some of the canyon stretches don't see the direct rays of the sun for months at a time. After a heavy snow and a deep cold snap, ice on the road can freeze as hard as a traffic cop's eyes.

The final descent into the valley that was home to the pioneer mining enclave of Gold Hill is a particularly spectacular section of trail. The road drops a few hundred feet in altitude—and about 150 years in time and attitude—in less than a minute.

Very few villages in the Rocky Mountains have managed to check the natural progression that leads from Old West town to Old West ghost town. Some of the ones that have managed to freeze themselves in time have become polished tourist magnets like Telluride and Georgetown, but only a precious few of the surviving nineteenth-century burgs have managed to remain invisible to the hordes of annual visitors who show up clutching tour books. Gold Hill was one of those few. Gold Hill was hard to get to, its fewer than two hundred full-time residents didn't exactly lay out a welcome mat for guests, and any attempt to find a location for a Golden Arches or Starbucks within the range of a .30-06 from town would likely be met by a crowd of passionate locals prone to carelessness with torches.

The Gold Hill Inn, the town's enduring fine dining destination, was open only during the summer months because too few Front Range residents could be counted on to make the drive up to nearly nine thousand feet in the inevitable springtime slush or the usually predictable autumn ice. Winter? For most people, casual travel to Gold Hill was too risky during an average snow year. I've always had the impression that four or five months of regular visits by curious flatlanders were about the maximum the residents of Gold Hill could tolerate anyway.

I hadn't asked Sam about his business in Gold Hill. The mountain enclave was in Boulder County, and Sam was a city cop, not a sheriff's deputy, so I suspected that his business was personal, not professional. But I also knew Sam well enough to know that if during the course of an investigation he wanted to talk with somebody who happened to reside a few steps outside the city limits, he would usually find a way to do so. The solution might be by-the-book legal, or it might be less-than-by-the-book creative. But the job would get done.

The fact that he was on medical leave from the police department? That would be no more of an impediment to him than the countless potholes we dodged in the dirt lane up to Gold Hill. Or the fact that I was certain he was under orders not to drive for a while after his heart attack.

Did I mention that to him? The driving restrictions? I didn't. When I arrived at his house, I had offered to drive. He had declined. That's as far as it went. I knew from experience that I could strongly encourage Sam's sense of self-preservation. But insisting on it only put my own at risk.

We parked on Gold Hill's main street across from the Gold Hill Inn. The street may actually have been called Main Street, but I didn't look for a sign. I was enjoying the gorgeous day and was reveling at being up in the mountains in a town that was so charmingly frontier yet didn't look as though it had been imagined by Disney set designers. As soon as I stepped out of the car onto the dusty dirt lane, I knew that, despite the fine autumn day, the air in Gold Hill—three thousand-plus feet above Boulder in altitude—held a chill that warned of imminent winter.

It should have felt ominous to me, but it didn't.

Sam led me across the road toward the ancient building I'll probably always think of as the home of the original Lick Skillet Café. My first wife and I had made frequent treks up the hill to the Lick Skillet for memorable meals in the late eighties before Dave Query packed up and trucked his culinary imagination down the mountain to Boulder and Denver.

The destination Sam had in mind was packed with locals. About half of the patrons seemed to make Sam for a cop before the cleft of his substantial butt cleared the jamb of the doorway. He pointed me toward an open deuce in a far corner. On the way we passed tables covered with platters that were plastered rim-to-rim with eggs and bacon and potatoes and flapjacks as big as hubcaps.

"Breakfast is hard for me," Sam said. "I miss meat that's been treated with nitrates. Outside of cheese, that's what I miss most. Brats, bacon, salami . . ."

I thought the waitress was just the slightest bit tentative as she approached our table. Sam waved off the menus and ordered an egg-white omelet, sans cheese, sliced tomatoes, and dry wheat toast. He asked her to be sure that the omelet was made with very little butter. Almost speechless, but eager to endorse his choices, I told her I'd have the same.

Although we both knew that we had just done the equivalent of going into a fine steak house and ordering steamed broccoli and brown rice, the waitress took the order with casual aplomb, as though the entire town of Gold Hill were already on the Ornish diet and our order was par for the course that morning.

"Wait here," Sam told me. "I have to go to the head. I won't be long." He stood and walked toward the bathrooms. Although I hadn't been back that way for most of a decade, I was guessing that the odds were about fifty-fifty that the plumbing Sam would find was still the kind that didn't involve copper pipes, or flushing.

I watched the choreography of turned heads that followed Sam's departure from the dining room. Just as the faces returned to their plates and their stained stoneware mugs of coffee, the waitress who had taken our order—a pleasant-faced young woman with close-set eyes and stringy brown hair—took the short walk toward the back of the house, too. She glanced over her shoulder before she turned the final corner.

Sam returned to the dining room first. He had been gone no more than ninety seconds total. The waitress followed him about ten seconds later and resumed her tasks behind the counter.

"Had to pee," he said as he sat down across from me. "Like to wash my hands before I eat."

"Yeah. You met with our waitress, too."

He nodded. "Wanted to remind her that the toast had to be dry. I'm off butter, you know."

"Yeah, I know. You want to tell me—"

"Maybe later."

Breakfast was bland, but then, we'd ordered it that way. Sam dug into his without complaint. I used the hot sauce on the table to add some zip to mine.

"Remember when we took the kids to Rocky Mountain National Park in September?" he asked.

"Sure," I said. Elk mate in the early autumn, and the beautiful dance concerts they produce at dusk prior to copulating draw hordes of human observers. Rocky Mountain National Park, northwest of Boulder, is prime territory for Front Range elk voyeurs. Sam, Sherry, Lauren, and I had taken the two kids, Simon and Grace, up the previous September for a cold picnic dinner and a visit to the annual elk show.

The elk had done their courting thing that night with philharmonic aplomb. Although the dance steps of the majestic bulls and their harems of cows were difficult to discern during the prime dusk time period, the acoustics that night were perfect. The bugling bulls sent their baritone calls bouncing off the granite faces in the park, and the eerie echoes quieted even the most restless *Homo sapiens* in the audience.

"That's when it hit me that Sherry was kind of unhappy. That night."

"Yeah?"

"Yeah."

He had wiped his plate clean and held up his mug for a refill of decaf before I realized he'd said all he planned to say about that night in the park. Me? I had a feeling there was more to discuss.

The waitress hustled over and topped off Sam's coffee mug. "There are a lot of rules after a heart attack. No caffeine for a while—that's one of them," he said. "As far as things I miss, it would be hard to choose between caffeine and nitrates."

"Sex?"

"I hope that's not an offer. If it is, you're a dead man."

I offered a grudging smile. Were I with a patient, clinical protocol would have had me waiting silently, feigning patience, for Sam to return to the topic of his troubled marriage. But with Sam I didn't have to follow any protocol. I said, "So that's it? That's all you're going to say about Sherry? That you knew she was unhappy?"

"She was showing me something. Maybe I wasn't able to see it. What more is there to say?"

"I don't know. That's why I'm asking."

"Did you notice anything?" he asked me.

"That night? No."

Sam caught the waitress's attention and pantomimed a request for the check. "Sherry said she was restless. That's the word she used. She was thinking of selling the flower shop. Maybe going back to school."

"I don't remember that."

"That's because she said it to me, not to you. You and Lauren and the kids were running ahead of us."

" 'Restless' for Sherry meant unhappy with you?"

"You know, you go back and look for clues. That's what I've been doing, anyway. I wonder what I missed. Whether I should have done something else."

"Like what?"

"I don't know. Something different. Maybe I let stuff slide that I shouldn't have let slide. Anyway, that's one of the things I'm thinking I did wrong. Other times I think it's all her shit. I go back and forth. I have a lot of time on my hands."

"That night? What did you say to Sherry?"

"Probably not the right thing."

I sipped some water. "Why? What did you say?"

The waitress brought our check, sliding it to an empty spot on the table pretty much exactly halfway between us. She stacked all the plates and mugs in a careful cascade up one forearm. I watched closely; not even a glint of recognition flashed between her and Sam.

He said, "I don't remember exactly. I'm sure it wasn't what she wanted me to say."

I grabbed the check. Sam dropped a ten-dollar bill on the table.

"You're paying. That's the tip," he said.

"What about you, Sam? Are you happy?"

Did I get an answer?

Did Gold Hill have a Starbucks?

Almost halfway back to Boulder I asked, "What's the story with the waitress? Your meeting in the back of the café?"

A quarter of a mile of contemplation later he apparently decided that he was going to answer me.

"Four weeks ago last night she was with some girlfriends at a club downtown. One of those places on Walnut, not far from your office. I'm not going to say which one. You can probably guess. Maybe you read about it in the *Camera*. But she was on my turf. She got drunk—she admits that. She met some guys—she admits that—and she agreed to go to an after-party at some frat house by CU. She admits that. She decided to let them drive her over there in their car. She admits that. Crappy judgment after crappy judgment after crappy judgment, and she admits every bit of it."

His left hand snaked from the steering wheel to his upper abdomen, his thumb pressing on his sternum.

"On the way over to the Hill for the after-party, she was sexually assaulted in the back of a Chevy van."

"Raped?"

"Sexually assaulted."

The distinction was obviously important. I was curious why. Prurient interest? No. Just enduring curiosity about the perverse imagination of assholes on alcohol. But I didn't ask for any more details. Sam wouldn't have wanted me to know any intimate details of the waitress's horror. I liked that about him.

"And?"

"And it turns out that of all the people she's had to deal with about what happened that night, she trusts me the most. Go figure."

Sam paused. I think he was giving me the opportunity to make the mistake of saying something snide. I didn't.

"I've been concerned that if I wasn't around to hold her hand as this thing got closer to trial, she might get shy and drop the charges. The cops and the DA? We try real hard to make it okay, but the truth is that it's a bitch to be a sexual assault victim in the system we have. So I wanted to tell this girl personally about the heart attack and let her know that I'd be gone for a while but that I'd be back on the job to, you know, help her before this thing went to court."

I wasn't surprised at Sam's generosity, though his sensitivity sometimes snuck up on me.

That moment a sharp gust of wind exploded out of the west, which was behind us. The heavy car seemed to levitate like an amusement park ride about to careen down some ersatz mountainside. The sheer eighty-foot drop five feet from my window served as a reminder that this particular mountainside wasn't exactly ersatz.

I craned my neck to look behind us and saw that a thick bank of clouds had popped up and begun to shroud the highest peaks on the Divide.

Sam didn't turn around.

He said, "Told you. We're going to get blasted. Weather here is goofy."

We beat the approaching front down the mountain, though not by much. From our vantage on the street in front of Sam's house where he had parked his Cherokee, the army of clouds marching over the Divide had the determination of the Allies assaulting Normandy.

We were about to get blasted.

"You have rehab today?" I asked.

"Not until Monday. You know what they do there? These young kids in these dorky matching sweatsuits hook me up to all this heart monitor crap, and I do calisthenics with a bunch of old people, then they watch me walk on the treadmill, and then—then—they act like I'm lying when I tell them what I ate the day before. That's the entire drill. I don't see how that's supposed to help my heart, unless terminal aggravation is their frigging goal."

"You'll give it a chance, though? The rehab? I'm sure a big part of rehab is attitude."

"Don't talk to me about attitude. I'm feeling a little better every day. I think the medicine is helping. The beta-blockers. I'm more mellow, you know? That can't be all bad, right?"

I recognized that he hadn't answered my question about giving rehabilitation a chance.

"Of course not," I said.

He changed the subject once more. "I heard you made an unscheduled appearance at the execution of that search warrant yesterday." After he spoke, he punctuated his words by finally pounding the shift lever forward into park. I noted that he wasn't terribly kind to his transmission.

"Is anything a secret in this town? Jeez. I'm surprised my picture's not in this morning's *Camera.*"

Sam laughed, first time all morning. I liked the sound of it, even if the joke was at my expense.

"I got a personal invitation from the search warrantee, Sam. Nobody knows that my friendly neighborhood cop gave me a heads-up. Did they find what they were looking for?"

He gazed at me over the top of his sunglasses. "You really think I'm going to tell you that?"

"Probably not. You wouldn't happen to know when she's going to, you know . . ."

"Accost you? No. But she will."

"Maybe not. I told her everything I know."

"No, you didn't. You told her everything you think it's okay for her to know. If Reynoso knows what she's doing, she knows damn well that you have more. And she's going to want to know what it is."

"What have you heard about her?"

He didn't answer that question, but he did answer my earlier one. "The search at the house didn't go too well. There's still plenty of stuff to go over—couple of computers and file cabinets full of paper— but they didn't find anything damning. That can't have been too much of a surprise after all these years, though, right? You got to look."

"What about her—the detective? Do you know anything? Is she sharp?"

"I'm on medical leave, remember? Totally out of the loop. Trying to keep my stress level down."

"Okay, then tell me what you hear from Sherry."

"Simon's missing too much school! And I'm missing him way too much. That's all I know."

"Come on, pick, Sam. Carmen Reynoso or Sherry. Tell me something about somebody."

"Okay. Word is that Reynoso has a chip on her shoulder. Some incident in San Jose a few years back forced her to leave that department before she had her fifteen. She's about as happy chasing tourists around Laguna Beach as I would be chasing tourists around Aspen."

That wasn't very happy.

"What kind of incident in San Jose?"

"Won't tell you."

"Can't tell me?"

"Won't tell you."

"Do you even know?"

"No. But I wouldn't tell you if I did."

TWENTY-FOUR

By the time Detective Carmen Reynoso tracked me down for an interview, her outfit of wools and leathers was perfect for the weather.

The front that was carrying Pacific moisture over the mountains had collided with some super-cold air that was blowing down from Saskatche-wan, and together the two weather systems became a fast and furious snow machine along Colorado's Front Range. What had likely been the season's final Indian summer interlude was history before anyone had a chance to bid it adieu. I'd managed to drive only halfway from Sam's house to mine before the winds moderated below gale force and snow started falling in fat flakes that left mela-noma rings in the dust on my car. I looked at the time.

Twelve-thirty.

I looked at the sky.

Winter.

At nine o'clock that morning, the day had

been as splendid as any November day in memory. And now it was snowing like a son of a bitch.

We were getting blasted.

Carmen Reynoso was parked on the shoulder right where the pavement ended and the dirt lane started winding along the hillside toward my house. She was sitting in the front seat of a rented GM coupe reading an Avis road map. I knew the odds were good that the dirt lane that came to a blunt end in front of my home wasn't marked on the map she was reading.

At first I wasn't a hundred percent sure it was Reynoso behind the wheel, so I pulled alongside to get a better look. Once convinced, I lowered my passenger-side window.

"Detective Reynoso?"

"Dr. Gregory? You've been expecting me?"

I shrugged.

"Interesting weather you have around here. We don't get a whole lot of this in Laguna Beach."

What would the tourist board want me to say? "Well, I hope you enjoy the change. The storm will make the ski resorts very happy. They always love a good dump before Thanksgiving." The meteorological reality was that Front Range upslope snowstorms often left the big ski resorts on the west side of the Continental Divide basking in bright sunshine.

"Can we talk? I'm sure you know about what." Her words said invitation. Her eyes said something else.

I knew I could refuse. But what was the point? I wanted Reynoso to know what I knew. What I didn't want to do was fence with her about the things I didn't have permission to tell her, although that is precisely what I anticipated we would spend our time doing.

"Sure," I said. "Do you have a place in mind?" I didn't want to have the meeting at my house.

"We could have done it yesterday at your patient's house. You know, after the search. But I heard you only stayed for the first act."

Was that humor? I wasn't sure. A snowflake the size of a moth blew in the open window and landed on the tip of my nose. It melted instantly, and I wiped it away.

"Give me a few minutes with this"—she lifted the road map—"and I think I could get us back in the direction of the Boulder Police Department. That's—where? Thirty-third Street? Off, what—Arapahoe? Am I right? I'm sure they'd give us a room we could use. Everyone's been so nice."

I'd seen the interview rooms in the Public Safety Building on Thirty-third Street. Not my idea of a great place to spend a Saturday afternoon, blizzard or no blizzard.

I said, "You want to get some coffee somewhere?" I was thinking of leading her east into Louisville and finding some chain place like Village Inn. I didn't know as many people in Louisville as I did in Boulder.

She fixed her eyes on my face. A deep cleft had formed above the bridge of her nose, as though she were smelling something foul or facing directly into a bright sun. After a pause long enough that I would notice that she had delayed, she suggested, "What about your house? It's close by here, right?" She lifted the map again. "I bet I can find it."

The pace of the snow suddenly accelerated. The lazy snowflakes that had been falling were replaced by millions of smaller, quicker reinforcements. A few superfrozen scouts started sticking to the windshield.

I was dressed in cotton cords and a light sweatshirt. Home had its allure.

"Yeah, it is," I said. "Follow me."

I led Detective Reynoso down the lane and then into our house.

Lauren had scribbled a few words on the bottom of the note that I had left for her about heading out earlier in the day with Sam. She and Grace were home from yoga and gone again to a birthday party in Lafayette for one of Grace's friends. I use the word "friend" loosely. One-year-olds don't actually have buds; they have other one-year-olds that their parents make them hang out with.

I closed my eyes and cursed silently. Taking Grace to the birthday party had been my job: I was supposed to get Grace some lunch and then take her to her friend's party and bring her back home.

Two outings in a row taxed Lauren's multiple sclerosis–depleted energy reserves, which meant we would all pay a price later in the day, probably increased fatigue, for my oversight.

Damn.

During my interlude of silent self-flagellation, Reynoso stood patiently in the entryway. I finally remembered my manners. "Can I take your coat?"

"Sure. Nice place."

"Thanks."

She tried some small talk on me. "Do you know that Baseline Road is the fortieth parallel? I read that on the Boulder website."

"No, I didn't know that. You mean exactly? No minutes, no seconds?"

"Exactly. That's what it says. The road is exactly forty north."

"Well," I said as I led her into the living room and adjusted the thermostat to bring us some heat. To the west the usual glorious panorama of the Rocky Mountains was nothing but a screen of swirling white dots. "It's usually a nice view. In fact, on most days you get a pretty good look at the fortieth parallel."

"Your wife's a prosecutor," she replied, unamused.

Reynoso had moved on; we were apparently finished chatting longitude and latitude. But I didn't especially want to talk about my family, so I didn't respond.

She noticed that I didn't respond.

"I'll take that coffee," she said. "Actually tea, if you have it."

I didn't trust Reynoso alone in my house. What did I think she was going to do? Nothing specific, but at that moment I didn't even like the idea of her reading the titles that were lined up in my bookcase. "Of course. Come to the kitchen with me while I make it." I didn't say, "*If you're curious, you can check out the cookbooks.*" But I thought it.

I made her a small pot of tea—Tension Tamer from Celestial Seasonings seemed an apropos choice. She sat on a stool and watched me. I could tell that she was enjoying our meeting more than I was.

When the tea was ready—she asked for milk, no sugar—I carried a mug back into the living room for her. She took a seat on the sofa, held the tea below her face—for the warmth, I decided, rather than the aroma—and took a tiny sip. After a moment she closed her eyes briefly and said, "Thank you."

I was settling firmly into the familiar security of therapist mode. I didn't say, "You're welcome."

Reynoso, I guessed, was a few years older than I. Her features were carved, and the ridge beneath her eyebrows was prominent and brooding. But what was most stunning about her appearance was the quality of her skin. Her complexion looked as soft and smooth as my almost-toddler daughter's.

"The other day on the phone? After your call? I wasn't cordial with you, Dr. Gregory. I'd like to begin by apologizing to you for that. The whole thing came out of the blue. I wasn't gracious."

"Accepted." My antennae were tuned for cynicism, and I immediately wondered whether she was disarming me or placating me or both with her apology. "You thought I was a crank, I bet."

"We get some crazy calls sometimes. You have a child?"

"A daughter." I still didn't want to talk about my family.

"This doesn't have to be difficult," she said.

"Although it's not a pleasant subject, I don't expect it has to be difficult, either, Detective Reynoso. I'm happy to tell you anything that I have permission to share with you."

"Ah," she said, and returned her attention to her mug. "That's the rub, though, isn't it?"

"The rub?"

"You deciding what you have the right to tell me. That's the complication for us, right?"

"Your profession has rules. My profession has rules. I'm sure that we can respect each other's positions."

Actually I wasn't at all certain that we could respect each other's positions, but it seemed like a cordial thing to say, and it was apparent that we were both trying hard to be cordial.

The posted odds in Vegas were a hundred to one against things remaining cordial between us, however.

Reynoso said, "My profession's rules are geared toward discovering the truth. That's all."

I didn't want to joust with her. But I was willing to, if that's what she wanted. I said, "Mine aren't."

"Really?"

"Really."

"You don't have a goal of helping your . . . patients learn the truth about their lives?"

I figured it was a trick question. "Psychologically? Yes. Factually? No."

"I was in therapy once."

What would the American Psychological Association want me to say? "I hope you found it helpful."

"Very."

"Great."

"I don't have much leverage with you," she said with her eyes averted and her hand reaching for her purse.

I thought, *Good.* The fact was, I didn't think she had any leverage with me. But in the interest of extending the cordiality as far as possible, I said, "You don't need any leverage, Detective. I'm happy to do whatever I'm able to do to help you solve this crime."

She took a notepad and slender pen from her shoulder bag along with a small tape recorder and a purse-size bottle of Tylenol. She set the recorder on the coffee table between us, threw a couple of pain relievers into her mouth, and washed them down with a gulp of tea. After flicking the recorder on, she pointed at the red light for my benefit, stated the date and time, and then touched the pause button. "Where are we right now? The address?"

I told her my address, adding, "You feeling okay?"

She touched her temple. "I've had a headache since I got here."

"It could be altitude sickness. Happens a lot. Drinking more water might help."

"Altitude sickness?"

I nodded.

"You have headaches all the time?" she asked.

"No, you get over it."

"Good." She returned her attention to the recorder, removed her finger from the pause button, repeated the address, explained the purpose of the interview, stated her name and mine, and asked me if I was participating voluntarily.

I had to think about my answer. Finally, I said I was.

"When did you first meet Gibbs and Sterling Storey?"

I considered that question carefully, too. "I'm sorry. I'm not at liberty to answer that one."

It was obvious that Detective Reynoso hadn't expected my response. She'd thought she was lobbing a softball my way.

She said, "What?"

"The circumstances of my meeting the Storeys—if, indeed, I have met the Storeys—might be part of a therapeutic relationship, and any details about a therapeutic relationship, even simply whether or not there is a therapeutic relationship, and if there is, when it may have begun, are things that I'm not permitted to reveal under Colorado law."

"What?"

The second "What?" was born of incredulousness. "Dr. Gregory, I know you know her. You've already told me you're treating her. Come on. Don't be difficult just for the sake of being difficult."

"You didn't ask me whether I know Gibbs Storey, Detective. If that is the question, the answer is yes, I know Gibbs Storey. If you would like me to tell you when I first learned the information that brought you to Colorado, I can tell you that, too. It was last Monday. What you asked me was when I met Gibbs and Sterling Storey. That is a question that I'm not at liberty to answer."

"Why not?"

"I can only answer questions that are covered by an affirmative release of information. I have a limited release from Gibbs Storey. I do not have a release of any kind from Sterling Storey."

She sighed. "Have you ever met Sterling Storey?"

"Next question."

"Am I correct in assuming that if the answer was no, you would be free to tell me so?"

I didn't respond. I wasn't having very much fun.

"I'll assume that, then."

"Assume what you wish. Whether someone is in therapy, and thus whether I know them professionally, is privileged information. I can't discuss it without a release. We'll get a lot farther a lot faster if you just limit yourself to questions that I'm free to answer."

My frustration was showing. I'd expected that Detective Reynoso would know the rules as well as I did. If she did, she wasn't letting on, and her attempt to frustrate me was intentional.

And it was working.

She said, "And you are free to answer questions that . . ."

I swallowed a sigh. "I'm free to answer questions that relate to Gibbs Storey's accusation that her husband, Sterling, is responsible for murdering a woman named Louise Lake in Laguna Beach, California, back in nineteen . . ." I'd forgotten the year. "Whatever. That's it."

"Ninety-seven. What is Gibbs Storey's current diagnosis, Doctor?"

"I can't tell you that, Detective. I'm sorry, but it's not covered by the release."

"The release is that specific?"

"Yes, Ms. Storey has been quite specific about what she would like me to tell you and what she would prefer to remain privileged."

Carmen Reynoso sat back on the sofa, crossed her long legs, and smiled such a big engaging smile that I reflexively smiled in return.

"Twenty questions with you just isn't any fun," she said. "How about this? Why don't you tell me what you can tell me?"

So I did.

TWENTY-FIVE

I knew only what Gibbs wanted me to know.

Louise Lake was a British flight attendant who had shared two homes with two other flight attendants. One of the homes was an almost-derelict, two-bedroom, to-die-for maid's quarters attached to a ramshackle, early-twentieth-century shingled palace high on the rocky cliff above Crescent Bay in Laguna Beach in the southern L.A. metro area. The woman who owned the property and rented out the apartment was an elderly Australian who spent most of the year in Sydney.

The other home shared by the trio of flight attendants was a tiny one-bedroom flat in the fashionably tony Hyde Park section of London. Louise and another woman, named Helena, owned the London flat together. Their third roommate, Paulie, paid them a healthy rent for the privilege of crashing occasionally at one place or the other and, when circumstances dictated, didn't complain about sleeping on the sofa in the front room of the London flat.

All three close friends typically flew the busy Heathrow–LAX run for British Airways.

Sterling had met Louise in business class while he was on the long trip back from doing the coverage on the British Open in the summer of 1997. She told him that she was looking forward at the time to an almost full fortnight of holiday at her Laguna Beach hideaway. Sterling revealed to her that they were practically neighbors—that he and his wife were only weeks away from completing renovations on a cottage in Corona Del Mar, just a few miles up PCH from Crescent Bay.

Louise was seeing a guy in L.A. at the time. His name was Scott and he was the personal assistant to a young director who was a favorite of Steven Spielberg and David Geffen. Louise was a little embarrassed by the way Scott flashed his cell phone and beeper and BlackBerry like a Boy Scout displaying his merit badges. She admitted to Sterling that she thought Scott was fun and pretty but was really just a "glorified freeway butler."

At the conclusion of the flight Sterling invited Louise and Scott to dinner. She accepted.

The meal was at a little French place that the Storeys loved on Balboa Island, and it went well. Scott turned out to be precisely as full of himself as Louise had suggested he was, and with precisely as little cause. Over the next few months as Gibbs, Louise, and Sterling became good friends, Scott was soon out of the picture. He disappeared to Europe with his boss, who was spending the late summer wooing a French actress in Brussels and scouting locations for "a period thing" he was about to start shooting in Budapest and Prague.

"The nature of the friendship, please. That's important," Carmen Reynoso prodded. "If you can, of course."

Louise was a working woman whose primary home was in Britain. When not in London she was usually traversing the North Atlantic doing her job, which left her mostly unavailable to accompany Gibbs on her frequent forays to her favorite haunts of Fashion Island or

South Coast Plaza. Louise's unavailability didn't seem to matter; Gibbs adored Louise and almost immediately counted her among her closest friends. Gibbs especially loved Louise's cosmopolitan manners and her London accent. Although she didn't say so exactly, it was apparent that Gibbs thought Louise was a better accessory in the South Bay social scene than either Kate Spade or Manolo Blahnik.

"Louise Lake was a beautiful woman. Where did that fit in?" With the question, I noted that the cleft had reappeared between Reynoso's eyebrows. She wanted to know about Sterling and Louise, the couple. The thought apparently caused her to frown.

Gibbs didn't suspect that anything was going on between Sterling and Louise until a Halloween costume party that Gibbs had long planned to celebrate the completion of the renovation of the Corona Del Mar cottage. Louise wasn't even planning to attend the party; she had sent her regrets weeks before because she was scheduled to work the overnight from LAX to Heathrow on the thirty-first. Some combination of factors—Gibbs thought it was a mechanical problem and a crew overtime issue, but who ever knew with the airlines?—conspired to keep Louise in L.A. for another night.

She arrived at the Storeys' party in Corona after midnight, still dressed in her BA uniform. The party was already in its death throes, and the few guests still remaining on the patio were so inebriated that a couple of them even complimented Louise on the originality of her costume.

Gibbs was decked out as Grace Kelly. By self-report, she'd looked the part. Sterling came as Joe DiMaggio, and Gibbs remained troubled about his late change of heart about costumes. She had been counting on Prince Rainier or James Bond, her early suggestions. If she'd known he was going to be wearing pinstripe flannels as Joltin' Joe, she would have tried to talk him out of it.

Failing that dissuasion, she could have done Marilyn just as easily as Grace.

All he'd had to do was tell her. Was that too much to ask?

Louise was one of the last to leave the party, shutting down the new great room bar around three. Gibbs volunteered Sterling, who never drank when he was hosting a party, to drive Louise down the coast to her home in Laguna. After a tepid protest Louise agreed to give up her car keys and accept the ride.

Sterling pulled his car out of the garage in Corona at three-fifteen.

He didn't return home until the sun was beginning to crest the string of coastal hills in the South Bay the next morning.

"That was October. What about November? Can we get there soon?" Carmen Reynoso asked. I suspected that she lacked a therapist's natural respect for backstory, but didn't say so. It was something we could discuss at another time. Or not.

Sterling had blown off Gibbs's concerns about the lost hours before dawn on Crescent Bay on All Saints' Day morning. He told his wife that he and Louise had talked for a while. That was it.

Gibbs didn't trust Sterling much, from a fidelity point of view. And she didn't believe him often, at least where other women were concerned. But she'd let the issue go. She'd watch for signs. With Sterling and other women she did that a lot.

Louise didn't spend much time in Laguna during the first three weeks of November, and although she spoke with Gibbs a couple of times on the phone, they didn't see each other during that period. Louise had bid for, and received, a month flying routes into De Gaulle and JFK because she adored being in both New York and Paris over Christmas. She didn't want to be in either city for Thanksgiving, though. She had four days off, Tuesday through Friday of the holiday week, and she was planning to spend them alone in Laguna. Helena was working, and Paulie and his latest partner were doing Ibiza.

Louise called Gibbs from her rental car on Tuesday afternoon to bitch about the traffic on the 405 and to gossip about an Australian tennis player she'd met while her actual date, an American lawyer, was in the WC at Les Deux Magots on the Left Bank in Paris. She reiterated her promise to come for Thanksgiving dinner on Thursday.

Gibbs reminded her that dinner would be early; the turkey would be carved at five.

And Louise reminded Gibbs that she didn't eat turkey and that she'd recently realized that she was only two minor obstacles away from being a true vegan.

Gibbs had asked what the obstacles were.

Louise had replied, "Paris, and meat."

"That was Tuesday?" Carmen Reynoso clarified. "Two days before Thanksgiving?"

"Yes," I said, recognizing that the calendar pages had flipped forward to almost the exact same spot in the current year. I went on. "Gibbs said Louise was killed that night, not the next day like the newspapers reported."

"Please go on with your story."

"Please remember, it's not my story. It's Gibbs's story. I'm just repeating what I was told. You can tell me one thing, though—is Gibbs correct about the time of death? Please tell me that."

"We'll get there, we'll get there," Reynoso said. When the issue was my ignorance and not her own, she was suddenly a very patient woman.

For some reason I thought of Sam.

The tape recorder snapped off. Carmen Reynoso fumbled in her bag for a spare tape. After she exchanged the tapes, she said, "Go on."

Sterling wasn't due home from New Orleans until Wednesday, late. Gibbs had completed the holiday shopping, supervised the house-cleaning, and done all the prep work she was planning to do in the kitchen before Thursday's meal. She had a Mexican woman whose name she didn't remember coming in to do most of the cooking on Thanksgiving morning.

By Tuesday afternoon Gibbs was bored. She decided to surprise Louise. She'd pick her up and welcome her home by taking her out to dinner somewhere in Laguna.

About a block from Crescent Bay, Gibbs spotted Sterling's car parked on the street.

She almost missed it. What caught her eye was the bright red hat with the network logo that he kept on the shelf behind the back-seat.

"A block away?"

"About a block away."

"She didn't tell you exactly where?"

"I don't know Laguna Beach, Detective. I wouldn't recognize any landmarks. I'm sure Gibbs will tell you."

"Did she say what kind of car?"

"I don't think so. She may have. If she did, I've forgotten."

"You forgot? Anything else you forgot, Doctor?"

Gibbs drove a few blocks away from Louise's home and phoned Sterling's office from her car. His secretary reminded her that he was still in New Orleans and suggested Gibbs try him on his cell phone.

To get to Louise's apartment, a visitor could use the public access path partway to the beach, then cut across an aging flagstone trail to the deck. Gibbs returned to Crescent Bay, parked near the top of the public path, descended a few yards, stopped, and listened.

She heard Sterling and Louise arguing. She couldn't tell about what. But she heard her name.

Gibbs.

Sterling had yelled, "I don't fucking care about Gibbs."

Gibbs headed back up the path in tears. Up near her car she heard a scream. She wasn't sure if it was Louise or not. At the time she thought it couldn't be. Why would it be? When she heard the news later, on Thanksgiving afternoon, she wasn't so sure.

Back at her car, she grabbed her phone and punched in the number of Sterling's cell. The distinctive sound of her husband's ringing phone traveled up the slope to where she was standing.

She killed the call.

"I think you know the rest," I said.

"I'd like to hear about his reaction when the body was discovered. Can you talk about that?"

"Yes. Yes, I can."

*   *   *

Sterling was home, as scheduled, late in the evening on Wednesday. Gibbs never said anything to him about what she had witnessed the previous afternoon.

On Thanksgiving Day, as was his practice, Sterling had all the TVs in the house tuned to football games. But he wasn't watching football; he was watching coverage, production. The competition. At three-thirty a local news update reported that a partially clothed female body had been discovered facedown in a tide pool at Emerald Bay in Laguna Beach. Stay tuned, more after the game.

Gibbs hadn't paid much attention. Sterling didn't stray more than a few feet from the television.

A few minutes later Sterling asked Gibbs what time Louise was due for dinner. Gibbs said any time.

He said he hoped Louise was okay.

" 'Okay'? That's the word he used?" Reynoso asked, frowning.

"That's the word Gibbs said he used."

The news report from Laguna Beach was repeated about a half hour later. This time there was a news crew live at the scene, and they were showing videotape of a wide shot of a body sprawled on the rocks on the north end of the horseshoe that was Crescent Bay. The tide was coming back in, and waves were lifting plumes of spray into the air as they crashed onto the rocks. The earlier report about Emerald Bay had been in error.

The body by the tide pool was draped with a sheet striped in pastels.

"I'm going down there," Sterling said to his wife.

"Why?"

"I have a bad feeling about Louise."

" 'A bad feeling'?"

"Yes, a bad feeling."

"Huh."

*   *   *

When Sterling got home, dinner was cold. As he ate a turkey and stuffing sandwich with cranberry sauce and lots of black pepper, he told Gibbs that he thought Louise had been strangled.

" 'Strangled'? "

"Yes."

"He said that?"

"According to Gibbs."

"That would have been when—six o'clock, seven?"

"You'll have to ask Gibbs."

"Anything else?"

"Sterling told her that he thought that somebody must have broken into Louise's apartment. He bet that the killer had broken a window and just gone in that rickety back door."

TWENTY-SIX

Carmen Reynoso sat back and crossed her arms.

"Why did you make the call? Why didn't Gibbs call us herself?"

"I'm not quite sure about the answer to that one, Detective. It has something to do with the nature of the betrayal she feels she's engaged in. Turning her husband in is one thing. Making the actual call is something else."

"You think it's psychology, then?"

"Isn't everything?"

"No. Some things are just criminal."

The distinction was obviously clearer to her than it was to me.

"Are we done?" I asked. I was tired, and the clock told me my girls were due home any minute. I really didn't want Detective Reynoso here when they walked in the door.

She stood. "Except for your earlier question. Time of death? Remember? You still interested?"

"I didn't think you were actually going to answer me."

The snow was coming down in waves. A curtain of white, thick enough to obscure the entire valley, would blow by over the course of a few minutes, and then suddenly a sparser fall would reveal the dark geometry of the fence posts and dirt tracks in the greenbelt below our house. After a brief interlude of visibility the curtain would shut, the angularity would disappear, and the world would again become white.

A couple inches of snow were already piled on the grasses and in places on the ground that spent the late autumn in shadows.

Carmen Reynoso stared at the winter spectacle, her lips parted. "I've only seen snow a few times in my life. I'm an Oakland girl. Didn't ever get to Lake Tahoe much. It's mesmerizing."

The sardonic quality of her Lake Tahoe comment was oddly alluring. I said, "There's a moment during every storm when I'm overcome by the beauty of it all. And a moment, usually a little later on, when I'm almost—almost—overcome by the aggravation of it all."

She turned back toward me, puzzlement in her eyes.

I explained. "Driving in it. Shoveling it. Walking through the slush of it. It gets old."

Her next words surprised me.

She said, "You're not a romantic, are you? I took you for a romantic. A knight-in-shining-armor-type guy."

"Wrong conclusion, I think. I am a romantic. I'll be romantic about this storm all day today and all night. Then tomorrow morning, sometime around five A.M., my neighbor will fire up her little green John Deere and start plowing our lane. That's when the romance will begin to disintegrate, with the sound of my neighbor singing Christmas carols on her John Deere at five o'clock in the morning."

"And that's so bad because . . ."

"You'd have to know Adrienne. She makes up her own words to the carols, and she can't sing to save her life."

Reynoso stepped away from the windows. "At least you get your driveway plowed."

"You have a little Pollyanna in you, don't you, Detective?"

"Very little, Doctor. Tomorrow's Sunday. Maybe your neighbor will take the Lord's day off."

"Maybe," I agreed. "That would be nice." I didn't bother to clarify

that if Adrienne was anything religiously, she was Jewish, and that
affiliation would make her Sabbath Saturday, not Sunday.

"The time of Louise Lake's death has never been made public."
Reynoso's change of direction was abrupt. Sam did the same thing to
me sometimes. I was beginning to suspect that cops in general have an
underappreciation of the value of segue in conversation. "The press
has always reported it was Wednesday, and we've never contradicted
them in any of our public statements. Gibbs's contention that it was
Tuesday, not Wednesday, is what hooked us—hooked me, anyway—
that her story might be . . . real. Because the coroner says it was
indeed late afternoon, early evening on Tuesday, and not late Wednesday, that Louise Lake was murdered."

I tried to keep my face impassive.

"But what really hooked me was something Gibbs didn't say, that
she only implied. We've left the public with the impression that Louise
was murdered on the beach and her body was pulled out into the water. Numerous reports from neighbors indicated that she walked the
cove and the tide pools at least twice a day when she was staying in
town, often at dawn or dusk. The public version of the crime is that
someone followed her to the beach, or waited and accosted her there,
and killed her. Maybe a crime of opportunity, maybe not."

"But she didn't die on the beach?"

"No. She died on the rocks. Her body had premorbid wounds
from the rocks. And the broken window in her back door? It's not public information, either. Therefore Sterling knew something he shouldn't
know."

"Why was the window broken? Is there is evidence of a struggle
in the house?"

"No comment."

"You haven't talked with Sterling yet?"

"No. He's in Florida. Something tells me he's going to lawyer up
anyway. I'm proceeding as though we're not going to have an opportunity to interview him."

"Do you have enough to arrest him?"

"If we did, he'd be in custody."

I tried a segue-free transition of my own. "Why a tide pool? The
killer must have known the body would be discovered soon enough."

"Louise Lake's body was not placed in the tide pool. It was dumped

into the Pacific, we think it got caught on something, and was in the
water for almost thirty-six hours before it floated free and back into
the tide pool during high tide."

We walked to the entryway, and I helped her with her coat.

"You can't repeat any of this," she said.

"Of course," I said. I was already wondering why she had told me
what she'd told me. I wasn't considering the possibility that her volu-
bility on the subject of Louise's murder was evidence of indiscretion.
Rather, I assumed that Reynoso had another motive for talking with
me. What? I wasn't smart enough to know.

She went on. "I heard from a couple of local cops that over the
years you've demonstrated some wisdom about forensic things—you
know, from a psychological perspective—so let me ask you something. From what you know about him—I'm talking Sterling Storey,
obviously—could he have done it? Could he have killed Louise Lake?"

I considered the flattery—the spoonful of sugar—and the question—the bitter pill—that she wanted me to swallow. I said, "I'm sorry,
but answering that would take me places that I'm not permitted to go,
confidentialitywise. I wish I could respond, although I'm not sure of
the value of what I might have to offer. Opinions are opinions, you
know."

That little crease reappeared above her nose. She said, "I think I'll
just take that as a yes."

Changing the subject seemed like a good idea. "Are you okay
driving in this? In snow?"

"How would I know?"

"If you don't know, then you're not okay."

"Any tips for a virgin?"

"Take it slow. Don't be afraid to use second gear. Ignore the assholes plowing by you in four-wheel-drive pickups and SUVs."

"And if I skid on the ice?"

"Don't. It's better if you don't skid."

"Thanks. I'll try to remember that."

TWENTY-SEVEN

Lauren and Grace arrived home less than ten minutes after Detective Reynoso departed.

Their arrival wasn't a pretty sight. They had both left the house dressed for a warm fall day, and both were wet from the storm and chilled to the bone. Lauren's violet eyes had taken on the gray-purple pall of extreme fatigue; whatever she and Grace had been doing since I'd left to meet Sam that morning had worn her beyond whatever limits she possessed that day.

How guilty was I feeling?

With Grace in my arms, I cranked up the heat in the master bathroom and began running a bath for Lauren. Then I took Grace into her room, and got her dry and clean and into fresh warm clothes. My daughter, sometimes a tough kid to put down for a nap, found the sanctuary of sleep moments after her head hit the mattress in her crib. I promised her, silently, that because of her compliance during this crucial moment in our lives, I would overlook at least one moderate-to-severe teenage indiscretion that was certain to occur in her future. She seemed to smile back at me from her sleep, as though she were already planning whatever it was I would need to forgive her for.

I shuddered at the thought.

When I got back to the bathroom with a steaming mug of tea, I found Lauren in the tub.

"No caffeine?" she asked.

"Mint. No caffeine. I'm sorry, I screwed up today."

"I know you're sorry."

"Sam—"

She shook her head, just a little, and asked, "He's okay?"

I nodded. She forced a smile in reply.

"You didn't look too good when you came in," I said.

She lowered herself farther into the soapy water. She was covered all the way to her chin. Her toes and colored toenails, painted a shade of coral that I was sure Grace had selected, popped out of the water at the far end of the tub. "Something's cooking, Alan. I have brain mud. I'm more tired than Bill Gates is rich, and in case you haven't noticed, my eyelids aren't blinking at the same time."

I tried hard to look her in the eyes but not stare at her eyelids. "So what can I do?"

"Let's give it a few hours, see what develops. The pin is definitely out of the grenade. We'll see what's going to blow up."

"Maybe it's a dud. Can I get you something to eat?"

"No, I'm not hungry. Some quiet, okay? Take the dogs, and don't let me sleep past five. I love you."

Multiple sclerosis roughly translates as "many scars."

When a new wound forms on the protective covering of a nerve in the brain or spinal column—apparently caused by the body mistaking its own neural insulation for a gremlin of some kind—symptoms develop. What symptoms? It depends on what nerve is involved. As the wound heals and scar tissue grows to replace nature's myelin, the symptoms either disappear totally, or they don't diminish at all, or—and this is most likely—something happens in between.

It's a total crapshoot.

Lauren and I didn't often use the word "exacerbation." To use it had the ugliness of a profanity. But as I left her toweling off after her quick bath—I stayed until then because I feared sleep would take her right there in the bathtub—we both knew that an exacerbation, a fresh wound on some previously unaffected nerve, was what we feared was happening.

If we were right? I didn't want to think about it. But I knew the list of potential consequences was as long as the list of the body's miraculous capabilities. Numbness, blindness, paralysis, weakness, bladder problems, GI problems—I stopped myself before the list grew any longer. And it could have grown much longer.

But repeating the litany of potential disabilities wasn't helpful.

Did I cause Lauren to have an exacerbation by not taking my daughter to her friend's birthday party?

No. Of course not.

I didn't. Really.

Really.

TWENTY-EIGHT

Sunday was full of surprises. None of them good.

Lauren never really woke up from her Saturday "nap." She opened her eyes for a while, but whatever was going on with her neurologically and immunologically was consuming enough of her energy that she didn't venture farther from the bed than the bathroom.

She declined dinner. Grace and I ate alone.

As was typical, I was the first in the family out of bed on Sunday morning. Instead of pulling on Lycra and Gore-Tex and heading to my bicycle—the pre-Thanksgiving snowstorm made my typical weekend morning ride impractical—I tugged on some fleece sweats and thick socks and carried the local paper and a cup of coffee to the living room.

The sky above the Front Range of the Rockies was the color of deep tropical water, the soaring granite slabs of the Flatirons were bearded with snow, and the earth was carpeted white as far as my eyes could see.

It was absolutely enchanting. I hoped Carmen Reynoso was some-place she could enjoy this view.

I listened for the sound of Adrienne mangling Christmas carols or the rumble of her John Deere. Nothing. Lauren had left some De-bussy in the CD changer. I flicked it on, turned down the volume, and lifted the hefty Sunday paper to my lap, fearing that the tale of Ster-ling and Gibbs Storey might have finally made it from the police files to the newspaper.

Below the fold, bottom right, some bold type caught my eye. But it wasn't an exposé about the Storeys. The headline read, JUDGE'S SPOUSE ARRESTED FOR POSSESSION OF COCAINE.

Huh, I thought, *I know about that.*

Jim Zebid had told me about it. I hadn't given his revelations about Jara Heller's husband's criminal activities a moment's thought since I'd heard them during Jim's regular session the previous Tuesday.

What was Judge Heller's husband's name?

I started to read the article. Jara Heller's husband's name, it turned out, was Penn Heller. I allowed myself to be distracted for a moment trying to figure out how someone ended up with the name Penn. Pennington? Pennsylvania? Penncroft? Couldn't. Nor did I recall any legal cocktail party chatter with a male spouse named Penn.

The article didn't have much information. Police, acting on a tip, arrested Mr. Heller, an investment banker with some firm I'd never heard of, early Saturday evening in a brewpub downtown, and they'd confiscated a "significant quantity" of white powder and an unspeci-fied quantity of cash. The reporter apparently attempted to reach Judge Heller for a comment, but his calls were not returned by press time.

Huh.

I felt a pang of sympathy for Jara Heller. She had a decent reputa-tion on the bench and was known as a hard worker who knew the law and played fair. I'd always thought she was personable and that she couched her ambition better than many of her colleagues did. Whatever her husband was involved in wasn't going to do much for her reputation. I wasn't smart enough to know what it would do to her future on the bench. I'd ask Lauren when she got up.

A distant humming sound intruded on my reverie about the Hellers. Within seconds the hum became an insistent rumble. Adrienne wasn't singing, but she had indeed fired up the Deere and was preparing to

plow the lane. Sunday or not, she loved the damn tractor too much to
allow a decent snowfall to melt of its own volition.

Solar energy was her sworn enemy.

The roar of the Deere awakened Grace, and within a minute I was
called to my daughter's room by her surprisingly mature lungs.

Diaper change for Grace. Take the dogs out, feed them. Waffles.
Sunday almost always meant waffles—from-scratch waffles—and lots
of chatter. Debussy ended, and the next disk in the changer fired up.
Tony Bennett and k.d. lang doing Louis Armstrong. Perfect.

The weekend morning routine was soothing but surreal. After
breakfast Grace played in her high chair. I tried to focus on the paper.
But below the surface calm lurked, I knew, the monster that lived in
the depths: the closed bedroom door and the precarious state of my
wife's health. I waited for the sound of the toilet flushing, or water
pinging against the tile in the shower, anything to indicate that
Lauren's day had started in a fashion that resembled normal. But
eight o'clock came and went without a hint of her condition.

The phone rang at 8:05.

I pounced on it.

"It's me," Sam said.

"Another field trip?" I asked. "I think I'm busy."

"I'm calling from the pay phone outside Moe's. The place is
crowded even after a blizzard."

Moe's Bagels was in a little shopping center on North Broadway
not far from Sam's house. I made an assumption that he was out for
his prescribed morning rehab walk and was seeking moral support
from me much the way that an alcoholic might call his sponsor from
outside a saloon. I said, "It's okay, Sam. But get something with
whole grain. And nonfat cream cheese. Not the good stuff. But lox is
okay. Omega-three oils."

"I'm not asking for help with the menu. I'm calling from a pay
phone outside of Moe's so that if somebody ever subpoenas your
phone records, they won't show that I talked to you at eight o'clock
on this Sunday morning." His tone was gruff.

I sat down. "Yeah? Why?"

"Because Sterling Storey is dead. And I'd rather people not know
that I'm the one who told you. Just in case that becomes important."

"What?" My exclamation had to do with surprise at the news of

Sterling's death. But I was also wondering how it could become important from whom I'd heard the news. Paranoia wasn't part of my friend's character, so I assumed that Sam was a step or two ahead of me. Although all the chess pieces appeared blurred on the board to me, Sam was plotting moves farther down the line.

"Lucy came by to see me last night, kind of late. You know, to check on me. She told me about it."

"Why is Lucy worried about you?"

"That's not why I called, either, Alan. Focus."

I considered pressing it; after all, he'd offered the opening. But I didn't. "Okay, then what happened to Sterling?"

"I don't know what happened to Sterling Storey. All I know is what I'm hearing."

Another one of those critical distinctions that Sam liked to make. I asked, "And the Storey story is what?"

His voice changed. It became a little louder, a little less patient. "Hold on. I'm waiting for a woman to stop staring at me thinking I'll get off the damn phone any second if she's rude enough. I hate that. Don't you hate that? Now she's like five feet away. She's staring right at me. I'm staring right back at her.

"Hey, lady, I'm going to be a while, do you mind? Get over it."

"Did she go away?"

"She's like sixty or something—she looks exactly like my aunt Esther—and she just flipped me off behind her back as she was walking away. What is that? I don't think I want to live in a society where old people are pricks."

"She's an exception, Sam. Tell me about Sterling."

"You know he was in Florida, producing coverage for some football game? Yeah, of course you know that. After his damn football game was over yesterday, he was driving from Tallahassee to visit an old college friend in Albany, Georgia. You know where that is? Me, neither. Personally, I think he was avoiding coming back here to face the music, but it's a free country, right? Until the cuffs are on, hey—he can do what he pleases. Lots of people want to talk to him, but nobody was ready to arrest him.

"Anyway, there was some freak rainstorm all across southern Georgia yesterday. Flash floods, the whole thing. A biblical-type storm. Witnesses say a car went off the highway and was about to slide into the Ochlockonee River. If I said that name right, I deserve a prize. I thought Minnesota had goofy names for places, but the South? It's like they had a goofy name contest and there were a thousand winners. No, ten thousand winners.

"Anyway, Sterling, being the sweet guy we all know he is, stopped his rental car and went to help this woman whose car was about to go in the river. He slipped on the bank, fell in, and went underwater almost immediately. His body hasn't been found."

"Wow."

"That's it? 'Wow'?"

"Sam, the man's about to be picked up for questioning for a homicide and instead he dies a damn hero trying to rescue a stranger from a car wreck? That's world-class irony."

"Warms your heart, doesn't it? Three witnesses to the whole thing, too. One of them is a damn preacher. The others are twin sisters. A social worker and a pediatrician."

"I take it you don't believe what you're hearing?" Sam often didn't believe what he was hearing. It wasn't evidence of a character defect so much as it was the foundation that made him a good detective.

"What do the lawyers say? Render up the body? Do I got that right? Well, when they render up the body, then I'll believe it. It's all too convenient as far as I'm concerned."

"How do you fake a rainstorm and a biblical flood, Sam? Sterling Storey isn't Moses."

"Moses? What Bible do you read? Moses doesn't fake any floods in the Bible I read. Forget my question—I don't want to know what Bible you read. No. All I'm saying about Sterling Storey is that maybe . . . maybe the guy thinks on his feet, that's all."

"I assume that the Georgia cops are looking for his remains."

"They are. The river he went into—I'm not going to try to say the name again—is pretty wild, apparently. Lots of things underwater—trees and shit—where a body could get caught up."

"Sam, why do you care about this case so much? You have plenty more important things to worry about."

He was silent for ten seconds before he replied, "I'm not sure. I think I'm going to go back home."

"Wait, Sam. Hold on. Do you know anything about Jara Heller's husband? Judge Heller?"

"I saw the paper. Nothing more than that."

"Will you do something for me? Will you check and see how they became suspicious of him? How they knew he was involved?"

"Why?"

"It's important."

"Somebody fingered him. You can count on it. Maybe he walked into a sting, but odds are somebody gave him up. You hang around with people who do drugs, especially people who buy and sell drugs, you come to realize that it's not the most honorable segment of our society."

"Just check for me, please. If somebody turned him in, I'd love to know that. I promise I won't ask who did it."

"You promise?"

"Yes, Sam."

"That means you already know who turned him in. You just want me to confirm it for you. Am I right?"

I stammered.

He said, "You should be seeing a higher quality of clientele. You hang out with a lot of scum." Then he hung up.

Across the room Grace—bless her—continued to entertain herself. She was absolutely captivated by the wrong end of a spoon.

I called my office phone and checked for a call from Gibbs. I wondered if she even knew what had happened to her husband the previous night, whether anyone had called her.

The only messages on my voicemail were from other patients. One was a cancellation; another was from a patient requesting an additional session. And one was a confirmation from a paranoid-obsessive guy I was treating named Craig Adamson. Craig always required confirmation that I hadn't forgotten his next appointment. Always. It was sad.

All in all, the messages on my voicemail were a zero-sum game and included no frantic calls from Gibbs Storey.

I was trying to decipher what that meant when, behind me, Lauren said, "Who was that who called?"

A big smile exploded across Grace's face, and she said, "Mom Mom."

I pivoted.

TWENTY-NINE

SAM

My eyes stayed glued on the cranky old lady until she was all the way down by the wine store. I didn't want her to think I was getting off the line for her. When she hopped from the curb to jaywalk over toward Ideal Market, I hung up the phone.

Sherry would tell me I was being petty. Maybe she would be right. I can be petty sometimes. Especially with people who flip me the bird when I'm not doing anything but talking on the phone.

A little bubble of gas erupted down in my gut and began a sudden northern migration that would take it directly into belch territory. I could feel it rise. As the capsule crossed the midtorso territory that I now knew—*knew*—to be my heart's domain, my hand rose involuntarily to my chest. I placed my knuckles on my sternum and pressed gently. It took no more than a second for the gas to rise the entire length of my esophagus.

I did burp, kind of loudly actually. After, I left

my hand in place below and between the boobs on my chest that looked just like my dad's, the man-boobs I'd promised myself I'd never have.

Never.

Well, I had them now.

I inhaled deeply and exhaled slowly. No pain rose in my chest. It was okay to move my hand away, to slide my big feet.

I stepped away from the phone and got into the long snaking line that led to the counter at Moe's. What had Alan said I could order? Whole grain? Nonfat cream cheese? Lox?

Damn.

I had man-boobs, a heart artery that looked like a muck-filled galvanized pipe, a wife who hadn't smiled in my general direction since the summer monsoons had passed us by, and a kid I adored who was a thousand miles away from my hug.

What had Alan asked me?

"Why do you care about this case so much?"

The woman in front of me was ordering nineteen different things nineteen different ways. She wanted an "everything" bagel without sesame seeds. Jalapeño this with white meat turkey that. "You mean you don't have veggie cream cheese without those orange things in it? . . . Oh, those are carrots? Ooh, red onions? You don't have white? Are they bitter?"

She asked for a spelt bagel. What the hell is spelt?

The girl waiting on her had an oblong ring the size of a carabiner through her right eyebrow. She didn't care a hoot about the woman she was waiting on, or her act. The clerk's eyes didn't frown. Her lips didn't smile. She was going to get minimum wage for the next hour of her life no matter what the hell the idiots on our side of the counter wanted her to do.

I could relate.

The girl shook her head at the spelt question.

I was glad Moe's didn't have spelt. I would have been seriously dismayed if Moe's had spelt.

"Why do you care about this case so much?"

I realized that my left hand was in my parka pocket, and I was twirling something round between my fingers.

The little brown bottle of nitroglycerin.

"Why do you care about this case so much?"

In my life I've known maybe five people who could make me think. Alan Gregory is one of them. I've grown to appreciate it—his ability to get me going—but I've also grown to recognize that it isn't an altogether comfortable state of affairs for me. Introspection, I mean. I don't much like Indy racing, but I love NASCAR. Why? Traffic is traffic, but most of the time NASCAR is all left turns. You just drive fast, control your speed, hit the pit, react to the other guys. You don't always have to prepare for a hairpin, you're not always slamming on the brakes.

Having Alan as a friend is like driving the damn Grand Prix. Left turn, right turn. Brake, downshift, gas, brake *hard*. It isn't always fun. Sometimes I just want to drive I-80 through Nebraska. The road goes straight, the car goes straight. And me?

I go straight. No doubt about it, life is best for me when I go straight.

Why do I care about the case so much?

Because she loved the asshole so much, that's why. Because this Gibbs Storey lady lived all these years with a guy she knew had murdered her friend, and she stayed living with him even after she knew the police were coming after him to throw him in jail.

I wanted to know about love like that. I wanted to know about a marriage like that. I wanted to know about a woman like that. Was it him, or was it her? What made her tick? Was it strength or weakness? Was it confidence or desperation? I had a guess, sure, but I wanted to know.

My Sherry? After my heart attack she couldn't wait to get the hell out of our house. Out of town. Screw Thanksgiving, screw my rehab, screw whatever this whole thing was doing to Simon. Screw our marriage.

Screw me.

I didn't understand any of it. I was thinking that Gibbs and Sterling Storey could teach me something.

My turn finally came at the counter at Moe's. The girl with the piercing raised her eyebrow. The metal ring levitated ominously. It was her way of telling me I was next. Speaking was an inconvenience for her.

"Whole wheat toasted, please. Low-fat cream cheese, lox, and whatever vegetables you got. Lots of them."

Her eyes didn't frown. Her lips didn't smile. She made me my breakfast, wrapped it in white paper, and dropped it in a brown-paper bag as though she'd done it a few thousand times before, thrust it over the counter at me, and looked for the next person in line.

Poppyseed toasted with butter. Smelt on spelt with a schmear. It didn't make any difference to her.

With one last glance at the girl with the heavy metal in her brow, I paid for my bagel and crammed a buck into the tip jar.

The girl didn't know it, I thought, but she was auditioning to play the role of somebody's wife after sixteen years of marriage.

Later, after I picked up a couple of things at Ideal and stopped back for a cup of decaf at Vic's, I started walking home. I wasn't ready to go home, really, but I couldn't think of anything else I could do to avoid it. It was Sunday morning, and I'd gone every place but 7-Eleven that I could think of that was open. Except for church. But I couldn't do that. Not that the spiritual solace of an hour at church wouldn't have been welcome. I didn't go because I didn't want to see all the familiar faces and hear the litanies of "How're you feeling?" and "Hey, where's the family?" And I really, really didn't want to hear another story about somebody's relative's heart attack and how they were dead in a week.

I didn't want to hear how, oh, lucky I am.

I wasn't feeling too damn lucky.

The walk wouldn't take long—it was only a few blocks from North Broadway to the thousand square feet of siding-covered box that we called home—and I could feel the heave-and-ho of my chest as I made the gentle climb. Not chest pain; no pain exploding below my sternum. Not even a little twinge. The heave-ho was just the rise and fall of excess skin and the sway of my fat.

My man-boobs.

In sight of my house I stopped and watched a teenage girl shovel her sidewalk. Her outfit was more appropriate for an early summer day at Boulder Reservoir than the first real day of winter. Shorts. Sweatshirt that said—what? I couldn't read her sweatshirt from thirty yards.

What was it with kids and clothes? I had to figure that out, had to. Simon was on his way. I had to get there first.

I made the decision to spend my forced medical leave of absence doing two things. I was going to begin to get rid of my man-boobs, and I was going to go looking for Sterling Storey.

I stopped and checked my pulse.

Eighty-four. That was good. Walking up the hill, holding an eighty-four? That was good. My cardiologist would be pleased. Those perfectly svelte physical medicine specialists who ran the rehab program would be pleased.

Or maybe they wouldn't be pleased. Their mantra seemed to be "I think you can do better, Sam." I had the sense that if you told them they'd won Powerball, they'd complain that the jackpot was only thirty million.

Sherry would like them. She thought I could do better, too.

What had Alan said to me? *"You have plenty of more important things to worry about."*

He was right. And finding Sterling Storey was going to be my way of worrying about them.

My man-boobs? I'd never laid eyes on the guy, but I was betting that Sterling Storey didn't have any.

THIRTY

ALAN

"I'm having some trouble with my leg," Lauren said.

I'd deduced that already. The walking stick in her right hand was a dead giveaway. I tried to remember the last time I'd seen the thing emerge from the closet, but I couldn't. I guessed that it had been years. I purchased it for her at a mountain equipment store in Ouray, on the Western Slope, during another health crisis. Or was it Telluride? I couldn't remember.

I did remember that the circumstances were similar to these and that I'd seen the decline coming. It seemed disease exacerbations always arrived after a drumbeat of warning.

"Come, sit," I said. I took her by the elbow and led her to a kitchen chair next to Grace's high chair.

"It feels like it weighs a ton. I'm just dragging it around." She was talking about her leg.

"Yeah."

She bowed her head toward Grace and was immediately lost in the vernacular of baby talk that allowed her to reconnect with her daughter and forget about whatever was going on with her myelin sheath. Grace was oblivious to her mother's malaise, but she was pretty interested in the walking stick. Were she developmentally able to stagger a few steps and simultaneously hold on to an object, I assumed I would see our daughter playing with a toddler-size version of the walking stick before the day was out.

I was examining Lauren for indications of other peripheral neuropathy. Her facial muscles were still unable to coordinate her blinks. Beyond that, my unskilled eyes found nothing anomalous.

"Any other weakness?" I asked. I wanted to hear her talk again, to taste the cadence for evidence of impairment in her speech.

She shook her head.

"Is that the same leg as before? You remember, that trip to help Teresa in Utah?"

"That was the other leg," she said.

She sounded okay. "Should I call the neurologist?" Lauren's neurologist, Larry Arbuthnot, liked to be aggressive with steroid treatment in the face of a fresh exacerbation that threatened serious consequences.

"I don't want to start steroids," she said.

Yeah, okay. "I know."

She actually smiled. "I'm due for interferon today. I'll take that and see how things develop."

Ah, yes, interferon.

Lauren's weekly interferon injection was preventive medicine; it was intended to protect her from waking up to mornings like this one. The IM injection that she plunged into her thigh once a week wasn't intended as a treatment in the event that a morning like this one occurred anyway. Interferon was a toxic prophylaxis against a rare event, akin, I sometimes mused, to lighting particularly noxious incense in an effort to keep elephants out of the living room.

In the case of interferon, burning the incense usually seemed to be effective, but it was inherently hard to tell. Last time I checked, the living room was devoid of elephants. But then again, it usually was.

Was it the incense?

Answering that question was the rub.

Regardless, interferon wasn't intended to deal with a rogue elephant that had snuck into our living room anyway. And that's what we had right now: a rogue elephant in the living room.

"You sure that's wise?" I tried hard not to say it in a tone that communicated that I thought her strategy unwise. I probably failed.

Lauren was almost totally focused on Grace. If it weren't for the walking stick she had clamped between her knees, I could have convinced myself that it was any other Sunday morning.

She finally answered me. "No, not at all. I'm not at all sure. Will you bring me half a cup of coffee, please? Maybe some juice."

I wanted to scream. I wanted to take the damn disease she had by the throat and tighten my grip on it until it died.

"Lauren, we're talking ambulation. It's a big risk."

She snapped back, "Don't you think I know that? I hate steroids. I want to give it a few hours, okay?"

I retrieved her coffee and juice. Her request for a few hours was reasonable. But then, so was my alarm.

Her voice was much, much softer when she said, "Was that Sam before? On the phone?"

"Yeah, there's a lot that's going on." I filled Lauren in on the events that had taken place outside Albany, Georgia, and Sterling Storey's ironic demise on the Ochlockonee River.

"That's convenient," she said, almost devoid of sympathy. Death a time zone away was so much easier on the soul.

"That's what Sam thinks, too. He said he wants them to render the body."

She laughed. "I think you mean render *up* the body. Rendering has something to do with separating out fat, doesn't it? It's a cooking thing, I think. Adrienne does it to chickens sometimes around the Jewish holidays. Is Sam okay?"

Her laugh warmed my heart. "He's doing the best he can. He's so off-balance. The heart attack. His family gone. I don't think he can really believe that Sherry took Simon away at a time like this."

Grace seized the moment to toss her spoon across the table. I caught it before it hit the floor. She thought the whole thing was

hilarious. If I gave it back to her, I was sure the game would get repeated. Piaget would have given it back. I kept it.

Lauren said, "I can't either." Panic crossed her violet eyes in a flash,
like the reflection of a lightning bolt in a pane of glass at midnight.

"Nor can I," I said. I didn't know if my wife wanted me to say
that I wouldn't leave her, to reassure her that the latest permutation of
her illness hadn't changed a single facet on the surface of my heart,
but I feared that the very mention of her vulnerability might make the
circumstances too real for her. So all I added was "I can't believe what's
happened with them."

I slid the newspaper across the table to her, pointing at the article
about Penn Heller's arrest for possession of cocaine.

She read the headline, gazed up at me, and said, "Really?"

I could have lied and said, *"I don't know anything more than I
just read in the paper."* But I didn't. I said, "Apparently."

She scanned the article quickly. "It sounds like they have him for
intent to distribute. That's not good."

"What's this going to do to Jara's position on the bench? How
damaging is it?"

She shrugged.

"Do you know her husband?"

"A little," Lauren said. "Just a little."

It was apparent that Lauren wasn't eager to talk about Jara and
Penn Heller.

A few minutes later Lauren hobbled back toward the bedroom with
her non–walking stick hand full of the supplies necessary to inject a
milliliter of interferon into her thigh. I glanced at the clock. I added two
hours. That was when she'd start getting sick from the medicine. I
added twenty-four hours more to that. That was when she would stop
being sick from the medicine.

A day, every week, deducted from her life in a valiant effort to re-
pel rogue elephants.

I waited until Lauren closed the door behind her before I turned
to Grace and said, "It's too late this time, I'm afraid, Gracie. The elephants are already here."

Grace tried to say "elephants." Anyway, I think what she tried to say was "elephants."

She pointed at the dogs.

Close enough.

I realized that Emily's paw umbrella needed my attention.

THIRTY-ONE

SAM

The list of people who were going to be pissed at me was longer than usual.

Alan? Absolutely. Top of the list. My captain? He'd kill me if he got half a chance—save my insurance company a lot of money and my doctor a lot of work. My cardiologist? I think he was coming around to the reality that I wasn't his normal post-MI patient. Still, he wasn't going to be happy about my extracurricular activities. I was pretty sure about that. And Carmen Reynoso? Eh, so? It'd just give her another reason to look down her nose at us mountain cops.

Who else?

I wondered what Sherry would think, but I finally decided that I couldn't really guess. I hadn't thought she was the type of person who could walk out the door with my kid less than a week after I had a heart attack.

Who am I kidding? Sherry wouldn't be

surprised. When she heard what I was up to, she'd make that noise that I hated that came from someplace far back in her sinuses, but she wouldn't be surprised.

The noise was her marital shorthand for "See what an asshole he is."

Or maybe it was "What can I do with him?"

I didn't know anymore.

But at that moment I was coming to the conclusion that being on medical leave from the department wasn't all bad. My check was still coming in. The mortgage was going to get paid. I even liked not carrying my badge. And not having a gun on my hip or strapped below my armpit? It was fine, good even, at least for a while.

Two phone calls, and I had her address. If I was smarter, I could have figured it out in one, but I used one of the calls to get an answer to Alan's question about how the cops were tipped about Jara Heller's husband's cocaine problems. I admit I frittered away a minute or two trying to figure out why Alan wanted to know, too.

Gibbs Storey's house wasn't that far from mine, geographically speaking. Ten blocks? Twelve? I could have walked over there easily, but I didn't. Too much slush on the sidewalks, too little motivation to fight the muck on my part. I took the Cherokee and parked half a block down from her place. Why not in front?

I was on the lookout for media, especially media with cameras.

The whole connection between current Boulder residents Sterling and Gibbs Storey and the old murder in Laguna Beach hadn't yet hit the papers, but I knew it would. Any minute, probably.

And Sterling's disappearance in Georgia?

That was prime tabloid bait. The frosting on the cake. When that news hit the wires, we were talking nonstop cable TV chatter and lots of reporters making their first trips ever to southern Georgia so they could do their pompous stand-ups on some obscure bridge over the Ochlockonee River. There'd probably be good footage of gorgeous old bloodhounds on long leashes snuffling along the riverbank and maybe even some shots of gruff rescue guys in wet suits searching eddies. And of course, there'd be plenty of on-camera interviews with fat cops like me saying they're doing the best they can, ferreting out every lead, examining every possibility.

So I checked the street in front of the house as carefully as I knew how. I didn't want to get ambushed by some reporter.

Not yet.

Gibbs Storey was home. To my surprise, she answered her door. To my greater surprise, she invited me inside as soon as I told her I was a friend of her psychologist. That's what got me inside her door: Alan. Whatever. I was grateful to be off the porch; I'd felt like I had a spotlight on me when I was standing outside like some Jehovah's Witness or some almost-homeless guy walking across lawns going house to house spreading doorspam.

The entryway of the Storeys' home was all rose-hued marble tile. Nothing was out of place in the part of the house that I could see from where I was standing. No dust, no dirt. No kids' shoes. No crappy tennis balls the dog dragged in. If my crazy grandmother had had a ton of money and a totally different sense of what was tasteful— actually the dear old woman didn't have any sense at all of what was tasteful—this is what her house would have looked like.

"You're Dr. Gregory's detective friend? The one he wanted to talk to about . . . my situation?"

That part couldn't have gone better if I had written her lines myself. I'd never said I was a cop—technically since I was on leave, I wasn't a functioning cop—but she'd generously gone ahead and granted me detective status. Alan had once told me that status was a simple thing, psychologically speaking. One person assigned it, and as soon as someone else agreed, the status became real. That's all it took. Well, Gibbs had assigned me detective status. And me?

I didn't contradict her. Thus, my status was real.

"Yeah. I'm Dr. Gregory's friend. The one he talked to" was all I said.

"How did you find me? He said he wouldn't tell you my name."

"He didn't. He kept his word; he's big on that. But there's a lot of other stuff going on—you must know that. Things that I'm in a position to hear about without any assistance from him. The search warrant here the other day? The cops visiting from the West Coast? It wasn't hard to put numbers on the players' backs, if you know what I mean. I sort of put two and two together on my own."

She stared at me as though I were some kind of bizarre math

whiz, and she feared I was about to do some jujitsu calculus on her.

I smiled back at her like a teddy bear. A big teddy bear with man-boobs.

I was wearing a coat, a nylon parka that had once had enough goose down in it to keep me warm in a blizzard. She wouldn't know about the man-boobs. Hell, maybe she would. Didn't matter. I wasn't planning on taking the coat off in front of her.

Why? I just wasn't going to do it.

Gibbs Storey was gorgeous, okay? I mean make-me-nervous, shift-my-weight, avert-my-eyes kind of gorgeous. The girls-guys-like-me-don't-even-get-to-talk-to kind of gorgeous.

Not pretty.

Gibbs was movie-star stuff.

If she hadn't been so pretty, or maybe if I had just been constitutionally more adept at being around someone so pretty, I might not have blurted out what I blurted out next. But she was, and I wasn't.

I said, "And of course, I heard about your husband. That's kind of why I'm here. Well, that is why I'm here."

Her face decomposed into tears. For a moment I thought she was going to run into my arms. Fantasy? Maybe. But she didn't turn to me; she turned and sprinted down the hall.

I decided that her rapid departure constituted an invitation, so I followed her.

It took about five minutes before things calmed down again.

We'd ended up in a long room that faced the greenbelt below the hogbacks on the western edge of town. Right where the Storeys' carefully manicured backyard stopped, the scrub of the greenbelt began. The previous owners of this place must have had a scary, scary night in July 2002 when the Wonderland Lake fire erupted and looked as though it were planning on turning this particular section of Boulder into raw material for Kingsford.

A quick calculation told me that the room we were in was almost exactly the size of my house. This family room/breakfast nook/kitchen combo was as spotless as the entryway, but it wasn't done in marble. This doesn't-it-look-like-a-ski-lodge? haven was all dark wood floors and wood-beam ceilings and plaid sofas and furniture converted from farm implements and a chandelier made out of a heck of a lot of deer antlers. A moss rock fireplace divided the view of the sharp hogback to the west almost exactly in half. If the fireplace had ever had an actual fire in it, somebody with a serious aversion to ash—I'm talking phobia—had taken on the responsibility of cleaning up after the blaze.

It crossed my mind that maybe that's why Gibbs Storey was seeing Alan. She was a neat freak, a pathological neat freak of some kind. He was trying to get her to loosen up, not dust for a day.

But who was I to say what was deviant, right?

While I was encouraging Gibbs Storey to stop crying—I do a surprising amount of that in my job day to day, and I'm pretty good at it—I was thinking that if somebody came and chopped off the rest of this house and just left this room standing, Sherry and I still couldn't afford to live here.

Why did we fight so hard to stay in Boulder? Why? We worked our asses off, together we made a decent amount of money, or what should have been a decent amount of money, and what did we get for it? A barely insulated frame box with a crappy furnace, a twenty-year-old roof, and wall-to-wall carpeting that smelled like a colony of prairie dogs used it for a few years before donating it to the Goodwill. If you're a cop, or a teacher, or a lady selling flowers in a little shop just off the Downtown Mall, that's what working your ass off gets you, if you want the privilege of living a dozen blocks away from Gibbs and Sterling Storey in beautiful, beautiful Boulder.

It gets you shit.

Maybe Sherry was right. Maybe it was time for a change. Back to Minnesota? I didn't know.

Gibbs was curled up in the corner of a big sofa. I was across from her on a chair made out of twigs and branches. Her sniffles seemed to be slowing. Finally, she whimpered, "I'm a private person. Soon everybody is going to know everything, right?"

Well, that gave me pause. I'm thinking I have a grieving widow on my hands, and that I'm going to be ladling out the comfort and tugging the tissues if I want to get anything out of her, but instead I'm wondering whether she's upset just because her family secrets aren't likely to remain secrets for too long.

That was a whole different state of affairs.

" 'Everything' being what exactly, ma'am?" I said. It was as innocuous as I could make the question sound. I hoped it was innocuous enough, because if Gibbs heard any semblance of the echo of what she'd just said to me—assuming she was one tenth as smart as she was pretty—I figured that my forward progress was going to be severely hampered.

She swallowed, opened her eyes a tad wider, and inhaled slowly. Yep, she'd caught wind of the echo.

"What is it that you want, Detective?"

"Please call me Sam. Sam Purdy."

She dabbed at her eyes with one of the tissues I'd handed her. It wasn't wadded; it was folded neatly. She used one of the sharp corners to do the dabbing. "But you are that detective friend of Dr. Gregory's, right? The one who works with the Boulder Police Department?"

Tricky question. "That is how I make my living, ma'am."

"Why are you here? Why did you come to see me this morning?"

"Something's been troubling me, I mean wake-up-in-the-middle-of-the-night troubling me about . . . your situation, and I'm hoping you can help me make some of my confusion go away."

She narrowed her eyes. "What?"

"You've lived with your husband a long time since you knew he had killed your old friend, right?"

"Yes."

It was a reluctant yes. Not reluctant because the facts didn't ring true to her, reluctant because she could spot the danger looming ahead if she accepted my premise.

"Well, I'd like to know how you could stay with him. It's important. To me, really important. I don't understand how you could go through the routines, you know, the daily . . . stuff that makes up marriage, knowing what you knew."

"He's my husband, Detective."

Yeah, yeah. But I heard the present tense. And knew she'd wanted me to hear the present tense.

"But wives leave husbands all the time, ma'am. All the time. They leave husbands over goofy things, over things that are much less consequential than murder. Money, booze, other women. Snoring, halitosis, sex—too much, not enough—you name it. But you didn't, and I'm trying to understand that."

What I didn't say was *"My God, woman, your options are limitless. I know twenty men who would bow down and lick clean the ground you walk on."*

"I love Sterling."

I wanted to touch my chest right then, press on my sternum with at least three fingers to see if the tightness I was feeling had to do with my heart or with my *heart,* but I was afraid it might freak her out to see me caressing myself, so I didn't. Instead, I reached into my coat pocket and fingered the bottle of nitro the way I used to stroke the velvety rabbit's foot I carried around in my pants pocket as a kid.

I said, "And that's enough?"

"It was for me," she said.

Past tense now.

I took a moment to look away from her and give myself a pep talk. I told myself that I could look her in the eye and not be weakened by her beauty. That my resolve wouldn't dissolve in her loveliness.

When I looked back up at her, I was pretty sure that I'd been wrong.

"Can I admit what I've been wondering about you?" I said.

In an endearing way that ambushed me, she said, "Please."

"I've been wondering whether you've been threatened, you know? Or maybe you've feared what your life would be like if you turned him in, what would happen to you. Is that what kept you from calling us?"

My mother collects Lladro angels. The smile Gibbs offered reminded me of the face of one of the angels, only prettier. "That wasn't it, Detective. I've gone over all this with that woman detective. With Miss Reynoso."

I waved off her objection. "Different departments. California, Colorado. It's a left hand, right hand thing. I don't mean to be repetitive—to force you to be repetitive—but in my business it truly helps sometimes to hear things yourself." I glanced away from her, then right back. Gibbs Storey was still gorgeous; that hadn't changed. "I'd understand those reasons. You know, if you were scared. If that's the reason it took you so long to—"

"But you don't understand that I love him. And that love made every choice difficult. Every option . . . complicated."

Is that what love did? Would Sherry say the same thing? I didn't know. I'd like to have asked her.

Maybe I would. Probably I wouldn't.

I said, "I'm having a little trouble with that, I'll admit."

Gibbs stood up and crossed the space between us. She leaned over, placing her hands on her knees so that the flawless skin of her face was only about a foot from my eyes. She said, "Would you like something to drink, Detective? Some coffee, maybe? It'll just take a minute."

She made me some decaf in a little glass coffeepot with a spring thing in the middle. It looked like something from a high school chemistry lab. The results were pretty good. I bet Alan had a pot just like it. Probably most of Boulder had a pot just like it. Sherry and I would be last. More likely, everybody would move on to another kind of coffee-making appliance before we got around to getting the one with the little spring thing in the middle.

We'd get ours on the sale table at Target.

She served the coffee in a cup with a saucer and a little platter of cookies. Often when I go into people's houses to talk, they offer me coffee, or a Coke, or even a beer, but I know it's fake polite, not real polite. They're seeking to grab some of my advantage; they don't really want me there. I didn't get that feeling from Gibbs. She seemed sincere with her coffee and cookies.

"About your husband's disappearance, ma'am? If you can bring yourself to discuss it—I'm sure it's painful—I'd very much like to hear your thoughts about what happened."

Her eyes filled with tears again. Was that grief? If it wasn't, it was a close approximation.

"I got a call just last night around bedtime. After eleven. It was from someone in Georgia, a policeman, I think. Maybe a firefighter. I don't recall. They're still looking for him, you know. I haven't given up hope."

"Yes, I know. That's why I called it a disappearance. I'm sure they're doing extraordinary things to find him."

"Thank you."

"You're welcome. Was last night like him? Like your husband? To stop and help someone like that? That was a courageous, selfless thing he did. An act of true heroics."

"What do you mean?"

"Maybe it's the work I do, maybe it's just some inborn cynicism— I admit that's a fault of mine—but I've come to believe that some of us are born with more of the Good Samaritan gene in us than others. I'm curious where Sterling fell on that spectrum."

She thought about it for a moment.

"It wasn't like him at all. Stopping to help someone like he did. Usually Sterling put his own self-interest first. It's not one of his best traits. Love doesn't require perfection, does it?" Her eyes found the small plate in front of me. "You don't like the cookies. Some fruit, maybe, instead? I think I have grapes."

I almost got stuck on that question. Not the cookies-and-fruit one. The one about perfection. Sherry hadn't done what she did because I wasn't perfect. No, that's not why she left. That had to be true. The day I said "I do," I knew I wasn't perfect. I went to bed every night knowing I wasn't perfect. I knew it the same way I knew that the stars felt like snowflakes under God's feet. I just knew it.

She knew it, too. Sherry left me for some other reason then, something more.

Or something less.

"No, ma'am. No thank you on the fruit, and no, love doesn't require perfection. So what evidently happened last night at the Ochlockonee River?" The name of the Georgia river rolled magically off my tongue. "Him stopping to rescue somebody. That would have been an exception then, what we might consider an anomaly?"

She nodded. "I've been comforting myself with the possibility that it was an act of . . . you know, contrition? Atonement?"

"Because he heard about the investigation that was going on? He was making up for what he had done?"

"Yes, I'd like to think so. I'd been keeping him informed of what was going on here, you know, legally. Sterling knew what kind of trouble he was in."

I lowered my eyes and allowed my expression to soften before I looked back up. "My understanding is that at the time of the . . . tragedy, he was traveling to visit a friend?"

"Yes, an old college friend. A man named Brian Miles. Brian lives just outside Albany, Georgia. He's a tech guy. An electronics genius of some kind. I don't know him that well. He and Sterling used to chase girls together in school—he's that kind of friend. They stayed in touch. We never socialized much together, though. I always thought Brian was kind of, you know, gay. Sterling says not."

Relevance? Got me; I filed it.

"And this visit? It was typical for Sterling to look up old friends during business trips?"

"No. Not male friends anyway, not just for the hell of it. Sterling likes women for company. He prefers women for company. Always has. He always will."

She managed to state it as though it were a simple fact, as though he preferred Hilton to Hyatt or Pepsi to Coke. But there had to be something more, didn't there? When people do unexpected things at unexpected times, it's important.

"Has that been a problem for the two of you? That Sterling prefers women for company?"

She stared at me again. She had quite a repertoire of stares. This one was an it's-none-of-your-business stare.

"All couples have issues, Detective. We have ours." She glanced at my stubby left hand and spotted the thin gold band almost disappearing in the lard on my finger. "You're married, aren't you?"

I was tempted to get lost with her. Tell her about Sherry and Simon and having Thanksgiving alone. But I don't tell stuff to strangers. Certainly not to strangers treading in homicide soup like Gibbs Storey. So I didn't tell her. But I knew I'd come close.

I came close because she's so pretty.

That was an ugly realization.

I moved my right hand so that the gold ring was no longer in view. What did I want to ask? I wanted to know how in the world a man could prefer the bed of another woman when he was married to the one who was sitting in front of me. I opened my mouth to ask at least twice, but each time I chickened out. Even rehearsing the words in my head, they sounded wrong.

I ended up asking a safer question. "So this whole sojourn from Tallahassee was unusual? The trip to see an old friend, a man? Then stopping to aid a stranger. Were you aware that Sterling was going to visit Mr. Miles?"

"Yes. Yes, I was. Sterling called me during the football game in Tallahassee. He knew about the search of our home, about the detective waiting here from Laguna Beach. He knew what was facing him here. He really wanted to talk it out—you know, his situation—with someone he trusts. Sterling doesn't have too many male friends, but Brian is someone he trusts. As much as he trusts anyone."

"Mr. Miles?"

"Yes."

"The one he chased girls with?"

"Yes."

"Was Sterling angry with you for your role in exposing him to the police?"

She maintained her balance and matched my steps as though she was accustomed to following bad dancers.

"He was, and he wasn't. I've been so torn—my loyalty to him, my love for him. An impossible choice. He understands that I've been placed in a difficult position by all this."

"And you have, haven't you?" I said. I meant two or three things with the question but figured she only heard one.

After a little sinus upshift she started to whimper again.

My decision-making process was abrupt, almost instinctive. I didn't plan to say what I said next. I just said it.

"I have some time off from work. Personal time. I'd like to help you find your husband. Try to find out what happened that night. At least go . . . to Georgia and do what I can to make sure everything possible is being done to . . ." I didn't know how to end the sentence.

Gibbs did. She said, "Find him."

"Yes."

She melted me with those eyes. "Please do that. Will you do that? Find him." I didn't know what to make of the stare she offered up next. But Gibbs Storey skipped third gear and went right into sniffle overdrive.

In seconds I had an arm around her, and she was leaning into my man-boobs. Want to know what it was like? Having her in my arms, having her delicate beauty against my fat flesh?

Comfort. Solace. Succor.

Giving, getting.

I felt like goddamned Shrek with the goddamned princess.

It felt like heaven.

Didn't feel right, though. I can tell you that.

And it didn't answer that question about why Sterling chose the bed of another woman. Or the question about why I'd volunteered to go ask him.

Nope, it didn't do any of that.

THIRTY-TWO

ALAN

The storm had departed and left the Colorado plains in bright sunshine, which was typically what happened after a fierce snowstorm along the Front Range. But our seventy-degree Saturday had become a high-thirties, low-forties Sunday. Less than a full day had passed, and we were in a whole different season.

Lauren slept most of Sunday, a bad sign. Grace and I ran some errands, played some toddler games for which neither of us understood the rules, built a snowman out of snow that was the consistency of a Slurpy, and the whole time I pretended that the big bad wolf wasn't really at our door getting ready to huff and to puff and to blow our house down.

Once I succeeded in getting Grace into her crib for her midday nap, I checked my messages at the office. I was anticipating that I would be receiving a call from Gibbs seeking my compassion about her husband's disappearance in Georgia. But the only voicemail wasn't from Gibbs; it was a long message from Jim Zebid.

"Hey, Alan. It's Jim. I assume you saw the *Camera* this morning. I have to admit I'm a little concerned about it . . . um . . . you see, my guy—I'm sure you remember the one I'm talking about—swears he hasn't told anybody about his, you know, his thing with the guy, the one in the paper. And I certainly haven't told anybody about it but you. And now the cops know, obviously, and it's in the news. So it's a concern, obviously, and I'm left wondering whether—this is hard to say—you might have been a little indiscreet after we talked earlier in the week."

His tone wasn't belligerent. It wasn't even heated.

"I'm not accusing you, believe me, but the position my guy is in right now is really precarious. I mean, if her husband talks, you know—about, you know, it could be real bad for my guy. Anyway, if you have any thoughts about all this, I'd love to hear them. I'm on my cell all day. I think you have the number."

He's not accusing me? What else would I call it?

I dialed his cell number. He answered after three rings. "This is Jim."

"Alan Gregory, Jim."

"Alan, hold on. I need to get someplace I can talk. It'll take a minute, I'm downtown." I heard the sounds of a soulful saxophone. I knew exactly where he was on the Mall. He was at the corner of Pearl and Thirteenth. Some cold air wouldn't keep throngs away from the Mall on a sunny autumn Sunday when the number of shopping days until Christmas was dwindling away like Girl Scout cookies in a firehouse.

"Okay, this is better. Thanks for holding. So what do you think about what I was saying before?"

"What do I think?" I wasn't about to start this conversation. That was going to be up to him.

"The article?" he said.

"Yes?"

"Were you, maybe, a little indiscreet?"

"No, Jim. Not even a little. Until I saw the paper this morning, I'd totally forgotten about that part of our conversation. I'm almost embarrassed to admit that before this morning I hadn't given what happened with your client a thought since you left my office."

"Yeah?"

"Totally." I was determined not to sound defensive. I wasn't sure I was pulling it off. Instead I feared I sounded callous.

Jim was quiet. From the change in the background sounds, I guessed he was walking around on Thirteenth Street, down from the corner where the old black guy played the saxophone weekends on the Mall. There wouldn't be as many pedestrians on Thirteenth as there were on the Mall.

"Well," he said, "my guy had no reason to talk. And he assures me that he's told nobody but me what happened."

"Cops have other ways of finding out things, Jim. I assure you that nobody heard it from me. Directly or indirectly."

"What about your notes?"

"I don't put things like this in my notes. Ever." So much for not sounding defensive. Should I have told him that I wasn't even certain I'd written any notes about the session? Nothing was to be gained by going down that road. "I think there might be something else going on here, Jim."

"Good, I'd love an explanation. I'm planning on talking with my guy later on today."

"I think it's something we should talk about on Tuesday during our regular appointment."

"This can't wait until Tuesday. What do you have Monday?"

"I have a cancellation at eleven-fifteen. You want that?"

"Fine."

"Jim, I suspect this has more to do with you and me—issues in the therapy; I suspect that trust is high on that list—than with whatever you told me during our last session."

"You're kidding, right?"

"No."

"Jesus."

He hung up. Or the signal died. Either way, the deadness in my ear let me know I wasn't talking with him any longer.

*　　*　　*

The bedroom was dimly lit, blinds tilted to filter the western sun. The air had already taken on the stuffiness and stillness of an infirmary. Lauren didn't lift her head from the pillow as I entered. But she said, "Hi, baby. How's Grace doing?"

"Good. She's down for her nap. She ate a good lunch."

For a long moment I listened to her breathing, watched the bedding rise and fall above her chest.

She said, "Would you call the neurologist for me? Set up the steroids? I'm ready to start."

"You're sure?"

"Yeah."

"Here, or at the hospital?"

"Here."

"He may want to see you. That's cool?"

"Of course. And call somebody at work, tell them I won't be in for—God, I don't know—a few days."

"Sure. Is Elliot okay?" Elliot was one of Lauren's favorite people at the office.

"Elliot's good."

I touched her through the bedding. "I love you. Know that."

"I know. I love you, too. And I'm sorry."

I sat on the edge of the bed and placed my hand against her cheek. I said, "Don't be."

"I just am."

The home care nurse the neurologist sent over to our house arrived at dinnertime. She was a young woman named Petra, and I tried to engage her a little as she was gathering supplies. It didn't work. My clinical antennae said she was battling chronic depression. For some reason—maybe it was the barely restrained scowl she shot my way when she learned my profession—I guessed that she had already suffered through a bad stint or two of psychotherapy and had been the unfortunate victim of multiple antidepressant failures—a couple of tricyclics, some SSRIs, and maybe even an MAOI or two.

The good news is that what Petra gave up in gregariousness, she made up in efficiency. The IV was running and taped in place within ten minutes of her initial knock on our door. Moments after that she loaded the first gram of Solumedrol into a fat syringe and began pushing the liquid in it hard into the tube that led to Lauren's purple vein.

How much is a gram of steroids? If a healthy person were to injure a shoulder, say, or a hip, and a physician determined that major anti-inflammatory drugs were required, the doctor might prescribe oral steroids. Over five days of treatment the dose would decrease from a high of maybe thirty milligrams a day down to zero.

Lauren had just received over thirty times that maximum dose, and she'd had it forced directly into her bloodstream all at once. And the exact same procedure—with the same megadose—would be repeated on each of the next three days.

As I watched the blood pressure cuff inflate on her arm, Lauren managed a smile. She mounted the smile, I knew, for me. The syringe had just relinquished its final drops of steroids into the IV tube. She said, "The first twenty-four hours aren't all bad, you know."

I touched her hair. *And after that?* I thought. After the first day became the second and the first gram of steroids was followed by another, and another, and then, damn it, another?

After that, well, after that we'll just jump off that damn bridge when we get to it, won't we?

It wasn't until after Petra had departed—she'd left a buffalo cap behind affixed to the indwelling IV in Lauren's forearm—that I realized that Gibbs had never called me about Sterling's disappearance and possible demise in Georgia.

I usually didn't waste even a solitary calorie of effort worrying about patients who *didn't* call me after hours. My consistent message as therapist to my patients was that I expected they could handle life's stresses without checking in with me. I expected them not to call me after hours.

But emergencies are emergencies. And missing husbands who are feared drowned are usually considered emergencies.

As I prepared Grace's dinner, I couldn't help thinking that Gibbs *should* have called. Since I left her at her house during the search warrant execution on Friday, she'd had to endure an uncomfortable interview by Carmen Reynoso. Her husband had disappeared and was feared dead in some river I'd never heard of in Georgia. That had to be stressful.

I couldn't help wondering why she didn't call.

I thought of calling her, checking on her. I really did. The very fact that I was considering it was so unusual that it caused me to recall Diane's admonition that I was treating Gibbs differently than I would treat some other patient, which for some reason caused me to jump to a very disconcerting association to Teri Reginelli and *hachas en cabezas.*

I had an appointment with Gibbs Monday morning near dawn. If she could wait until then, I could wait until then.

THIRTY-THREE

My best guess is that Lauren hobbled out of bed after a few fitful hours of sleep somewhere around three A.M. The primary short-term side effect of high-dose steroids is agitation, and she was agitated. Not wide awake, but agitated. I followed her out to the living room to check on her but never looked at the clock. She got herself settled on the sofa with the remote control and sent me back to bed. Did I sleep after that? I don't know. I do know that the alarm jangled at five forty-five.

Grace started squealing at five forty-seven. She was my snooze alarm.

Viv, our daytime nanny, arrived at six thirty-five. I filled her in before I kissed Lauren and Grace and ran to my car at full speed.

Emily's paw umbrella *clack-clacked* on the floor as she chased me to the door. I apologized to her because I didn't have time to make repairs.

*   *   *

Gibbs looked much better put together for our seven o'clock appointment than I did. The morning was brisk, and she was modeling her fall things. The autumn forecast, fashionably speaking, apparently called for snug black jeans, tight sweaters, and large beads of silver and gold. Gibbs wore it all well, no surprise.

I'd brought coffee from home. Gibbs had stopped at Starbucks. Every time she sipped, she left a slightly wider lipstick stain on the plastic cover of the paper cup.

"Whew, interesting weekend" was her opener.

I suppose. I tried to read her face for signs of what she might be feeling, but no clues jumped at me.

I did, however, check "distressed" from my list.

"Tell me," I said. I could just as easily have chosen silence or said "go on" or "yes," but "tell me" is what I chose.

"I talked with that detective, finally."

She lifted her latte and took a baby sip. I expected her to continue with her tale of her meeting with Reynoso, but she returned the cup to the small table between us and looked at me expectantly.

I sat holding my mug just below my chin with both hands, and I waited. Gibbs had apparently decided that this appointment was going to be more dental than psychological and that it was going to be my job to pull the teeth. In turn, I decided that it wasn't going to happen. In therapy, when things go according to plan, the patient sets the pace.

On good days in the therapist's chair, I could outwait Job. And I felt like having a good day.

I needed a good day.

Two minutes, maybe three, later, Gibbs blinked. "Oh, and I met that friend of yours. Detective Purdy? He stopped by my house yesterday for a visit. He's so nice. Don't you think he's nice?"

I thought, *You have to be kidding.*

But I kept my face impassive and said, "Tell me." Steam blossomed up from the mug below my chin.

I allowed Gibbs to go on uninterrupted. She sensed, I think, that her story was causing me consternation, but I doubted that she understood why I was feeling almost cataplectic at what she was telling me.

If Gibbs was to be believed—and I admitted to myself that I was experiencing more than a few instances of severe doubt about the veracity of her story—Sam was probably well over halfway, or more, to Georgia as she and I were speaking. I'd been on road trips with Sam before. The image in my head needed no further developing. He was crammed behind the wheel of his Jeep Cherokee, listening to some music that was as full of lament as was his current life. He was hungry. He was cranky. Road maps were spread out on the passenger seat beside him. Maybe they had already crumpled into heaps on the floor. He'd marked his preferred route with a pastel highlight pen, then marked an alternative in a different color. Something you could count on when traveling with Sam was that every time he stopped for gas, he would decide that there was a better way to get from where he was to wherever he wanted to be.

If it was more than an hour from his last fuel stop, he probably needed to visit a bathroom. But he wouldn't pull over again until he needed gasoline. Highway rest stops were for wusses. Sam was a velocity traveler, not a comfort traveler. Bladder be damned, full speed ahead.

I was willing to make a guess that he was someplace in Arkansas or, if he was making particularly good time, had already crossed the border into Louisiana.

I had a fleeting wish that I was beside him, riding shotgun. Sam grows reflective on long trips. The monotony of the road or the infinity of the sky or something about the miles passing below his feet causes him to consider opening windows into his life that were otherwise nailed shut and hung with blackout curtains.

There was so much for Sam and me to discuss right then: Sherry. Simon. Heart disease. Rehab. Cop work. Lauren's exacerbation. The future.

God, the future.

And of course, Gibbs and Sterling Storey.

But the real reason I had a yearning to be sharing the Jeep with him was that I wanted to be a fly on the wall, a silent spectator, as the inevitable collision occurred between the recalcitrant Iron Ranger and the southern good old boy. I wanted to watch as Northern Minnesota, personified by Sam, said hello to Southern Georgia, personified by any number of unwitting volunteers. I would have paid good money for a chance to witness what happened as Sam Purdy tried to reconnoiter Dixie.

I blinked myself back to the present. Gibbs was still talking, oblivious to the extended holiday my attention had just taken.

"He said he'd call when he got to Albany, but I don't expect that will be before tonight. I'm thinking thirty hours minimum."

"Tonight," I repeated for no other reason than to get my bearings. I didn't bother telling her that Sam would be doing the trip nonstop; that his head wouldn't see a motel pillow between here and there. I didn't know the mileage, but Gibbs should be dividing by seventy-five-plus miles per hour, not any pedestrian fifty-five.

"You think sooner? You know better than I do, I'm sure. Cops don't have to drive the speed limit, do they? He could just flash his badge and make the ticket go away, couldn't he?"

With those words she grew silent.

I used the interlude to consider the obvious. What was it Sam hoped to accomplish in Georgia? I knew him well enough to suspect that his motive had nothing to do with what he had told Gibbs: that he wanted to help her find her husband in the Ochlockonee River.

In usual circumstances Sam wouldn't have driven to Denver to look for Sterling Storey in the shallows of the South Platte.

So then, why?

The silence spread between us like a little pond of fetid water. We each sat on an opposing shore.

Gibbs finally said, "He used to think he was falling. Sterling did. That's when he used to say 'catch me.' Isn't it ironic? Isn't it? And now he goes and . . . disappears trying to catch somebody else. He really was falling, and there was nobody there to catch him."

The abrupt change in direction threw me, once again, off balance. The invisibility of the silent associations that had helped Gibbs traverse the undoubtedly rich affective territory between Sam's arrival time in Albany, Georgia, and her husband's beseeching her for support while he fantasized himself falling perplexed and frustrated me.

Catch me. Yes. Gibbs had once told me something about Sterling saying "catch me."

But what?

Sex. Was it sex? It was probably sex. But I couldn't remember. My brain was on full overload. I felt as though I had *un hacha en mi cabeza.*

It probably had been sex. An awful lot of what Gibbs ended up talking about seemed to ultimately be about sex. Maybe Diane was right: Maybe I just had a difficult time hearing it.

I asked, "Literally falling? Or figuratively falling?"

"Gosh, that's an interesting question," Gibbs said. "I never really thought about that. I always thought he meant falling like that first time on the balcony. Do you remember?"

Do I remember? Do I remember what?

"He was leaning against the side railing, and I was in front of him, you know. . . . I was wearing a skirt. But I wasn't wearing any . . ."

She blushed a little. I finished her sentence in my head. The next word was going to be "underwear."

Diane would have corrected me. She would have maintained that Gibbs's next word was going to be "panties."

"Well, I don't have to paint a picture for you, do I?" she said.

I considered whether the comment was flirtatious or seductive. Although it probably was, a conclusion escaped me. This was not my morning for clarity. I could blame it on the early hour, but that wasn't the cause.

No, of course not, I said to myself, *you don't have to paint a picture for me. I already have one:* New Year's Eve party, Wilshire Boulevard. The balcony of a friend's condo. You and Sterling, the first time you had sex. You weren't wearing any . . .

"That was the first time Sterling said 'catch me,' " I said. My words sounded insincere, even to me. I knew I was saying them to offer proof that I remembered what she had told me.

"Yes," she murmured, reflecting on something I couldn't fathom, perhaps my insincerity.

"He said it again last week," I pointed out.

She nodded. "When we were . . ."

She stopped herself, searching for the correct verb. For that particular activity there were a lot of choices.

Then I remembered. Gibbs had already told me that she could see another couple in the bedroom that night. They were . . . doing that verb, too. I said, "There was another couple, too. That night in L.A. In the bedroom next door."

"Yes. Yes, there was."

She seemed surprised that I knew. Had she actually forgotten telling me? Had she?

"Sterling was so afraid he'd lose control. Lose his balance. That he'd fall, somehow. We were ten stories up, at least. That's when he said 'catch me.' He said it like he meant it."

In my head I was playing with the geometry and the anatomy and the physics and the possible erotic acrobatics. I didn't see how Sterling could have been at much risk of actually going over the railing backward—he wasn't that tall, and Gibbs had the body mass index of a large butterfly—but then my personal experience in such matters was limited. Diane would be able to explain it to me: She'd be the kid in the back row with her hand in the air, yelling, "I know that one. I know that one."

I said, "Really? He was really frightened of falling? Or was it, perhaps, something else?"

"That day, really. Later, I think it was something else. Afraid of falling, you know, metaphorically. He'd say 'catch me' when he was feeling down. Lost. He was asking for my help. To save him, I think."

"Was it always sexual?" I asked. Immediately—I mean instantaneously—I knew I'd asked the wrong question. At the very least I'd asked a question when I should have sat as mute as a bronze Buddha.

"Was what sexual?" she asked in return.

I tried to recover. "Sterling's concern about falling. Did he only say 'catch me' in sexual situations?"

She lifted the Starbucks cup, popped off the lid, and drained whatever remained of her morning coffee. Mocha-stained foam coated her upper lip like sea froth on a glossy red shore. She used her tongue to wipe her lip clean. She did it slowly, deliberately. Out first, then side to side.

Seductively? I just didn't know. I wanted to see the replay. Sometimes I just needed to see the replay.

She said, "We're back there again, aren't we?"

"Back where?"

"I told you once we needed to talk about sex, didn't I?"

I remembered that. "Yes, you did."

"Well," she said. "The truth is, I enjoyed it."

"Excuse me."

"I enjoyed it. It turned me on."

*Talking with me about sex turned Gibbs on? Uh-oh. It's too early
in the morning for this.*

"And it has ever since that night on the balcony," she said.

I was grateful for the clarification. But her words, I thought, carried a hint of defiance. Or maybe it was provocation. Did the difference make a difference?

"Sterling saying 'catch me' while you two were having sex turned
you on? That's what you're saying?"

She shook her head.

Damn.

"No, no. God, no. Watching the other couple that night. That's
what turned me on. I told you about the night on the yacht in St.
Tropez, didn't I? When we met? I did, right?"

"Yes." She knew she had.

"That was the first time I'd ever seen anybody else . . . do it." She
laughed. "Everybody else do it, actually. The feeling that I had that
night was . . . indescribable. It was so unexpected. Then came New
Year's Eve on the balcony and the couple in the bedroom, and I . . . I
was watching him and he was watching me and . . ."

Her words drifted away. She was breathing through her mouth,
and her chest was rising and falling visibly.

The coffee in the mug in my hand had gone tepid. The light in the
room had transformed from dawn to day, and stringy shadows from
the naked branches of the leafless trees were streaking across the floor.
Gibbs's perfume marked the air.

I was thinking, *Weren't we talking about Sam? I'm pretty sure we
had started off talking about Sam.*

"Yes," I said. "Go on." Two heartbeats later, before she'd responded, my train of thought skipped back, then forward once more,
and I added, "Gibbs? You said Sterling was asking for your help when
he said 'catch me.' Help with what?"

"I think he wanted me to help him stop killing the women."

Ah, yes. That.

THIRTY-FOUR

As strange as it may sound, the fact that Gibbs was confident that Sterling Storey had killed a number of women had to remain my secret.

Legally, I not only didn't have a responsibility to tell anyone—for instance, the police—about the other women whom Gibbs suspected her husband had murdered, but I also didn't have the right to tell anyone about them. If Gibbs had informed me that her husband was about to kill yet another woman, well, then that would have left me sailing in murkier waters. But even in those circumstances I probably couldn't breach Gibbs's confidentiality without her permission.

That's right. The only circumstance that would have allowed me freedom to spread the word about the other murders was if Sterling himself came into my office and told me that he was about to kill yet another woman, then proceeded to conveniently identify that woman.

Given the events on the Ochlockonee River on Saturday night, that didn't seem too likely.

But morally?

In the field of mental health, ethics and morals are an odd couple. Despite their differences, though, they get along most of the time. Sure there are occasional quarrels, but most controversies eventually get ironed out because their goals are so similar. Sometimes there occurs, however, a set of circumstances that creates a chasm between ethics and morals that is the size of the Mariana Trench.

This was one of those.

Morally, I knew I had to tell somebody that Sterling Storey had killed other women.

But ethically, it was just as clear that I couldn't.

Look up "quandary" in the dictionary. In the margin beside the definition there will be a picture of me sitting across from Gibbs Storey wondering what the hell to do next.

THIRTY-FIVE

SAM

I used my cell phone to call Simon from a truck stop outside Montgomery. While I talked to my son, I was strolling along the border of the property, kicking at weeds I didn't recognize and swatting at insects I didn't know lived on the planet with me. I didn't tell Simon I was calling from the South. It wouldn't have bothered me at all that he knew I was in Alabama—with his limited worldview he'd have figured I was at the U of A for a football game, and he'd have a question or two about the Crimson Tide—but I didn't want him to start conspiring with me to keep secrets from his mom, so I kept the news about my travels to myself.

Sherry didn't want to talk to me. Her father, a gruff, kind, barrel of a man whom I'd always liked, was the one she'd tapped to tell me she didn't want to talk to me. Angus had always been fond of me, and after I'd bulldogged my way a few years back into a position to help my niece—his granddaughter—get some medical care she desperately needed, he thought I was the son-in-law from heaven. I'd always tried hard to do nothing to dissuade him.

"She's still being a bitch, Sam, what can I say?" was the way Angus described the situation to me. Angus was never one to mince words about his progeny. When one of his girls acted heroic, he called her a hero. When one of them acted bitchy, he called her a bitch. Angus taught me good things about being a dad.

"How about you and I cut her a little slack, Angus? How about that? She's working stuff out." Sherry and I had our problems, but gang-tackling her with her father didn't seem like a fair way to confront them.

He harrumphed. "You okay? Your ticker?"

"It's ticking fine. I'm following all the rules, and the docs think I'm a star. Simon sounds good."

I didn't like lying to Angus, but there it was. Not the part about Simon, the part about following all the recovering-from-a-heart-attack rules. Buried somewhere in the fine print there had to be a rule about no nonstop road trips to the land of deep-fried everything.

Yep, that was probably prohibited. That's the one I'd broken. That one and maybe a few others.

"Simon's good. He's a great kid. A little on the wild side, but a great kid. Though he should be in school. You and I both know that."

"Stay cool, Angus. This will all work out."

"Ask me, it's goofy. They should both be in Boulder with you. But nobody asks me. You get to be seventy-five, and everybody thinks you're an idiot. You wait until you get old."

"You know I agree with you," I said. "And I don't think you're an idiot."

"Now there's an endorsement." He laughed. "There's something I got to ask you, Sammy."

"Yeah."

He laughed again, a deep roar. "Are those Avalanche of yours ever going to score more than one goal in the same game? I mean ever? The point of the game is to put the puck in the net, isn't it?" Angus's laugh exploded into a guffaw.

All I said in reply was "Let's see whose team is still playing in June, Angus, what do you say?"

He was laughing so loudly, I'm pretty sure he didn't hear me.

The bathrooms in the truck stop were surprisingly clean. The restaurant seemed to be run by a group of women my mother's age—two black, two white—who were suspicious about a guy my size ordering egg whites and grapefruit and decaf coffee. As soon as my order made it over to the kitchen, one of the waitresses came by and asked me where was I from, honey. When I told her Colorado, she nodded knowingly.

I didn't even have to say "Boulder."

She'd seen my kind before, apparently.

The matrons kept a careful eye on me after that. I figured they were waiting for me to call them over to the table and order some tofu, or a kiwi smoothie, or maybe a grande cappuccino.

Despite their suspicions they were kind women, all in all. Even brought me a side of grits I didn't order. There was a big fat orb of butter melting like a setting sun right in the center of the grits. I ate around the circle of butter so that what was left on the plate when I was done looked like a cool caricature of a sunny-side-up egg that my kid might have drawn at school.

I dropped enough money on the table to leave the ladies a hundred-percent tip on the meal, filled the tank out at the pumps, checked my maps, and pointed the Cherokee toward Georgia.

I hadn't looked in my rearview mirrors—not intentionally, not once—since I'd headed east on I-70 out of Denver. I didn't look at the mirrors when I pulled away from that Alabama truck stop. Nor did I bother to wave good-bye to the matrons who'd made and served my meal.

I'd told myself from the beginning of my trip that I would only know that I'd really finished leaving someplace when I passed a sign that was promising me that I'd arrived at someplace new. That was the way my life seemed lately, so that was how I was going to travel.

My current plan, always subject to revision, was to cross the border into Georgia right about where Phenix City, Alabama, ended and a highway sign said that Columbus, Georgia, was beginning. Then I would drift southeast toward Albany. Farther south than that, Rand McNally said I'd find the legendary wilds of the Ochlockonee River.

When I got there?

The answer to that question eluded me, I must admit. For well over a thousand miles I'd been trying hard not to think about it. Instinct had rarely failed me in life, and I was counting on a visit from the instinct fairy sometime after I crossed the border into Georgia.

On the short stretch of frontage road between the truck stop and the highway I drove over some railroad tracks that were protruding high above the roadbed. I felt the sharp jolt from the rails as a punch below my sternum, and my pulse immediately popped up a good twenty percent.

Since I'd left the hospital, it seemed that I felt almost everything that happened to my body right in the center of my chest. It was as though any physical sensation was amplified and focused right below my ribs, centered a couple of inches down from my man-boobs.

A belch? Heart attack.

Indigestion? Heart attack.

Roll over in bed? Heart attack.

I knew that the next time I stubbed my toe, I was going to finger that damn brown bottle of nitro.

I thought about my injured heart, and about my broken heart, until I saw the sign for Phenix City. What I was close to deciding was that neither assault on my heart was going to kill me.

I was thinking maybe I was going to be okay after all.

THIRTY-SIX

ALAN

I didn't know where Gibbs had grown up. I didn't know what her family of origin was like.

Siblings? Dog? Cat?

Didn't know, didn't know, didn't know.

Had her parents loved each other? What did her dad do? Had her mother worked? What was school like for her? Did she wear braces? Had she lived in the same house her whole life or had she moved a dozen times? Did she play the piano or enjoy playing any sports?

Did she yearn for children?

Or a career?

Had her heart been broken? Had she endured wrenching losses?

I didn't know.

Typically, after a handful of conjoint sessions and a few individual appointments, I would be able to construct a pretty reliable social history of any one of my patients. But not with Gibbs.

With Gibbs, I didn't know much at all that didn't have to do with St. Tropez yachts and Wilshire Boulevard balconies.

I gave that state of affairs some thought.

What did I know?

I knew about an old murder that purportedly involved her husband, and I knew that voyeuristic sex turned her on. I knew that her husband sometimes said "catch me" during lovemaking. I knew about a magical night in St. Tropez.

And oh yes, I knew about Louise Lake and the other dead women. Gibbs kept reminding me about them.

Did I actually forget about the victims in between her reminders? Hardly. I just kept telling myself that when the chaos quieted, Gibbs and I would get back to it.

The chaos? Yes.

Murder, sex, multiple murder, sex, search warrants, sex, coffee with my friend the detective, sex.

In psychotherapy that kind of progression constitutes chaos.

And now she'd moved us again back to multiple murder.

Damn.

Psychotherapy rule number six: If you want to understand the motivation behind an act, first examine its consequences.

The consequences of Gibbs's chaos-creation proclivities? Her therapist—me—would end up way too off balance to focus on the big picture, whatever the big picture was.

Was that Gibbs's intent?

I didn't know.

But I suspected that my not knowing *was* her intent.

"Gibbs?" I waited until she focused her eyes on me.

"Yes?" she said pleasantly.

"Why don't you tell me about the other murders?"

She fingered her wedding ring. "Just between us?"

An interesting response. I replied, "Of course."

"What difference does it make now? If Sterling is really gone, what difference does it make?"

"I could answer that question for you, but I think it's better if you answer it for yourself. You keep bringing up the other women whom you think Sterling killed. You brought them up again just now. It apparently makes a difference for you that he killed more than one woman. That's what difference it makes."

Psychotherapy rule number eleven: Follow, don't lead.

Had I just broken it?

"They are all women he was involved with at one time or another. At least that's what he told me. I'm not sure I believe him."

I waited. I couldn't follow if she didn't take another step forward.

"You don't believe what? That he was involved with them?"

"I don't know. Sterling lies a lot. He . . . betrayed me. You know?"

"No," I said. "I don't know. The reality is that I don't know anything that you don't tell me, Gibbs. But I don't understand why he would admit to affairs that he didn't have."

"He probably had them." She glanced at her hands before she continued. "The first one he told me about was at Augusta."

"Augusta, Georgia?"

"Yes. He met her at the Masters."

I waited, wondering why it was important that he met her at the Masters. "She was the first one he . . . killed?"

"She was the first one he told me about. But there was another one at West Point, too."

"The military academy?"

"She was a hostess he met. At the Army-Navy game."

I was still following her, but now I was on my tiptoes, trying to look over her shoulder.

"And then Indianapolis," she added.

I thought I was getting the swing of it. Sterling met women while he was producing the broadcast of sporting events. "The Indianapolis 500? The car race?"

She shook her head. "No, the College Combine. The NFL draft? She worked for the arena people."

I took a few steps back to give Gibbs room to lead. "Why just between us? Why not share this information with the authorities?"

"I don't want people to think he was that kind of man."

"Even though he was?"

She glowered. "He has demons, Dr. Gregory. Women make him crazy sometimes. Crazy. He's been fighting it his whole life. He really has. I don't think people will understand."

I couldn't argue with that. Gibbs was absolutely right: People wouldn't understand.

"Women make him crazy?" I asked. It wasn't much of a question. I could have just as easily have said, *"I'm going to skip my turn, why don't you just keep going?"* But instead I said, "Women make him crazy?"

"He was afraid that they wouldn't let him go, that they would ruin what he had. All the good things he'd accomplished . . ." Her voice trailed away.

I was confused about the good things. I asked, "His career?"

"Yes, but . . . no. I was talking about his marriage to me."

"So he killed these women because . . . they threatened your marriage? I'm not sure I follow."

"I don't know very much about any of it." She wriggled and tugged on her sleeves, finally looking back my way as though I were a vanity mirror and she was checking her reflection. "It's not like we talked about this all the time."

I had a thousand questions. I asked none of them.

Her voice was pressured when she resumed. "Just once. We only talked about all this once, okay? Right before we moved back here to Boulder. He admitted the affairs with all the women—there were others, too, many others. I don't know the details. Ones he didn't . . . you know, kill, but I think felt an impulse to . . . There was one in South Bend, a sports information something"—she shivered—"and a girl in Flushing Meadows—she was a publicity something with the women's tour, I think. And Daytona Beach, maybe. I forget. I try to forget."

South Bend was Notre Dame University, probably football. Flushing Meadows was tennis, the U.S. Open. Daytona Beach was NASCAR, I thought. Some car race. Sam would know.

She exhaled deeply. "That wasn't a surprise to me. The affairs. I knew he was . . . seeing other women. I just did. It's who he was. But he promised me that he was done. He told me he had changed, that moving back here would be a new start for us. That he valued our marriage too much to ever cheat on me again."

A tear moved a centimeter down her cheek, paused, and then tracked at an angle toward her nose. She touched it with the tip of her finger. Another tear soon followed the same track. Her chest heaved a little.

"Take your time," I said.

"He said he was going to prove his love for me all over again by putting his life in my hands. That's when he told me that the women were gone. The ones who were a threat . . . to us."

"Gone?"

"That's what I asked. He said they wouldn't bother us ever again. I asked him what he meant."

The tears on her cheeks were leaving silky tracks in the powder on her skin.

" 'Louise is at peace. They are, too.' That's what he said. Those were his exact words. What do you think he meant?" Gibbs's hands were rolled into fists.

I slid the box of tissues closer to her. She appeared not to notice.

I didn't have a prayer of knowing exactly what Sterling had meant with his words. But every one of my guesses chilled me.

Gibbs continued. "We made love that night. And he said 'catch me' again. He was trusting me with his secret, begging me to keep him from falling." She paused for a good hunk of a minute before she confessed, "His life was in my hands for a few weeks. That's how long it took me to betray him."

THIRTY-SEVEN

SAM

The bridge over the river where Sterling Storey disappeared wasn't much to look at.

I'd been working under the assumption that it was a major highway bridge on the stretch of Highway 19 that connects Thomasville and Albany, but it wasn't. For some reason, when Sterling had cut off the main road out of Tallahassee, which was Highway 319, he'd ended up on a smaller road, a two-laner that I guessed was a county road, marked Georgia 3, heading northwest just about parallel to Highway 19. The bridge on the smaller road was a concrete structure that had been doing its job for a lot of years, almost too many. The local cops figured Sterling had gotten lost in the storm and had taken the wrong turn out of Thomasville and ended up on the county road instead of 19.

It was a reasonable assumption, but assumptions trouble me.

The details of the accident weren't what I expected. The minivan that had gone off the highway and that had been in danger of sliding into the swollen river was traveling southeast, not northwest, before it went off the road. I couldn't figure out how Sterling had even seen it down there. It was on the opposite side of the road, on the opposite side of the bridge.

That wasn't all that I couldn't figure. After living in the high desert for as long as I had, it was a constant revelation to me how lush everything was in southern Georgia, even the week before Thanksgiving. With the accident having taken place at nearly eight o'clock at night, with all the woods and vegetation camouflaging everything, and with torrential rains obscuring anything that wasn't camouflaged, I didn't know how Sterling could have seen a damn thing out the windshield of his damn rented Camry.

Standing near the top of the bridge abutment, I stared at the placid river below my feet. The water in the Ochlockonee was more yellow than gray, and I suspected that with global warming and all, there were glaciers that moved faster than that river was flowing at that moment. It took every bit of my imagination to conjure up a picture of the biblical flood that had recently coursed down that channel.

Before I left the riverbank, I reread the police report that my partner Lucy had smuggled to me. The report was okay. Better than many I'd read. Written clearly, decent chronology, good descriptions. In most circumstances it would have sufficed. These weren't most circumstances, though, and standing on the bridge, I realized what wasn't spelled out in the report.

Who had arrived at the scene first? Was it the Baptist preacher, the twin sisters, or Sterling Storey?

According to the police report, the preacher who had witnessed Sterling's disappearance into the river was Reverend Nathaniel Prior, who served the faithful at a church in Meigs, a little town a short stretch northeast on Georgia 3 from the accident scene.

That's where I would start.

*   *   *

The drive from the river to Meigs passed through thick woods that alternated with fields harvested clear—I was guessing—of cotton. I didn't see much else that would support the local economy. I assumed I was in a poor county.

I drove up to a recently whitewashed church and asked a young man who was out in front raking leaves on the ragged lawn if he knew where I could find Nathaniel Prior.

"You've already found him. I'm Nathaniel Prior," he told me. "I'm pleased to meet you."

Nathaniel Prior was no more than twenty-five years old. He was smaller than me by a few inches but matched my weight pound for pound and then raised me a few for good measure. He had a voice that resonated like a diesel in a tunnel. The pile of leaves at his feet covered him up to midcalf.

He had big ears.

He tugged off a canvas glove, and we shook hands. I said, "Sam Purdy. Shall I call you Reverend?"

"That's fine, or Nate's fine, too. There are moments when I'm convinced I'm called worse things behind my back, but you've barely met me, so what reason would you have to insult me? What can I do for you this fine day?"

It was a fine day. The afternoon sun was shining, and the moisture in the southern air had already softened up my cuticles and the tender skin inside my nose. Those are the first parts that turn to papyrus after even a few days in the Colorado high desert.

"Do you have a minute to answer some questions about last Saturday? The accident at the bridge?"

Prior looked over my shoulder at the Cherokee. He said, "Mr. Purdy? Do I have that right? Why don't we sit a spell and get a glass of tea? I have a feeling you've come a long way to ask me these questions, and these leaves are probably more than content to wait to be imprisoned in Hefty bags."

"Sam," I said. "Some tea sounds great." I sat on the wooden porch of the church while the reverend retrieved the tea from inside. At least three people walking down the quiet lane waved hello to me while he was gone. I waved back to every one of them.

The tea was sweet, flavored with mint, and was delivered in painted glasses fat enough to hold a Big Gulp with room to spare.

"Thanks," I said after a long draw.

"Colorado, huh? You ski?"

"Snowboard, actually, if you can believe it. I have a kid I try to chase around as much as I can. The snowboarding is his idea. He thinks skis are dorky. For his benefit, I try not to be any dorkier than comes naturally."

"Copper? Winter Park?"

I didn't expect somebody in Meigs, Georgia, to be asking me about ski resorts on Colorado's Front Range. "Winter Park and Breck, mostly. You know—"

"I did a semester in Denver. At the Denver Seminary. Went up skiing whenever I could afford it, which wasn't very often. A bunch of us got those cheap Buddy Passes at Copper. That was a good winter."

I almost said, *"No shit."* But I didn't; I was on God's front lawn. "How long you been in Meigs?"

"A couple of years. I'm loving it. I have a wonderful congregation. My family's in Atlanta, close by. I'm doing what I've always wanted to do. Life is as sweet as this tea." He placed his glass between his feet. "So what caused you to drive all this way to ask me what happened at the bridge?"

"The man who disappeared? I'm assisting his wife. I told her I'd try to figure out exactly what happened to him."

"You an investigator of some kind?"

I considered lying to him but didn't want to lie to a preacher. I don't know why, exactly; in most circumstances I'd be happy to lie to the pope to advance an investigation. "Yeah, I am. I'm actually a police detective in Boulder. But I had a heart attack a while back and I'm on medical leave. So technically, at the moment, I'm nobody. Just somebody trying to help a friend."

This was the moment in conversations with strangers—the moment they learned I was a cop from Boulder—when they asked the did-you-work-on-the-JonBenet-case? question. I steeled myself for it.

"You don't look like Boulder."

I smiled at him, grateful that we'd skipped right past the Ramseys. I replied, "You don't look like Meigs."

"Touché," he said. "Fire away. What can I tell you?"

I took a battered notepad out of my pocket, flipped it to the next empty page, and clicked open my pen. "When did you arrive at the accident?"

"I was the last car to stop before Mr. Storey disappeared in the water. When I arrived, he was already there, the two sisters from Ochlockonee were already there, and of course, Mrs. Turnbull's minivan was already down the bank."

"Pretty dark that night?"

"As Satan's heart."

"Raining?"

"Buckets."

"And you saw Mr. Storey go into the river? Personally?"

"I'd parked my car so my headlights were pointing toward Mrs. Turnbull's minivan, so even with the rain there was some light down there. Though most of the beam went above her car. She was hung up on a tree branch on a steep section of the bank. It was leaning—at least thirty or forty degrees would be my guess—"

"Mine, too. I saw the river this morning. That bank is like a slide. The other side, where the tree was, there was more vegetation over there."

"Exactly. Well, Mr. Storey was already easing his way down toward Mrs. Turnbull when I first saw him. He was only a couple of yards away from the minivan when his feet went out from under him and he slid down the bank."

"You saw that?"

"Sure. The whole thing happened in the blink of an eye. I didn't see him go into the river. There was no light down that far."

"But he slipped, and then he slid? That's definite?"

"Absolutely."

"He was on the mud side of the car, not the tree side?"

"Correct."

"Did he call for help?"

"He did not. We—the Wolf sisters and me—guessed he was in the water before he knew what happened. He could've been downstream a hundred yards by the time he inhaled. Or tried to inhale. It's awfully easy to hit your head in raging water like that."

"You think he's dead, Reverend?"

"In my heart? Yes, I do. I prayed for his soul that night before I left the riverbank. I felt death around me while I prayed." He gritted his teeth as though a fleck of ice cube had come to rest right on top of a cavity. "You don't, do you? Think he's dead."

"I'm not convinced, no." What I didn't add was that if Sterling Storey was dead, my whole trip to Georgia would dissolve into futility. I wasn't in the South seeking justice; I was in the South seeking understanding. Sterling was going to be my unlikely professor.

I placed my empty tea glass two steps below my fat butt.

"Anything else?" I asked.

"I pray for Mr. Storey daily. Please tell his wife that. He sacrificed himself doing a Christian act of mercy."

"I will pass that along. She'll be comforted, I'm sure."

"Thank you."

I think he could tell I didn't mean the part about Gibbs being comforted. I sat silently for most of a minute reviewing my questions and the reverend's answers, looking for omissions. I couldn't find any.

"If your church has a bathroom, I'd love to make a pit stop. Then I'll be on my way. I'm grateful for your generous help. And for the fine tea. Meigs looks like a pleasant town; the people are friendly."

"It is and they are. You're going to go see the Wolf twins now, aren't you?"

"Yes, I am. I like to hear everyone's stories."

"They won't be home before supper. Go then. They'll feed you well. Your patience will be rewarded."

"I appreciate the tip."

"You're a Christian, Mr. Purdy?"

"I am."

"Doing Christian deeds?"

"I try."

"That's all the Lord asks."

"Is it?" Usually my faith in God was strong enough that such a question would never have occurred to me. But I was in Georgia on a wild-goose chase, and the question appeared on my lips and escaped before I could trap it.

The reverend looked at me in a kindly manner as though he could read the doubt in my eyes, as though he could tell that my faith was suffering.

I didn't ask him why, if I was doing all the Lord asked, I'd just had a heart attack and how come my wife had left me and taken my son away from me a week before Thanksgiving. Why didn't I ask the reverend? I supposed I didn't want to hear him speak about faith and about God acting in mysterious ways. And I didn't know whether or not I would have felt any better when we were done.

But my faith was weak right then, and I doubted it.

Reverend Prior must have sensed that misgivings were clouding my vision. He said, "Don't make the mistake of measuring God's love by the yardstick of your own life, Mr. Purdy."

"What else do I have?" I asked.

He was busy pulling his canvas gloves back onto his hands. I wondered if he was planning to answer me.

"If you question God's plan when life is spitting in your face, you must be willing to accept Him without question when He blesses you with a child who snowboards and doesn't want you to be a dork." Prior bent down and lifted the leaf rake. "Come by for services if you stay in the area. You're welcome here, Mr. Purdy. There is abundant love here."

"Thank you."

"It's nothing. The bathroom is right through there."

THIRTY-EIGHT

Julie Franconia didn't usually get to set these things up the way she wanted. Far from it. She didn't have that much experience, but the few times she'd tried something like this, it had seemed that her fantasies usually got lost in the jungle of some man's choosing. That's the way it was the first time with him, too.

But this time his message said that she got to pick the time, the place, the setup. He just wanted to "control the mood." The last time with him was the best ever. He'd taken her over the moon. The mood? He could have the mood.

That's not all he could have. From the moment she'd spotted him at the RCA Dome, she'd been dying to make him hers. It had turned out better than she could have hoped.

She fit the headphones on her head and snapped the tape into the Walkman.

Beethoven.

An otherworldly voice-over said, "You have twenty minutes to get to the campsite. That's all. Go, baby."

Her heart was swollen. Anticipation. Pure anticipation.

Beneath her hiking clothes she was all silk. Everywhere.

Everywhere.

She knew the spot; she'd picked it carefully. Morgan Monroe State Park, north of Bloomington. A favorite trail. She wouldn't have any trouble getting there in the dusk light. Getting the tent up? She could do it in three minutes.

The piano concerto ended, and some old rock 'n' roll filled her ears. She thought maybe it was the Animals, but she wasn't sure. That was before her time.

Before his, too.

"Okay, babe, get the tent up. Hurry. I can't wait. I'm close by; can you feel me? Can you? I'm watching."

She threaded the fiberglass poles. One, two, three. The tent was up.

"Into the woods, to the west, ten steps. Go on now."

Her hiking boots sank half an inch into the marshy soil. She smiled as she saw the picnic basket.

"Now set everything up in the tent. Everything."

She did.

Wine and chocolate. Two cans of whipped cream. A disposable camera. It didn't take too long to set things up.

The music changed. The Doors.

Jim Morrison sang, This is the end, my friend, the end.

And it was.

When the police found Julie's body, they concluded that she was a hiker who had been pulled off the trail and shot by a madman.

Her body wasn't in a tent.

And she wasn't surrounded by a picnic of wine and sweets.

THIRTY-NINE

SAM

The twins.

Identical, by my reckoning. One padded around their house in the little town of Ochlockonee in Acorns ancient enough that all the dye had worn off the leather soles, the other in tattered Reeboks. The footwear choices made any height differential between the sisters difficult to determine, but the one in the Acorns looked me right in the eye when she greeted me at the front door. She was tall. Real tall. They were light-skinned African American women, each had a highlight of gray hair above her left ear, both wore baggy jeans and bulky sweaters knitted from the same skein of yarn, and each was as skinny as a hose, with fewer curves on their bodies than any two women I'd ever seen in my life.

But they were friendly and kind and generous the way my aunt Josie was friendly and kind and generous. I was in the twins' home for less than

two minutes, and I was already sitting in their best chair eating sliced
carrots from their root cellar. They served them ice cold with lime
juice and more salt than my cardiologist would have liked, but the
treat was tart and fresh, and I was enjoying it immensely.

The twin in the Reeboks said, "We picked that idea up in a bar in
Jalisco a few years ago. So simple, so good."

I assumed Jalisco wasn't a suburb of Thomasville or Valdosta. I
didn't know what it was a suburb of. Alan would probably know,
though I wasn't always sure that was one of the things I liked about
him. He wouldn't shove the fact that he knew it down my throat,
though, which was one of the things I did like about him.

To my untrained eye, Ochlockonee appeared to be a smaller town
than Meigs, if that was possible. Poorer, too. But the Wolf sisters'
home wasn't particularly modest, at least not inside.

From the street the house appeared to be similar to the few others
that were close by—a lot of weathered wood yearning for more paint
than most people had the inclination to apply—but inside it was an
ethnic showplace for artifacts that I quickly deduced the twins had
collected on frequent travels abroad. I guessed that Africa, Central
America, the South Pacific, and Mexico were among their favorite
places for holidays. The bookcase closest to me contained cookbooks
from cuisines I couldn't identify, and on a lower shelf were tattered
guidebooks alongside titles from Naipaul, Forster, Theroux, and
Darwin. This was the home of world-wise women.

CNN was on somewhere in the house, but I couldn't exactly tell
where the TV was located.

It was about the time a glass of wine arrived in my hand that I
came to the conclusion that Mary Ellen Wolf was the pediatrician in the
Acorns. Her sister, Mary Pat Wolf, was the social worker in the Reeboks.
I said a silent prayer that they didn't change footwear during my visit.

The wine was offered by Mary Ellen, who informed me that it
was from Chile and seemed to be waiting for me to be surprised. I
couldn't have distinguished a Chilean wine from a French wine and
could barely tell either from Manischewitz, but living in Boulder, I
was way past being surprised by food I didn't understand. Half the
people in Boulder ate food I didn't understand.

Truth was, I probably ate food that half the people in Boulder
didn't understand. Or at least I used to, before the heart attack.

I said, "Really? Chile?"

She could tell I was just being polite, but she didn't call me on it. That, by itself, was different from Boulder.

Mary Pat led me from the comfy chair toward their dining room table and delivered a platter of toasted bread that was covered with chopped tomatoes, some dark, woody mushrooms I didn't think grew in my neighborhood, and some kind of fat white beans I'd never seen before, and she handed me a napkin. "That's bamboo," she said.

"The bread? Really?" I thought only panda bears ate bamboo. Or was that eucalyptus and koala bears? I couldn't remember.

I worried that the heart attack had made me stupid, or stupider. I worried a lot those days about what the heart attack had done. Or would do.

"No, silly, the platter."

Her reply made it sound as though my gaffe had been an intentional stab at humor. Her gesture was a small kindness but much appreciated at that moment. Sherry wouldn't have done it. Few people I knew in Boulder would have done it.

I asked, "Do you always have this kind of greeting ready and waiting for unexpected guests?"

They smiled identical smiles. I found it disconcerting.

"Reverend Prior phoned and said you would be by," Mary Ellen admitted. "He explained about your quest to assist Mrs. Storey. What can we help you with, Mr. Purdy? Please."

"I only have a few questions, really." That was my cue to take out my notepad and pen. I could take notes without my reading glasses, though I couldn't read what I'd written.

"Let's have them then." They were both sitting at the table with me, and I could no longer see their footwear, so I wasn't a hundred-percent sure which one of them actually said that. It was the twin on my right.

"It's about Saturday night and the accident at the river."

"Of course it is." That was the sister on the left. She handled my next few questions, too.

"You were traveling together?"

"Yes."

"What direction?"

"We were coming home from seeing a movie in Thomasville.

Denzel's new one? Have you seen it? I swear I'd pay to watch that man cut kudzu."

"I don't get to the movies much," I said. "Videos sometimes. But I agree Denzel is something special."

"Well, we both work in Thomasville. Ochlockonee doesn't have much commerce."

I didn't know what to say in reply that might not be interpreted as inadvertently insulting to Ochlockonee, so I returned my attention to the Storeys and asked, "Were you the first to stop at the bridge?"

"Well, poor Mrs. Turnbull stopped first, if you wish to split hairs. And I have a feeling you are the type who wishes to split hairs, Mr. Purdy. Though she didn't exactly stop the way she might have wanted to stop."

The other twin spoke. "We saw her car leave the road. Her headlights went, swoosh, right down the side."

"Of course, we stopped," said her sister.

"Of course. And Mr. Storey was right behind us."

"Right behind us. He'd been following too closely, if you know what I mean. Especially in that kind of storm, on wet roads. With that visibility. His driving left a lot to be desired."

I wasn't there to give Sterling Storey a traffic ticket. I said, "But he stopped, too? Right behind you?"

The twin on my right stood and went to the kitchen to retrieve the wine bottle. I glanced down at her feet. She was Reeboks. I told myself *right = Reeboks, left = Acorns.* I repeated the mantra so that I had a prayer of committing it to memory. On my notepad, for insurance, I wrote "R-R, L-A" in large letters.

Mary Ellen, on my left wearing Acorns, answered, "Well, not exactly. He drove right on past us at first."

"He did?"

"That surprises you?"

"Yes, it does," I admitted. I don't think I could have lied to these two women if I'd wanted to. Fortunately, I didn't want to. "That's not in any of the police reports I read."

"He drove at least a hundred yards—"

"At least," Mary Pat agreed.

"—before he stopped, did a three-point turn, and came right back and parked beside us."

"What? As though he'd had second thoughts about driving by?"
I said.

"That's exactly what we thought. That he found some generosity
in his heart over that hundred yards. I'd like to think that's what happened."

"And then?"

Dr. Wolf—that was Mary Ellen in the Acorns—said, "I was already on my cell phone by then, calling nine-one-one, trying to get us
some help. We were terrified that the minivan was going to slide the
rest of the way into the river."

Mary Pat said, "I jumped out and ran to the riverbank. But I
couldn't see a thing, not a thing. The accident had caused Mrs.
Turnbull's headlights to go out, and it was totally black down that
bank. And after I'd taken two steps from the car, I felt like I'd fallen
into a swimming pool with all my clothes on. Drenched to the bone. I
actually had to throw away my shoes when I got home. They were
hopeless.

"Anyway, Mr. Storey appeared beside me on the bank. He said,
'Can you see it? Is that where it went down?' I said I thought so. And
that's when Mrs. Turnbull started screaming for help for her baby."

"And?" I said.

"We just stood there, for"—she turned to her sister—"what
would you say? A minute? A full minute?" Her sister nodded. "We
were just standing there, wondering what to do. It was dark and wet
and none of us had ropes, but we knew the fire department rescue
people wouldn't get there for too long a time. Finally Mr. Storey
leaned over to me, and he said he was going down."

"Those words? 'Going down'?"

She grinned at me. "I knew you were a splitting-hairs type of
man, Mr. Purdy. I knew it. I can't honestly say that he used those exact words. But something very close to 'I'm going down.' "

"And then?"

"He did. He started down the bank."

"Not over on the other side, by the tree, where the bushes are?"

"No, down the bank. That's when Reverend Prior drove up. He
moved his car so that it gave us some light."

It took me a minute to catch my notes up to the story. When I looked back up, I made sure that both sisters were looking at me before I continued.

"You saw Mr. Storey go into the river?"

Mary Pat said, "No. I saw him go into the dark. The river was just part of the dark."

Mary Ellen smiled approvingly at her sister's description. "Mary Pat puts it well, Mr. Purdy. We saw him go into the dark. Have you been out there? To that spot on the river?"

"Yes, I have."

"Then you know that from the spot where Mr. Storey slipped and fell, it's a straight shot into the water. And that night, the Ochlockonee was quite swollen. I mean it was as high—"

"It was way high, as the kids say," added Mary Pat, the social worker. "Where he fell on that bank, it was just like being on an amusement park mud-slide ride straight into the river."

"So you both believe that's what happened? That he lost his footing and slid into that river?"

They looked at each other and nodded. Simultaneously, they said, "We do."

"But you didn't actually see it happen?"

This time, when they looked at each other, they both shook their heads, but they said nothing.

Mary Ellen said, "You don't think he drowned? Is that what you're saying? He never went into the river?"

I said, "The odds are high that he slid right on down the bank into the river. Just like you both believe. But so far I can't find anyone who actually saw it occur. I'm thinking that maybe it didn't happen that way. His wife is certainly hoping that maybe it didn't happen that way."

"Then where is he? The rescue people were at the bridge about ten minutes after he disappeared down that slope. He never called out for help. We never heard him. The rescuers had lights and boats, and they looked everywhere for him. They searched downstream for miles with dogs. They even had scuba divers out the next morning after the storm passed." Mary Pat's tone was slightly conspiratorial.

"And no one found anything, right? Not a trace?"

"Nothing," Mary Ellen agreed.

I said, "It's been my experience that occasionally people have a reason to want to disappear."

Mary Ellen dropped her voice most of an octave. "Are you suggesting that Mr. Storey was one of those people who had a reason? Why on earth would a man like that want to disappear? An important job like he has, a wife who cares enough to send someone like you all this way."

"Just between you and me?" I said. They nodded vigorously. "Mr. Storey is wanted for questioning about a murder."

"Oh my," said Mary Pat.

"So you think . . . ?" asked her sister.

"He might have . . . ?" Mary Pat again.

"Well," I said, "you have to wonder."

You do. Sometimes you have to wonder.

FORTY

ALAN

Viv, our Hmong immigrant nanny, worked part time, squeezing care of our daughter and us into her crowded school schedule. She saved our parental asses on most normal days. On crisis days, and those days were crisis days, her presence in our home was an undeserved gift from the parenting gods.

It was Viv who answered the phone when I called home after Gibbs's appointment. Lauren was busy cleaning the master bathroom. I had to picture it in my mind: One hand was on her walking stick and one hand was in a vinyl glove, clutching a rag. She was scrubbing surfaces that an obsessive microbiologist would probably have already deemed surgically sterile. By the end of the day, I knew, the motor on the vacuum cleaner would need new bearings, our entire supply of cleaning fluids would be depleted, and virtually every square inch of our home would be a whole new category of clean.

I'd seen it before in the wake of previous exacerbations. I had a name for it. I called it *steroid clean*.

Steroids don't provide virgin energy; they aren't some gentle super-caffeine. No, steroids, especially megadose steroids, provide agitation with all the negative consequences of the word. Impatience? In spades. Irritability? God, yes. Steroids are pure rocket fuel. I knew from experience that Lauren's management of the extra horsepower that was coursing through her veins would be relatively adaptive for about twenty-four hours—thus the steroid clean house—but after that the agitation and the resulting sleeplessness would overwhelm her coping ability, and she would take on a few of the assorted characteristics of the Seven Dwarfs on amphetamines.

Grumpy on Speed would be the dominant Dwarf. He—or in this case, she—would be around virtually the whole time, only reluctantly sharing the stage with Sleepy on Speed and with Dopey on Speed. If Sneezy on Speed showed up, we were all in a fresh mess of trouble; during a previous steroid treatment his arrival had caused my poor wife to sneeze something like thirty-seven times in a row with hardly time for an inhale in between. Emily, our Bouvier, hated human sneezing and had barked in concert with Lauren's honking for the last dozen sneezes or so. It was a memorable duet.

Sadly, Happy on Speed would make only the briefest of cameo appearances. If history were a guide, the cameo would take place during a narrow window in the first act.

I felt a stab of self-pity. For the next couple of weeks I'd be married to a most distasteful subset of the Seven Dwarfs on methamphetamine. Fortunately, my corrosive self-pity was swiftly dissolved by the solvent of compassion: Lauren not only had to live with the meth Dwarfs for a fortnight; she had the misfortune to be possessed by them.

She broke from scrubbing the beleaguered bathroom germs long enough to tell me what time she was seeing her neurologist later in the day, then gave the phone back to Viv, who informed me that Grace's cold was almost all better and that she'd even managed to add enough filament tape to Emily's paw to keep the clacking sound from driving Lauren even closer to distraction.

Viv also told me not to worry; she would take good care of us.

I told her she was great. And I started plotting ways to thank her.

Since I'd seen Gibbs so early that morning, Sharon Lewis was my second appointment of the week, not my first. The continued media attention that her breach of security at Denver's airport was generating still haunted her. As did the fear of imminent arrest.

"Am I really the most selfish person in America?" she demanded.

Needless to say, I didn't cast my vote on the question.

Obsessing was one of Sharon's things, so she obsessed. Should she turn herself in? Should she get a lawyer? Was what she did so wrong? Really? Wouldn't other people have done the same thing? Wouldn't they?

Would I?

I didn't answer that one, either.

Once the legal part of the crisis was resolved whatever way it was going to be resolved, Sharon had a long stint in therapy ahead of her. I was responding to her in the short term so that I would be prepared for what the future would inevitably bring.

Jim Zebid was late for his rescheduled appointment. He didn't arrive until half our allotted time had vaporized into the therapeutic ether.

"Damn prosecutors" was how he started. "I swear they argue things just to waste my time."

I tried not to allow my face to reveal anything back to Jim. My wife was one of those "damn prosecutors." I knew it and he knew it.

After that prelude he dove right into the topic of the day. "I need to tell you that it's hard for me to believe that you weren't indiscreet with that little tidbit I told you last week. My guy's firm that he didn't tell anybody about selling blow to the judge's hubby. I tend to believe him; he has no reason to be shooting his mouth off. I certainly didn't tell anybody other than you. So that leaves you."

The pointed implication was that I did have a good reason to be shooting my mouth off: to gossip with my wife. "Are you asking me something, Jim? Or is that just a flat-out accusation?"

He shrugged.

I registered some surprise at the fact that he didn't seem particularly angry. Although his words were sharp, his tone was the same one he might have used to order take-out Chinese.

What did I do? I took the bait.

"I will repeat my earlier assurance. I told no one—no one—about our conversation last week. And I will repeat my earlier suspicion, Jim, that your accusation about the incident has to do with something between us—something in the therapeutic relationship."

"Like what might that be?" These words were delivered in a tone that was totally dismissive. Litigators, in my experience, are more skilled at being dismissive than most people on the planet. They are able to imbue layers of nuance into their dismissiveness that most of us can only dream of. A law school trick of some kind, I suspected.

"Trust, maybe?" I tried to keep sardonic echoes from my own voice, but I wasn't totally successful.

"Trust?" He slumped back and crossed his ankles. His wingtips were the size of river kayaks.

I waited.

"Yeah, well. Like my client trusts me right now? That kind of trust? Sure, sure, we can talk about trust, Alan—after I somehow end up convinced that you're not just covering your ass. How's that?"

The remainder of my Monday was more or less routine from a patient point of view.

Midafternoon I reached Lauren again. Her neurologist was hopeful that the steroids would arrest the exacerbation and felt confident that her good history of recovering from previous flare-ups boded well for her this time, too. To boost prophylaxis even more he started her on a statin, something she'd been discussing with him for a while, and he gave her some Ambien samples to help her try to get some sleep until the Solumedrol loosened its grip on her psyche.

She said, "I hope it works."

"The Ambien?"

"Everything. The steroids, the statin, everything."

"You scared, babe?"

"Yes. I'm afraid you're getting tired of this."

"Don't worry about that. Worry about getting better."

"Sam wasn't worried."

"I'm not Sherry, Lauren."

"You must have second thoughts about marrying me. Everybody has limits," she said.

I felt my pulse jump. I wanted to bark, *"Of course I have limits. Of course I hate this. Of course I feel sorry for myself."*

I didn't.

"Be honest," she pleaded.

¡Dios mío. Hay un hacha en mi cabeza!

Lauren didn't want my honesty. She wanted my reassurance. In all my years in clinical practice treating couples, I'd seen honesty wielded much more often as a *hacha* than as a caress. There was a time in the eighties when the relationship mantra from the women's magazine gurus was *"All honesty, all the time."* What a disastrous few years of misguided advice that was. Since then, whenever I heard a romantic partner whine for unabashed honesty in my office, I tested the waters for one of two things. First I listened for the call of insecurity begging for reassurance. Alternately, I listened for the diseased call of someone begging to be hurt or begging for the license to inflict pain.

With her earnest "be honest" I decided that Lauren was seeking the former and not the latter, and I prayed that I was right.

I wished I could touch her or kiss her nose. I couldn't. So I said, "I'm not even close to my limit." I didn't say *"I'm full of doubt,"* or *"I wish I were as good and generous a person as I'd like to be."* I didn't say *"I don't know my limit, but I think it's within range of my vision."* I didn't.

No, I reassured her. Why? Because the reassurance was at least as true as my doubts and a whole lot truer than my fears.

She made a noise in response. Disappointment? Dismissal? Relief? I wished I knew.

The cream of reassurance that I was whipping was already in stiff peaks. I added more sugar until it tasted just right. "I'm not going anywhere, sweetie. I love you."

It was all true. A little less than totally honest, but all true. Imperfect honesty in an imperfect world. Nobody, least of all Lauren, would have to spend the day removing any *hachas* from their *cabezas*.

But the telephone was a terrible instrument for gauging the effectiveness of comfort, and I feared that my words were barely palliative.

I was packing up to go home when my pager vibrated on my hip. No message, but I recognized the number. I threw my briefcase and jacket back down on top of the desk and dialed deliberately, giving myself time to pull my thoughts together.

I wondered whether the state of Georgia was in the Central or Eastern Time zone. I guessed Eastern. It took me most of a minute to find a place where I could balance my current annoyance with my compassion and my friendship.

Sam answered. "Hey, Alan."

I said, "Hi, Sam. What's up?"

"I'm in Georgia."

"Yeah." I wanted to say I knew that already, but confidentiality rules. "What time is it there?"

"A little after eight. How pissed off are you?"

"Lauren's sick. I don't have enough energy to waste any of it being pissed off at you."

"What's going on with Lauren?"

I explained Lauren's predicament as though I were talking to a friend, and Sam said all the right things in return. I felt better. Then I asked, "What about you. You feeling okay?"

"This—this road trip—has been kind of good for me, I think. Takes my mind off things. No chest pains so far. I'm watching my diet. Taking all my damn pills."

"Exercise?"

"I walk when I can."

"It's important, Sam."

"Yeah."

The "yeah" was his way of indicating to me that it was time to move on.

"Nothing from Sherry?"

"Nothing. Simon's okay, though; I talked to Angus."

He paused long enough for me to respond. When I didn't, he said, "She loves me. I love her."

"You still worried that it's not enough?"

"Things are complicated, you know? Life, marriage, relationships— it's all complicated. Listen, I thought you might want to know that I think he might be alive. Sterling."

"What? Really?"

"The whole accident/rescue thing is too goofy for words. Nothing came down in a way that gives me any confidence in a scenario of him rushing to help someone and accidentally ending up drowning in a raging river."

"Like?"

"I'll tell you later when I have more time. A for-instance, though— on one side of the car he was trying to reach was all this brush and trees and crap—you know, stuff to hold on to—on the other side was a muddy riverbank, real steep. Which one do you think he chose?"

"The mud."

"Yeah. Like I said, goofy. I think if your IQ is anywhere near your golf score, you choose the side with the bushes on it. I keep trying to come up with excuses for him, but I'm failing."

"You think he planned it so he went into the river, or maybe just found himself swimming and took advantage of serendipity?"

"Good question, Alan. I'm impressed. Turns out that he hesitated at the top long enough to think it all through. Actually drove past the accident scene once and then came back. So yeah, I'm thinking pre-meditation. I got Lucy checking to see what kind of swimmer he was."

"I bet she finds out he was pretty good." I was thinking that any-body who crewed on a big expensive yacht and gave diving demos had to be more than a little comfortable in the water.

"What do you mean?" Sam asked.

I realized how close I'd come to an unwitting disclosure. "Nothing. I just think Lucy might find something."

"You could save her some work."

"Maybe, but I won't."

He let it go. "In case you're wondering, I'm planning on keeping my suspicions to myself until I have a little more evidence."

He was telling me he wasn't going to tell Gibbs he thought Sterling was alive. "Does that mean you're coming back home now?"

"No, I'm not done looking."

I allowed the buzz on the line to dominate for a few seconds before I asked, "Why, Sam? Why are you doing this?"

"This'll sound goofy, but I figure Sterling can teach me something
about marriage. Sterling and Gibbs both, actually."

"What?" My "what?" was undiluted incredulity.

"Yeah."

He was serious. I could tell. "That's the craziest thing I think I've
ever heard. And considering what I do for a living, that's wild indeed."

"Maybe it is crazy," he said. "But it feels okay to me."

"Sam, what if you're right about Sterling? What if he's not dead?
What if he comes after her?"

"Gibbs?"

"Yeah."

"I didn't think about that." He was silent for a moment. "No, I
don't think he will."

"I do."

"Why?"

"He has reasons," I said.

"Things I don't know?" Sam asked.

"I don't know what you know."

"You know exactly what I don't know. Just tell me, there are reasons?"

"Yes, for sure there are reasons," I said. I counted the dead
women on the fingers of my right hand. *At least four reasons,* I said to
myself.

"Then I'll call her and tell her that I'm not convinced he's dead.
And she should be careful. Can you get her someplace safe to stay?"

"Let's say that offer is on the table."

Again he grew quiet for a few seconds before he said, "I hate
situations like this. I hate 'em. The exact same woman who wouldn't
let her kid walk out the front door to ride a bike without a damn bicycle helmet won't take the simplest step—the simplest step—to keep
her own head from getting bashed in by some guy she's sure loves her.
I hate those situations."

"Yeah. Thanks." I didn't know what else to say. Silently and involuntarily my brain was busy translating "to keep her own head from

getting bashed in" to a pidgin Spanish version containing *cabezas* and
hachas. Silently but totally voluntarily, I cursed Diane.

"By the way," Sam added, "I forgot to tell you: The tip the police
got on that judge's husband? About the cocaine? It came from inside
the DA's office. That's all I could find out. Hope it helps."

Helps? No, not exactly. All that meant to me was that Jim Zebid, if he
learned the same facts that Sam had just disclosed to me—which he
most likely would—would have more reason than he already did to
believe that it was indeed I who had leaked the information about
Jara Heller's husband's cocaine problems to Lauren, who had in turn
acted on it through some colleague in the DA's office.

Great.

My second attempt to get out of the office ended almost the exact
same way the first had ended: My vibrating pager interfered just before I made it to the door. Once again I dumped my things on the
desk. Once again I recognized the phone number on the pager screen.

Gibbs was breathless. She answered before I was certain her
phone had even rung. "She just left. Just now! Two minutes ago! How
could you? How *could* you? I trusted you!"

"Gibbs," I pleaded. "Slow down, slow down. I don't know what
you're talking about."

"She just left. I can't believe you told her!"

"Who is 'she,' Gibbs?"

"Reynoso. That—that—"

"What is it you think I told her? I haven't spoken with her since
Saturday. I didn't even know she was still in town." My defensiveness
was too reflexive; I was getting frustrated about the repeated accusations from my patients about my indiscretions with their secrets. And
it was showing.

Half a beat passed. Hesitation? A pause to reload? I wasn't sure.
But Gibbs's fury was turned down a notch when she resumed. "You're
saying you didn't tell her about the other women? You didn't tell her
what I told you this morning?"

It was apparent from her voice that she wasn't particularly pre-
disposed to believing that I hadn't spilled the beans.

I, too, hesitated. The "other women" could have been the ones that Gibbs told me Sterling had slept with during their marriage, or they could have been the ones she told me he had killed. But a quick review convinced me that I hadn't told Carmen Reynoso about either group of other women. I replayed the events in my head thoroughly enough to convince myself that I hadn't even known about either group before that morning's session with Gibbs.

Then I remembered that wasn't exactly true. I had known about Gibbs's concern about other murder victims for most of a week; I just hadn't known details until that morning. But the reality was that I hadn't revealed the facts of Gibbs's concern to anyone. I was certain of it.

I said, "No, not a word."

"You didn't talk with her today?"

"No, Gibbs. I've been here at the office since this morning's appointment with you. I haven't shared the information you told me this morning with anyone. I wish you would give me permission, but until you do, I won't share that information with anyone."

"Well, I've never told anyone but you about these other women. How does she know?"

Damn good question.

Damn good.

Gibbs said good-bye after she asked me to change her regular appointment time on Tuesday. I offered her a slot that had just opened up on Wednesday.

I left my things on the desk and wandered around my office.

It wasn't a small room, nor was it palatial. Fifteen by twenty-two feet, maybe. Space enough for a chunky desk, a file cabinet, a seating area, and a couple of bookcases. Three windows and a solitary French door brought in abundant light. Double doors—not side by side, but back to back—one opening in, one opening out, provided security and soundproofing to the interior hallway that Diane and I shared. We'd spent a bundle during remodeling constructing the interior walls of offset studs and had even set the extra-sound-retardant Sheetrock in channels, all in an effort to reduce noise transmission from the office to the hallway and from office to office. The entire back hallway was separated from the waiting area by a door with a deadbolt lock. After an intrusion years before, Diane's husband had installed a sophisticated alarm system in the building, too.

I assured myself that there was no way someone could eavesdrop on a psychotherapy session in my office.

What about someone in Diane's office? Could they have eavesdropped? No, that wasn't possible. During the course of an average day the only sound I heard through our acoustically deadened adjoining wall was an occasional burst of Diane's sharp laughter. I couldn't recall a single instance of overhearing one of her patient's words. The tones of normal conversation just didn't make it through the walls.

I plopped down on the sofa and reviewed my day.

No matter from what angle I examined it, I couldn't remember a solitary indiscretion on my part regarding Gibbs's admissions to me about the other women. I hadn't written any of the data in my case notes. And I hadn't spoken a word about it to anyone.

Not even Sam? No, not even Sam.

Which meant one thing: The cops were developing the same information on their own.

What other conclusion was possible?

The answer to that question would come, unfortunately, soon enough.

FORTY-ONE

SAM

Before I left their home, the Wolf sisters invited me to come back in a few days for Thanksgiving supper. They explained that they usually deep-fried a turkey for the large group of family and friends that gathered in their home, but this year they were planning to slow-roast something they called a turducken for the first time, and thought that I would be a perfect addition to their holiday table.

"You deep-fry your turkey?" I said. When I'd first heard about people preparing their birds that way, I thought it was an urban myth, like jack-alopes. Then the Boulder Fire Department started answering calls for turkey-fryer fires, and I accepted that it was a real thing, though I still couldn't figure out what people did with all the leftover oil.

Mary Ellen said, "It's the best way to do it, absolutely. Moist? Oh, Mr. Purdy. But we're going to try something new and finally do a turducken this year. Mr. Prudhomme, Mr. Paul Prudhomme from New Orleans"—when she spoke the name of the Louisiana city, it was only one word, and it was absent the *w*, and when she spoke Mr. Prudhomme's name, it was with a reverence customarily reserved for heroes or saints—"recommends a very slow oven, so we'll actually have to start roasting that delight before we go to bed on Wednesday evening. The house should smell like the Lord's own grandmother's kitchen when we awaken Thursday morning."

Mary Pat was the one who recognized the ignorance in my eyes. "A turducken is a Cajun treat, Mr. Purdy. Oyster dressing and andouille sausage and a few other goodies are stuffed into a chicken that is then stuffed into a duck that is then stuffed into a turkey. More dressing is added between each bird during the assembly. It's all boneless. It's all delicious."

I tried to imagine the cascade of flavors that Mary Pat was describing, and I was momentarily lost in the fantasy. My hand crept up the contours of my tummy until my thumb found the lower edge of my sternum. Sculpted in place, my hand could have been a monument to my ambivalence: Part of my hand—the part caressing my gut—honored my usually indulgent appetite, part of it—the thumb on my sternum—honored my cardiologist's admonitions.

"And you roast this . . . thing for how long?" I asked. "It must weigh most of a ton."

"We are doing a large one. Fourteen hours should bring it close to perfection. Then it will need to rest a while to stitch the flavors together before we carry it to the table."

With a smile as warm as apple pie, Mary Pat said, "And you haven't had a real Thanksgiving supper until you've tasted my sister's gravy, or her cornbread."

Mary Ellen savored the compliment. "Red pepper," she explained. "Our mother's secret. Abundant red pepper."

"Can I let you know?" I asked them. "My plans for Thursday are still a little up in the air."

"No need to call. You just come by if you can. We'll have a place all set at the adult table for you, and you can be certain that the good Lord willing there will be no shortage of food beneath this roof on the day we give thanks. Mary Ellen will start carving right around two."

*   *   *

Less than a mile from the twins' home I stopped on the shoulder of a fallow field of what I was still guessing had been cotton and called Alan Gregory to catch him up on what I was up to in Georgia, and then I called Gibbs Storey to tell her that I thought it was premature to assume her husband was dead.

"He's alive?" she replied, of course. What else would she say?

I'd told her I thought that was a premature conclusion, too. But I suggested prudence might be warranted, and counseled her to temporarily move someplace where her husband couldn't easily find her.

"Sterling won't hurt me," she said.

"If I had a dollar for every time a woman's told me that in the past twenty years, I'd be driving a Lincoln."

She sighed at me and told me she'd think about it.

"Trust me, Gibbs. You're not thinking straight. After what you've been through . . ."

"I'm fine."

It's what I expected. I'd done what I could do. I folded up my phone and started driving again.

An hour later I was on the outskirts of Albany, Georgia, trying to decide between two adjacent motels for a place to spend the night when Lucy paged me using our personal code that indicated an emergency. At full arm's length I could barely read the code: 911 followed by the phone number. Imaginative, no. But it worked for us.

I picked the motel that wasn't a national chain and finished checking in before I used my cell to return Lucy's call. The motel room was full of my grandmother's oldest chenille, the air was musty, and the background smells in the shadowy room were born of burnt tobacco and constant humidity and were as unfamiliar to me as the accents of all the people I was meeting in Georgia.

Lucy had left me her own cell number, not her office number. I figured that was important.

"Hey," I said. "It's me."

"Hi, Sammy. I really miss you. You okay?"

"Later, what's up?" She didn't 911 me to ask me how I was doing.

"Listen, you're not going to believe this, but Crime Stoppers— yeah, I'm serious: Crime Stoppers—got a tip, anonymous, of course, that Sterling Storey may be responsible for as many as four murders. All women, all in towns where he's worked over the years. He travels around producing sporting events on cable."

"I know about his job. Does the story check out?"

"At least one piece of it seems to. There's a woman in Indianapolis who went missing in the same circumstances that the tipster reported. She's the same general description as Louise Lake—single, attractive, late twenties—and she worked where the guy said she worked. Donald and I have just started putting it together. There are other teams tracking down all the other women, but I haven't heard anything about their progress."

"You have a name?"

"Julie Franconia. She worked in PR or marketing or something for the Indiana Dome or—"

"It's the RCA Dome now, I think. The Colts play there. Peyton Manning. Good kid."

"Whatever. She disappeared in 2000. Late March, I think. Just a sec . . . yeah, March twenty-third, 2000."

"Remains?"

"We just got on this."

"Circumstances?"

"She told her co-workers she was going to meet some girlfriends for a drink after work. Disappeared."

"No body?"

"That's what we're trying to confirm. It was dumped on us as a typical without-a-trace, but a local cop told me he doesn't know what all the fuss is about, that they have it as a cleared homicide. We're waiting to hear back from the homicide guy. You know what it's like with the holidays coming."

"Is the press on this?"

"Nobody's called me personally, but I think yes, probably."

"Four? You said four?"

"Four total, including the California murder."

"Where are the other two?"

"Augusta, Georgia, and West Point, New York."

"That would be, what, the Masters and . . . I don't know, the Army–Navy game?"

"I guess," Lucy said. Other than occasional Broncos football, she didn't pay much attention to sports she didn't participate in, and she didn't apologize for it.

I asked, "Any progress on the river search down here? Did Storey's body show up today? Tell me yes. If you tell me yes, maybe I'll come home."

"I wish I could tell you yes, Sam. They're still looking, but nobody seems hopeful about finding the body. The search is winding down. Oh, and in case it matters, you were right about Storey. He is, or was, a swimmer—a star on his college water polo team."

"Water polo? Didn't play that a lot when I was growing up in Minnesota."

Lucy knew me well enough not to respond to my sarcasm. She asked, "You're not in touch with the local authorities down there?"

"I made a courtesy call when I first got here. They're looking for a body. I'm looking for something else."

"You think he's alive?"

"I'm not ready to think out loud. I assume someone interviewed Sterling's friend Brian Miles."

"Georgia State Police talked to him. Miles said Sterling called from Tallahassee and said he was coming to visit but never showed up. The story checks out." Through the phone I heard an overhead page in the background.

"Where are you right now, Luce?"

"Whole Foods, getting something for dinner. Why?"

"You going back to the department?"

"I'll be eating at my desk. For now, this case is all computer and phone work."

"I'll keep my pager on. Enjoy your dinner."

"You okay, Sam?"

"I'm meeting some nice people down here. Luce? Send some patrols past Gibbs Storey's house. Can you do that?"

"Sure. You do think he's alive?"

"I forgot, one more thing. Is Reynoso still in Boulder, or did she go back to California?"

"Her? None of the above. I heard she was leaving for Georgia to look for Sterling. You haven't run across her yet?"

"I think I'd recall that."

She laughed. "I imagine she'll be trying to find you."

"We'll see how good a detective she is. Thanks, Luce. Talk to you."

I leaned back against the headboard of the motel bed. My mass caused it to crack hard against the wall, and I imagined what a percussive racket an energetic couple could make on this bed. The thought froze me for a moment, as I wondered when the last time was that Sherry and I had rocked a bed. I mean really rocked it.

I couldn't recall.

Lucy had said that there were suspected victims of Sterling Storey in Augusta and Indianapolis.

Augusta was closer, but I'd be flying blind if I went there. Indianapolis was farther, but at least Lucy would have facts to feed me. What did I hope to find?

I didn't know. Maybe when I tripped over it, I'd know.

The guy at the desk didn't use a wheelchair as much as he wore one. It was hard to imagine him without the aged, rusting contraption that was pressing hard against his fleshy hips as he rolled back and forth behind the motel's counter. A tiny color TV—maybe three inches across—hung upside down on a braided nylon rope around his neck. He was watching a game show, occasionally tipping the little television toward the ceiling and staring down in the general direction of his navel.

Wheel of Fortune? I wasn't sure.

I tipped him ten bucks when he let me check out without paying for the few minutes I'd actually used the room.

"The way I see it, you're not checking out. What you're doing is unchecking in" was how he put it. "Where you off to in such a hurry?"

"Indianapolis, I think. Got a call, so I gotta go."

"Never been there."

"Me, neither," I said. I turned to leave but had a thought, so I stopped and asked him, "You ever had a turducken?"

"Sure, sure." He smiled so fast, his cheeks shook and his triple chin momentarily became one. "I have, I sure have. Three years ago. Thanksgiving supper. My aunt Totsy's—she's my daddy's little sister— her place on the Delta. It's a meal not to be missed, not to be missed."

"This trip I have to take up north means I'm going to lose what may be my one and only chance to savor a turducken. And I'm beginning to think that's a minor tragedy. Well, I do hope you have a good Thanksgiving, sir," I said.

"I'll be right here," he said, as a way of letting me know he didn't expect to enjoy his holiday much or get anywhere close either to a turducken or to a family gathering at his aunt Totsy's on the Mississippi Delta. When he said "here," he didn't point at the office he was in or at his wheelchair.

What he did was, he touched his TV-on-a-rope.

A minute or two communing with Rand McNally left me with the impression that I could get to Indianapolis in ten to twelve hours of hard road time. I planned to drive for six, sleep for six, drive for six more, and then find someplace for lunch close to the RCA Dome.

By then Lucy should know something new.

And I might have a clue what I was doing.

FORTY-TWO

ALAN

Tuesday morning found Lauren solidly in hyper-energized zombie mode—think the Energizer Bunny meets *Night of the Living Dead.*

Her affected leg was no worse, maybe a little better. Less weakness. That was the good news.

But there wasn't enough good news. Worry about Lauren and the future—hers, Grace's, ours—stabbed at me incessantly, but she and I didn't talk about it during the duration of the extended steroid fog. Neither of us once mentioned the bull elephant that had pitched a tent in our living room.

We'd made it through the night—me with little sleep, her with less than that—and thanks to Viv's early-morning assistance with Grace, I managed to get to the office in time for my first appointment.

Tuesday's workday was remarkable only for its normalcy. I spent an entire day at work feeling almost effective. Going home that evening, I faced the more daunting task of trying to be an effective husband and father in a home that was quaking from the aftershocks of illness and treatment.

Together—Grace and Lauren and I, with a full assist from Viv and the puppies—we made it. Wednesday morning came. The respite of a four-day holiday weekend was only one workday away.

How hard could that be?

The local media had begun feasting on the Storeys' troubles. The morning TV news shows and the Boulder and Denver papers had pieced together most of the details of Gibbs's and Sterling's ties to Louise Lake. Now they were busy fleshing out the more lurid parts of the tale, including the details of the fruitless search of the Ochlockonee River and the revelation that authorities suspected that Sterling Storey might be involved in the deaths of three other women.

I anticipated that Gibbs would be overwhelmed by the public revelations. Reactive hibernation wasn't out of the question, and I wasn't a hundred percent sure she would show up for her early-morning appointment.

But she did.

"Not Safe House. I don't want to go there, I just don't think I'd fit in."

That was actually Gibbs's opening gambit, her first words after a perfunctory "good morning."

Had I expected it? No, not really. Was I surprised? No, not at all. The insidious nature of battering caused the pendulum of hope to swing from reality to denial and back again. This was Gibbs's denial talking. The way she introduced it told me that she had been busy having a conversation with me in her head and had just then decided to allow me to mouth my own lines. I was more than content to let her go on without me for a while, if she would.

"They followed me here. I'm sure they did. They were waiting outside this morning when I opened the garage."

"They?"

"Those newspeople."

I nodded. I could have encouraged her to go off on a rant about those newspeople, but I chose to look down the other path she'd offered. "You don't think you would fit in at Safe House, Gibbs?"

"I'm not a battered woman."

Arguing the point was a tempting option, but I made a quick judgment that it was neither the right issue nor the right time. Gibbs, I suspected, was protesting a different kind of "fitting in." And the truth was that her rationalization wasn't the real issue; her denial was.

Gently, I tried to draw her back. "But you are in need of a safe place to stay—you accept that?"

"I'm trying to be . . . cautious. Detective Purdy suggested it. Just in case there's a chance that"—she took a moment to decide how she wanted to complete her thought—"that I might be in some danger. He said he talked to you, too. Right?"

I nodded. I reminded myself that it had been I who had invited Sam into this conundrum; I shouldn't be too surprised that he was complicating it. At least his advice to Gibbs was sound.

"And now, with all the cameras, I can't stay at home anyway. I can't. I'm not even going to go back. I have some things in the car, and I have to find someplace else to stay."

"What are you considering?"

"I was hoping you would have an alternative . . . for me." She lifted her eyebrows. "Someplace besides Safe House."

Were there other options? Of course. Many women in vulnerable circumstances turned to friends or family for shelter. I usually didn't think that it was a good idea. "I think Safe House is where you belong. They know what they're doing. It's not just the shelter that they offer. It's the support, the counseling, and their experience. Everything. They work well with the police. They're the pros. When the stakes are this high, I think you go with the best."

Watching her face as I made my speech, I realized that it was as though I hadn't been speaking at all. She waited until the aggravating noise of my voice subsided before she said, "I'm actually thinking about going to a hotel. I'd be more comfortable there, I think. You know, more privacy?"

Not to mention a private bath, maid service, nice linens, room service, and maybe a chocolate on her pillow.

I stated the obvious: "Isn't that the first place Sterling would look for you?"

"He's dead, Dr. Gregory. Dead."

I softened my tone a little. "Is that what you believe, Gibbs?"

"No, not really," she said without any contemplation. "But it would be so much easier, wouldn't it? For everybody?"

I didn't respond. It wasn't a tactical silence. I just didn't know what to say. She leaned over and touched the handle on her purse. For a moment I thought she was going to grab it, stand up, and go. She didn't.

She settled back, crossed her legs, and said, "He went back to kill them, you know."

No, I didn't know. "I don't think I understand."

"Sterling met them one year. Had his little flings with them. And he went back to see them again the next time."

"The next time?"

"The next time he was covering the event, whatever it was. The golf tournament, or game, or race, or whatever it was. A lot of this stuff he produces is annual, you know? He goes back to some of the same places, and he does basically the same thing every year."

"And . . . he continued his affairs? He saw the same women each year in each city?"

To me, it sounded exhausting.

"If he . . . liked them. If their first encounter was . . . you know. Then, yes, he saw the same women again."

I tried to gauge her discomfort at our discussion of Sterling's serial infidelity. I thought it was high. Or maybe I just thought it should be high.

"And then he killed them?" I asked. I knew the beginning of the story, and a lot of the middle, and the very end, but it felt as though somebody had ripped out a chunk of pages just before the conclusion.

"Not usually. Just sometimes."

Great, I thought, allowing myself the luxury of some irony. *Maybe he can be rehabilitated.*

"Go on, please, Gibbs. Was there a method to his . . . a way to understand the motivation he used to . . . I mean, how did he, um—"

"Decide? Some of them wanted more from him. That wasn't the arrangement. That's why I think he . . ."

Killed them.

"They were the ones who wouldn't let go, who insisted. That's what put them at risk."

The arrangement?

Was Gibbs implying that the women were responsible for their own murders by violating some agreement they had with Sterling? Reaching such a conclusion would not have been that atypical for a battered woman.

Damn, I said to myself. Gibbs had once again distracted me. I'd been confronting her about her decision to stay in a hotel, not Safe House, and she'd managed to change the subject to murder. A compelling change, I had to admit: This misdirection was not the work of an amateur.

I prepared to point out the process when her face displayed sudden alarm. "You're not going to tell anyone what I just told you, right? Not the police? If anybody learns this, Dr. Gregory, they will have learned it from you. No one else knows about it. I couldn't bear it if any of this got out. I couldn't."

I'd been expecting Gibbs to revisit her distrust of the reliability of my silence from the moment she'd walked in the door, but the timing surprised me, and an undertow of accusation sucked at me. I said, "I haven't broken your trust, Gibbs. And I won't."

"Good." She smiled at me. "No matter where we go—you and I—we end up talking about sex, don't we?"

Were we just talking about sex? Or had I just been witness to yet another one of the greatest illusions since Penn and Teller?

"Sex. It's not just for procreation anymore."

In the ensuing minutes, in case I required it, I received a refresher course in the resilience of denial and the elasticity of resistance. Gibbs and I covered no new ground. The topic of Sterling's affairs? It was of no apparent interest to her. "Old news," she declared. "I prefer to look forward."

Sterling's being alive, or dead? "I think Detective Purdy is right. He's alive. I would know if he were dead. I would. That changes things. It does. I have decisions to make. Different ones."

The danger she was in? "He wouldn't hurt me. He did it once and he apologized. He won't do it again. I just need to get away from all the media."

I prodded her resistance directly. I went after the soft flanks of her denial. Nothing seemed to work.

Sometimes that was the nature of psychotherapy.

After Gibbs left her session—her exit was marked by a promise to call me once she was settled into a hotel—I ran into Diane in the hallway as we were both on the way to the bathroom. She was wearing jeans and a sweater: not office garb.

"I just came in to get my appointment book," she explained. "I have jury duty. Have to be at the courthouse in ten minutes. God, I hope I get sequestered. It would be so great to get sequestered."

"No lawyer in this town is going to let you sit on a jury."

"Why not?"

With the frequency with which Diane testified on custody and child abuse issues, she knew the county's judges and clerks, and the law, better than half the members of the bar. Every attorney wanted to believe that at the conclusion of a trial what ruled in the jury room were the echoes of the lawyer's own words of wisdom. But any lawyer who had ever crossed paths with Diane Estevez knew that she wouldn't think of allowing that to occur. Were she seated on a jury, what would rule in the jury room was what Diane wanted to rule in the jury room—which meant that the odds of Diane being chosen as a juror in Boulder County were about the same as Al Gore spending Christmas on a ranch in Crawford, Texas.

She tilted her head back toward my office, sniffed the air, and said, "Do I smell the Dancing Queen?"

I flared my nostrils and tested the air but didn't detect anything. Was I immune to my client's perfume? As a way of changing the subject, I asked, "You can't hear anything in your office, can you? When I'm in my office doing therapy, you don't overhear my sessions?"

"With your voice? You speak so quietly, I'm surprised sometimes that your own patients can hear you. Why, did I miss something good?"

"Nothing? You can't hear a thing?"

"No. Why? Can you hear me?"

"I hear you laugh."

She laughed. "Why are you asking?"

"I've had a few accusations from patients in the last few days that I'm divulging information that I heard during therapy. They're . . . concerning; they're accusations about serious things."

"Accusations? Not just worries?"

"Accusations."

"Oh, the Dancing Queen? Are you the anonymous tipster? You're the one who called Crime Stoppers on Platinum?"

"Diane."

She had really perked up. "Well, are you?"

"No. Of course not."

"Nothing inadvertent?"

"No."

She squeezed past me and slipped into the bathroom. As she shut the door, she said, "Maybe your office is bugged."

I said, "Ha. Very funny."

But I'd barely shifted my weight from one foot to the other before I thought: *Sam.*

Rhymes with *damn.*

FORTY-THREE

It was surprisingly easy to find someone to sweep
my office for bugs. I called a couple of lawyers I
knew through Lauren, who put me in touch with
the private investigators they used, and the two
investigators both pointed me toward the same
company: West Security.

The electronic security specialist I talked to at
West was a woman named Tayisha Rosenthal.
She explained that I had my choice between a
cursory sweep of my office for about half of my
practice's daily earnings, and a thorough sweep,
which would cost me twice what my practice
typically generated in a day. If I chose the thorough examination, she would give me a 99.99
percent assurance that my office was not being
monitored by listening devices.

I said I would take the deluxe package.

She asked when.

"As soon as possible."

"Can you do noon?" she said. "I can squeeze
you in at noon."

I looked at my calendar. It would mean canceling a patient, maybe two. I said yes and I gave her the address.

I'd made a bad error in judgment when I'd asked Gibbs for freedom to consult with Sam about her suspicions about Sterling. That was certain. And it was clear that Sam had gone too far when he'd approached Gibbs himself and decided to take off on some ill-thought-out quest in Georgia.

But bugging my office?

He'd gone too far.

Way too far.

I picked up my address book and began looking for the phone numbers of the two patients whose appointments would have to be rescheduled.

Like neighbors everywhere, Diane and I kept keys to each other's office. Highly doubtful that what might be said in my own office would ultimately remain confidential, I took advantage of Diane's tour in jury duty limbo and saw the rest of my morning's appointments in her hopefully uncorrupted space. When my patients asked me about the change, I explained that my office was being fumigated. It was as close to the truth as I was willing to get.

Right at twelve o'clock I paced out to my waiting room where I spied an unfamiliar woman reading a copy of *Sports Illustrated*. She was a young African American with close-cropped hair and soft features. When she looked up, I saw that her dark eyes were brilliant, like fire and onyx.

"Tayisha Rosenthal?" I said. "Alan Gregory."

I invited her back to my office. She grabbed a fat metal aluminum briefcase, and I allowed her to precede me down the hall. "It's not this whole place, right?"

"No, not unless you find something in my office. Then I suppose you'll have to search the whole building."

She tapped her watch. "Won't be today."

"I understand."

She stood in my office for a moment reconnoitering the place, then took long strides across the room to my desk, opened her case like a giant clamshell, and started fishing out equipment.

I waved her back into the hallway and pulled the door closed. "Let's talk out here. Just in case."

"You sticking around? You want to watch me work?" she asked.

"Why? Is that extra?" It was a lame attempt on my part to find humor in the experience.

She laughed. "Nah. I'll give you a running commentary of what I'm doing if you want."

"That would be great."

"Good. But the commentary is extra. Make it fifty, cash." She held out her hand. "Up front."

"Excuse me?"

She laughed again. "Kidding. You're a shrink, right? I thought you people were supposed to treat paranoids, not become one yourself. And here you are thinking that people are listening to your every word, just like some nutcase. Aren't you supposed to be the healthy one?"

"Yeah, that's the way it's supposed to be."

"There's some irony there, don't you think?"

"Yes," I admitted, "there is." I was eager to change the subject. "How does someone end up doing this—what you do—for a living? Sweeping buildings for bugs?"

"Army intelligence. I did this same kind of thing for Uncle Sam's Army of One for four years."

She looked too young to have completed four years in the army. Apparently, she could tell that's what I was thinking.

"I'm twenty-four," she said. "Old enough. Do the math."

She stepped back inside the office and went to work.

The equipment she'd pulled out of foam rubber compartments in her metal case seemed to have been cobbled together from the detritus of a few visits to Radio Shack. Microphones, earphones, and a little machine that looked like what I thought a modern Geiger counter would look like. Gauges with long, jumpy needles. Digital scoreboards. A few knobs and switches that required some fiddling.

After about ten minutes of poking around and setting and resetting her electronics, opening drawers, and moving my furniture around, she said, "Hot-cha!"

By then I'd settled into a place on the floor by the office door, leaning against the wall reading the same *Sports Illustrated* Tayisha had been perusing in the waiting room. Tiger Woods was apparently still winning golf tournaments.

Tayisha's exclamation startled me. I looked up at the mess she'd made of my office and said, "What?"

She pointed toward the hallway, but she didn't look my way; she was totally focused on one of her little digital gadgets.

We stepped out of the office.

"Yo, Doctor? You paying attention? Good. On these private gigs, like this—by private, I mean I'm not out doing one of my routine sweeps for corporate security purposes, just a one-time for somebody who thinks somebody's listening in on him—on these private gigs I meet some of the craziest human beings ever. Nutsos. People with tinfoil all over their apartments. Husbands sure their wives are listening to them over the radio in their cars. Those guys always have mistresses, by the way. They're always getting something on the side. It's the guilt that makes them whacked; that's what I think. But crazy? You bet. I do a couple, three of those a month. Most of the time I feel like I should keep a syringe of Thorazine in my briefcase, you know, just in case?" She smiled. "And—and—you want to know what? I've never found a device on one of those jobs. Not one."

"Good, I'm glad to hear that." Maybe Tayisha's track record of ubiquitous failure boded well for me. Right at that moment I would rather have been judged crazy than discover that I'd been right about the bug.

"Until today," she said.

"What?"

She pointed at the equipment she held in her left hand. "This says that there's a device in there sending out a signal. Mmm-hmmm. Something's generating a fairly healthy signal that's going out of that room. It appears to be voice activated."

"What?"

"Don't worry, now that I've detected it, I'll locate it in a minute or two. You be real quiet while I finish up, okay? I'm concentrating."

Although in my fantasies I was already raising Sam by his thumbs, via pulleys, to some very high ceiling, the truth was that I had thought that I was being overly paranoid, too. I really hadn't expected that Tayisha Rosenthal would discover any devices in my office.

Locating the bug took another five minutes. Ninety-nine-plus percent of the device was inside one of the throw pillows on the sofa where my patients often sat. The electronics were buried deep in the batting.

"That's the transmitter. I just turned it off." Zipping open the pillow, she pointed at a tiny box about the size of a pack of gum. "And this here"—she pulled the batting apart and revealed a braided wire—"is the antenna. Like little strands of hair.

"And this little baby—can you see that, right there?" She used the tip of a pencil as a pointer. "See how tiny that is? That's the microphone. Good stuff. Quality equipment."

The lead of the pencil was pointing directly at a small gray dot about the size of a lentil that extended out at the edge of the pillow, near the zipper. If you weren't looking for it, you would never notice it.

"Really, that's the microphone? What's the range? How far can . . . a device like this transmit?"

"We could test it if you want, but I'd say not too far. I would guess that whoever's listening has a car parked nearby with a good receiving antenna and a digital recorder for the output."

The "output" was my therapy sessions. I waved at the pillow. "Who has stuff like this?"

"Lots of people. You can buy listening devices over the Internet these days. Easy. Equipment this good is pricey, though. Somebody invested some serious money going after whatever it is you have to say in here. The battery in the transmitter alone costs some serious bucks."

"What do I do now?" I asked.

"How about what do I do now? What I do is I document this— what I found and where—and I take some good pictures of the equipment in place. You'll get a fair-size stack of glossies for your photo album. Here's your part: Then you authorize me to remove the device. After I do, I screen one more time to be absolutely positively certain that there isn't a second device. Don't worry, there isn't. I'm ninety-eight percent sure already. Then you call the police to report the intrusion. There've been some laws broken in this room. Mmmm-hmm."

"Yes," I agreed.

"Then you sit down and have a long, hard conversation with yourself about who might do this to you."

"And why," I added.

"Yeah. That, too." She glanced at her watch. "I'll be out of here in ten minutes max. But hey, we're going to have to find a time to do a sweep of the rest of the building now, too."

She watched me swallow. The act was involuntary.

Tayisha was reassuring. "I'll give you a good rate, don't worry. This has been fun."

I wasn't having such a good time.

After punching in Sam's pager number, I listened for the beep before I dialed 911 and my cell phone number. Then I sat on Diane's desk and waited for my phone to vibrate. I used the dead time to try to compute the number of secrets from the number of patients that might have been intercepted by the jumble of sophisticated electronics that was stuffed in my sofa pillow. I quickly realized that I was missing an essential variable: I didn't know how long the bug had been in place.

The earliest accusation I'd received from one of my patients was the one from my attorney client, Jim Zebid, the previous Sunday accusing me of leaking the story about Judge Heller's husband selling cocaine. He'd told me that story the previous Tuesday, so the bug had been in place for at least eight days. Maybe longer.

I was seeing thirty-six patients a week. Which meant thirty-six unique sets of secrets were at risk of having been revealed.

After cursing silently for half a minute, I took Tayisha Rosenthal's advice and began to have that long, hard conversation with myself about who might do this to me.

And why.

FORTY-FOUR

SAM

Nashville was one of those legendary American cities that I'd always wanted to visit, but when I finally got there at a quarter after one in the morning on a dark, misty night a couple of days before Thanksgiving, all I wanted to see was the lumpy synthetic pillow waiting for me on a Nashville motel room bed. I begged a Mountain Dew–distracted clerk for a five-thirty wake-up call and was in bed three minutes after I slid the plastic card into the lock on the door.

DO NOT DISTURB sign on the door. Strip, pee, meds, bed.

I slept like a dead man.

By the time five-thirty came, my car was chilly, Dixie dew coated the windshield, and pre-holiday Nashville was still as sleepy as I was. I walked a couple of blocks to a little convenience store to try to scrape together some breakfast. Satisfaction wasn't in the cards. I was learning that one of the places where post–heart attack patients can't conveniently dine is a convenience store. Breakfast choices at the gas station were limited to doughnuts—a pretty good variety, actually—or Danish, or a sad-looking egg-and-sausage thing on a croissant. I settled for a dry bagel, burnt decaf, yogurt, and a carton of orange juice and walked back to the motel with every intention of eating my ascetic meal, climbing into the Jeep, and pointing it vaguely north toward Indianapolis.

It didn't happen.

I woke up later on only because I had to pee. The light outside my room said dusk. I used the bathroom, took off my clothes, killed my cell phone and pager, and fell back into bed. "Tired" didn't come close to describing my fatigue. "Exhausted" wasn't enough of a superlative.

The next change in light that registered in my consciousness was the wink of dawn. After a long shower I felt quasi-alive. In a fashion that reminded me, sadly, of Bill Murray in *Groundhog Day,* I retraced my steps to the convenience store of the morning before, bought the same food, and returned to the motel with the same intentions.

Practice makes perfect. The second time I pulled it off. Before Nashville was awake, and certainly before I'd had a chance to taste any of her charms, I was on my way out of town in the Cherokee.

Later on I stopped for some real food at a roadside café near someplace called Orlinda and lingered there for a while considering whether I was driving to Indianapolis, Indiana, to be a detective or to Rochester, Minnesota, to be a father. I climbed back in my car unaware that I ever quite reached a decision.

After my late breakfast some truckers and I convoyed together up into Kentucky. I figured that the long-haul drivers were hurrying to get home to their families for Thanksgiving supper, so they were maintaining a speed that was far enough over the speed limit to make me reasonably content.

The countryside south of Louisville was as pretty as a calendar. The whole thing was much better than rehab for me and my injured heart. A day asleep, peaceful landscape, uncrowded roads, strange accents on funny radio stations, and problems that seemed a thousand miles away.

Or at least five hundred.

*   *   *

If you look at a road map of Indiana, Indianapolis looks like the spot where an award-winning sharpshooter left his first and only pop at an imaginary bull's-eye that had been pinned on top of the map. The state's largest city is almost perfectly centered north to south and east to west. As you approach Indiana from any direction, you feel a sublime confidence that you couldn't miss Indianapolis even if you fell sound asleep at the wheel. All roads may not actually lead to Rome, but in this part of the United States it sure seemed like they all led to Indianapolis.

The convoy of truckers and I were making good time as we cleared the northern boundary of Columbus. Out in front of us, Highway 65 was gleaming in the November sun like the Yellow Brick Road that was going to carry us nowhere but to Oz.

A while later my beeper vibrated on my hip, and I fumbled to find my Kmart reading glasses so I could read the little screen. I saw the 911 before the phone number and felt my heart rate jump. I reached down and shushed the volume on Faith Hill's lament, and signaled to pull the Jeep into a rest stop. Two of the truckers blasted a good-bye with their air horns, and I honked my reply. After I exited the highway, I settled into a parking place beside a big recreational vehicle full of gray-haired women. For some reason they made me think about Sherry, which caused a twang in my heart over Simon, and I let my mind wander in that neighborhood while I allowed myself a minute or two to decide whether to return the call.

I punched in the number.

Lucy said, "Is that you?"

"Yeah, what's up?"

"Where are you? Don't you ever answer your phone?"

"Just south of Indianapolis somewhere. A rest stop full of strangers."

"Don't bother going any farther, Sammy. Get back on 70 and keep an eye out for the mountains. Just before you run into them, that's home. The Julie Franconia mystery is solved. We got that one cold, I think. There's nothing for you to do in Indiana."

"Yeah?"

"A body was found in some woods outside Martinsville—

that's just south of Indianapolis—three or four days after our Ms. Franconia disappeared. It was hers. The local police had originally cleared the thing by attaching the homicide to a serial killer who was traveling about that time from Chicago to Texas. He was one of those guys who maintained he'd killed scores of people since he was, like, eleven. You know the ones. Cops and reporters from *Dateline* follow him around the country with shovels and backhoes as he points out all the places he left bodies. I have his name somewhere; you want it?"

"Not unless it's relevant."

"It's not. A close comparison of the VICAP reports on the serial killer's known victims—there are six or seven; the guy was a killer for real even if he's a little boastful about the numbers—shows that our girl doesn't belong in his group. MO of her death wasn't really anywhere close to his known MO. Circumstances of her disappearance aren't right, either. Personally I think somebody around Martinsville was looking for a cheap clear. They got it. Anyway, that body was found. They're going to reopen now."

"Cause?"

"Single gunshot to the base of the skull."

"Front or back?"

"Back. They think a nine-millimeter."

"Mutilation?"

"No."

I grumbled at the news. That wasn't the work of any garden-variety serial killer. The feds would be working overtime to tie the case back to Sterling Storey. I had been hoping to do something useful in Indianapolis. As soon as I heard Lucy's news, I knew that wasn't going to happen.

Lucy said, "You can come home, Sammy. Start now, and you'll be here in time for Thanksgiving dinner."

"What about Augusta?"

"No body discovered down there yet. But it turns out that some clothing that might belong to that victim—the locals have soft ID on a shoe from a girlfriend of hers—was found dumped outside town in a place called the Phinizy Swamp around the time of her disappearance. Police still have the clothing, fortunately. They're revisiting the forensics."

"Revisiting" was a Lucy word. "This swamp—a good place to dump a body?"

"That's what I hear. Alligators live there."

"Yuck. What about West Point?"

"Progress there, too. Previously unsolved murder. But the pieces are fitting the Sterling Storey puzzle."

"Nothing actually ties any of this to Storey, does it, Luce?"

"Opportunity, opportunity, opportunity. Records from his network show that he was in the right place the day each woman disappeared. What are the odds of that, Sam? The same guy being in each town when the vics go missing? Those are bad facts, come on."

"Yeah? What else?"

"Means is easy. I bet we can end up proving he knew these women, you know, carnally. And motive? As far as I'm concerned, the motive for serial killers is always just smoke."

"Evidence, though? Back when I was a real cop, convictions tended to take evidence."

"Everybody's only been on this for a little more than a day. It'll develop. You're not going to be of any help to anybody in Indiana, Sammy. The local cops and the feds are all over these cases. You're not going to get anywhere close to the principals. Come on home."

"Georgia cops find Sterling's body?"

"No. In fact, they called off the search yesterday afternoon. A searcher found a hat with his network logo about a mile downstream. For all intents, he's presumed dead."

"That's convenient. Cops all over the country get to close old cases and blame it all on a Good Samaritan who disappears in a river in Georgia. No trials, no appeals. Everybody ends up looking good. This is fairy-tale stuff. I smell a documentary cooking on this one."

"Don't be snide. It's not good for your heart. One more interesting thing, though. Brian Miles—remember him? Sterling's friend in Albany, Georgia? The one he was on his way to visit? FBI went by to interview him again. Gone. Neighbors are baby-sitting his dogs. He apparently didn't tell anybody where he was going."

"What are you thinking?"

"Coincidence?"

"Yeah, right."

"Sammy, come home."

"I'll consider it."

What I was really thinking was that Rochester, Minnesota—which was where my son and his grandfather were hanging with my sullen wife—was closer to Indianapolis than Boulder was. Sherry wouldn't be thrilled to see me, but Simon would. We could watch the Lions' Thanksgiving game together on TV.

"Heard anything from Reynoso? Is she bagging it and going home to California or what?"

"I haven't heard anything since I heard she was going to Georgia. But I don't think I would, necessarily. I'll ask a few questions and let you know next time we talk."

"Yeah."

"You feeling okay, Sam?"

"Like a million bucks, Lucy."

"That means what—I shouldn't ask? I'm worried about you. You should be home resting, watching football, getting ready for your turkey dinner. You shouldn't be out there alone."

"It's true, I'm fine. Maybe a little tired. But I got another call coming in, so I have to go."

"Call me when you know what you're going to do."

"Yeah."

"I'm serious. Promise me."

"Okay."

"Sam—"

I killed the call. Lucy was sweet, and her heart was in the right place, but nobody knew what I should do next. Not her. Not me. Nobody. Anyway, the truth was, my pager was going off again. Another 911: Alan.

I was really tempted just to get right back on the highway and find my way to Rochester and ignore his call. But if I did, I'd ruin Angus's Thanksgiving for sure. And Simon would have to watch his mom use all her willpower not to kill me for showing up uninvited.

So I didn't. Although I doubted that whatever Alan wanted warranted a 911, there was always the possibility that Lauren had gotten worse, or something bad had happened to somebody, you know? So I called. Within seconds I wished I hadn't.

"Sam?" he said.

"Yeah. What's up?"

"I'm at work, and, uh . . . I'm here with a woman—she's a security specialist—who just swept my office for listening devices . . ."

I thought *That's pretty goofy.* Alan had paused at that point like he was thinking that I was supposed to take over from there or something. I wasn't feeling terribly cooperative, so I just waited him out.

". . . and it turns out she found one."

He paused again once he'd succeeded in getting the entire sentence out of his mouth. It was becoming apparent that he was planning on telling his story in fits and starts. Me? I was standing in a highway rest area next to a bunch of old ladies who had set up a card table outside their motor home to play bridge. At that moment they were finding something hilarious about diamonds and the women's rest room across the way.

Although I was mildly curious about the odd fact that my friend had a bug in his office, I wasn't feeling particularly patient with his storytelling pace. I didn't know what help he wanted from me, but I hoped he got around to asking for it before moms and grandmoms all over America started taking turkeys out of their ovens.

"Sam, did you put that bug in my office?" he asked.

I screamed, "What?"

The old ladies scattered away from the little card table. They were moving so fast, I was afraid one of them was going to fall down and break a hip.

"What the hell are you accusing me of?" I yelled, even louder.

The women reacted to my outburst by scrambling back into their Winnebago clone as though they were thirty years younger.

"I just asked a question," Alan said, smug as shit.

Yeah, right. "You're lucky you're a thousand miles away from my fist."

"I take it that's a no."

"I don't believe you, Alan."

"I guess the feeling's contagious," he said.

I hung up on him.

The old ladies were peering at me through the windows of the motor home. They had fear in their eyes. One of them had tossed her cards in the air before she ran for the safety of the RV. I picked the cards up, dusted them off, scanned them, and placed them back on the card table. She'd had a damn good hand. I smiled up at the women and mouthed, "Four spades."

Then I took my pulse. One-twenty. Too high.

I reminded myself that I had choices.

I considered heading to Albany, Georgia, to have a chat with Brian Miles, but that felt like a dead end. And I admit I was briefly tempted to find my way back to Ochlockonee for a holiday date with a pair of twins and a turducken. I even thought about a long drive to Colorado to be with Gibbs. But the strongest pull? The due north on my emotional compass?

Simon.

I climbed back into the Cherokee.

FORTY-FIVE

ALAN

Maybe I didn't handle things well with Sam.

When I heard the yeah-whaddya-want tone in his voice on the phone, I immediately figured I'd tracked him down in one of his infamous constipated moods. The way I was feeling I just didn't have the patience for it. In retrospect, I immediately topped that miscalculation with another serious mistake: When he returned my call, I wasn't allowing for the possibility that Sam was not the person responsible for planting the bug in my office.

The truth is that I actually didn't get around to seriously entertaining that likelihood until long after I'd talked to him. In fact, I was halfway through my one-thirty appointment, later that afternoon.

My one-thirty was an elderly woman with severe posttraumatic stress syndrome from the unlikeliest of causes. She was perhaps the sweetest, kindest, most genteel person who had ever come to see me for treatment. Ironically, both she and I were currently obsessed with bugs. Hers were the microscopic kind that make people sick. By her account, she had barely lived to be able to tell me the tale of her atrocious treatment on board a bug-infested Caribbean cruise the previous fall.

Her story, which she insisted on recounting in excruciating detail, was now in its fifth weekly installment. The ship she was on the previous November had aborted its scheduled island-hopping itinerary and rushed back to Miami after suffering its second sailing in a row plagued with an epidemic of Norwalk virus, a severe gastrointestinal malady not uncommon in North America. According to my patient, the cruise line had known about the epidemic—which had also infected a huge percentage of passengers and crew on the previous sailing of the same ship—for over a week and had made a corporate decision, despite the severity of the outbreak, to disinfect the ship and immediately sail again. That decision had put a whole new group of twelve hundred passengers, including my patient, at risk of exposure. She maintained that none of the passengers on board the second doomed sailing had been forewarned about the ongoing epidemic until moments before boarding. Certainly my patient hadn't been forewarned before she'd made the thousand-mile-plus trip to the dock in Miami.

"Why?" she kept asking me. "Why? What did I do to them that they would risk putting an eighty-year-old woman in the toilet for most of a week? Why? Don't they know what they did to me? Why?"

She answered her own question. "Greed," she said. "They made me sick as a rabid dog and they almost killed me because they're greedy bastards. They care about money, not about people. That's what I think."

If I had to guess, I would have guessed that she hadn't actually used the word "bastards" before in her eighty-two years.

My poor patient was at the part of her story where a fellow passenger threw up on her in the elevator—"and I was at least five feet away from him."

Her seagoing tales of explosive emesis, institutional rudeness, and Olympic-size lack of compassion by cruise line employees had just begun, I knew. The excruciating story had thus far only progressed to cover day three of her voyage; she and I had three additional long,

long days at sea ahead of us. Covering them at our current pace would take us a month of weekly appointments.

"I don't blame them for the virus," she said. "I blame them for just about everything else they did." She'd said that before. I was certain she would say it again. And again.

"Greedy bastards," she repeated. "Do you know what they offered me for compensation? Do you?"

I did. But I also knew she'd tell me again anyway.

"They'd let me do the same darn death cruise a second time, and then they'd let me do another one at twenty-five percent off. That's it. That's the going rate for almost killing an old woman."

It was at that interlude in her session that I had the wisdom to cut Sam some slack. The thought I was allowing to ferment was: *Maybe he didn't do it. Maybe he was telling the truth about the bug.*

But if Sam didn't plant the damn device in my office in order to find out what Gibbs knew about her husband's murderous tendencies, who did? And why?

My dear patient, I knew, would have gladly blamed the whole fiasco on the greedy bastards from the cruise line.

The truth, I guessed, was not going to be so simple. Who had planted the device in my couch pillow? I didn't know and probably wouldn't know until I figured out why it had been placed. Knowing why meant discerning exactly what one of my patients might have had to say in the confines of therapy that was worth committing a felony to overhear.

I spent some time mentally reviewing my roster of patients, imagining which of their secrets, mostly mundane to me, was so prized by someone else. Although Jim Zebid's accusation about Judge Heller's husband selling cocaine was intriguing, and Sharon Lewis's identity would have certainly caused a tabloidish stir, Gibbs's story was the one that definitely had the most universal allure.

That's what led me to thinking that the culprit was the cops, and to Sam. The police would certainly have some interest in what Gibbs said to me.

So, I imagined, would Sterling. Had he somehow gained access to my office and planted the device before he left for Florida to cover the football game in Tallahassee? If he had—considering the likelihood that his corpse was caught on some debris beneath the surface of the

Ochlockonee River—I'd probably never know. But at least everyone's
secrets would be safe.

But I was overlooking something important: a possibility that I
had to rule out. I phoned home. Lauren answered. I checked in on her
battle with Solumedrol and commiserated as she reluctantly shared
the details of her travails.

Then I asked, "Do you have time for a work question?"

"Sure, sure," she said.

Her voice was pressured, as though her vocal cords were too taut.
I asked, "Is there any way the police could get a warrant to put a listening device in my office?"

"What?"

"Is there any way—"

"I heard you. You're serious?"

"Yes."

"No."

"No? No way?"

"No, no way."

"I just had one removed. A listening device was hidden inside a
pillow on my sofa."

"If this isn't your idea of a joke, I can assure you that it wasn't the
Boulder police who put it there."

"Thanks, I needed to hear that. I have to go."

"You'll fill me in on all this later?"

"Yeah. Love you."

If I could have answered the who and why questions, I might have
been able to predict the complications that were to develop over the
next few hours.

But I couldn't, and I didn't.

FORTY-SIX

SAM

Sometimes momentum rules. I'd been pointing toward Indiana's bull's-eye, so I kept going that way. I had some lunch in a Shoney's by a gas station, went and saw the Speedway just for the hell of it, and then backtracked downtown so I could be near the RCA Dome. I parked the car in a motel lot a few blocks away, checked in for one night, and started strolling over toward the immense sports stadium, waiting for some inspiration from the dead woman who had worked there. What was her name? Julie Franconia. Yeah.

But I got no inspiration.

Nothing. Julie wasn't talking.

My pager vibrated once again against my hip.

I knew it was him. I walked another hundred yards or so before I bothered to look at the screen.

It was him. Another faux 911.

First I kept my promise to Lucy, called her,

and told her where I was spending the night. She didn't have anything new for me. Then I called Alan.

The second the phone started ringing, I was already regretting phoning him back. "What?" I said.

"I'm sorry," he said.

I was still walking. It turned out that the Dome butted right up against downtown Indianapolis. I liked that. Sports should be part of things, part of a city's life, not some suburban reverse-doughnut thing where the arena is surrounded by acres of open space that are used to park a gazillion cars twenty times a year. There was even a nice green park with a big fountain outside the front door of the RCA Dome.

Cool.

"I'm sorry," Alan said again.

By then I'd walked around the corner, ducked under a sky bridge that linked the stadium with a garage, and stopped in front of a nice old church with twin copper steeples. I sat on the steps.

"I'm in a church," I said to Alan, lying. "I'm hoping it will make me be nice to you."

"I'm sorry, Sam."

"You said that. Next."

"If that was being nice to me because you're sitting in a church, I'm glad you're not sitting in a topless bar."

I laughed. It was a good comeback. "A titty bar would be way too much stress on my heart. Truth is, I'm actually on the stoop of the church. Not inside. God may be occupied with the folks who made it all the way inside, so be careful."

"I shouldn't have accused you."

"Accused me? You shouldn't have even considered me. I play hard, but I don't play dirty. I might be tricky, but I don't cheat."

"I know. I was wrong."

"Is that it? I got to go."

"Where?"

It was actually another good comeback, although Alan probably didn't realize it.

"I don't know. I'm thinking of going up north and seeing Simon."

"Is that a good idea?"

"Seeing my kid? It's always a good idea. Always."

He didn't skip a beat. He asked, "You want to tell me what's going on with Sherry?"

"Nope."

My pager vibrated again. I was about to turn the damn thing off. I lifted it off my hip and held it at full arm's length from my eyes. Even that far away I could barely read it. I said, "Gibbs is paging me. Now I do have to go."

"What does she want? Call me back."

"Right."

"Detective Purdy? I'm scared."

Her voice did something to me.

It was something unfamiliar. I stood and moved two steps higher on the church stoop. That didn't feel quite right, so I moved back down and settled my fat ass one step lower than when I had started. I wasn't sure precisely what I wanted God's help doing at that moment, but I was aware that it might be something He wouldn't be eager to assist me with.

"Yeah?"

"I think he's alive. I do."

I assumed we were chatting about Sterling. "You think he'd come after you?"

She said, "No, not really. But maybe, I guess. God, what a thing to say."

As she implored the deity, I craned my neck upward toward the pointy ends of the steeples.

"Where are you, Gibbs? Are you at home?"

"No, I checked into a hotel."

I guessed she would be at the Boulderado. I saw her standing near one of the tall windows in the new wing of the downtown hotel, her body softer than soft behind the gauzy curtains. "Which one?"

"The Boulderado," she said.

Arguably Boulder's finest, and the first place Sterling would look for her after he determined she wasn't at home. The very first. Gibbs's judgment was impaired. That wasn't news. A lot of experience had convinced me that all battered spouses have impaired judgment.

Just like all squares have corners.

"Maybe not the best choice," I suggested.

"Do you think he's coming?" she asked.

"What do you think?"

"Over these years he hasn't hurt me, he's hurt them."

"Them?"

"The women he was . . . you know."

"Screwing?" I felt my pulse jump as though my heart had a turbo-charger. Seventy to one-seventy in three seconds flat.

I thought she mumbled, "Mmm-hmmm," or something like it.

"The women he killed . . . he was . . . having affairs with them?"

"I don't want to . . ."

I found a fleece-lined version of my don't-fuck-with-me voice and used it like an exposed blade against her throat. I said, "This isn't the time to get coy with me, Gibbs."

"Yes," she blurted. "Yes."

"Do you know of others? Other women? Besides the ones who are in the news already?"

"No one else."

She had hesitated. Damn it. The pause was subtle, but it felt like a stomp on the foot to me. She was lying.

I didn't want her to be lying to me.

Her next words seemed to come out of her like a tabby's purr, all soft and comforting. She said, "I don't want anyone to get hurt. Do you think he's out there? Do you?"

I inhaled slowly, as though I could somehow detect the scent of Gibbs's perfume in Indianapolis's air. All I got was a lungful of bus exhaust. "Until someone finds his body, you can't be sure he isn't. I always tell people to trust their fear. It's usually pretty good advice."

"The FBI called and asked me about Brian Miles."

Gibbs's change of direction was abrupt. I felt like I'd just tripped over something. I regained my balance and asked, "Yeah? What did you tell them?"

"What I told you already. That Brian and Sterling had whored around together. And that I didn't like Brian."

"You didn't tell me that. That you didn't like Brian."

"He wasn't nice to women."

"No?"

"No."

"How wasn't he nice to women?"

"Maybe I should go to Denver instead of staying here. Or go up into the mountains."

Way out in front of my eyes I spied a couple of dots that needed connecting. I asked Gibbs, "What business is he in? Brian Miles?"

"Electronics."

"Huh? Like TVs? Stereos?"

"No, microelectronics. Stuff I don't understand. Do you like the mountains?"

I stumbled again trying to keep up with her. Gibbs was clearly accustomed to having men follow her wherever the hell she decided to go. So what did I do? I followed her, too. I asked, "Have you considered Safe House?" but I was still pondering Brian Miles and microelectronics.

"Actually, I was thinking Vail. Or maybe going back to Corona Del Mar and staying with friends."

Gibbs was definitely Vail. Not Aspen, Vail. Not the mountain, the village. She'd be right at home in Vail Village.

Through the phone I heard a horn honk loudly.

"You have a room on the Broadway side?" I asked.

She hesitated. "Close. I'm on the alley."

A siren blared by.

"That ambulance was really moving," I said. "They usually don't go that fast on Broadway."

Gibbs said, "I wish you were here, Detective. I'd feel safer."

It was the tabby's purr again, vibrating gently against my fragile heart. I stood and stepped down the church steps. My feet felt like they were disappearing into sand. Lifting them—left, right—took extraordinary effort.

I made her feel safer. I made her feel something good.

I made her feel.

"Call me Sam" was what I said. Or just call me glib. Was I tempted? Yeah. Heading back to Colorado's high country to play bodyguard to Gibbs's princess sounded just fine to me. The impulse to go felt wrong. It did. But the sense that it was wrong came and went fast, like the roar of a passing stock car.

A homeless guy was sitting hunched over in the recessed doorway of a building just a few yards from the church steps. *That,* I thought, *is what hope looks like as it's dying.*

I tried, but I couldn't pry my eyes off him.

As a way to break free from the suction of his gravity, I pulled out my wallet and fished out ten bucks. I dumped the bill into the hat that sat upside down between his antique Air Jordans. He didn't even look up to check the identity of his benefactor, but a remarkable sleight of hand allowed him to suck the bill up into the sleeve of his ratty corduroy coat so fast that my eye lost track of the money.

I realized that quick-as-a-burp he'd replaced the ten with a single and that I'd been had. I hadn't contributed some needed charity to a homeless man, I'd made an unwitting payment to a skilled urban busker.

Gibbs broke into my reverie. "Detective?" she said. "Sam?"

She called me Sam.

"Yeah," I replied.

"If I decide to move somewhere else, I'll call you from Vail or wherever I am. I hope you have something for me when we talk again."

Me too. Me too. "Me too," I mumbled.

"I can pay you, you know, to protect me. I can. I'd like you . . . here."

"That's not it," I said. "I'm working on something here that might help."

She sighed. " 'Bye, Sam."

" 'Bye."

Where was I planning on finding whatever information it was that I planned on giving to Gibbs? That I didn't know.

I found myself again distracted by the costumed magician who had my hard-earned money up his sleeve. An elegant, elderly woman wearing a fox stole walked by, slowed, and threw a handful of coins into his hat. For a brief moment his hand hovered above the money. But her contribution apparently didn't equal the price of admission; this guy granted no magic show for a mere handful of change.

Then I remembered: Alan wanted me to call him back. It was just as well that I'd forgotten. If I'd remembered, I would have had to make a conscious decision not to do it. Then I would have ended up feeling guilty. And that would have been bad for my heart.

I pulled a five out of my wallet, folded it the long way into a V, and slid it into the magician's hat. Faster than my eyes could follow, the bill was gone and replaced in the hat by a solitary buck.

The surrogate bill wasn't folded down the middle.

I took a step back and applauded quietly and politely, as I might if I attended the symphony, which I don't.

The homeless impersonator lifted his head an inch or two and mimed a tip of the hat for me.

All in all, it hadn't been a bad way to spend fifteen dollars.

FORTY-SEVEN

ALAN

Despite Tayisha's reassurance that my office was clean, I made the stroll to the waiting room to retrieve my four o'clock without feeling a whole lot of confidence in the sanctity of my workspace.

My four o'clock was the twenty-three-year-old named Craig Adamson who had called earlier in the week to confirm his appointment. Craig was one of those patients who kept me up late trying to find ways to help him. He was a terrific human being who spent every waking moment battling a whammy of mixed character pathologies—a moderate obsessive/compulsive disorder alongside a severely paranoid character. In his unfortunate circumstances the two problems coexisted about as well as quarreling neighbors. The DSM diagnostic code that I'd cobbled together to describe his condition looked like a European phone number—way too many digits—because it required that I tack on additional numerals to account not only for his depression but also for his occasional psychotic interludes.

A surprise greeted me as I opened the door to the waiting room. Craig was right where I expected to find him: in the corner chair, which was the location farthest from any other seat in the room. But sitting closest to the door was another patient of mine, one who didn't even have an appointment that afternoon. It actually took me a moment to recognize her. She'd dyed her hair so that it was a shade of red that nature tended to reserve for flowers and fruits, and she'd cut it short enough that she wasn't going to need a blow dryer for a while.

Sharon Lewis.

She shot to her feet, glanced at the hypervigilant man in the corner—apparently concluding that he wasn't much of an adversary—and with enough pressure in her voice to power a hydraulic lift, she announced, "I need a minute. I'm sorry, I'm sorry, but I just do." Then she squared and faced Craig. "May I have five minutes with him? I know it's rude, but this is an emergency. You don't mind, do you?"

Without waiting for either of us to reply, she squeezed past me into the hallway that led back to my office and disappeared from view.

Craig was having a difficult time comprehending what had just happened. I couldn't blame him for that. Finally, he said, "It's okay. Really." But his eyes were jumping with incipient panic.

"It's not okay," I told him. "This time is yours."

Despite a daily cocktail of psychotropic medications prescribed by a psychiatrist who knew what she was doing, and despite twice-weekly psychotherapy with me, Craig remained one of the most disturbed patients I'd ever tried to manage in outpatient therapy. I'd begun seeing him as a favor to my neighbor Adrienne, who worked with Craig's parents, both local anesthesiologists. They thought I would be the ideal therapist to treat their son, one, because I wasn't a colleague of theirs, and two, because my office was only a little more than a block from the town house they rented for Craig on West Pearl Street. Craig's pathology severely limited the geographic territory in which he felt comfortable traveling.

Sharon Lewis could not have picked a more vulnerable person to intrude upon if she had plotted her assault on my waiting room for weeks.

"No, no," he said. "It's okay. I'll wait. She needs . . . it . . . you . . . more than I do. I'll wait—wait here." He didn't look at me as he spoke. Not even a glance.

"I'll take care of this as quickly as I can."

"Fine. Fine." Exhale. "Fine, fine, fine."

"I'll be right back out," I said. A blind person could have read his body language. Craig was anything but fine.

He stuck his face closer to his magazine. I noticed that he was reading *Popular Mechanics*. It wasn't a title that Diane and I supplied to the waiting room, which meant that he had brought it along with him. It could have been, of course, that he wasn't fond of any of the magazines we provided for the waiting room. But I suspected the reality was that Craig wasn't comfortable picking up a magazine not knowing who might have touched it before him.

Would he admit that to me? Not yet. But we'd been making progress on the trust issue lately. Progress that I was afraid this event might annihilate.

Sharon Lewis was waiting on my sofa. She appeared as though she'd been hooked up to a Starbucks IV for most of the day. Her acute agitation made me think of Lauren's recent Solumedrol jolt.

"I should just go back to Ontario and hide."

"Ontario? California?" I felt an imperative to adjust my therapeutic gyroscope. Asking an inane question or two would buy me a few seconds of calibration time.

"I'm from Canada," she explained.

"I didn't know." I didn't.

"Well, they know," she said. "God damn it. They know. They know everything."

I took a slow, deep breath trying to find words that would challenge her without being accusatory. "What you just did out there in the waiting room, Sharon, is the same thing that got you into such a mess at the airport a couple of weeks ago. It's what we've been talking about. You impulsively decided that your needs were more important than anyone else's, in this case the other person in the waiting room. You once again allowed a sense of urgency"—I could have added, but didn't, "and a sense of grandiosity"—"to cause you to decide that the rules"—I omitted "of decency and compassion"—"don't apply to you."

"I said I knew it was rude. And I apologized to him."

"The problem is that knowing that the behavior is rude doesn't serve to deter you at all. And your apology sounded about as sincere as—as a campaign commercial."

Her jaws were clenched. Despite my bluntness my words hadn't dented her Kevlar facade. I hadn't expected they would.

"They know who I am. Today on the noon news, Colorado's fucking News Channel reported that the mystery woman who inconvenienced a million airline passengers—you know, *the most selfish woman in America*—they're reporting that her name is Sharon, that she lives in Boulder, and—get this—they said she's getting mental health treatment for her 'condition.' My 'condition'! Jesus."

The blood drained from my face. I guessed what was coming next. And I wasn't disappointed.

Or I was.

"Did you tell someone?" She almost spat the words at me. "Did you tell someone about me?"

"You would like to blame me for the situation you're in?" I thought I managed to ask the question evenly, with just the slightest hint of confrontation.

"Who else?" The subtext of her retort was *You imbecile! Nobody else knows but you!*

Yogi Berra once said that he couldn't think and hit a baseball simultaneously. His point? Some things happen so fast that they must be done by instinct.

My reply to Sharon should have been one of those instinctive things. But it wasn't. Why? Because I was absolutely frozen in place by the fact that one of my options was admitting to Sharon that I'd just had a listening device removed from the office in which we were sitting, and that it was likely that the little microphone and transmitter had carried her secrets out my windows or through my walls out into the world.

The fact that one of the local television news channels knew only her first name convinced me that the leak had been from one of our sessions. Rarely did I ever use a last name during treatment. But if I made the admission to Sharon about the listening device, I was certain that she would, rightly, accuse me of destroying her hope of confidentiality. Were she to accuse me in public, the notoriety of the case would bring me almost as much misery as she was about to suffer.

I sputtered to find words. Although I knew I'd eventually have to tell Sharon and all my other patients what I'd found in my cushion, I wasn't ready to start right at that moment.

In ten quick seconds of therapeutic silence I saw my precious career vaporizing before my eyes.

What did I end up saying? I said, "I don't know, Sharon."

She actually started to cry. "I was going to turn myself in. I was. Now? It will look like I did it because they found out it was me. Hell, I'm screwed. Screwed! I'm leaving—I have to talk to a lawyer."

A minute later I was on my way back out to the waiting room to retrieve Craig. I opened the door to discover that he was gone. I wasn't surprised, and I began considering the words I'd use that evening when I called Craig's home trying to repair some of the damage. I actually felt some hope that if he and I could deal with what had happened in the waiting room that day, it might ultimately be helpful in his psychotherapy. Nevertheless, I didn't take much comfort in being the unwitting foil in the provocation he had suffered.

I spent the dead time before my final appointment of the day making a list of all my patients and all their recent secrets, big and small. I couldn't keep myself from making tortuous detours as I imagined the admissions that I would have to make to each one about the possibility that their revelations to me were soon going to be in the public domain.

A few minutes before five Diane tapped on my open door. She was mugging a pouty face. "None of them wanted me. I got voir-dired to death on an arson case, but nobody wanted me. I'm crushed."

"Hi," I said. "It turns out you were right."

"Of course I was. About what?"

"The bug in my office."

"That? Right. Anyway, there was this one guy in the jury pool—"

"I'm not kidding."

She snapped her mouth shut, and I explained about Tayisha and the listening device and about the continued revelations about my patients' lives that were finding their way into public view.

She couldn't tell whether to believe me. Finally, she asked, "How many is that total?"

In my head, I counted. Jim Zebid and his story about Judge Heller's husband's cocaine. That was one. Gibbs Storey and her accusations about Sterling. That was two. Sharon Lewis and her ignominious behavior at Denver International Airport. That was three.

"Three that I know of," I said.

"That doesn't make sense."

Why it didn't make sense escaped me. "What, Diane? You don't like odd numbers?"

"Why would somebody plant a bug to discover something about one of your patients and proceed to broadcast information about three of them? It doesn't make any sense."

"I don't follow."

"One person walks into a park and paints a statue pink, you think there's something wrong with the painter, right? A wacko?"

"Yeah." Although I replied in the affirmative, my tone conveyed more doubt than assurance.

"But if three different people walk into the park at different times, and they each paint part of the statue pink, you have to begin to think that there's either a conspiracy going on—"

"Yeah." Less doubt that time.

"Or . . . there's something weird about that statue. Does anything—anything at all—tie those three patients of yours together?"

The possibility of a conspiracy was novel to me. "I can't see anything. As far as I know they don't know each other. They're all in different professions. Different social circles. They've never mentioned each other to me, that's for sure."

"Well, then take a look at the statue."

"Me? I'm the pink statue?"

"Exactly."

"What are you saying?"

"Somebody's out to get you."

"Me? What are they planning to do, Diane? Humiliate me publicly by revealing what I say to patients in therapy? I may not always be pithy, but I don't think what I say is *that* bad."

"Pithy? Did you say pithy? God, you're something. Whoever planted that bug didn't expect you to find it, Alan. Right? So why was it there? Not to embarrass you. A simple tape recording of your clinical wisdom would have embarrassed you. And I don't think it was to learn some deep dark secret that one of your patients might be telling you. Don't you see? Not with three different stories leaked already. Why would somebody do that?"

I'm sure I looked confused.

She went on. "If it was just one patient whose story was revealed, you could say that patient's secrets were the target, but if there are three—with maybe more to come—you have to assume that you, and not your patients, are the target."

"Then what? I don't get it." I was hoping we weren't on our way back to the pink statue.

"What was it you once told me in one of your rare fits of perspicacity? You said that if I want to understand someone's motivation for an act, then I should take a look at the consequences. Well, what are the consequences of all these leaks going public?"

"It's going to ruin me."

She walked close enough to me that she could rest a hand on my shoulder. "Exactly. Somebody's been trying to set you up as a therapist who can't keep secrets. You have an enemy, dear."

I tried to inhale. I failed. "Diane, if somebody did that, it—"

"It sure would. Once people in town think you can't keep secrets, you're dead meat."

"Hell."

"Just a guess on my part," she said. "But I would think that we've discerned the motivation. All you need to do is figure out who might want to destroy you."

FORTY-EIGHT

SAM

Want to know dead? Dead is the downtown of any major midwestern American city on the eve of Thanksgiving Day.

If the whole center of Indianapolis erupted in a spontaneous conflagration and burned to the ground that night, it would have to be considered a cremation, not a fire; that's how dead it was downtown.

If there were twenty people in downtown Indianapolis that evening, I somehow managed to miss fifteen of them. Even the faux-homeless guy with my money up his sleeve had packed up and gone somewhere for the night. Probably a suite in a fine hotel.

The clerk manning the desk at the motel where I was staying was a Sikh with a turban and an accent that made me smile. He suggested I try to find something to eat at the Marriott over by the RCA Dome. "Go there. They have to be open" was the precise nature of his melodic culinary recommendation. If he ever decided to change careers and shun all the opportunities available in the motel desk clerk business, I thought he had a promising future with Zagat.

I walked over to the Marriott, found an open restaurant inside, and got a table and a menu. A waitress wasted no time in ambling over and smiling a sincere midwestern smile. She asked, "You from out of town?"

I looked up and made good eye contact with her. "What, you get locals here? Like ever?"

She laughed.

"Didn't think so."

"Let me guess," she said. "I'm bored, okay. It's a slow day. Do you mind? I'm pretty good at this. Not as good as Wendy. She's like a champion, but she's off through Sunday. I'd say you're from Wisconsin. Maybe . . . Michigan—but northern Michigan, like Traverse City."

"Not bad, Christy." Her name was written in capital letters on a plastic tag above her ample left breast. "Born and raised in Minnesota. But I've been in Colorado for a while now."

She snapped her fingers. "That's what threw me. The Colorado part." She said "ColoRADo," emphasizing the penultimate syllable in a way that made me want to grate my teeth.

Behind her a woman stood in the restaurant's entrance craning her neck this way and that. I figured she was checking the room for her husband, or her date, or her girlfriend. I nodded in the direction of the foyer. "There's somebody over there who needs your help. I'll be ready to order in a minute, I promise. I'd love a beer when you get a second."

"What kind?"

"Surprise me." I'd already managed to forget that alcohol was on my post-MI do-not-consume list. Truth is, it wouldn't have made any difference had I remembered.

"You're nice," she told me.

"Nah, I'm not really," I said.

I could tell she didn't believe me. A bad judgment on her part. I had no doubt that if I had a beer with Christy, the first thing I'd learn from her was that all her boyfriends had been assholes.

Growing up, my family always had soup the night before Thanksgiving. It was part of our tradition. My mother, bless her heart, could throw together a big pot of soup faster than I could say, "What's for supper?" She considered soup a light meal that was appropriate in anticipation of the richness of the coming holiday feast. But Mom's soups were never really light—she wasn't a consommé kind of gal. Her soup was always something thick and chunky, hearty with sausage and white beans or kidney beans and plenty of rich cheese.

I endured a moment of sadness as I realized that all the love she'd put in her soups was now coating my arteries like spackling on a wall.

I'd returned my attention to the menu, looking for some soup not too much like my mom's, when I felt the waitress approach again.

"Almost ready," I said. "How's the minestrone? Come from a can?"

She didn't reply. I looked up.

The woman from the doorway stood with a hand on the top of the other chair at my table.

"May I?" she asked.

She was pretty. Well dressed. Polite. And tall. I was bumping into a run of tall women on my road trip. I thought of the Wolf sisters and the turducken that was about to begin roasting in their slow Georgia oven, and I lamented that not a single bite would cross my lips the next day.

I opened and closed my mouth a couple of times like I was some old fool who just realized he hadn't remembered to replace his dentures, before I said, "Actually, I'm fine all by myself, thanks."

She pulled back the chair and sat down.

Christy the waitress had a fresh place setting in front of her within seconds.

I stared. The pieces of the puzzle floated in front of my eyes. But they didn't come together.

My uninvited guest said, "You're having the minestrone?"

Two weeks ago I would have sent her packing. Two weeks ago I thought I had a healthy heart and a marriage that would survive until Christmas. Two weeks ago I wasn't sitting alone in a restaurant in a faceless Marriott in Indianapolis. Two weeks ago I hadn't met Gibbs Storey, and I'd never heard of a turducken.

"Have a seat, why don't you?"

"You don't know who I am, do you?" she said.

I hated questions like that—questions that taunted with I-know-something-you-don't-know. I reconsidered my decision not to send the woman packing. To buy some time to contemplate, I answered her first question. It had been more civil than the second. I said, "I like minestrone."

She held out her hand. "I'm Carmen Reynoso."

I made a little *ptttt* sound with my lips. The sound was part of my recognition that I hadn't made her as a cop. That troubled me. I thought I could make a cop in the fog with plugs in my ears and my hands tied behind my back. I didn't shake Reynoso's outstretched hand. Nothing personal to her; it wasn't one of my things.

The waitress brought my beer.

Detective Reynoso said, "I'll have one of those, too, please."

"You here looking for Julie Franconia?" It wasn't so much a question as it was my way of letting Reynoso know that I wasn't a complete dummy. I added, "The case is closed. Body was found south of here near Martinsville. Looks like your boy Sterling did it. If you get up and hurry over to the airport, I bet you can be home in sunny southern California in time for your turkey."

She nodded, so I thought she was going to agree with me. But she didn't. She said, "Actually, I'm here looking for you."

"Did I do something . . . particular . . . to interest the Laguna Beach PD?" I was thinking maybe surfing without a permit, or illegally parking my Range Rover, but I didn't say it out loud.

Once, after Alan observed me talking to a citizen about a crime I thought she might have committed, he complimented me on my interrogation technique. I said something to change the subject, which he ignored. He ended up going on and on the way he does sometimes, and told me that where conversation was concerned, I was good at making repetitive move ones, not falling into the trap of making reactive move twos. He said it served me well.

I didn't know what the hell he was talking about.

He, of course, explained it all to me. His lecture boiled down to this: In order to maintain control of a conversation, psychologically speaking, a person needs to make repeated assertive moves, not merely reactive moves. If someone says, "How are you?" the other person doesn't need to respond, "Fine," the other person can say, "Where

were you last night at eleven?" He said I was good at that, at keeping
control of conversations, at not making move twos.

I'd never thought about the linguistic structure of it all before. But
he was right. I am good at that. It isn't tactical on my part. I just don't
like feeling that somebody else is running the show.

It turned out that Carmen Reynoso was good at that, too. She ignored my sarcastic question about why the Laguna Beach Police Department might be interested in finding me. Instead she chose a fresh
move one. She said, "I came looking for you because people say you're
good."

I shrugged. "Doesn't happen too often, but sometimes people are
right." That, by the way, was a classic move two on my part, which
meant that Reynoso was firmly in control of this conversation.

It was okay with me for the moment. I was confident I could take
back the wheel whenever I felt like it.

She said, "We're the only two people I know who believe that
Sterling Storey is actually still alive."

"How do you know what I believe?"

"I'm a detective."

She didn't yield an inch of territory. I smelled Lucy. "My partner
told you I was here?"

She smiled for the first time. Her lips were sealed during the entire
grin. I was thinking she didn't like her teeth. Yellow or crooked? I
guessed crooked, then instantly reconsidered my conclusion. Maybe
she was a smoker. I sniffed at the air, didn't detect anything foul that
wasn't coming from the kitchen. Still, she struck me as someone
who'd maybe once smoked.

She said, "I'm picky about revealing my sources."

"You mean your snitches? What do you want with me, Detective
Reynoso?"

"You Catholic?"

"I thought you were a detective. You should already know the answer to that." I wasn't sure whether my response had been a move
one or a move two. But I thought it was pretty clever.

"I am. I'm Catholic. My father considers St. Peter's—you know,
in Rome—the holiest place in the world. Notre Dame—the university,
not the cathedral in Paris—comes in a close second. In my family
Saturday afternoons in the fall are just as holy as Sunday mornings.

Fighting Irish football? Anyway, this is a roundabout way of wondering if you'll accompany me up to South Bend."

I'm not Catholic. To the contrary, I hate Notre Dame University with the same kind of passion that heretics despised the Inquisition. Why? Lots of reasons. But mostly because Notre Dame stole Lou Holtz from the University of Minnesota.

Some things aren't forgivable. But I'd learned over the years that it wasn't a safe area of discourse with Notre Dame fanatics, who tend to be about as rational about their beloved Fighting Irish as the real fighting Irish are about the British, so I kept my enmity to myself.

"Why?" I asked. My resolve about not revisiting the Coach Lou hijacking was weakening already; I was sorely tempted to go into my well-practiced Notre Dame harangue.

"If Sterling's alive, I think that's where we'll find him."

I left half my beer on the table. She left slightly less of hers. I never got a chance to taste the minestrone, but I suspected that it wouldn't have satisfied like my mom's bratwurst and cheese soup with ale. As Reynoso and I were walking out of the Marriott, I said, "There are three, by the way."

"Three what?"

"People who think Sterling's alive. His wife does, too."

I had to hustle to keep up with her long strides. "Actually," she said, "that would make four."

"Four?"

"I'm thinking Brian Miles."

Sterling's pal in Georgia. Smart lady. I said, "Gotcha."

Two more steps. "Gibbs is a piece of work," she added.

To that, I thought, *Amen.*

I was going to South Bend. That was the bad news. The good news? Carmen Reynoso had rescued me from my impulse to drive even farther north to Minnesota. Every objective part of my brain was telling me that the trip to see my family would have been a bad thing to do.

How did Reynoso convince me that going to Notre Dame with her on Thanksgiving was the right thing to do?

The Crime Stoppers tipster in Colorado had called again. People who listened to both tapes thought it was the same guy as the first call. This time he'd told the volunteer who'd answered the phone that if Sterling Storey had happened to survive his swim in the swollen Ochlockonee River, he might be going after another victim, a woman he may have been planning to kill all along. The tipster suggested that the next victim would be found in one of three towns: South Bend, Indiana, Flushing Meadows, New York, or Daytona Beach, Florida. The tip also revealed that the South Bend woman worked in the Sports Information Office at Notre Dame. Reynoso had already done the footwork necessary to identify her. There was only one woman on the Sports Information Office staff who fit the correct profile: twenty-five to thirty-five, pretty enough to turn heads, a widow.

"Why you focused on that one? She's the only one at risk?" I asked.

"There're two other women on the list. The one in New York does advance work for the women's tennis tour. But we think she's in Australia at the moment setting up a tournament, so we're not as concerned about her. The other woman has something to do with Daytona Beach, Florida—maybe the car race—but so far we don't know enough to figure out who she is. So I'm here."

"The South Bend woman, what's her name?"

"Holly Malone. Good Irish girl."

I asked the obvious. "Isn't it likely the tipster's a crank?"

"He got the others right, didn't he? The other three homicides after the one in Laguna?"

"Still."

"Let's be real. You doing anything else for the holiday, Sam?"

It was the first time she'd called me by my first name.

"Not really," I admitted.

"Me, neither," she said.

"Why," I asked, "doesn't the South Bend PD take care of this?"

Reynoso was in the passenger seat of my Cherokee. We'd backtracked and dumped her rental car back at some no-name agency at the airport and had started driving north. Unless we got seriously distracted, we'd be in the hometown of the Fighting Irish just before we arrived at the Michigan state line.

Reynoso answered my question. "I called the local cops when I was still in Georgia, explained the situation real politely, and I requested some assistance. Hold on—let me try and get this next part exactly right."

She took a moment to collect her thoughts, and then she adopted an accent that was part something and part something else. I wasn't good with accents. It was one of my few liabilities as a peace officer.

" 'Ma'am,' " she said in character, then went back to her everyday voice and explained that "the detective I spoke with in South Bend called me 'ma'am.' I always find that improves my mood considerably, being called 'ma'am.' " She resumed her soliloquy with " 'Ma'am, you want us to go out and protect a woman from a killer who's already been declared dead by the Georgia authorities? You actually do that sort of thing regularly in southern California? Up here we don't get a whole lot of spirit homicides. We actually haven't had a good ghost killing in, dear Lord, aeons. And my memory is that the last one we did have got the death penalty. Well, we hanged him. Recall we had the darnedest time finding a good place for the rope. It got all tangled up in the sheets. But we managed.' "

"I bet he thought he was pretty funny," I said.

"The man thought he was hilarious. One of his buddies was cracking up, too. I could hear him. I hope we get a chance to meet both of them when we get to South Bend. That would please me."

While she was talking, she'd started fiddling with my radio, which wasn't pleasing me too much at all. The fine country station with the clear signal that I'd found south of Indianapolis disappeared in a sharp crackle, and suddenly I found myself listening to late seventies pap. I couldn't imagine a worse choice—I didn't like to be reminded that I'd actually been in the prime of my life during disco. It was a source of long-term humiliation for me. I worried how I would explain it to Simon when the time came to discuss the music of my youth. If rap hung around long enough, that would help; rap was at least as hard to defend as disco. Maybe harder.

I asked, "Who do you think the tipster is, the guy who's calling Crime Stoppers?"

"Don't know."

"Who'd know what he knows? Can't be too many people."

"It's a fair question."

"You're not curious?" I asked.

" 'Course I'm curious. I just don't know. Do you?"

I was thinking that I had a pretty good idea, but I didn't feel much like sharing right then. It was probably a side effect of the toxic music that was being forced into my ears like a watermelon suppository. So I said, "Sure don't."

We were skirting Kokomo when she asked me about my heart.

"You feeling okay? You want me to drive, I will."

"I'm cool," I said, trying to be cool.

"Hear you had a heart attack."

"Just a little one."

"Still," she said.

"Yeah," I admitted.

The tires hummed along on the highway.

Carmen Reynoso knew when conversations were over. I was already liking that about her.

Half a mile or so later I asked, "What have you been able to learn about Holly Malone?"

"Not much. She's an assistant director in the Sports Information Office at Notre Dame. Started in the office as an intern when she was just out of school. She's twenty-nine, attractive. People like her."

"You said she's single?"

"No, widowed. She has a four-year-old son."

"How did her husband die?"

"Cancer."

"Can't blame that on Sterling, can we?" I said. "Have you spoken with her?"

"I called. She was relatively pleasant until I mentioned Sterling. That's apparently a sore spot for her."

"Sore?"

"She wanted to know how I knew about him. My take was that she knew he was married when she did whatever it was she did with him. I thought she was embarrassed that I'd found out about their . . . history."

Kind of like having people know you lived through disco and didn't do anything to stop it, I thought. *Felonious stuff.*

"Got a photo?"

She retrieved a folded eight-and-a-half-by-eleven from her purse. "Pulled this off the Web. That's her on the left. First row."

I put my glasses on the end of my nose. It was a crappy picture of a group of people standing in front of a building. Holly Malone stood out as though she were Technicolor and everybody else was black-and-white. "She's cute. Has a nice smile."

"Yeah."

"You wouldn't happen to have a picture of Brian Miles, would you?"

Carmen pulled another crappy picture out of her bag and handed it to me.

One glance, and I knew there were no man-boobs on Miles. Nope. I kept that thought to myself while I stuffed my glasses back in my pocket. "We going to find Holly in town for the holiday?"

"We are. She's cooking for her two sisters and two brothers-in-law. They're all coming down from Chicago with their kids."

"Yeah?"

"She told me all that before I mentioned Sterling. Holly's chatty. If you're interested, she's doing a traditional bird and is poaching some salmon for her sister, who doesn't eat meat."

"Given the circumstances, I bet the salmon would consider itself meat."

Carmen chuckled. After her laughter quieted, I let the whine of the road fill my ears for a minute or two. I was thinking, *This is okay.*

I asked, "For argument's sake, why would he risk it? I mean Sterling. Let's say he survived the river. Why put himself in a position to be caught? Why not just run for it?"

"Odds are he'll do just that, Sam. Odds are we're wasting our time. Five years from now he'll get picked up on a DUI in Idaho, and his prints will get flagged by AFIS. That's the only way we'll know where's he's been since he crawled out of the Ochlockonee."

"I can tell you don't really believe that."

"Serial killers—and maybe especially serial killers who don't choose strangers as their victims—they don't think like you and me. They just don't. Why would Sterling go back and kill Holly? I don't know. Why did he kill the other four women? We don't know that yet, either. But I don't want the fact that I'm slow to the draw to cost some young widow in South Bend her life."

Slow to the draw? I wondered what she meant. I felt regret hanging on to her words like an anchor.

FORTY-NINE

ALAN

I bumbled my way through my last session of the afternoon. Diane, bless her heart, was in my office seconds after my patient departed. "So who wants to destroy you?"

I knew Diane loved me, but I also thought I detected a troubling touch of glee in her tone, a rub-your-hands-together, muted Wicked-Witch-of-the-West-type cackle.

"I can't think of anyone."

"God, I can."

"You can?"

She went into a staccato litany of some of my more public cases of the past ten years, eventually, and probably accurately, identifying a long roster of people who might be prone to seeking some redress for wrongs they could have been convinced they suffered because of me. It wasn't a pleasant list for me to contemplate. As Diane's soliloquy

began to take on Elizabethan dimensions, I found myself wishing I'd
walked out to my car and gone right home.

"You done?" I asked when she paused to come up for oxygen.

"I think so," she said. "Are you going to be able to remember all
that, or do you want me take some notes for you?"

"Oh, I'll remember."

It turned out the pause was only Diane's version of a pit stop.
Within seconds she was gaining speed again. Unfortunately for me,
my seat belt wasn't fastened. She asked, "What about your current
patients? You really pissed any of them off? Any of them want your,
you know?"

I didn't know. Nor did I want to know, particularly. I said, "Not
that I know of. Other than the leaks over the last few days. The three
people whose information leaked aren't too thrilled with me. Other
than that, my caseload is reasonably content with my efforts."

"Then what about nuts? You treating anybody really crazy right
now? Any psychotic transferences creeping up on you? Ooooh, or
any really hot erotic transference? Those can get wild. That might do
it."

Despite the irreverent tone, her questions were reasonable. I
thought seriously about my answers before I said, "No, nothing."

"Damn."

She seemed disappointed. I wasn't sure what to make of that.

"I have to get home. I have baking to do for tomorrow. Raoul has
developed this thing for pumpkin pie. Who would have guessed? You
sure you don't want to come over for Thanksgiving?"

"Thanks, but Lauren doesn't feel up to being with people. She's a
little . . . irritable."

"Which we know is the Anglo-Saxon word for 'bitchy.'"

"Yes."

"Alan?"

She was in the doorway to my office, staring right at me.

"Yeah?"

"Stop feeling sorry for yourself. Jump this hurdle. Move on."

I wished her a happy Thanksgiving before I retraced my steps to
my office and called Craig Adamson to discuss our fractured appointment that afternoon. His machine picked up. I left a message, packed
up my things, and headed home.

*   *   *

The weather was pure Front Range autumn. Sweater-cold, hands-in-pockets, gusty-wind weather that came along with a promise of snow that is fulfilled less often than you'd think along the eastern face of the Rockies in October and November. I usually found the fall totally exhilarating, swollen with provocation.

But not that day.

The next day would be Thanksgiving. As I drove away from downtown Boulder, I reminded myself to count my blessings. It wasn't a short list—and Grace was firmly ensconced at numero uno—but I found myself distracted somewhere near number two or three by some of life's recent challenges.

My wife's feet were so full of edema, they wouldn't fit into Bozo's shoes, let alone her own. Somebody had bugged my office. My career was hanging by a thread. My best friend was alone somewhere in the Midwest, trying to find a way to recover from a troubled marriage and an angry heart. I had a patient whose husband might be trying to kill her.

And I had an enemy I couldn't identify.

I stopped on the way home to finish up the last of the holiday shopping. Bakery, groceries, wine. Everything took twice as long as it should have, of course. The butcher had our turkey listed under Allen, not Gregory, and I wasted almost half an hour trying to help him track down the bird while at least a dozen other joyous citizens waited behind me for their turkeys.

They expressed their holiday cheer to me via a well-rehearsed melody of sighs, nasal snorts, and whispers of "dear Lord" and "Jesus."

They weren't praying.

Sam once warned me that I would rue the day my parents decided to burden me with two first names. Maybe he was right. It wouldn't be the first time Sam had been right.

I wondered how he would spend the holiday.

The buffalo cap was out of Lauren's arm when I got home. That was her holiday gift, although the steroid misery wasn't completely over. She'd go from getting a gram a day of Solumedrol directly into her veins to getting eighty milligrams of prednisone into her mouth. Gradually eighty would become sixty and sixty would become forty and forty would become . . . and two or three weeks from now—I hoped by Christmas, for sure—she'd be completely finished with the steroidal assault on her metabolism. A few weeks later the side effects would dissipate to zero, and she and I would begin the familiar low-grade worry about the next time the elephant would camp out in our living room.

We had a light dinner as a family—actually I had a light dinner; Lauren was suffering the kind of munchies usually associated with chronic cannabis use but also common among steroid users, so she put down an unusual quantity of food—and then I read stories and got Grace down for the night. Lauren spent the whole time playing pool—the repetitive, endless nature of the game was one of the few things that seemed to help her outlast the Solumedrol.

After Grace was asleep, I joined Lauren in the dining room, where her pool table took up the space that an architect once envisaged for a dining room table. She didn't invite me to join her game. Lauren was once a highly rated amateur pool player. Let's just say that I wasn't. My opposing her in pool was as ludicrous a match-up as my lining up against Lance Armstrong for a quick sprint up Coal Creek Canyon to Wondervu on bikes.

Her strokes economical, Lauren dropped ball after ball into the leather pockets.

Through the steroid clatter in her brain she listened as attentively as she could to my story about Tayisha and the surreptitious device that was discovered in my sofa cushion. Other than offering empathy and wondering why I hadn't already involved the police, Lauren didn't have much to say in reply.

She was still playing pool when I retired to bed around ten.

I missed her.

The phone rang minutes after I flicked off the lights. I pounced on it so the ringing wouldn't stir Grace. As I lifted the receiver, I could still hear the *thwop-crack* of the pool balls coming from the dining room.

My "hello" earned me a "hey, buddy" from Sam.

"You okay?" I asked a little too urgently. I'd already convinced myself he was calling from some emergency room in some hospital. I was in a state of mind where I didn't have any confidence that anyone I cared about was okay.

"Yeah, fine, considering. Guess where I am?"

Given the mood I was in, I didn't want to play along, but Sam sounded happier than I'd heard him sound since his MI, so I tried to remember where he'd been the last time we talked. I thought Georgia, so I guessed, "Atlanta."

"South Bend."

My pulse jumped, just like that.

I was tired, but not so tired that my brain was unable to make the associations necessary to take me back to Gibbs's psychotherapy session the day before and to her revelation that Sterling had once been involved with a woman who lived in South Bend, Indiana.

Notre Dame University. The Sports Information Office.

Sam went on, filling the void. "Carmen Reynoso tracked me down. Remember her? It was her idea to come to South Bend."

Sam was telling me something. Given the hour, I had to believe it was something important. Maybe because of how close I'd been to REM time when he phoned, I wasn't getting it. Not quite.

"Yeah? How's South Bend?"

"I'm not a big Notre Dame fan. I liked Indianapolis, though. I didn't expect to, but I did."

"I'm not a Notre Dame fan, either. It's like the Yankees, I think. You either love the Irish or you hate 'em." I was still drawing a blank. I wished I weren't so tired. God, I was tired.

Sam said, "There's a woman here that Carmen thinks we should go see."

Carmen? Sam called her Carmen. That's when I got it.

Carmen Reynoso knew what I knew about South Bend. My next line in the script? "I guess I'm wondering how Carmen heard about the woman in South Bend."

"Tip from Crime Stoppers. A guy."

"Anonymous?"

"You know how people are; they don't like to get involved. Listen, I don't need any details or anything, but—you know me—I'm curious whether you've had any conversations at work lately about any women in South Bend."

"Turns out I have, Sam. Just yesterday, as a matter of fact, I had a conversation about a young woman who lives in South Bend. Can't say any more, because of how I heard it, but yeah."

"Any reason to believe she might be in some danger?" Sam asked.

"The woman in South Bend or the woman who told me about the woman in South Bend?"

Damn! I'd just exceeded the parameters of the game I was playing. I'd told Sam that I'd heard about South Bend from a woman. He could have guessed it on his own. He probably had, of course. That would have been okay. What wasn't okay was that I'd told him.

"Either. Both," he said. "Listen, you ever heard of a guy named Brian Miles?"

"Don't think so. Why?"

"He's some old friend of Sterling Storey's. And it turns out his background is in microelectronics. Given your conundrum, that might be important."

Yeah, it might be. "An awful lot depends on what really happened in that river in Georgia, doesn't it?"

"The Ochlockonee," Sam said. "Funny, but it's gotten to the point where I like saying it. Och-lock-onee. Ochlockonee. You know it's yellow? The river?"

"No, I didn't know that."

"It is. Anyway, I figure it about the same way you do. It's all going to come down to Sterling and the Ochlockonee." He paused. "How's Lauren feeling? Any change?"

"Her leg's a little better. The medicine's making her nuts, though. Thanks for asking."

"Tell her I'm thinking about her."

"I will. Sam, it was Crime Stoppers, huh? That's how you knew about South Bend?"

"Yeah."

"Hard to trace, those Crime Stoppers calls?"

"We don't trace them. Did I say it was a guy who called?"

"Yeah, you did. And you said that this Brian Miles guy is in microelectronics. I'm grateful."

"Well, I hope it helps you with your puzzle."

"The fact that it's a guy cuts the number of suspects in half, roughly."

"There you go. Process of elimination. Just like a real cop."

*   *   *

Did I fall back to sleep right away? Hardly. I was consumed with thoughts of Gibbs and Sterling and St. Tropez and a balcony on Wilshire Boulevard and women in Augusta and Indianapolis and Laguna Beach and West Point and a guy named Brian Miles in micro-electronics and mostly—mostly—Sterling saying "catch me."

"*Sex. It's not just for procreation anymore.*"

Maybe Sam would catch him after all.

Maybe in South Bend.

Maybe.

I listened to the muted *thwop-crack* of the pool balls for a while and toyed with counting sheep.

Instead, recalling Diane's admonishment, I conjured images of me jumping hurdles, and I numbered each one as it passed beneath my feet.

FIFTY

SAM

Carmen Reynoso had an address for Holly Malone
and a little map to the Malone house that she'd
printed off the Internet. Although we didn't get
into South Bend until after eleven, we decided to
drive by Holly's residence just to make ourselves
familiar with the area. We found the bungalow
on a corner in a neighborhood more upscale than
I thought that a university sports information officer could afford.

Carmen said, "Craftsman style. Nice."

I think I surprised her by saying, "This is the
territory for it. Stickley worked around here
someplace, didn't he?" The truth was that I knew
damn well that Gustav Stickley's furniture company had been just up the road in Grand Rapids,
but I didn't want to come across as a smart-ass. I
figured Reynoso took me for a fat, dumb cop—
most people did. Partly I cultivate that impression
for strategic purposes: I like the advantage that

comes with being underestimated. But partly I do it because I'm most comfortable hanging with people that fat, dumb cops get to hang with. Talking Stickley and Frank Lloyd Wright and Elbert Hubbard doesn't go over too well in most areas of my life.

That's okay with me. The point of knowing stuff isn't so you can let other people know you know it. Occasionally feigning ignorance is a small sacrifice for the companionship of good people. And in my life I got to hang with more than my share of good people.

Carmen smiled at me after my comment about Stickley's furniture company. She didn't just smile; she smiled at me. Her lips stayed smoothly together, though, so I still didn't get a chance to see her teeth. But I wondered if the quick smile was her way of telling me that she cultivated the angry Hispanic persona the way I cultivated the fat doofus persona. We would see.

The Malone bungalow was an Arts and Crafts classic. It had a shingled roof, a wide front porch supported by small clusters of efficient pillars, elegantly grouped windows, and a solitary second-story dormer that faced the street. The lights were all off downstairs, but the flickering glow of a TV screen was playing shadow games on the curtains in the dormer.

I circled the block once, hoping Sterling was stupid enough to be waiting in a car parked on the street watching Holly through binoculars. No such luck. I ended up parking on the corner opposite the house beneath a big tree that was totally naked of its leaves. After a second or two I killed the headlights and the engine on the Cherokee. The valves clattered loudly as they tried to find someplace comfortable to rest. I shifted my ass and did the same.

"She's still up," Carmen said. I could see Carmen's breath in the dark car. South Bend was colder than Indianapolis. I inhaled a little more deeply than usual to try to taste Carmen's scent. Failed.

"Watching Leno," I said.

"Letterman," she corrected.

I smiled, turning my head and parting my lips, letting Carmen see my teeth. It was an effort at modeling. "Yeah, you're right, probably Letterman. He's from Indiana, too, right? What do you think, should we go over, pound on her door, tell her about Sterling, ruin her evening?"

"She's not going to be happy to see us, Sam."

"Nope," I said. "I don't know about you, but I find most people aren't happy to see me at times like this."

"It is pretty late."

"Murderers work all kinds of hours."

"You really think he's going to kill her tonight?" she asked.

" 'Course not. But are you a hundred percent sure he isn't? This could be one of those times when being a little wrong has serious consequences."

Carmen yawned. "Why do I get the impression that you go through partners the way I go through panty hose?"

"Lucy's been my partner as long as I can remember."

"Is she a saint?"

"No. Lucy has issues, too, just like me. The rocks in her head fit the holes in mine almost perfectly."

Across the street Holly Malone killed the TV, and the light in the dormer died along with it.

Carmen noticed the change in scenery the same second I did. She said, "I guess we have a decision to make."

"Coming here was your idea, Carmen. It was a good idea, or I wouldn't be here with you. I think whether we ruin Holly's holiday tonight or tomorrow morning is up to you. I'll back you up either way you want to go."

She gave the puzzle fifteen, twenty seconds of thought. "We passed a motel a few blocks back. I vote that you and I go get some sleep, and we talk to her tomorrow morning when she's chopping celery and onions to stuff into her turkey."

"Okay, that's what we'll do." I started the car. "Tell me something, Carmen. Are you a Raiders fan?"

"What?"

I pulled a U-turn in the intersection before I switched on the headlights.

"Football? You a Raiders fan?"

"As I matter of fact, I am. How did you know?"

"Intuition. Did you have tickets when you lived up north?" What was I guessing? I was guessing that she had season tickets and that she owned a good-sized wardrobe of Silver and Black.

"Yes, I did."

"Thought you might."

"What else do you know about me?"

You like disco and the Oakland Raiders. That's about it. Don't necessarily like what I know, but I don't know as much as I'd like. That's what I was thinking.

I decided to circle Holly Malone's block one more time, slowly, searching for any sign of Sterling Storey. Why? Criminals almost always end up proving themselves to be a lot smarter or a lot dumber than people give them credit for. I was still hoping that Sterling was a lot dumber. That was why.

Halfway around the block I finally responded to Carmen's question. "Nothing," I said. "I don't know anything else about you. You have kids?"

"One. She's a freshman at UC Santa Cruz. She's spending Thanksgiving with her boyfriend's family."

I did the math, figured Carmen was maybe a little older than me. "I have one, too. He's a sophomore in grammar school. He's spending Thanksgiving with his grandparents."

She laughed before she said, "I know."

She knew.

"You married?" I asked. I didn't think about asking, I just asked. I don't like it when my mouth gets ahead of my brain. It doesn't happen often. Usually my mouth is pretty slow, my brain a little faster.

"No," she said, without explanation.

She didn't ask me if I was married.

She knew.

Or did she?

I sucked in my gut, knowing damn well the act did nothing to disguise my man-boobs.

What did I spend the next few blocks wondering? I spent the next few blocks wondering what it would be like to get one room at the Days Inn instead of two.

FIFTY-ONE

We got two.

I hoped I hadn't been obvious when the woman at the desk had asked, "One room or two?" I'd hesitated a beat too long—I knew I had. I was waiting for Carmen to say "two," but she didn't. Or hoping she'd say "one" or something. It might have been my imagination, but I thought she was waiting to hear what I was going to say.

After that beat-too-long passed, we both blurted, "Two."

My room had little NO SMOKING signs just about everywhere I looked, but it had recently been occupied by a smoker, no doubt about it. The fetid air caught in the back of my throat with each slow breath I took.

I took a minute to call Alan on my cell to let him know that Carmen, and therefore the Boulder Police Department, knew about the woman in South Bend and that they seemed to have a conduit that ran straight into his office by way of the Crime Stoppers program.

He sounded dismayed at the news. I felt bad for him. The guy's plate was pretty full.

Carmen and I had been assigned rooms right next to each other; they even had a pair of those odd connecting doors between them, as though the desk clerk thought it might be fun to tempt me with trespassing all night long.

She sang soulful songs as she prepared to sleep. Except for my shoes I was still fully dressed, and I lay on the bed as motionless as I could so that the bed wouldn't squeal and I wouldn't miss a muted note. I was almost certain that I'd never heard any of the songs she was singing before in my life.

That, I thought, was fitting. It seemed that all the melodies I'd heard since she sat down opposite me in the Marriott were composed of fresh notes.

Except for the disco.

She sang three songs, paused, I guessed, to brush her teeth, and then sang one more tune, something so full of lament that it brought tears to my eyes about Simon and Sherry and the holidays and my heart. I thought of Lauren and the fears that enveloped her, and even of Gibbs and what her life was going to be like when the dust settled, and I shed a tear for her as well.

I fell asleep right like that with my clothes on and woke at one-thirty, stripped in the dark, brushed my teeth, and fell back into bed. I listened for a while to the silence, pretended I could hear the soft percussion of Carmen's breathing through the walls, and replayed the songs I'd heard only once a short while before, and they worked for me once again like lullabies. I was back to sleep before two and stayed that way until she pounded on my door at a quarter to eight.

When Carmen busted me awake, she'd torn me from a dream about the Wolf sisters and their mostly cooked turducken. The details of the dream evaporated instantly, but I woke thinking that if I inhaled deeply enough, I would be able to smell the intertwined birds roasting in an Ochlockonee, Georgia, oven. A deep breath and a quick look around the room brought me back to the reality that all I was smelling was the stale smoke of some inconsiderate fool's Marlboros.

I chided myself for my juvenile romantic fantasies all through breakfast. What had I been thinking?

Whatever intimacies I had imagined the night before had disappeared with the darkness. If we'd been flirting at midnight, we weren't flirting anymore. Carmen played nothing but business at breakfast, and I ran along next to her, trying hard just to keep up. I returned to the buffet line in the motel's little breakfast room a couple of times, not just to get more food, but also to get a break from her intensity. The meal wasn't bad; I ate yogurt and fruit and Cheerios with nonfat milk. After two cups of decaf I switched to regular coffee. If the morning was any indication what our day was going to be like, I was going to need some rocket fuel to match her pace.

My cardiologist would just have to understand.

"What do you know about Sterling and Holly? Their relationship?" Carmen asked me when I indicated I was done eating by pushing the plastic cereal bowl and the plastic spoon away from me. I thought that her saying "Sterling and Holly" was particularly ironic; it managed to make the two of them sound like they were the cute couple that'd been crowned king and queen at the Homecoming Dance.

But Carmen's question caused me take a sharp breath, too. Or maybe it wasn't the question; it was the answer I was about to give. "They were having an affair," I said. Which was exactly what I'd been thinking about doing the night before. I tasted hypocrisy with my next sip of coffee.

I don't like hypocrisy in others. I hate it in myself. Hate it.

"Yeah, but that's not enough. When I talked to her yesterday, she was obviously upset that I knew about her and Sterling. If all the two of them did was mess around a couple of times, why would she be so upset? She's not married, so what did she do that was so wrong, other than show some bad judgment by sleeping with a married guy? That particular sin is committed about a million times a day in this country."

It couldn't have been clearer if she'd been shouting at me. Carmen was announcing to me that she'd almost made the exact same mistake eight hours or so before and that she wasn't feeling particularly good about how close she'd come to yielding to the temptation.

But I didn't see the issue she was describing with Holly Malone. "I don't know that it's that confusing. She's Catholic. She's Irish. She has a young kid. She lives in a small town. Maybe she's the guilty type, or maybe she's just afraid of scandals. Most people don't like to be reminded of their indiscretions. Or—wait, better—she met him through her work, right? Maybe there's a Fighting Irish Sports Information Office prohibition against sleeping with people they're doing business with. She's scared of losing her job."

"That's possible. It sounds Catholic enough. But I think there's something more than that going on."

"Why does there have to be something more than that?"

"There doesn't have to be, Sam. There just is. I feel it. Who did you call last night?"

"What?"

"The second you stepped into your room, you made a phone call. Why? What was so important? Who was it?"

I sat back and felt my man-boobs jiggle beneath my shirt. It was clear that I wasn't making much progress on the man-boobs segment of my self-improvement program. I tried to look her in the eyes, but I couldn't quite corral her gaze. "Are we on those kinds of terms, Carmen? Where you can ask me who I call on the phone?"

She sat back, and her boobs jiggled beneath her shirt a little bit, too— although it was an altogether different phenomenon. "You're right, you're right. I'm sorry. I don't know what I was thinking. I'm sorry."

She had been asking me something, but she had been telling me something, too. What did I conclude? I concluded that she was telling me that her songs the night before had been a private concert just for me. I chewed on that. "The shrink who called you about the Storeys? The one you met in Boulder? He's a friend of mine."

"I know," she said.

She knew a lot about me.

She hadn't looked back at me since her intrusive question about the phone call. I said, "I called him. He has a . . . problem. I had an idea that I thought might help him with it. So how do you want to play this with Holly later this morning?"

She finally looked back up at me. She smiled. "If you're up to it, I'd like you to talk to her. Yesterday didn't go too well on the phone with me and her. You can start fresh. Is that okay?" My eyes were locked on her smile. There was nothing wrong with her teeth. They weren't crooked. They weren't yellow. They were just fine.

"That's okay," I said.

FIFTY-TWO

She was talking to herself more than she was talking to me.

"Twenty-two pounds. Dinner's at four. I'd like the bird out of the oven by three, maybe a little after. Eighteen to twenty minutes a pound—that's because it's stuffed, otherwise it would be only fifteen. That means five hours, give or take, so I need to get this in the oven—oh my God!—in the next few minutes. Aaaagh."

Holly Malone was kind of cute. She would be the darling kid in the sitcom—the one you really liked, the one with the charm. Pretty, but not the kind of drop-dead-beautiful that made me nervous. Like Gibbs.

I was enjoying watching her flit around her little linoleum-tiled kitchen searching for utensils and roasting pans and ingredients that it was apparent she hadn't laid a hand on in months. Or longer. But she possessed enough enthusiasm for an entire cheerleading squad, and her positive energy was better for my heart than anything I'd run across recently.

I was also enjoying being in a kitchen on Thanksgiving morning, getting the opportunity to be a spectator at an event that I'd been privileged to witness almost every year of my life since I was old enough to remember. I was surrounded by tradition; the countertops in Holly's kitchen were upholstered with celery and onions and broth and butter and parsley and dried bread crumbs and a big fat naked turkey, and for a moment all was right in my world.

I looked at the clock that hung on the wall by the door that led from the kitchen to the living room, which was where Carmen Reynoso was waiting while I was doing my best to bond with Holly. The clock read ten-fifty. I did some arithmetic, considered for a moment the consequences of keeping my mouth shut, and said, "Relax, Holly. Dinner won't be until six-thirty or seven. Maybe later. You have all day."

"What are you talking about?" she said playfully. She thought I was teasing. "Everyone's coming shortly after two. Dinner's at four, promptly. My sister's husband Artie would have a fit if he thought his meal would be even a minute tardy." Holly had a trace of an accent of some kind that caused her to elevate the last syllables of her words as though she really, really liked them. The accent was cute, too.

I was having a very good time.

Reluctantly, I explained the turkey dilemma. "Twenty-two pounds at twenty minutes a pound is exactly seven hours and twenty minutes of cooking time, not five hours give or take. That sounds like a long time to me, but what do I know about turkeys? If you stick it in the oven right this second—and you and I know that's not going to happen—then that bird won't be coming back out of the oven until almost six o'clock this evening."

She froze and stared at me as though I had screamed at her not to move, she had a tarantula on her nose. I could tell she was using the interlude to check my facility with numbers.

"Oh my God," she whispered. "Oh my God!"

"What can I do to help, Holly?" I asked. "Chop something?"

Her shoulders dropped. She put a devilish look on her face and said, "Can you go and arrest Artie for something or other? Throw him in the slammer for a while? That'd slow him down."

* * *

Half an hour later the bird was finally in the oven, and Holly and I were sipping fresh coffee at her linoleum-topped, chrome-framed kitchen table.

"This is going to be the kids' table later on," she told me. "This and an old card table from the basement."

"I like the kids' table," I said. "Conversation's usually better."

She sighed and looked at the clock. "I was a math major at Williams. I swear I was," she said.

I assumed that Williams was one of those eastern colleges that I was supposed to recognize by reputation. I didn't. I'd gone to St. Cloud State and didn't hang a whole lot with kids who didn't.

I said, "Thanksgiving meals never happen on time. It's part of the whole tradition. Don't worry. If Artie gives you any trouble about it, he's a jerk. Dinner will be wonderful."

"Artie is a jerk. I don't know what the heck my sister was thinking. She has this thing for anal men."

I saw my opening. "Don't be so hard on her. We all make decisions in relationships that we'd like to do over. I know I've made a few. I bet you have, too."

She was staring into her mug. "Yeah," she said, "I have." She stood, walked over to the oven, and peered in on the bird. She and I both knew it was just as pale as it had been ten minutes before. And she and I both knew that she was getting some distance from me. We were getting a little too close for Holly's comfort.

I pulled the photo of Brian Miles from my pocket. "You know this guy?"

She took a serious look at it before she said no.

My first reaction was that I believed her. I reminded myself that that didn't mean she was telling the truth.

"Sure? He hasn't been around?"

"I'm sure. Who is he?"

"Not important."

She moved some things around on the counter. Finally, she said, "This is where we talk about Sterling, isn't it?"

"Stuffing's made, turkey's in the oven, the first round of dishes is done. Coffee's hot. Guests won't be here for hours. It's probably as good a time as any."

"I should check on my son."

"He's fine. Detective Reynoso loves kids." Or she hates kids. Or she can take or leave kids. I didn't know. All I knew was that she'd managed to keep one alive until the kid was in college.

"You're sure?"

"I am."

"Is Sterling dead? The papers say he's dead."

"I was down in Georgia a couple of days ago. They think he's dead. Me? I'm not convinced." I went into a long explanation about the Reverend Prior and the Wolf sisters, the precise order they all arrived at the bridge over the Ochlockonee during that terrible storm, and I even slid into a little digression about the turducken that had already been in the Wolf sisters' oven for over half a day.

I could almost taste it right that second.

Holly was much more curious about the construction of the turducken than she was in the logistics involved in Sterling's fall into the Ochlockonee River. At her behest I did my best to explain the precise way a creative butcher nested the birds together like a set of those weird little Russian dolls that fit inside one another.

"Artie wouldn't like it," she said. "All those meats in the same meal? He likes to keep his foods completely separate on his plate." The thought of disappointing Artie made her smile.

"Do you know about the other women?" I asked. Enough about poultry, enough about Artie. If I was still around when Artie showed up, he and I were going to have a chat.

She gestured at the morning newspaper. "I don't believe it. I don't believe what I've been reading. It's just—it just can't be true. Not Sterling." She'd been waiting for me to ask the question about Sterling and didn't spare a second in answering it.

"You don't believe it?"

She looked at me, which was good. Her eyes were tight with something; I wasn't sure what. She said, "Sterling is . . . pretty, I mean—God, who am I kidding—he's really gorgeous and . . . he's . . . smooth. You know, he's not the Sylvester Stallone macho-type guy, he's more like a short—God, I probably shouldn't say that. Oh, what the hell—he's like a short version of George Clooney. Sterling's really charming, not the kind of guy I usually meet through the—" She stopped herself.

"Yeah?"

She went on firmly. "He wouldn't kill anybody. No, no. Sterling is just not that type of guy. I know men. I do."

I whispered a prayer of gratitude for the opening. "So what type of guy is he, Holly?"

I'd been traveling for four days plus through I'd-lost-count-of-how-many-states hoping to get the answer to that question. And now here it was. I was about to hear what kind of guy Sterling Storey was, what kind of guy could cheat on a woman like Gibbs over and over again.

Holly's phone rang. It was her sister, Artie's wife.

"You got my message?" Holly said, stepping away from me across the kitchen. "Is Artie going crazy with the delay?" She raised a finger to warn me that she was going to need a minute.

I stood and poked my head into the living room. Carmen had Holly's son in her lap. She was reading him Christmas stories. I recognized a funny little book that I always read to Simon over the holidays called *Bialosky's Christmas*. Simon thought Bialosky was one terrific bear, which was something I never really understood.

Carmen's storytelling style was full of melody, and she imbued each character with a distinct voice. She was making it sound as if one of Bialosky's friends was from the barrio. Carmen was good. I listened for half a minute, but only with the periphery of my awareness. Front and center? I was replaying the last few moments with Holly.

Behind me I heard her place the phone receiver back on the cradle.

"Sorry," she said. "My sister."

Before I stepped back into the kitchen, I killed the power on my cell phone so we wouldn't be disturbed, and I changed the weight of my voice, reducing it the way my mom used to reduce the gravy before bringing it to the table. The act was pure instinct, like a big cat flexing her muscles before she pounces. I was about to pounce.

My prey was a cute blond widow who was cooking Thanksgiving supper for her extended family.

"Sterling Storey's not the kind of guy you usually meet through . . . what?" I asked Holly.

She took a step back, literally, and bumped against the stove. "I hoped you hadn't heard that. I've been wishing I hadn't said that."

"Maybe. Or maybe you hoped I did. Regardless, here we are. I heard it. You said it."

"I'm a widow," she said.

"Got that. I'm sorry."

"People talk. You know what it's like. My . . . options are limited. In my personal life."

"Are we talking about sex, Holly?" I managed to ask the question with a certain panache, as though I talked about sex with cute young widows all the time.

Yeah.

My question amused her. "Yes, Sam, we are indeed talking about sex. Hello."

I said what, to me, felt obvious. "You're a lovely girl, Holly. Bright, funny. I don't see how your options are limited." I didn't say, *"You could have any guy you might want, any guy at all."* I didn't say, *"A guy would be lucky to be with you. A guy like me would . . ."*

I didn't allow myself to finish the thought.

"Before he died, my husband and I had an . . . imaginative sex life. We enjoyed a variety . . ."

Holly turned away from me.

Holly wasn't bashful about sex. That's not why she turned away. She turned away because she instinctively knew I was bashful about sex.

I tried to focus. *A variety of what?*

"We were careful. Always careful, especially after Zach was born. We didn't take unnecessary risks."

At the moment she said that she was talking directly to the turkey. Unlike me the turkey didn't blush.

"That's good," I replied. "You and your husband, what you did together in your private time is . . . was . . ."

"Our business. Yes. Is this important? I'm not really comfortable talking about all this with you."

Neither am I. Trust me, neither am I.

"Your husband's name was?"

"Mark."

"Thank you. Detective Reynoso and I are trying to determine what kind of danger you might be in from Sterling Storey. How you know him and how you met him are important parts of that determination. We'd like to leave here today able to assure you that you're safe."

She considered my argument. She looked in her hand, pulled out a card, and held it up for me to see. "I don't have to talk to you, though, do I? Legally, you don't have any authority here, do you?"

The card she'd chosen from her imaginary hand was a good one. I acknowledged that she held it. I said, "Nope, I don't."

"But then," she said, "you don't have to be here at all, do you?"

"Nope, I certainly don't. I'm a volunteer in this fire department."

She turned back toward me. The fact that I was there on my own time and on my own dime carried a lot of weight. She said, "Who will know about this? I mean, if I decide to tell you?"

I sipped at some coffee. It was cold. "This is where I could lie to you and tell you nobody but us, me and Detective Reynoso, but the truth is I don't know who'll end up knowing. Secrets are like puppies. Once you let them out, they tend to be pretty hard to control."

"South Bend's a small town. Notre Dame's a Catholic university. A very Catholic university. I'm a mom. Some of the things I do in my private life aren't acceptable here. I have no illusions about that."

"I understand," I said. "I know about small towns and secrets. In case you've never been, Boulder is more small town than big city. I grew up in a much smaller town in Minnesota. So how did you meet him?"

Instantly, she entered a little time warp. I recognized it. It was a little Jules Verne moment where time stopped and she tried to decide whether to tell me the truth. Ten seconds later she exited the warp with what sounded to me like honest words. "I have personal ads on the Web. Adult personal ads. I try to meet men with . . . similar interests . . . who are traveling, you know, who are in town on business. Mostly I end up going to Chicago to . . ."

Part of me was grateful that she left the sentence unfinished, part of me was just the smallest bit curious about what happened when she went to Chicago. "But Sterling came here to South Bend?"

"Yes, he did. His work brought him here—brings him here. You know about that, don't you? His work?"

"I do. You didn't meet him through his job, though?"

"No, we met, if you can call it that, over the Internet. We never ran into each other on our jobs. Even after. My job concerns primarily women's sports. I don't deal much with the men's teams."

"See, I didn't know any of that. You have a copy of the ad you run? May I take a look at it?"

"*What?*"

Holly had heard me just fine. Her exclamation was understandable, about what I would have expected had I asked if I could fish through her underwear drawer. I softened the request. "I'd like to know what exactly Sterling responded to. It will help me . . . understand him a little better."

She exhaled, her eyes wide. She dropped her arms to her sides and spread her legs a couple of inches farther apart. "He responded to a revealing picture of an attractive woman who said she likes sex with strangers. It's not that complicated, Detective. Getting people to respond to my ad wasn't difficult—isn't difficult. Finding someone I can feel safe with . . . that's a whole different problem."

I blushed. "How do you—"

"E-mail. I set up temporary Hotmail accounts, and then I e-mail back and forth with the guy until I'm comfortable. If I don't get comfortable with him, I close the account and start all over with somebody else."

I didn't know what a Hotmail account was. Hell. I'd ask Simon when I talked to him later in the day. My kid would probably know. "How long did the process take with Sterling?"

Carmen chose that moment to step into the room. "Smells great in here. You guys making progress?"

"We're doing great, Carmen. Maybe a few more minutes?" I said. The expression on my face was intended to shout "bad timing." *Real bad timing.*

She backed out.

Holly said, "I don't like her."

"Yeah, well. She's great with your kid. That's good, right? You were saying how long it took to—"

"Not long."

"So you met him . . . where?"

"On campus."

"And you . . . ?"

"Jesus, Detective. Do you really need to know? Really?"

I said yes. I didn't feel yes, but I said yes. Some things you want to know even if you don't want to know them.

This was one of those.

Holly stepped over next to me, lowered her mouth to my ear, and whispered what it was she'd done with Sterling Storey.

Maybe it was the moist heat of her breath, maybe it was what she told me, but I blushed all over again.

FIFTY-THREE

This was going to be a first. Holly and her husband had talked about doing something like it a couple of times, but the discussions were always more joke than anything else. But this guy from California? He was serious. Right from the start, she could tell.

Totally serious.

She thought about his proposal overnight. Excitement overcame fear, fear became excitement, and she e-mailed a simple lowercased yes.

It had been a Saturday afternoon in September a year before. Notre Dame was playing Michigan in Ann Arbor. The date for the date was Holly's idea. The university campus would be empty. The students and faculty and staff who weren't in Michigan for the football game would be holed up watching the annual tussle anyplace that had a big screen and plenty of beer.

One-thirty to two-fifteen. That was the window she'd given him. She'd be there by one-thirty.

She'd leave by two-fifteen. They had to be gone before Saturday after-noon confessions began.

In between? For Holly, the sweetest of all aphrodisiacs: anticipa-tion.

"What are you going to do while you're waiting for me?" he asked in one of his e-mails.

He knew all about anticipation. She'd figured he would.

"Pray," she'd responded.

Some secular universities have chapels; some Catholic universities have elaborate churches. Notre Dame University has a basilica.

Holly was waiting for Sterling opposite the Chapel of the Reli-quaries in the vaulting nave of the Basilica of the Sacred Heart.

Ten minutes before two o'clock he knelt in the pew that was right behind her. She hadn't heard him approach. He was the church mouse.

"Don't turn around," he whispered. "No, don't."

Her lungs felt bottomless. She was breathing so deeply that she had to open her mouth to get enough air.

She already knew from experience that the fire of anticipation consumed immense quantities of oxygen.

She hadn't spent the time praying. No, she'd been counting the other people in the church. Currently, there were thirteen. One lovely woman in a dreadful purple suit was only a few feet from her in the Chapel of the Reliquaries. Thirteen was just right. Not too many, not too few. Just right.

"Sex in churches shouldn't be reserved for priests," he whispered to her in an over-the-top Irish brogue. "Should it, now?"

She'd been thinking that they'd use the confined space of the con-fessional for their tryst, but she wasn't so sure she wanted to be in the dark with him.

Fear? No. That wasn't it. Not at all.

She wanted to be able to see him.

Without a word Holly stood, walked down the length of the nave, and climbed the stairs toward the pipe organ. Her idea.

A few minutes later he followed.

She knew he would. They always did.

As his footfalls brushed the stairs, one by one, she knew that what she'd been thinking about, fantasizing about, since she was a thirteen-year-old schoolgirl was about to happen.

Holly didn't actually see his face until they were finished. Until anticipation was nothing but sweat on the cold church floor. When she finally turned toward him and saw the white slash of his Roman collar and the ruby light from the stained glass that limned his profile, his physical beauty almost took her breath away again. She thought, Mark would have vetoed him for sure.

For sure.

FIFTY-FOUR

Carmen and I left Holly's house before I had a chance to meet Artie. That disappointed me.

We were out the door and all the way down the porch steps when I thought of something else, told Carmen to go ahead and get in the car, and returned to the screen door. Zach was playing with a pile of those oversized fat Legos in the living room, making something that looked like Frankenstein's dog.

"Holly," I said, calling her back to the door. "I'm sorry, one more thing." I lowered my voice to a whisper. "You're not frightened of him? Of Sterling?"

"No, I'm not."

"The other women he's suspected of murdering? They don't—"

"I'm not convinced. Far from it."

Her expression changed just enough that I guessed that whatever came next was going to be at a different level of intimacy than what had come before. I found myself struggling to tune my antennae.

"Listen," she told me, "I e-mailed him again a couple of weeks ago. I asked him if he was interested in going to church with me again sometime. That's how not-frightened of him I am."

"You would see him again?"

"Before this week and all the news in the papers? Before you and Detective Loves-Kids-Lacks-Social-Graces started trying to scare the bejesus out of me? I would have seen him, yes. We had a great time together."

Sometimes people ask me why I'm a cop. I don't usually answer with the public service/public welfare refrain. I answer with the truth: People are endlessly interesting.

Holly Malone was a damn good example.

"Did Sterling respond to your e-mail?"

She shook her head convincingly. Even a little ruefully, I thought.

"I gave you my cell phone number, right? Just in case? You'll call if you see him around here, or even if you get a feeling?"

"Yes, Detective. You did. And I will."

I reached into my pocket and handed Holly the crappy photo of Brian Miles. "Him too. Keep it. Call if you see him."

"You're not going to tell me who he is, are you?"

"His name is Brian Miles. He's somebody you should avoid."

She held the picture loosely in her hand. "I told you, I'm careful. No matter what you think about my lifestyle, I don't take chances with my safety. You haven't convinced me that Sterling's a killer, but you've convinced me that seeing him might involve taking an unnecessary risk."

"Might?"

She smiled at me in a way that seemed full of understanding and wisdom. The wisdom was bearded with just the slightest tease. I found it all quite disarming. Me and women? What a frigging mess.

With my thumb and index finger I spread my mustache away from the center of my lip. Holly was watching me carefully, waiting to see where I was heading next; I thought she knew that I hadn't come back to her door to ask her about Sterling and Brian Miles and to make sure she had my phone number.

Holly probably knew things about men that I wouldn't know for the rest of my life.

In the grand scheme that was probably an okay thing.

I said, "You and your husband, you and Mark? Did your, what did you call it before, your 'imaginative' sex life—that's right? I got that? Did it include, you know, other people, other couples? Sexually, I mean. I don't know if I'm asking that exactly right. But what I'm wanting to know is . . . well . . ."

My voice disappeared like stormwater down an open manhole. *Swooosh.*

"Is this a professional inquiry?"

"Actually, no, no, it's not. It's, um, . . . it's personal. It's something I'm struggling with . . . myself."

I watched muscles change in her face. Her mouth softened, and the tendons along her jaw slackened. Fine lines erupted alongside her eyes. She said, "Yes, it did. It included other people sometimes. We were active swingers long before we were married."

"And it didn't . . ." Some questions are harder to ask than others. Those seemed to be the only kind I was asking. Or trying to ask. I wasn't doing a bang-up job.

"Didn't what?"

"Cause problems? For the two of you? In your marriage? Fidelity, and trust, you know? Feelings weren't hurt?"

She shook her head. "Far from it. This may sound funny, but it was all about trust for us. Mark knew every man I was involved with sexually, and vice versa. We each had total veto power over the other's partners. What we did enriched us." She glanced back to make sure Zach was still engaged with his Legos. "This is a hard thing to explain. Sex with other people brought us closer."

"It did?"

"Yes."

"It helped with trust?"

"No. We had trust going in. Honesty. Respect. That never wavered."

I was perplexed the way I'm perplexed by Stephen Hawking. The words he uses are English, but after one or two paragraphs I feel like I'm reading Armenian. Same thing right then with Holly. The arithmetic of the coupling was simple enough. Two plus two equals four. I shouldn't have been so mystified by the equation. But I was.

"Trust?" I said again, and then I sighed away some of my exasperation. "I wish I understood it better. I really do. It seems that . . .

with you being . . . and him . . . I just don't quite get it. I'll think about it some more, though. I will."

"I appreciate that. I appreciate that you try to understand. Some people don't. Most people don't."

"Artie?" I said.

She laughed. "Artie, indeed. Have a happy Thanksgiving, Detective. I'd invite you to join us for supper, but under the circumstances . . ."

"Of course, of course. Artie wouldn't be happy I was there. You, too, Holly, you have a good holiday, too. Don't let Artie ruin it for everybody."

I pivoted to leave but stopped and looked over my shoulder. She was still at the door.

"Would Mark have been okay with Sterling? As a sexual partner for you? Just curious."

The face she made was rueful. "No. No, he wouldn't. Sterling is . . . firmly on the wrong side of the Brad Pitt line. That's where Mark's comfort level stopped. At the Brad Pitt line."

She leaned out the door, took a step toward me, and touched her lips to my cheek. That was good-bye.

Carmen waited for me to get settled, pull my seat belt on, and start the engine before she said, "Holly seems like a nice girl. I'm sorry I got off on the wrong foot with her."

I smiled at the irony. "She is a nice girl. My mother maybe wouldn't think so, but she is. She's nice."

Carmen didn't want anything to do with my comment about my mother. Wise on her part. "Did you get what we needed?" she asked.

"To decide if Holly's in danger? I don't know. How about we'll decide that together? Let's go someplace, and I'll tell you what she said, and we'll put our heads together and decide if we should spend Thanksgiving hanging around South Bend waiting for Sterling or whether we should spend it doing something else."

"Do you want to go back to the Days Inn? We can talk there. There's some kind of coffee shop on the corner."

"Nah. I don't think so. Where's the campus from here? I'd like to see that. That way you can tell your dad you've been there, and . . . anyway, I've heard some interesting things about the basilica."

FIFTY-FIVE

ALAN

Dawn broke on Thanksgiving with a cold front blowing furiously over the Divide. The pressure change was preceded by winds that caused the big panes of glass in the living room to hum ominously. I wasted a few minutes standing on the warm side of the humming glass watching the morning sun light up the sky and reflect off the quartz crystals embedded in the granite planes of the Flatirons.

Special.

I'd awakened with a plan. My plan was to make a plan. I tracked down an index card, no lines, and listed all the things I had to do that morning. Most of the items on the list were domestic—*Grace, bath! Dogs, walk*—or culinary—*Turkey, clean & dry.* One was fantasy—*Bike ride??* And one was business—*Gibbs?*

Although I wasn't usually a list-making guy, I felt better knowing that I had a battle plan for the day, which promised to be convoluted, and enjoyed a flash of empathy for my old college roommate, who had always carried an index card with a to-do list in his shirt pocket. When each list's tasks were completed, he would immediately grab a fresh card and scrawl a single line at the bottom: *Start a new list.*

With Diane's admonition about hurdling in my head, I began to leap over the items on my list one by one. I'd made a good head start on the day's complicated kitchen preparations before Grace announced, loudly, that she was ready for her holiday to begin.

Midmorning Lauren joined Grace and me in the kitchen. Lauren had managed a few hours of sleep after her pool-playing marathon, and her mood was softer than I'd seen since the previous weekend. I could see my wife reemerging from the nefarious cocoon of Solumedrol in which she'd been imprisoned. It felt great. She sipped some juice and coffee and offered a couple of gentle suggestions about my cooking techniques, and our little core-family-size turkey found its way into the oven just about on time.

That's when my pager informed me that someone had left me a message at the office. I picked up the phone and checked my voicemail. Gibbs. The number she'd left was for her cell.

I excused myself from my girls and called Gibbs back from the living room, adopting an office demeanor before I spoke my first words. The wind had quieted to less than gale force, and the glass had ceased humming. The sky was as clear as my daughter's conscience, and the mountains were close enough to touch. I said, "This is Dr. Gregory."

"Hi, it's me. Gibbs. Thanks for calling back. I'm up in Vail."

At that moment I was gazing vaguely southwest toward Vail. Fifty miles of mountains and one imposing Continental Divide stood in the way, but I was pretty sure I was looking almost exactly in the right direction. Between here and there, cake-batter clouds seemed to be shadowing all the high valleys. "You're safe?" I asked. It wasn't a great question, but it was better than my first impulse, which had been to ask "Was it windy up there this morning, too?"

"I wanted someone to know where I was. In case something happens. You know, in case Sterling shows up."

That thought gave me a chill.

"Safe House is open on holidays, Gibbs. I'm happy to make a call for you."

"The nice hotels were all sold out. I'm in a crappy place by the highway. Do you hear the noise? The trucks going by? Sterling would never look for me here." She giggled. "Never."

Just for the record, I thought it was important to remind myself that crappy hotels in Vail aren't exactly like crappy hotels in Baltimore or Detroit. I told myself to imagine a cheap cabin on an expensive cruise ship.

"You're okay?" I said.

"Yes, I am."

"I appreciate that you checked in with me. We're set for Monday morning, right? Same time?"

"Sure, yes. I'll be there. Do you know where Detective Purdy is? Is he coming home for the holiday? I haven't heard from him. I'd feel much better knowing he was close by."

The purpose of a psychotherapist is not—is not—to provide information to a patient that is unrelated to her care. The fact that Sam was in South Bend was definitely unrelated to Gibbs's care.

"I can't help you with that," I said.

"If you hear from him, would you ask him to call me? His cell phone isn't working. I can't reach him."

"It's not an appropriate role for me. To deliver messages to people for you. If I'm going to prove helpful, it's important to recognize the unique nature of our relationship." My voice was even, but I was thinking, *I'm not your damned errand boy.*

I caught myself. Why was I so annoyed? Was this high school revisited? Was Gibbs playing Teri Reginelli, wondering if I knew where she could find my friend Sean?

And was I reacting now the way I reacted then, by being a spurned fool?

If that's what was happening, that was countertransference. Textbook countertransference. It was not a pretty picture.

She huffed, "I'm not asking for a big favor, Alan. Just pass along the message, please."

"I'm sorry, but I can't do that."

Clinically, I was standing on solid ground. Communicating with a patient about the location of one of my friends was not an appropriate therapeutic role. But experience had taught me that when countertransference melded perfectly with what appeared to be appropriate treatment, danger often ensued.

"You *won't* do that," she corrected.

"Okay, I won't do that. It's not an appropriate role for me. That you're asking me to do it might be important in terms of understanding some of the issues we've been discussing in your therapy. We can talk about it more during your appointment on Monday."

"Am I being dismissed? Is that your way of telling me that you and I are done talking for now?"

"Gibbs, I'm glad you're safe. But I think anything that is not an emergency can wait until we meet on Monday morning."

"If Sterling shows up and knocks on my door, I'll call you. That would be an emergency, right? My murderous husband at my door? You'll be able to find a couple of minutes to chat about that, right?"

She hung up.

I thought, *That went well.*

Forty minutes passed before I realized what I'd missed. I'd completed one basting cycle with the turkey and was about to go back for the second when it hit me out of the blue, even though I hadn't spent the interim consciously thinking about either Gibbs or her phone call.

The important clinical issue wasn't that Gibbs wanted my help tracking down Sam, that she apparently wanted to alter the nature of the therapeutic relationship so that my status devolved from helper to mere errand-runner.

No, the issue was that she was so desperate to find Sam at all.

Why?

"Are you going to baste that thing or just stand there letting all the heat out of the oven?"

I turned. Lauren had bathed and put on some makeup, and what was much more important was that she'd put on a smile. She was limping, but she wasn't carrying the walking stick.

I closed the oven door and said, "Hi."

FIFTY-SIX

SAM

The Basilica of the Sacred Heart was a monument to something. Had to be. I spent ten minutes walking around inside the giant church like a tourist at some midwestern Vatican, but I couldn't decide precisely what the pompous shrine was intended to honor. God? I came from a tradition of simple prairie churches with inadequate heat in the winter and nonexistent air-conditioning in the summer. I wasn't raised to pray to a God who sat around in heaven with His saints counting His cathedrals and basilicas like Midas counting his gold; a God who cared whether the glass in His windows was stained or the bronze on His altars was gilded.

Certainly not a God who gave a hoot whether Notre Dame beat Michigan. My old man once told me that if God cares who wins a football game while people are starving in Africa, we can all just give up. That hell on earth is just around the corner. My old man was not a genius, far from it, but he got that right.

Carmen was an observant lady. Being observant, she didn't waste any time before she asked why I seemed so interested in the massive pipe organ inside the basilica. I told her it was a thing I had, a fascination with organs and organ music. The truth was, I didn't know a division from a manual or a pipe from a stop. But it didn't make a whole lot of difference what I knew or didn't know: Carmen liked disco. I figured arguing musical taste with the woman would be about as fruitful as trying to teach a dog to gargle.

All that mattered to me at that moment was that the precise location where Holly and Sterling had had their profane tryst was going to remain their secret, and mine, and maybe God's—that is, if during their coupling He hadn't been too occupied watching the Notre Dame–Michigan game or hadn't been totally blinded by the quasi-Gothic glitz of His Indiana basilica.

Memory told me that one of God's commandments to Moses had to do with coveting thy neighbor's wife, so I was assuming that He maintained some interest in marital fidelity and duly noted the fact that Sterling and Holly had fornicated in front of His fancy pipe organ.

Carmen and I moved back outside and stood for a moment beneath the vaulting spire that dominated the front of the basilica. I said, "I hope God cares what happened to those four women, and I hope He cares what happens to Holly Malone and to Gibbs."

She touched my hand. "Feeling philosophical, Sam?"

I couldn't tell whether my hand was cold and she was all heat or vice versa. But the thermal contrast between her flesh and mine had all my attention. I said, "Kind of, I guess."

Carmen had listened carefully to my edited version of Holly's story—I transformed it from an X-rated melodrama to a suggestive PG-13 and totally omitted any reference to the Basilica of the Sacred Heart—on the way over to the Notre Dame campus. I was ready to hear her thoughts on how we were going to spend the rest of our day.

"Is she in danger?" I asked. "What do you think?"

"Maybe."

I laughed. The campus, deserted for the holiday, chewed on my guffaw and spit it back at me in fractured echoes.

"Well," I said, "that settles it."

Carmen laughed, too.

Our hands were still touching. The top of my hand rested against the side of hers. It was either an accident, or it wasn't. I figured that was just the way we had planned it. Total deniability. Know this: Cops are better at deniability than just about anybody but politicians and corporate executives.

Carmen grabbed two of my fingers and tugged me away from the church. When I chanced to return the pressure, she pulled away and stuffed her hands into the pockets of her coat. I did the same.

Didn't mean a thing.

She yanked us back to the work we were doing. "Let's assume that the way Sterling met Holly is similar to the way he met the other women. Can we do that?"

"Not Louise, the stewardess."

"Flight attendant."

"Don't get me started. I liked stewardesses. I liked waitresses. Turns out I'm not so fond of flight attendants and servers. Why is that? Sterling met Louise on a flight she was working, right? Isn't that the story? And he met Holly on the Internet, right? But I don't think it really matters. I don't think the meeting-them part is as important as the sex-with-them part."

"You're probably right. He met them. By chance, socially, at work, on the Internet—whatever. He met them. He made a point of meeting them. And he had sex with them."

"I don't think it's that simple," I said. "The sex with Holly wasn't . . . pedestrian. She made it clear that that was important. Not only to her but to him, too. He wasn't just into infidelity, he was into . . . sexual adventure. He was into women who might be as adventurous as he was."

"This another interest of yours, Sam? Like pipe organs?"

With the tease, her voice tingled a little.

"Don't make this more difficult than it already is for me."

"Holly's that adventurous?"

"Mmm-hmm," I said. Not only did I not want to violate Holly's confidence, I didn't want to have to repeat her story out loud to another human being. Especially not another human being of Holly's gender.

Carmen could tell. She Cliff-Noted the thing for us. "He met them, he gauged their interest, and he joined them on some sexual adventure. So why are four of them dead?"

"We know some things about Louise and Holly, right? We know they both survived their first sexual encounters with Sterling. Can we assume that the other women did, too? That there was an initial encounter—mutually satisfying—and that he went back a second time, or a third or fourth, and that's when he killed them?"

We covered a good chunk of dormant Notre Dame turf before Carmen answered. "Yes, for now we can assume that. We almost have to."

"That means that Holly's now in danger. Pure and simple."

"Maybe," she said.

"Maybe?"

"Sam, nobody was looking for Sterling when he killed these other women. He had the cover of anonymity. Now? He has to assume that we're after him."

"Is this devil's advocate time?"

"The risk factor has changed. He has to think that some cop—somebody like you and me—doesn't believe he drowned. If I'm him, I'm lying low."

"Why? The Georgia cops think he's dead. My guess is that your superiors have already suggested you go home, too. Or even ordered you back to work." Her eyes confirmed my supposition. "I bet you're using vacation days right now, aren't you?"

"Yes, I am."

She could have lied to me. Would've been easy. I said, "Sterling might think he's home free, Carmen. That this is like a free play in football, you know? After an offsides call?"

"We still don't know his motive, Sam. And we don't know where Brian Miles fits."

She was right about that. We certainly didn't know where Brian Miles fit. But the possibilities concerned me. I said, "Half the collars I get I never understand what the idiots were thinking, Carmen. Criminals are goofy."

"Goofy? Is that a Colorado word?"

"Nope. Minnesota." Intentionally, I said Minnesota the natural northern way, accentuating the "so" syllable so that it became "soooo."

"That's what that accent is? Minnesota? That's where you're from?"

"The Iron Range. That's up north."

"Interesting," she said.

"Not really."

I wasn't sure she was going to let it rest there.

She did. I was impressed.

Ten more steps. I asked, "Do you think they call this the Quad?"

"Don't know," she said.

On the way back over to Holly Malone's neighborhood, Carmen said, "Since I left San Jose, this is the most time I've spent with another cop without being asked why I left town without my pension."

"Some things are personal." I was thinking about Sherry and me, but I was also thinking about Alan and that bug in his office, and about Sterling and Holly and their time down near the pedals of the pipe organ. Secrets? They don't mean shit. "You want to tell me what happened before you changed jobs, that's cool. You don't, I understand completely. I'm sure you had your reasons."

Traffic was light on the streets of South Bend. Everybody was either watching football or cooking a turkey or taking a nap or playing with nieces or nephews or grandkids that they hadn't seen in way too long. In a perfect world I wouldn't be spending my holiday driving through the streets of some strange midwestern town with a California cop who liked disco.

In a perfect world Simon and I would be cuddled up in front of the TV making fun of the Detroit Lions.

But in the imperfect world where I spent most of my time, being with Carmen wasn't the worst of alternatives.

Carmen seemed to read my thoughts, sort of. "This your first holiday by yourself?"

"My wife took our kid to see her parents."

"Yeah, right, that's the reason you're alone. And I left San Jose because I like the beach."

It was a good comeback. The traffic light changed to red over the intersection in front of me. I thought of running it—mine was the only car in sight—but I braked instead. I tried to think of something smart to say back to Carmen, but nothing came to mind.

"It's mine," Carmen confessed after we'd been sitting at the light for a while. "My first holiday without my daughter. And it's not going to be the last, either."

I admitted something to her that I hadn't even admitted to myself. "Probably won't be my last, either."

She touched my knee. A quick little fingertip thing. There, and then gone.

"It's easier to be working," I said.

"Yes," she agreed.

I pulled into the parking lot of a gas station so we could both use the john. As we walked inside, I was thinking that Carmen and I had covered a lot of important emotional ground in that one block of West Angela Boulevard Road in South Bend, Indiana, and we'd done it without using too many words.

If damn Alan had been in the backseat, he would have made us jaw on and on until we reached the Canadian border and probably wanted to kill each other.

Until we definitely wanted to kill him.

I wondered how he was doing with his problems. The office thing. How Lauren was feeling. Whether that thing he'd made for his big dog was still keeping her tongue off her paw.

I'd call him later on, after I called Simon, probably just about the time they were sitting down to their turkey dinner.

FIFTY-SEVEN

ALAN

Lauren was trying. She was really, really trying. As I cleaned up the kitchen counters and readied Grace for her afternoon nap, I knew that behind my wife's beautiful closed lips her white teeth were busy biting down on the tip of her soft tongue over my various venial sins of omission or commission in the kitchen or the nursery.

I could tell that she was grateful for the way I was picking up the domestic load. And I was grateful for her diligent effort at smoothing out the speed bumps that figurative boatloads of Solumedrol had injected into her mood.

While Grace slept, Lauren and I snuck in a quickie. The urge surprised both of us, I think.

An embrace became a kiss became hands beneath shirts became a jog to the bedroom.

It was amazing to me how tentative two married people could be with each other while they were rushing headlong into compressing a familiar, intimate act into an unfamiliar window of time after an extended period of tension. While we were stripping each other naked we were simultaneously sprinting across a field of eggshells. Thankfully, we reached the finish line before the time limit, which, of course, was Grace's awakening.

In the naked moments after—naked both literally and figuratively—Lauren said, "You know Dennis, right? He's one of our paralegals."

"Sure." Dennis Lopes was happily gay, buff enough to be selected Mr. January on a firefighters' calendar and, as far as I could tell, solely responsible for the fiscal well-being of Ralph Lauren's clothing empire. In a field that's replete with professionals who have more agendas than a cut diamond has facets, Dennis was a hell of a nice guy who said what was on his mind.

Nonetheless, I couldn't fathom what he was doing making an appearance in our bed at that particular moment.

While I considered the destination of Lauren's segue, I couldn't help but notice that her diet of IV steroids was beginning to turn her usually svelte frame more Rubenesque.

"He was walking between the Justice Center and the Court House earlier in the week, and he went down Walnut."

Dennis was a fitness nut. That he walked, rather than drove, between the two county buildings was no surprise. "He went right past my office," I said.

"Yes." She paused. "He was on the opposite sidewalk, and he saw Jim Zebid park his car and walk into your building. He mentioned it to me yesterday."

Instinctively, I pulled the sheet up to my waist. But I didn't reply.

She went on, her tone full of caution. "I hope you're not seeing him for therapy, babe."

"You do? Why?"

From the way she blinked—she held her eyes closed for a split second too long—I could tell that she had been hoping that Jim had been in the building to see Diane, or even to visit the funny Pakistani man who ran his software empire out of our tiny upstairs, and that she no longer had the luxury of that illusion.

"Jim and I have a history."

Reflexively, I teased. "Like Muhammad Ali and Joe Frazier?"

"What?"

I stopped teasing. "Yes, I know you have a history. I know you've beat him up a few times in court. That assault thing at Crossroads comes to mind. The one where his client was claiming self-defense after he threw a hot dog at the counter girl at Orange Julius."

"That's not what I mean," she said softly.

"What do you mean?"

"Lots of things happen at your office that you don't tell me about. Your work, your patients, right? Confidential things?"

"Of course."

"Me too. There are lots of things that go on at the Justice Center that I don't tell you. Things I know because of my position that I shouldn't, or can't, share with you. You know that?"

"Yes."

"Well, one of them involves Jim." She stood and began to pull on some clothes. "I wish you weren't seeing him."

From my earlier reaction, she knew that I was.

"You sound serious."

She opened her purple eyes wide and forced a sick smile. "I am. I wish you knew what I knew."

I stood, too, and began to pull on some boxers. While I did, I worked out the choreography to a little two-step that would allow me to tell Lauren something important without telling Lauren anything at all. All I said was "That problem I told you about at my office? With the bug?"

She was in the process of pulling a camisole over her head. "No?" she said into the silk. "He's not . . . Don't tell me he's . . . ."

Ethically, I couldn't respond to her question. Practically, we both knew I didn't have to.

She turned her back to me while she tugged a thick cotton sweater over her head. I admit I was having trouble staying focused on the topic at hand. Steroids or no steroids, I still liked her ass.

"Alan, you need to call Jon Younger. Today, at home."

Jon Younger was an attorney friend. He handled civil matters. Like, say, malpractice.

I said, "On Thanksgiving?"

She sat on the edge of the bed and began to slide her legs into some fleece tights. "Yes."

"Why?"

"Because I don't know what Jim might have planned."

"Planned?"

"Look at me," she said.

I did.

"Your first appointment with Jim? Was it after the Fourth of July?"

I blinked.

"That's exactly what I was afraid of."

Okay, Jim had come to see me for therapy after some confrontation with Lauren in the DA's office that occurred around Independence Day.

"Lauren, your history with Jim? He has reason to be . . . I don't know . . . angry at you?"

"Call Jon. He knows the background. Give him a heads-up. I'll feel better."

From down the hall came the not-so-soothing trill of a tear-laced "Mom Mom Mom." Grace tended to throw the few words in her repertoire together in unfettered strings, oblivious—or disdainful—of punctuation.

Emily stood at the sound of Grace's call, and her paw umbrella immediately *clack-clacked* on the wood floors.

Lauren said, "I got Grace."

I said, "I'll get some tape. I got Emily."

Lauren and I and the two dogs all ran into one another in the doorway on the way out of the bedroom. Lauren hugged me and said, "I'm really sorry."

She took off for the nursery.

The gravitas of Lauren's alarm about Jim Zebid wasn't quite registering with me. I didn't see anything about the mess I was in that couldn't wait until Monday. Interrupting Jon Younger's Thanksgiving to warn him that I had a pissed-off patient didn't make much sense to me at all.

*   *   *

While Lauren played with Grace, I made a different call, to a different attorney. I called Casey Sparrow.

Casey was a criminal defense attorney. She was smart, brazen, and fearless. She had a head of red hair that she'd had no more luck taming than most prosecutors had had taming her.

As I punched in the long string of numbers, I knew that an even longer rope of electron activity would be carrying my voice up thirty-five hundred feet of the Front Range to Casey's rustic home on the Peak-to-Peak Highway below the Continental Divide.

"Casey? It's Alan Gregory."

"Oh, no. Not tonight. Who is it this time? You or Lauren?" Casey had once defended Lauren against murder charges. That chain of events had started with an after-hours call not too unlike this one.

"Don't worry, neither of us has been arrested. Listen, I'm sorry to call on Thanksgiving, Casey."

"But?"

"Do you have a minute to gossip with me?"

"Gossip?" Her voice went suddenly girly. I imagined that she curled her legs beneath her and stripped an earring from her ear to get more comfortable with the telephone.

I stepped out onto the deck and closed the door behind me. "Yes."

"My partner's family is due for dinner any minute. You can have me until they arrive. After that I'm going to be the best damn hostess in the high country."

I didn't waste any time. "You know Jim Zebid?"

Hesitation. Then, "Yes." The yes wasn't the least bit girly. The yes was almost totally "oh shit."

"Something happened with him and Lauren last summer."

"We're gossiping, right?" she asked.

"That's right. That's all this is, just gossip."

"Lauren won't tell you, right?"

"Right."

"I shouldn't, either."

I knew she probably shouldn't, but I shut my mouth while she did whatever carnival act she felt she needed to do to juggle the moral aspects of her dilemma. Given her role with the defense bar, I figured whatever Casey knew about Jim and Lauren she knew because of courthouse gossip. Thus, her hands weren't tied with the same ethical twine that bound Lauren's.

Gossip is gossip.

Casey said, "Okay. I heard . . . I heard she turned him in to the Supreme Court last summer for disciplinary action."

"For?"

"Serious stuff."

I said, "He's still practicing law."

"These things take time."

"What did he do?"

"Do I have to?" Just a little girly.

"Unfortunately."

"He had a client who was accused of forgery, a petty thing. I don't know the details, but I don't think the facts are important. Lauren was prosecuting."

"Yes."

"Leave me out of this, Alan."

"You know I will, Casey."

"The rumor is that . . . hell. In lieu of legal fees, Jim was *schtupping* the guy's wife."

I was speechless.

I heard a doorbell ring in the background. Casey said, "Oops, got to go pull on my hostess's apron. Jim's defense, by the way, is that it was her idea. His client's wife's. She proposed the bargain. Have a good Thanksgiving. Best to Lauren."

"Casey?"

"Yes."

"Thanks, and good luck with Brenda's parents."

She laughed. "I'll need it. Domestic, I'm not."

I clicked the phone off and stared out toward the mountains south of town. The sky that enveloped the mountains near Eldorado was the color of an old quarter. The wondrous rich colors of autumn were almost gone; the beiges and grays and blacks and whites of winter filled the entire landscape from mountains to plains.

Jim Zebid's first appointment with me had taken place during the beginning of August. In the intervening weeks he'd never mentioned anything about an investigation into his conduct. He'd certainly never mentioned a conflict with my wife.

Why had he come to see me? I hadn't been sure before, but I'd been working under a clinical assumption that it was because his chronic anxiety was becoming increasingly dysphoric.

That old assumption was mutating into something new. I was guessing that Jim had been hoping to trap me into doing something that could be construed as malpractice so he could get even with Lauren.

Now he had me by the balls. And I didn't see a way to free them from his grasp.

FIFTY-EIGHT

SAM

"Somebody's going to see us sitting here and call the cops."

Carmen and I had pushed the seats all the way back on the Cherokee. We were parked on the same block as the night before, diagonally across from Holly Malone's house. But this time we were a couple of houses farther away. It wasn't a neighborhood where people sat in cars parked on the street. Inconspicuous we weren't.

"That's always a risk on this kind of stakeout, Sam."

"This is different, though. Usually you and me, we're the cops. Here we're persona non grata."

"Okay, you're a Craftsman-style expert, and you speak Latin. What do I have on my hands here?"

I went through the list in my head: Fat-ass cop. Iron Ranger with man-boobs. Schlub whose family dumped him for the holidays. Post-MI jerkface who's running around the country like he has the heart of a teenager.

Don't know why, but right then I reminded myself that Gibbs liked me. It helped a little, as sad as that fact was.

"I am what I am." Until the words were out of my mouth, I didn't realize I was quoting Popeye.

Carmen tried hard to swallow a laugh.

I laughed first. She followed immediately. "Go ahead," I said. "Say I'm a complete idiot."

"A cop who's a Renaissance man. Quick as a wink from Frank Lloyd Wright to Popeye—I'm impressed."

"You done?"

She was wiping tears from her eyes. "Yeah, I'm done. Almost. So what are we looking for exactly?"

My neck was as far out as I was planning on sticking it. "This was your idea, Carmen. Remember?"

She reached into her bag and took a reprinted five-by-seven from her purse and stuck it to the center of my dashboard with some gum I didn't even realize she was chewing.

The photo was of Sterling. He and his buddy Brian looked like a couple of male models.

"Who names her kid Sterling?" Carmen mused.

I didn't know the answer to that question. "He's pretty, right?" I asked. "Holly called him pretty."

Carmen gazed at the picture as though she'd never really looked at it before. "Yeah. He's pretty-boy pretty."

"Not your type?"

"No, unfortunately, he is my type. My type—historically speaking—could best be described as 'assholes.' And from everything I hear about his life until the moment his rental car crossed that bridge over the Ochlockonee River, Sterling Storey was an asshole. Is an asshole."

"Assholes?" It wasn't much of a response, but it was the best I could do.

"Sad as it sounds, that about covers it. If I'm into a guy, he's going to turn out to be a bona fide asshole."

"Assholes have bona fides? Like diplomats?"

She found that pretty funny. "The ones I fall for do. I only take them in if they're credentialed." Her laughter stopped as fast as it started. "That's what happened in San Jose. My asshole that time was a judge. He had credentials up his wazoo."

Carmen had pushed open the front door. I walked in. "Yeah? What did he do to you?"

"My daughter and I had just moved in with him, were just getting settled in his house. I was in love." She spread out the lone syllable of "love" so that it sounded like a crowd. "She called me from school, said she'd forgotten her calculator—it was one of those fancy ones with all those buttons, you know? I gave her a hard time about her irresponsibility and then I went home to get it for her. I'm a softy."

"He was there?" I asked. The fact that he was there was necessary to the story, but it wasn't sufficient to explain walking away from a pension. I knew there would be more.

"With my daughter's best friend's mother. I'd introduced the two of them at a volleyball game a couple weeks before."

Nasty situation. But it still wasn't sufficient.

"On the stairs of all places," she added. "He was doing her from behind."

Interesting detail, though it didn't compare with what I'd heard about Holly and the basilica. But that wasn't it, either. "It got ugly?" I asked.

"You could say that. I went berserk—I could take what he was doing to me, but what he was doing to my daughter and her friend? Shit! I screamed the woman's naked ass right out of the house, but that was just a warm-up for what I wanted to lay on him. I started yelling and cursing—did I tell you I have a temper? Well, I do. And he took one step forward and . . . the asshole hit me. A hard slap right across the face. It was such a shock, it took me a second to recover, but then I started up again, and he slapped me again, harder still. I couldn't fucking believe it."

"That's when you should've left, huh?"

"Would have been better, yeah. But I didn't, I wasn't ready to walk yet. So I started yelling all over again. He made a fist, showed it to me—shook it at me, really—and came at me again."

"You shot him?"

"You already know this story?"

"No. But I know if you just beat the crap out of him, you'd still have your pension, and you wouldn't be living in Orange County."

"I shot him."

"Nuts?"

"Foot. Nuts was tempting, though. Real tempting. Think I might've gotten time for shooting him in the nuts."

"He's still on the bench?"

"Of course." She sighed, the exhale carrying a full cargo of cynicism. "He was indifferent to hurting me, Sam. He didn't care. About the affair, about the slaps, about the pension. None of it. He didn't care."

"How's his foot?"

She smiled just a tiny bit. "He doesn't play squash anymore."

Across the way a car pulled to a stop in front of the Malone house. An SUV, one of those little stubby Lexus SUVs that were scampering all over Boulder like Japanese roaches. I hated them less than I hated the really big ones, the Fords and the Cadillacs and the Lincolns, but I hated them nonetheless.

No particular reason. I just did. Actually, it was one of the few things that my friend Alan and I agreed upon.

"I bet that's Artie."

"Who's Artie?"

"The brother-in-law I told you about. He's an asshole."

Carmen perked up. "Really?"

"Not your kind of asshole, I'm afraid. No bona fides, and I suspect that Artie's the kind of asshole who doesn't like his women to be packing heat."

She sat back again. "Ahhh. One of those."

While we chatted, I was checking the parade of clowns climbing out of the little silver Lexus. Artie had been driving, no surprise there. A slightly older, severely less perky version of Holly climbed out of the front passenger seat, and three way-too-well-behaved, way-too-well-dressed children exited the rear.

Carmen said, "No Sterling in that bunch."

"Afraid not. We wait." I touched her hand. "Sorry about San Jose."

"Yeah."

Twenty minutes later I said, "Shit."

We'd been silent the whole time, and Carmen was startled by my exclamation.

"What?" she asked. She was staring out the windshield as though she figured she'd missed something important at the Malone house.

"I forgot to turn my phone back on. Damn." I hit the little on button, and the phone came alive and immediately started probing the atmosphere for a cell tower to mate with. Once the slutty little thing had finished getting intimate with some new anonymous electronic partner, I checked my voicemail.

The first message was from Simon.

"Hey, Carmen," I said. "Give me a minute? I want to call my kid."

"Sure, be good to stretch my legs. I'll walk around the block again, see what I can see."

Simon and I talked football and relatives and hockey and snowmobiles—that part was new for us; he'd never ridden one before this trip—for about three minutes, which was about all the conversation he could ever manage on the phone. But the contact with him eased something inside me that desperately needed easing. When he was saying his version of good-bye, he asked if I was going to be at his grandpa's in time for turkey, and the question almost sliced me in two. In my heart I felt that awful sucking thing you hear when the cranberry sauce is sliding reluctantly out of the can.

To distract myself from the reality of the fact that I was in South Bend and Simon was up in Minnesota, I went back to my cell phone and scrolled through the other messages.

Lucy, just wishing me a happy Thanksgiving.

Yeah, you too.

And Gibbs. Sounding a little frantic, letting me know she was in Vail. I tried her back but didn't get an answer.

No call from Alan. That surprised me.

Carmen climbed back in the car. She was shivering just a little. She should have worn her coat.

"Anything?" I asked.

"Nothing. No Sterling, no Brian."

I said, "Gibbs called, left me a message. She's anxious. One of us should be watching her, you know."

I expected Carmen to disagree with me. She didn't. "Probably. She's as much at risk as Holly is, but she wasn't as cooperative about being watched as Holly is. Gibbs should be in Safe House."

"Yeah, she should. Maybe Holly should be, too." I liked that idea. Hell, if we could talk Holly into going to South Bend's version of Safe House, I could drop off Carmen at O'Hare and maybe—just maybe—get to Minnesota before Simon crawled into bed. I could read him a Bialosky or two, and he could explain to me what he found so fetching about that little bear.

But Holly wasn't about to go to Safe House. Part of me knew that a part of Holly was enjoying the current situation. Where sex was concerned, she was a roller-coaster, bungee-jumping freak. In this situation there was more than enough danger to get her sexual heart really pumping. Add in a heavy dose of anticipation—it was clear that anticipation stirred something in her that had been dormant in me for a long, long time—and for her this could be almost as big a rush as sneaking into the pope's bed in the Vatican.

Carmen and I cooling our heels out here on the curb meant that there were strangers watching Holly's every move and, even better for her, the possibility of judgmental Artie walking around any corner. Yep, the setup was almost as good as that afternoon in the Basilica of the Sacred Heart.

All that, and a turkey in the oven, too.

No Native Americans. No Pilgrims. But nonetheless, for Holly it had the makings of a Thanksgiving to remember.

The dashboard clock informed me that it was exactly three minutes after four o'clock.

Why was that important? Sometime in the last couple of hours, a world or two away from South Bend, Mary Ellen Wolf had carved a long slender knife through the crisp skin on the outside of a beautiful Georgia turducken. After a little downward pressure—it would take just a little because after eighteen hours in a slow oven those nested birds would be as tender as a grandmother's whisper—the sequential beauty would be revealed. Turkey, duck, chicken, followed by some dark andouille, and then all the glorious components of oyster stuffing.

There are times in life when you just know that the train has left the station without you and that it's not coming back around, ever. A county fair and a girl you could have kissed. A job and a promotion you might have had. Some friends in a beat-up old car and a trip you might have taken.

Twins, and a meal you might have eaten.

The Wolf sisters and that turducken were going to haunt me for a while. I was 110 percent sure about that.

A foot away from me Carmen was doing something with her fingernails and a sharp wooden stick. Sherry did the same thing occasionally, but Sherry doing it never captured much of my attention. Carmen doing it did. She distracted me even more when she started humming the melody of one of those tunes she'd sung the night before at bedtime in the Days Inn.

FIFTY-NINE

ALAN

While the turkey was resting on the cutting board prior to carving, Lauren asked me if I'd spoken with Jon Younger.

"Maybe after dinner," I said. "But I'm still not convinced this can't wait until Monday."

She kissed me. "Call him. Please."

Dinner? The turkey was dry, the gravy a little salty, and the cranberries overcooked, but the caramelized Brussels sprouts were perfection, and the merlot that Lauren had picked was as supple as a young dancer. Jonas, our neighbor Adrienne's son, and his nanny joined us for the meal because Adrienne was taking call at the hospital. Grace made it through the entire affair without a meltdown, and Lauren fought her steroid malaise with a determination that was inspiring.

The dogs slept like dogs.

It was a pretty damn good Thanksgiving.

Lauren and I cleaned up the kitchen together. I grabbed my pager off my hip a moment after I started the dishwasher and promptly excused myself to make a couple of phone calls. Five minutes later I tracked Lauren down at the pool table in time to watch her rerack the balls and begin to fondle the white cue ball in a way that made me just the slightest bit jealous.

I said, "Our guests are gone?"

She nodded. "Jonas was approaching a cliff at high speed. We thought he should have a mattress under him when he went over it."

I pointed at my pager and said, "Emergency, unfortunately. I have to go into the office for a couple of hours."

She narrowed her eyes. "Yeah?"

I said, "Yeah."

She didn't believe me.

She leaned over the table and with a single powerful stroke turned the triangle of pool balls into a physics lesson in vectors.

I didn't make the third phone call, the crucial phone call, until I was in my car on the way downtown to my office.

"Jim? Alan Gregory."

"Alan. This is a surprise."

"Are you out somewhere, Jim? Am I disturbing your dinner?" The truth was that I didn't really care whether I was intruding, but feigning politeness was called for, and I was feigning politeness.

"I'm with some friends. We just finished. What's up?"

"It's about the problem with . . . your client's secrets. I have some information that you should know."

"I'm listening."

"I'm not comfortable going into it on the phone. Could you drop by my office later on? Maybe five o'clock?"

"On Thanksgiving? This is necessary?"

"I think you should know what's going on. Some of what I want to talk with you about other people already know, so I'd like to bring you up to speed as soon as possible in case some of it becomes public, Jim."

"Really. Five o'clock?"

"I'm heading into the office now, and I have an emergency—something with another patient—that I need to take care of first. She and I should be done by five at the latest."

"See you then," he said.

When I arrived in downtown Boulder, I detoured into the parking lot of one of the banks on Walnut near Fourteenth and withdrew the maximum amount that was permitted from an ATM. My plan required cash. Quite a bit of it, actually.

A few blocks farther west I pulled down the driveway of the building that held my office. She was waiting for me on the steps that led up to the French doors at the rear of the building.

"You got the money?"

I flashed the thick pile of twenties.

"Let's go, then, get this done. They're holding dessert until I get back. My sister makes a sweet potato pie that . . ."

Tayisha's words just faded into the night.

"Shouldn't take long?" I asked.

"Nope." She smiled at me in a way that made her sparkling white teeth jump out of the darkness. "My boss never hears about this, right?"

"That's right," I said.

"Then we're on. Where's my baby?"

SIXTY

SAM

Only one other house on Holly Malone's block seemed to be having people over for the holiday celebration. As far as Thanksgiving was concerned, this was a neighborhood of guests, not hosts.

Carmen and I took turns dozing off for the next couple of hours. On one of my turns awake I walked around the block, not so much because I expected to find anything going on as because everybody had been telling me that it was good for my heart to get my pulse up every once in a while.

I was beginning to suspect that Carmen was good for my heart, too, though the fact that she was sleeping right beside me in the car was distracting me in ways that left me uneasy. The minutes passed especially slowly as she napped, but it was okay. I spent a portion of the silent hours lost in a familiar cop reverie about evil, an evil that I felt was hovering over that South Bend neighborhood like a dark cloud in still winds.

Somewhere around six o'clock Carmen and I got confused about whose turn it was to nap. The second I opened my eyes I knew something didn't feel exactly right. It took me longer than it should have taken to realize that she, too, was snoozing.

"Activity," I said.

Carmen's eyes popped open. "What, what?"

"Activity."

The activity was the arrival of a minivan, an older Plymouth that had those tacky fake wood panels on the sides. It hadn't been washed since water was invented. The minivan had parked right behind the little Lexus, so our view of the ensuing disembarkation was partially obscured. Still, I could tell that a small crowd was forming on the sidewalk.

"The other sister," I said.

With some wonder in her voice, Carmen said, "My, she's fertile. Look at the size of . . ."

I counted five kids congregating on the sidewalk, but anyone who was shorter than three feet or so in height probably remained invisible to me because of the angle and the intervening Lexus.

"Two adults?" I asked.

Carmen said, "Yes. One mom and one dad. One, two . . . five kids. Or six? What do you get?"

I counted again. "I get six. How old is Holly's sister? She tell you that when you talked to her yesterday?"

"If this is the one I think, she's five years older than Holly. Jeez, Sam, think—that poor woman has been pregnant almost every other day of her life since her eighteenth birthday."

The members of Holly's oldest sister's brood were dressed like kids, in sharp distinction to Artie's offspring, who were dressed as though they expected a relative to die during dinner and Artie wanted to be certain they were prepared to attend an immediate funeral.

The newly arrived posse broke ranks as they moved toward Holly's front door. Running. Laughter. Teasing.

"Wait," Carmen said. "I get three adults now."

"Yep, me too. The blonde is Holly's sister?"

"I guess," Carmen replied. "Who's the other one, then, the woman with the dark hair?"

I didn't answer. Holly answered the door, and the passel of nieces and nephews funneled inside, followed by the blond woman and then the rotund brother-in-law with the big smile. Everybody got either a hug or a kiss or both. The woman with the dark hair stood patiently on that classic Craftsman-style porch holding a covered dish, waiting for her turn to arrive. Once her relatives were safely inside the house, Holly stepped out to speak with the woman. Holly's head was tilted to one side the whole time.

After listening for about thirty seconds, Holly took the woman by the elbow and guided her farther from the door. They talked for another minute or so, their faces only a foot apart.

"A friend? Neighbor?" Carmen conjectured.

"Maybe." I didn't want to come to any conclusions at that point. I wanted to observe.

The covered dish finally changed hands, some final words were spoken, and the woman stepped down from the porch without a hug or kiss from Holly. She walked down the sidewalk away from the house, which was also away from me and Carmen. Holly hesitated a second at the door before she stepped back into the house. Had she looked our way before she went inside? I wasn't sure.

I figured she figured I was close by.

I checked my cell phone to make sure it was on. It was.

"Want me to follow her?" Carmen asked.

She was talking about the covered dish lady. That didn't surprise me. She was asking me what I wanted her to do. That did. "Don't think so. You're probably right. Just a neighbor."

Carmen said, "I'm getting hungry. You?"

"Always. You think maybe we could get Holly to bring us a plate? Her turkey will come out of the oven soon. I bet they end up eating around seven, maybe a little after."

She reached into her purse and offered me an energy bar. "You might get a plate, Sam. Not me."

I shocked myself; I took the bar. "If I get any turkey and stuffing, I'll share," I said. "Promise."

* * *

Six forty-five. Night had arrived under slate gray skies.

I said, "Turkey's coming out of the oven right about now. I'm going to do a stroll around the block again, see if I can work up an appetite."

It had been a joke, but Carmen missed it. She put a hand on my arm. "We wasting our time?" she asked.

"Probably."

"How long can we last? Just the two of us, I mean? Tomorrow morning? What then?"

I'd thought about that, too. "I'm hoping something new develops with the investigation, something we can use to get the local police willing to help keep an eye on Holly. If that doesn't happen, I'll go talk to Holly again, see if I can get her to go stay with one of her sisters in Chicago for the weekend."

"I know which sister I'd choose."

"Yeah. Artie doesn't seem likely to have a dominant good-host gene, does he?"

"I'm sorry about your holiday, Sam."

"Company's good, Carmen. That helps."

She didn't miss that I said that. Her hand was still on my arm. The pressure changed. "Sam? Before you go, call Gibbs. Do you mind?"

"I didn't think you were that attached to Gibbs's well-being."

"I'm not. I was just thinking that if Gibbs has seen Sterling in Colorado, then we're all done here, right? You and me, we can pack up and go someplace together and, you know . . . eat."

My heart hiccoughed during the hesitation at the end of Carmen's sentence. Missed a beat? Double beat? I couldn't tell. "I can do that." I pulled out my cell phone, fit my reading glasses on my nose, checked for Gibbs's number in the memory, and dialed. She answered after three rings.

"Hello," she said.

The sound of Gibbs's voice moved me like the refrain of an old song. I knew it wasn't right that it happened that way. But it did.

"It's Sam. Hey, how you doing?"

"Did Alan Gregory tell you to call?"

What was that about? "Nah. Just wanted to be sure you're safe. We haven't talked. Where are you?"

"Vail. A motel."

"Is it pretty?"

"Low clouds. It's okay."

"Here, too. Low clouds. Gray."

"I hear the South is like that sometimes."

She sounded cryptic. Maybe she was aggravated to be alone on the holiday in a motel. I could relate to that.

"I'm not in Georgia anymore. I drove north. I'm up in Indiana."

"You are? Why on earth would you go to Indiana? Where?"

"Currently, South Bend."

"Really? Do you have family there? Is that it?"

"No, my family's up in Minnesota for the holiday. I'm following up a long shot. A tip we got. Probably a waste of time. You're okay? You haven't heard from Sterling? Seen him anywhere?"

"I guess I'm okay. I feel terrible that my problems have kept you away from your loved ones on Thanksgiving. You shouldn't have to do that. I wish you'd just go get on a plane and go be with your family. I'll pay. That would make me feel better. Will you do that? Just go to the airport right this minute?"

"No Sterling?"

"No."

"Well, I'm fine, Gibbs. Don't concern yourself with me. You try to make the best of your holiday, but stay vigilant, okay? You'll do that? Keep an eye out for Sterling. Give me a call if anything makes you nervous?"

"I promise. Good-bye, Sam."

I closed the phone. "He's not there."

Carmen said, "Thanks for trying."

I'd stiffened up. Let's say pulling myself from behind the wheel to get out of the car wasn't one of the most graceful things I'd ever done.

Holly's house had a three-foot chain-link fence around the backyard. Since the house was on a corner, it was possible to get a real good look around the entire property by strolling the sidewalk. With ten kids inside I could hear noise and laughter from the house half a block away. I turned around at that point and retraced my steps toward the house.

On my first pass around the corner nothing had seemed amiss. On the way back, though, the latch on the backyard gate had been moved to a different position. The gate hook was one of those horseshoe latches that raise up to allow the gate to swing open and then slide back down to horizontal to lock everything into place. I was sure it was down during my first pass.

It was up during the second.

I crossed the street and phoned Carmen.

"It's me. The latch on the back gate. You know the one?"

"The chain link?"

"That's the one."

"Yeah, I know it."

"Was it up or down when you last came by?"

"Couldn't tell you. Why?"

"It's up now. I thought I remembered it being down."

"There's a houseful of kids in there, Sam. One of them must have run outside for something."

"I guess. Can you see it from where you are?"

She hesitated. "No, I don't have a good view of the gate from here."

"I'll get back to you."

I crossed back across the street, waiting in the dark shadows of a big tree I thought might be an oak, and I watched the rear of the house. Laughter, chatter, kitchen activity. An occasional child's yell. Just what you'd expect.

Nothing more, nothing less.

It took me a few minutes of watching to recognize that something was missing.

Holly.

Holly was missing. Her two sisters were making frequent appearances at the sink that was under the kitchen window. But Holly hadn't made a single appearance since my first pass around the corner.

Not one.

I felt a sharp tug just below my rib cage and reflexively reached into my pocket to find the little brown bottle of nitro.

As I rolled it back and forth between my fingers, I continued to stare at the kitchen window. It had been dark for a while. Now it wasn't.

I saw one blond sister. Then the other blond sister.

No Holly.

I listened to the cacophony of voices.

No Holly.

That wasn't right.

I checked my watch. Four minutes after seven. I figured it was just about time to carve the turkey. I was guessing the brother-in-law who wasn't Artie would be doing the honors.

I strolled closer to the house and leaned against the corner of the detached garage that was about ten yards away across the little backyard. *Come on, Holly. Come on. Show your face.*

Talk to me.

I called Carmen again. "Holly go out the front door for any reason in the last few minutes?"

"No. What's up?"

"Maybe nothing. I've lost track of her."

"Sam, she's inside with her family."

"Yeah, I know that."

I flicked my reading glasses down, hung up, and searched for another number in my cell phone's memory. Found it.

Holly's number.

Four rings. Finally, a kid answered.

"May I speak to Holly, please?"

"Hold on," the child said. He or she threw the phone onto something hard. The resulting explosion in my ear was painful.

Come on, Holly. Come on.

A minute, a dozen different voices. A loud call of "Aunt Holly?" Another. Then, "Anybody seen Aunt Holly?"

Holly's voice anywhere in the mix? I didn't think so.

The child came back on the line, finally. "I can't find her. Can you call back, please?"

"Sure."

Just then someone shoved a dull knife up under my rib cage. Rotated it side to side. Did it again. Deep.

That's what it felt like, anyway. The pain took my breath away, literally. I did an inventory.

Pain in my neck or jaw? No.

Down my arm? No.

Sweaty? Yes, a little. Okay, quite a bit.

I unscrewed the top of the little brown bottle, popped a nitro under my tongue, and braced myself for the inevitable flush.

Here we go, I was thinking. *Here we go.*

SIXTY-ONE

ALAN

Tayisha was finished in five minutes.

She joined me where I was waiting for her in Diane's office.

"Don't be looking like your hemorrhoids are acting up," she said. "I won't charge you the whole thing. Tell you what, we'll make it . . . we'll make it two-fifty. How's that?"

For five minutes? I should have been grateful. Tayisha had cut her original price in half. It still seemed like a lot of money for five minutes of anything.

I started unpeeling bills. "I only have twenties. You know, the cash machine."

"We'll make it two-sixty, then. That'll work."

I finished counting to thirteen and held out a thick stack of bills. She snapped them from my hand, folded them once, and stuffed the wad into the back pocket of her jeans.

"The thing is going to work? You're sure?"

Any enterprise that required me to turn over a large quantity of cash in total secrecy tended to leave me feeling a little bit anxious.

"I tested it; it's all good." She eyed me the way people eye a friend after he insists he can drive just fine after a night out drinking. "You know what you're doing, right? You're not planning something stupid?"

I shrugged.

"Figures. I'll be back next week to sweep the rest of your building. Just save the equipment for me. Don't rough it up; it's fine stuff."

"Sure," I said. "Thanks. I appreciate your doing this on Thanksgiving."

She patted the back pocket on her jeans. "That's a car payment. It's a pleasure doing business with you."

Diane's office, like mine, has a solitary French door leading out to the backyard. That's the way Tayisha left the building.

Five minutes later it was also the way that Adrienne arrived.

Adrienne was my neighbor, she was Sam's urologist, and she was, most important, my friend. I'd chosen her to assist me that night for two reasons. One, she was a conspirator by character. Her life as a respectable, and respected, physician was a cover for her true calling as an anarchist. Second, she was on call for Thanksgiving anyway and had spent a good chunk of the day at Community Hospital, which was only ten or so blocks away. Since I'd already fed her son, I knew I wouldn't be pulling her away from a holiday dinner with him.

She was dressed as though she'd awakened in Boulder that morning and discovered the whole town had been moved to the Arctic. Scarf, hat, gloves. A down parka that made her look like the Michelin Man's little sister.

"This sort of thing doesn't happen to normal people, you know." That was Adrienne's version of hello.

"I never claimed to be normal people."

"A bug? Somebody planted a bug in your office?"

"I'm afraid so."

"Do you know who?"

"I do. A lawyer."

She perked right up. "A lawyer? We're trapping a lawyer? Hell, I'll get naked with you for that."

"That won't be necessary, Adrienne." She would have. I had no doubt. I was more curious about the associative stream that led her to make the offer than I was about the prospect of seeing her *au naturel*.

She sat down on Diane's sofa and said, "What do you want me to do? If I get a page from the hospital, though, I'm out of here. Just so you know. Today I'm the catheter queen. Who knew? If the nurses can't thread the needle, they call me. Sometimes I don't do a single emergency Foley in six months of call. Today I've inserted three Foleys in five hours. Must be a turkey thing. Whatever it is, one more and I'm calling Guinness."

I didn't want to hear about any dubious urological records. Foley catheters made me squirm.

"You're going to play a doctor," I said.

"It's a bit of a stretch, but I can do that. What kind of doctor am I?"

"A shitty doctor who just screwed up a procedure."

"Hardly," she said. "Who's my patient?"

"You'll see."

Her face lit up. She'd started playing along with me in earnest. That was when I knew I had her cooperation. "Am I a urologist? Precisely what did this mystery patient come to me to have examined?"

"You're a Denver urologist, but you live here in Boulder."

"Which means I'm a Denver urologist with taste."

"You screwed up a vasectomy. You cut a nerve or something, made a guy impotent."

She shook her head at my ignorance. "Sorry, hon, but that's not exactly how the anatomy works. To make a guy impotent during a vasectomy, I'd have to use a tomahawk instead of a scalpel." She proceeded to explain the complex physiology of erections and the precise surgical maneuvers involved in completing a vasectomy in much more detail than I ever wanted to know. Erotic it wasn't.

"Once we get started in there, could you simplify it a bit, Adrienne? This is for a lay audience."

"Don't worry, even though your way is pure science fiction, I'll play along. But you'd better hope there are no doctors in the front row of the theater."

We rehearsed for a few minutes. I checked my watch. It was fifteen minutes after four o'clock.

I'd told Jim Zebid that I would be handling an emergency prior to our Thanksgiving evening appointment. If he was planning to eavesdrop on the emergency session, he'd be in place outside already. I imagined him sitting in a darkened car on Walnut Street with his receiving unit finely tuned and a pair of good headphones over his ears.

"You feel ready?" I asked Adrienne.

"Just show me the stage."

"This way, madame. Break a leg."

Adrienne whispered, "You know this would never happen in real life? Me screwing up a procedure like this?"

"I know. Goes without saying."

SIXTY-TWO

SAM

The rules of nitroglycerin are simple. If one tiny tab under your tongue doesn't make your chest pain go away in a few minutes, you throw another little white pebble into your mouth. The instructions don't tell you to pray, but if you're still caressing that minuscule brown bottle after those first few minutes of center-of-your-world, center-of-your-chest agony, then it's likely you've already made contact with whatever version of God that you consider might be the most influential.

I was sitting, leaning up against Holly's garage, when I popped the second nitro. As a general rule, standing and nitroglycerin go together about like beer and chocolate. Not too well. That's why I was sitting.

I started thinking about Simon. That freaked me out.

As a way of distracting myself while I waited

for the second nitro to kick in and the pain under my ribs to ease, I re-focused on Holly's house. Artie was at the kitchen sink. I didn't take him for a roll-up-his-sleeves, get-his-hands-dirty kind of guy.

But no Holly. Still no Holly.

My head was pounding. After the flush and the disorientation, the next side effect of nitro is the headache. An ice-cream brain freeze and a big bass drum. It's that kind of thing, and it comes on instantly.

Artie walked away from the window. One of Holly's sisters took his place at the sink.

Holly?

I phoned Carmen.

"Any sign of her yet?"

"Sam, where the hell are you?"

"Behind the house."

"You don't sound too good."

"A little indigestion."

"How can you have indigestion? You haven't eaten anything."

"It was probably that energy bar thing you gave me. My body's not accustomed to healthy crap like that. Any sign of Holly?"

I heard a car door open, then slam shut. I turned my head and spied the Cherokee, but I could only see the front end from where I was sitting.

"No," she said. "Nobody's gone in or out of that house." Her tone announced that she was pissed off.

I could hear her walking. First the sounds came through the ear-piece of the phone, then gradually I could hear her footfalls through my other ear, the one that was uncovered. The steps grew louder, more determined. Finally, Carmen emerged above me. God, she was tall.

"I'm calling an ambulance," she said.

"No, no. It's getting better. I swear. The nitro's working. It is."

Was it? I couldn't tell. The pain wasn't gone. But I could almost breathe without gasping. That had to be a good sign.

I didn't want to get into another ambulance. Not on Thanksgiving. Not in South Bend.

She squatted beside me, adopting a posture that I knew I couldn't have managed after a year of dieting and daily yoga sessions.

She touched my face. "You're clammy."

"No, I'm Sammy."

She slapped me. A true little love pat.

"If you die out here after you talk me out of calling an ambulance, I swear I'll come to your funeral and piss on your grave."

"I'd love to see the surveillance tape on that."

She slapped me again.

The pain was easing. It was. The knife was out from below my ribs.

"I'm good," I said. "Just a little angina. Doc said I might have some angina every once in a while. That's what the nitro's for." The doc hadn't said that, but it sounded like something a doc might say.

She stared at me as though she didn't believe a word out of my mouth.

"I have a feeling Holly's not alone," I said.

"Don't change the subject."

"I'm serious. I think he might be in there. Sterling."

"Why?" Her solitary word was a simple question, but given its inflection, it was also a statement. The statement was *Don't be an asshole. Not with me.*

Not now.

I explained about watching the kitchen window and about my phone call to the house.

"Okay, how would he have gotten in?" she asked. Her inflection? I recognized it. It was the one I used to employ with Simon when he was younger and he blamed mishaps around the house on his imaginary friend, Tank.

"Maybe he went in when everybody arrived, you know? He snuck in the back door when the family was at the front. Isn't that possible?"

"Anything's possible."

Carmen was staring at me, not at the house. She thought my sneaking-in-the-back-door scenario was about as likely as Gibbs going to Wal-Mart to buy her winter wardrobe.

"Or Holly might have let him in," I added.

"What?" she said. The tenor had changed. It was more like: Now you're saying something interesting. Tell me.

"She likes danger—risk might be a better word. We know that, right? Sexually speaking, Holly Malone likes risk. That was the whole thing with Sterling in the first place."

Carmen nodded. She completed my thought as though we'd been partnering for years, not hours. "And doing it with an accused murderer while her family is gathering for Thanksgiving . . ."

I visualized Artie's disapproving eyes. "Yeah, that sounds risky enough. That would qualify."

"How long since you've seen her?"

"Ten, twelve minutes."

We were both staring at the house. My eyes were plastered on the window wells that led to the basement. That's where I figured they'd be, Holly and Sterling. In some room down there. For some reason I decided that it was the laundry room. An image of Holly propped up on the dryer began to develop in my consciousness until I shooed it away like some aggravating insect.

But like a yellowjacket in late summer, it came right back.

I was ready to move, to go inside the house, but I wanted Carmen to arrive at the same conclusion herself. While I waited for her to come around, I hit a speed-dial number on my phone. Lucy. "Hey, Luce. I just have a second. The feds ever find Brian Miles? . . . No? . . . Thanks. . . . Yeah, fine. Seriously. I'll call you in a bit." I hung up. "Miles is still missing."

Carmen nodded as though she expected the news. "You think they're together? Sterling and Miles?"

"Can't rule it out."

She said, "What about the car? Maybe they're doing it in the car. Have you checked the garage?" She nodded at the wall I was leaning against.

I felt stupid. I was so focused on the basement that I hadn't even considered the detached garage. And no, I hadn't checked the garage. I shook my head in response to Carmen's question, suddenly not wanting to risk having my voice carry through the bricks.

"Shall we?" she whispered.

I stood. My balance problems were gone. My headache wasn't.

Carmen hopped the three-foot fence as though it were the height of a curb. I stepped over using a more conventional scissors maneuver. Carmen's revolver was in her hand when she got to the side door of the garage. I pulled my gun, too.

I don't like my handgun. Some cops do. Some don't. I've never felt right with the damn thing in my hand. I'm a pretty good shot; that's not it. It's something more intrinsic that I've never understood. I'm more comfortable with a rifle or a shotgun pressed against my shoulder.

Carmen, on the other hand, held her Smith & Wesson with the comfort of a good cook holding her favorite knife over an onion. No ambivalence there at all.

Holly's vehicle was a late-nineties GM sedan. Through the hazy glass pane in the side door, I couldn't have identified whether it was a Pontiac or a Chevy or an Olds if my life depended on it. I could tell that it didn't seem to be moving—moving, as in rocking side to side.

Carmen turned the doorknob and entered the narrow garage in a single fluid motion that reminded me of a ballroom dance move. I was right behind her. Despite my adrenaline surge, I was thinking that I wouldn't want to be screwing in that car and have us burst into the garage with our guns drawn.

It could change a person's view of sex forever.

We covered the perimeter of the little rectangular space and the interior of the car in seconds and came to the same conclusion at the exact same time: The garage wasn't Holly's love nest.

"Okay," Carmen said. "I'm convinced. Let's go ruin a lot of people's Thanksgiving supper."

SIXTY-THREE

ALAN

As an actress Adrienne was a little over the top. I shouldn't have been surprised.

"Thanks for coming in to see me on Thanksgiving," she began. "I know it's a terrible inconvenience. The reason I needed to see you is that . . . I did something last week that . . . well . . . I can't get off my mind."

"I assumed it was important for you to have come all the way in from Denver." I realized my role in this drama was going to be entirely ad-libbed. And with Adrienne as the person responsible for hitting the ball over the net for me to return, I knew I was going to need to stay on my toes.

"I'm having trouble living with it, with what I did. And I don't know exactly what I should do next."

"Yes?"

If Jim Zebid was sitting outside listening, he

was—thus far—hearing a pretty convincing presentation. If he was somehow watching, however, he wouldn't believe a word of it. When she wasn't choking down some laughter, Adrienne was leaning over, talking into the couch pillow like Maxwell Smart with his shoe phone.

"I was doing a vasectomy on Tuesday in my Cherry Creek office—I do a thousand of them, they're no big deal. First a little poke, a little cut, snip-snip, burn-burn—"

Burn-burn?

"—stitch-stitch."

"Stitch-stitch" I understood just fine. I was still stuck on "burn-burn."

"Burn-burn?" I asked. I shouldn't have asked—it wasn't germane to the trap I was setting—but I really wanted to know.

"Cautery," she explained with a frown.

"Cautery," I repeated. A rapid personal inventory didn't reveal any pieces in that vicinity that I would be eager to have fried during the "burn-burn" segment of her operation.

Adrienne went on. "During the procedure I cut one of the guy's nerves."

"You cut a nerve?"

"By accident, just after the first little cut. One of my snips? My hand slipped a little."

"Your hand slipped during a snip?"

"Are you just going to repeat everything I say? Is that all you're planning to do? I say 'my hand slipped,' and you add a question mark? I could go talk into a tape recorder and just play it back and add my own question marks, save myself a lot of money."

I glared at her. My nonverbal admonishment didn't faze her, though; she was having a great time.

"What did he say?" I asked.

"He doesn't know. I didn't tell him. How the hell would he know? You think guys watch while I do vasectomies on them? There are some things a guy likes to see done to his genitals, but that isn't one of them. You're going to have to trust me on this."

I almost said, *"You didn't tell him?"* but thought that another repetition might be too much provocation for Adrienne to ignore. Instead, I said, "It was an important nerve?"

That question cracked her up. She took five seconds to compose herself before she was able to say "Down there? They're all pretty important. That's what I hear, anyway."

It was my turn to swallow laughter.

"Is he going to be . . . impotent?"

"It's possible."

"Likely?"

"Maybe likely." She rolled her eyes.

"Won't he know you did it?"

"I'm sure he'll suspect I had something to do with it. But it'll be hard for him to prove. He's had trouble raising the flag before. And he knew the risks going in."

Raising the flag?

She ruffled a piece of paper. "You know what this is?"

I did, of course, but I said, "No."

"His phone number. I know I should call him. That's what I should do. That would be the right thing. To let him know what happened. But then the next thing I know I'll be getting served some stack of incomprehensible papers by some damn bloodsucking lawyer who'll make one little mistake seem like the assassination of King Ferdinand."

That last line—the World War I allusion—was pure ad lib. It was definitely not in the script. Not even close. I was tempted to ask Adrienne to defend Francis Ferdinand's posthumous promotion from archduke to king, but restraint was indicated and discretion ruled.

She leaned directly over the pillow and made a great show of ripping the paper into shreds.

"So you've decided not to call him?" I asked. That line was in the script.

"I've been staring at that number for two days. I have it memorized." That's when she recited the phone number in a lovely, melodic little singsong. She couldn't have delivered the line any better if she'd rehearsed it for days.

I mimed some silent applause for her benefit.

A beeper chirped. It wasn't mine, which was set to vibrate.

Adrienne responded to the interruption by diving at the little backpack/purse she carried and said, "Shit, that's my pager. I have to

go, sorry. You've been . . . I don't know . . . 'helpful' isn't exactly the
right word, is it?"

I sat openmouthed.

She grabbed her things and skipped toward the door. The skip-
ping part wasn't in the script, either.

SIXTY-FOUR

SAM

"Back or front?"

I was standing with Carmen beside the gate in the chain-link fence in Holly Malone's backyard. Carmen had stopped my forward progress by placing her palm against my chest. To be more specific, her hand had come to rest on top of my left man-boob. A couple of inches below her hand my upper abdomen still ached from the angina or whatever it was. But the ache was dull, not sharp. I could live with it, I thought.

Figuratively, if not literally.

"The adults are all in the kitchen," I said. "We should probably just knock on the back door. We'll spook 'em a little bit, which is a good thing. And that way we don't have to fight through the whole bushel of kids at the front of the house." While I was speaking, I was also involuntarily sucking in my gut and tightening my chest muscles.

Carmen removed her hand from my chest. "You want the honors?"

"No, no. You go right ahead."

She pulled back the screen door and knocked. Artie opened the door with a carving knife in his right hand and a stern expression plastered on his face, as though he suspected that he'd just discovered that one of his dressed-for-church kids had snuck outside for something sinister, like fun, and he was planning to Jack-the-Ripper the child into submission as a lesson for the surviving siblings.

Through the open door I spotted Holly's two sisters lined up behind Artie. The other brother-in-law? Elsewhere.

Carmen said, "I'm Detective Reynoso. This is Detective Purdy. We'd like to speak with Holly Malone, please."

"I don't see any badges." For a moment I thought Artie might be a lawyer but quickly decided that he had merely watched a lot of TV. I was having more than a little trouble getting past the dancing-teapots apron he was wearing and the fact that he had his hands on his hips in some semblance of indignation. With the knife at the ready, he looked a lot like an angry, aging transvestite on a day that he forgot to put on his wig.

Carmen and I both flashed our badge wallets for Artie's benefit. All we offered was a bored, quick little flip/close. Nobody ever reads the damn things. I had forgotten mine one day in Boulder and just flipped open my regular wallet instead at someone's house. It turned out that my driver's license and a school picture of Simon worked just fine to get me in that door.

"Holly Malone, please." Carmen's voice was suddenly clipped into a no-bullshit tone that caused Artie to take a step back from her. "It's important. We spoke with her earlier; we know she's home."

The older of the two sisters appeared appropriately sobered by our presence at the door. She said, "A few minutes ago she went to take a quick bath and get dressed. I'll go find her."

With a what-did-she-do-now tone the younger sister, Artie's wife, asked, "Is she in trouble?"

Poor thing, she was actually asking Artie.

Before he could make a total fool of himself by pretending he knew how to answer her question, I intervened. "For something she did? No, ma'am. We just want to ask her a few questions."

Carmen leaned back toward me and whispered, "She's taking a bath, Sammy. I'm feeling kind of stupid."

"Yeah, well," I said.

I'd noticed that she'd called me Sammy.

But I wasn't feeling stupid. Not yet. There would be plenty of time for that later. The bath? What was I thinking about that? I was thinking, *What else was Holly going to tell her sisters? To please excuse her so that she could go down to the basement for a quick poke with a stranger who's probably a serial killer?* Tugging along immediately behind the locomotive of that thought came the unedited laundry room image of Holly on the dryer, followed by a cabooselike graphic still of what happened up in the organ loft after Holly and then Sterling climbed the stairs from the Chapel of the Reliquaries in the Basilica of the Sacred Heart.

Fortunately, all it took to make the prurient images vanish again was a quick glance at Artie in the dancing-teapots apron.

"Sir?" I said to him. "Feel free to go finish carving your turkey. This shouldn't take long, shouldn't interfere with your meal." I smiled. "We came to the back door so we wouldn't alarm the children."

My suggestion about returning his attention to the turkey served as a reminder to Artie that he was holding a long thin knife in a provocative manner while speaking with a pair of police officers. He glanced at the blade, then at us. His face at that moment was priceless—he was the guy going through security at the airport who'd just remembered he'd forgotten to take his Mac-10 out of his carry-on.

Oops.

Artie slowly moved the knife behind his back, as though Carmen and I wouldn't notice he was still holding the thing.

Good move, Artie.

Sometimes I really love my job. Put them under enough stress, and most people are endlessly entertaining.

Big sister returned ten seconds later, breathless. For the first few moments after she reentered the kitchen, she couldn't make her mouth work. I had already started looking around for the basement stairs when she finally cried out, "I couldn't find her. And the bathtub was dry."

Carmen was halfway through the door. She demanded, "The basement stairs? Where are they?"

My cell phone rang. I should've been following after Carmen and grabbing my handgun in order to mount a search-and-rescue mission to the basement, but I grabbed the phone instead.

The caller ID? I held it at full arm's length from my aging eyes. What did it read?

To Carmen, I said, "It's Gibbs."

Carmen instantly recognized the possible implications. She stopped in her tracks and stared at me. Her big gun dropped from the ready position until it was pointing vaguely at my feet.

Artie's wife asked, "Who is Gibbs?"

"Yeah," I said into the phone.

"He's here, Sam! Sterling is here. Oh my God. Oh my God. Help me!" Gibbs was frantic.

I pulled the phone away from my ear, covered the microphone, and said to Carmen. "Sterling's in Vail."

Artie's wife asked, "Who is Sterling?"

Carmen said, "So where's Holly?"

The big sister said, "She didn't take a bath. The tub's dry."

I lifted the phone back beside my ear just in time to hear Gibbs's frenetic whisper, "Help me!"

SIXTY-FIVE

ALAN

The house was calm when I got home from the two-act farce I'd produced at my office.

The meeting with Jim Zebid had been brief and relatively cordial. He seemed surprised by my revelation that some of the same lapses in confidentiality that had been plaguing my practice were also plaguing my partner's practice next door. I went into a long explanation about the design of the soundproofing of the interior walls of the offices and why we had ruled out the possibility of eavesdroppers. I then revealed that my partner and I were planning to interview the couple who cleaned the offices for us the next day, and that we suspected that one or both of them may have found a way to get into our locked filing cabinets.

I promised to let him know the results of our inquiries.

He thanked me as he left. Truthfully? I didn't

see a sign that he was playing along with me. He was a better actor than I was.

I helped Grace into her pajamas and told Lauren to keep playing pool, that I would happily read stories to Grace before bed. I checked the charge on my cell phone battery, stuffed the phone into the pocket of my corduroys, and settled into the big chair in Grace's room to read. She picked the same books that she picked every night—she was in a phase where she liked the idea of cardboard characters popping up at her as she turned the pages. Her current favorite was a tall skinny book full of multicolored, pop-up monsters. We read it twice—I admit that I did most of the reading—and her delight was no more muted the second time through than it had been the first.

That's when the phone rang in my pocket.

I kissed Grace, lowered her into her crib, opened the phone, wrapped it hastily in one of my daughter's lilliputian T-shirts, dropped my voice an octave, took a deep breath, and said, "Yeah?"

"You don't know me, but . . . but don't hang up."

"What?"

"How's your sc-scrotum feeling? Your . . . balls?"

"What the— Who's this?"

"Just listen to me. The doctor who did your vasectomy? She—"

"What the— How do you—"

"No, no, listen to me. She screwed up when she did it. She clipped a nerve. No, snipped, snipped a nerve. You may be . . . impotent. You need to get a lawyer, sue her ass. She's . . . out to get you."

"Who are you?"

"A friend. You can . . . trust me."

My friend hung up.

I did, too.

While I tried to still my pulse, I kissed Grace again, told her I loved her, and made sure her favorite stuffed toys were within her sight.

I walked back out to the pool table, told Lauren that Grace was tucked in and waiting for a good-night kiss, and then plopped down on the sofa in the living room.

The lights of Boulder twinkled in the dark at my feet.

Emily waddled in, her stubby tail darting around on her butt in a parody of wagging, her paw umbrella clacking on the wood floor with each fourth step. She stood in front of me for a moment, looked me right in the eyes, and then lowered her head onto my lap. Prior to joining me in the living room she'd apparently just completed a visit to her water dish, and her long beard was dripping with enough water to wash a small car.

She was telling me that things were going to be all right.

Her instincts about such matters were usually infallible, but this time I couldn't figure out how it was all going to turn out okay.

SIXTY-SIX

SAM

"Calm, Gibbs. Calm. Did you call nine-one-one?"

"Yes."

"What did you see?"

"In the parking lot—he—he got out of his car. I saw him."

"Sterling's outside? Is he alone?" I said, repeating some of what Gibbs told me so that Carmen would know what I was hearing. Carmen was standing three feet away. I watched her eyebrows jump up at the news about Sterling. "You're not sure. The lights in your room, are they on or off?"

"On."

"Turn them off. The TV, too. Shhhh. Quiet now."

"I'm scared."

"The door's locked, right? The chain, too?"

"Yes. Help me, Sam. Help me."

"Do you hear sirens yet?"

"No, no!"

Carmen's eyes told me she was puzzled, the kind of puzzled usually reserved for those times when you think you just heard your cat ask you for a beer.

"Shhhh," I told Gibbs. "Quiet voice. What floor are you on?"

"Um, uh. Third. Third story."

"Third story. Get on the floor, okay? On the far side of the bed, away from the door. Can you do that?" As soon as I told her to get on the floor, I remembered that she was on her cell phone and wished I'd sent her into the bathroom.

"Yes, yes. Help me."

"Sirens yet?"

"Uh, no. No."

The commercial section of Vail is a few blocks wide, a few dozen blocks long. That's it. A cruiser in a hurry could get from one end to the other in seconds. Where were they?

"You're on the floor, right, Gibbs?"

"Yes."

"You're doing good."

"Come help me."

"I'm in Indiana, Gibbs."

"I know. Come help me."

"Someone will be there any second."

I heard pounding. Gibbs said, "He's here, Sam. He's here. Oh no, oh no."

"Someone's there?" I mimed the act of knocking so that Carmen would know what Gibbs was saying. "It might be the police, Gibbs. Stay still. If you know it's him, run for the bathroom."

More pounding.

This time Carmen mimed the act of knocking. Then, inexplicably, she pointed down toward the floor.

For a long moment I was confused by Carmen's charade and then, suddenly, I got it.

Holy shit.

I lowered the phone from my ear, and my pulse rocketed as though my heart had a turbocharger on it.

I moved the phone back to my face and said, "Gibbs? Stay quiet until you're sure who it is. Don't open the door. Shhhh."

With the pad of my thumb firmly over the phone's microphone, I leaned over to Holly's oldest sister and whispered, "Get the kids and get out of the house. Now! Front door, everybody. Got a cell?"

She nodded.

"Call nine-one-one when you get outside. Tell them cops are in the basement and guns are drawn."

I looked at Artie.

His mouth was open. His brain wasn't.

He was staring at the big gun that was filling my hand.

"Artie?" I said, careful not to raise the hand with the pistol. "Put the knife down on the counter and follow your sister-in-law. Go on, get out of here."

Artie followed my directions robotically. I raised the phone back to my face.

"Gibbs, are you there?" I asked.

Nothing.

Shit.

SIXTY-SEVEN

ALAN

Maybe it was something she saw in my eyes, maybe it was something else entirely, but Lauren didn't even flinch when I told her I had to go back out on Thanksgiving night to see someone. She caressed my neck for a moment, kissed me in the lingering manner that more often than not constitutes an invitation, pulled away only an inch, and said, "Be careful. Please." Both dogs stayed by her side as I headed out the door.

Since my errand required that I pick something up at my office, I parked the car there before I strolled the short distance over to Pearl Street. I didn't take my usual pedestrian route, which would have led a block or more northeast in the direction of the Mall, but instead ambled westward toward the sleepy part of Pearl, the part that's on the side of Ninth nearest the mountains.

The wind was gusting from Wyoming that evening, the collar on my coat was up, and my hands were stuffed in my pockets to thwart the chill.

I walked slowly, trying to find a reason not to do what I was about to do. Whatever that reason might have been, though, I wasn't able to walk slowly enough to find it.

My destination was a cluster of condos on the north side of Pearl that had been designed to mimic a grouping of Victorian row houses. Wedding cake trim, different on every home, was painted in colors that had aged to a palate that resembled the range of hues of an Easter basket. Lights from the waning moments of holiday celebrations brightened windows in about half of the units that I could see from the sidewalk on the far side of Pearl. From the way the numbers were running, I figured I would find the town house I was looking for at the west end of the front row.

The lights in that unit were on.

Each week, when Lauren injects a long needle full of interferon into her thigh to protect herself from a double-cross from her own immune system, she uncaps the needle and plunges it straight into her thigh. "Every second of delay makes it harder to do," she says. "No delay."

So I didn't delay at the door. I didn't want this to be any harder to do than it felt like it was already. I took my left hand out of my pocket, extended a finger, and touched the doorbell.

He came to the door quickly, within seconds. I could see the shadow of his eyeball as it darkened the peephole. He didn't open the door quickly, though. He stood behind the closed door and watched me, and watched me, and watched me through the tiny lens embedded in the door.

I checked my wristwatch after a while and began timing our little standoff. In other circumstances, with another person, I might have chosen a strategy other than dawdling, perhaps peppering the doorbell with repeated pushes, or maybe calling out, "Come on, open the door."

But not then. Not with him. With him I stood back a step and allowed him to see me clearly. Every couple of minutes I pulled my hands from my pockets and turned completely around so that he could be confident that I wasn't hiding anything behind my back.

Six minutes and ten seconds passed before he finally relented to some internal pressure I probably couldn't fathom and opened the door. When the time came, he didn't open it just a crack. He flung it wide open as though that had been his plan all along.

His physical appearance was a bit of a shock to me. He was wearing gray cotton sweats on top of a nylon running suit, had dark glasses over his eyes, and had a bandanna tied over his mouth and chin like he was Jesse James preparing to knock over a bank.

"Hello, Craig," I said. "I think I have something of yours. Can we talk?"

"You're the one," he said. "You're the one."

Craig didn't invite me inside, which didn't surprise me. I sat on the steps leading up to his town house while we talked. The whole time he stood a few feet from me with his back to the front door. He was more wary of me than he was during our office visits, but I'd anticipated that he might be. The therapy session that Sharon Lewis had busted in on and aborted late the previous afternoon was certain to take a considerable toll on someone like Craig, especially in the trust-your-therapist department.

Within minutes of sitting down on Craig's porch I reached a clinical decision about what I needed to do, but I didn't decide exactly how to go about doing it until another fifteen minutes passed. When I explained my thinking to him, Craig was so agreeable with my plan that I guessed he'd arrived at some version of it himself long before I'd arrived at his door. I'd hoped he would be cooperative, but I was prepared to do it the hard way if I had to.

His anesthesiologist parents lived in a lavish house they'd recently built a few blocks away on Third Street. To their credit, they both rushed to their son's home within minutes when I phoned and told them what I had in mind.

Craig chose to take an ambulance to the psychiatric hospital across town, not to ride over with his parents. Although I didn't understand his reasons, I supported his decision. Reluctantly, his parents did, too. When I phoned for the ambulance, I requested that a police patrol car come by, as well. I hadn't placed a person on a seventy-two-hour mental health hold for a while, and I had to ask the patrol officer for remedial instruction on how to go about it. Despite the fact that Craig was agreeable to being admitted to the hospital, I didn't want him changing his mind and discharging himself before he was stabilized by the combination of medicine and a safe, controlled environment.

I didn't accompany the Adamson family to the hospital. As the ambulance drove off, I turned my collar back up, stuffed my hands back into my pockets, and commenced the short stroll back to my office. I had a few calls to make to assure medical backup for Craig's admission and to get initial orders to the nurses on the unit.

I'd see Craig again the next day as an inpatient. I thought I knew where the psychotherapy session with him would begin. Craig had already admitted calling me that night about Adrienne's fake malpractice case. He'd denied, however, that the listening equipment that had been planted in my office belonged to him.

That troubled me. That's where I thought we'd start.

SIXTY-EIGHT

SAM

Carmen and I could have lost some important seconds by engaging in a how-could-I-be-so-stupid contest, but we mutually decided not to bother. We both knew it would have ended up a draw.

If the Malone home was a good example of the breed, whatever elegance and purity of design the Craftsman-era architects had built into the floor plans of their bungalows did not extend into basement layout. Holly's basement was a dark, confusing warren of tiny rooms with low ceilings. The aroma in the cellar was of moist concrete, standing water, and air freshener. I thought it was the same flowers-in-a-can Glade that Sherry liked to make such a show of spraying after I used the bathroom.

On our way down to the basement I was a few risers above Carmen. The stairs didn't squeak as we descended. Not a peep, which I thought was evidence of rather impressive construction.

Rooms opened up onto each side of the postage-stamp-size landing at the bottom of the stairs. We paused at the landing, our bodies touching at our hips. The phone was still at my ear. Once again I whispered, "Gibbs?"

Nothing came back into the earpiece. I shook my head at Carmen. She nodded and tilted her head to the left, so that's the direction we headed first.

She was still walking point.

Cellar noises? Nothing I didn't expect. Furnace sighs, plumbing burps, old-house creaks. But no more pounding. Above us the scampering of feet as children and parents rushed from the house had stopped.

The first room to our left was a furnace room with an alcove that had a workbench built in under a window well.

In the dark basement my eyes found shapes but no details. As I followed Carmen toward the door that would take us to the next surprise space in the maze, my foot brushed something on the floor that I hadn't seen. Carmen heard the noise I made. She stopped.

I crouched down and felt along the cold concrete surface with my hand.

I lifted a woman's shoe. A clog. Not really a clog; Sherry used another name for shoes like it, but I couldn't remember what. Why? I really didn't care.

Had Holly been wearing clogs in the kitchen that morning? I should have remembered, but the picture in my head of Holly preparing the turkey didn't go all the way down to the floor.

Carmen leaned over to touch the shoe. Feeling what it was, she took it from me and set it aside. With her head close enough that I could feel her breath on my cheek, she said, "Let's go."

The next room was small and seemed to be full of stuff. Holly probably called it her storage room. But I could tell from the haphazard pattern of shadows that it was the place she stashed the junk she didn't know what else to do with. Storage is one thing. Sticking stuff in a room is another thing entirely. There's a big difference. Sherry did storage. I stuck stuff in rooms.

Carmen's eyes must have adjusted to the dark better than mine.

She found a path through the stuff, and we were across that room and through another door in seconds.

The next room we entered was a bathroom. A window well provided enough light that I realized that "bathroom" was a generous description for the space. It was a tiny concrete room with inelegant plumbing and a couple of fixtures that existed in the time warp between modern and antique. Despite the shadows I could see streaks of rust on the porcelain surfaces of both the sink and the toilet.

Carmen reached behind her and held out her hand to stop my progress. Her fingers found me just below my belt.

It certainly stopped my progress.

Through the open door in front of Carmen I could see a square shape emerging from the darkness.

A washing machine. Maybe a dryer.

Here we go, I thought. *Here we go.*

I retraced all my steps to the landing at the foot of the stairs and opened the door that Carmen and I hadn't taken the first time. The room I entered was the largest room in the basement and was furnished with somebody else's things. A night-light spread a shadowy brilliance across its lowest reaches. From the looks of the bases of the pieces, I guessed that these were Holly's grandmother's things. Every one—sofa, chest, chair, table—was ornate, heavy, grandmothery.

Four long strides, and I was across the room and standing at the door that I was almost certain led into the laundry room. Carmen was waiting at the other door on the far side of the basement.

My role was straightforward. I was to keep anyone from exiting through this door until I went in on Carmen's signal. That was the plan.

From then on we would improvise. And hopefully try not to shoot each other in the process.

The phone call with Gibbs was over. I'd stuffed the cell back in my pocket.

My handgun was ready.

I was wondering precisely what the signal was going to be when I heard Carmen yell, "Police! Freeze!" and figured that was probably it.

I pulled open the door and stepped inside the laundry room in a flash, though it turned out there was little cause for hurry.

SIXTY-NINE

ALAN

It was a night of front porches.

Diane and I have an ancient oak swing on the porch of our building, and from half a block away I could see that it was moving to and fro in a tight arc. A solitary person sat smack in the middle of the seat.

I was guessing it was a homeless man. I pulled five bucks from my wallet, remembered what day it was, and replaced the five with a twenty. I held the bill folded in my hand. In my Thanksgiving fantasy the man would use the money to sit at a nice table in a nice restaurant and treat himself to a bountiful plate of turkey and stuffing.

The porch was in shadows. From the end of the driveway I couldn't make out the age or gender of the visitor.

Nor did I recognize the voice when he said, "I didn't expect to see you here tonight. You should be home with your family. I know I wish I was."

I stopped walking. "Excuse me. Who are you? Do I know you?"

The swing stopped moving, and the man stood. He was still in the shadows, but I could tell that he wasn't tall. "I brought you something. An explanation." He waved some paper at me. An envelope, maybe. "I thought it might help save somebody. I was just going to stuff it through the mail slot when I saw your car. Felt the engine; it was warm. I thought I'd take a chance that you'd be coming back."

"I still don't know who you are." I hadn't moved. I remained right where I'd been on the narrow driveway. Ten yards of drought-starved lawn and a border of unhappy euonymus separated me from the stranger on the porch.

He moved forward inch by inch, and with each inch the light from the streetlamps seemed to crawl up his body like water rising in a flood.

As the light moved up from his shoulders and began to paint his face, I said, "Oh my God."

"Hi," Sterling Storey said. "What a week it's been, huh?"

What did I think?

I thought, *Catch me.*

SEVENTY

*At first, Holly didn't even notice the woman with
the covered dish. The chaos associated with the
arrival of her oldest sister's family for Thanksgiving dinner was demanding all of her attention.
The woman with the dark hair and the perfect
skin and the casserole waited patiently through a
procession of hugs and kisses, waited until no one
remained on the porch but the two of them.*

"Holly?" she said.

"Yes."

*"Remember your friend from church? From
the basilica?"*

Holly hesitated. Could she mean . . . ?

"He said to mention the organ."

She could. "Uh, yes. I remember."

*"He's around the corner. Right this minute.
He'd like to see you again."*

She stammered, "I have guests."

*"He knows. He wants to see you while they're
here. In your house. He thinks it will be fun.
Especially fun."*

Holly took the woman's elbow and guided her a little farther from the door.

"Who are you? What do you want?" Holly emphasized "you."

"I want to watch. That's what I want."

"Watch?"

"At Notre Dame I was the woman in the purple suit. Remember me?"

Holly remembered. "My family . . . what—"

"Move them into the living room for a picture. Everybody. He and I will come in the back, go down into the basement. We'll know when, because you'll turn off the kitchen lights."

"And then . . . what?"

"Before dinner you excuse yourself, say you're going to take a bath. He'll be waiting downstairs. Me too."

At that moment Holly felt an explosion of anticipation. She felt it as she might feel the wind, or an ocean wave. It washed over her, covered her completely, engulfed her.

"Take this," the woman said, handing over the casserole.

"What is it?"

"Some music. Some directions. Put it on, and turn it on as soon as you get to the basement. I should go. Someone may be watching us."

Holly could barely breathe through the moist heat of expectation. She watched the woman go down the sidewalk and chanced a glance at the Cherokee with Colorado plates on the next block.

She went back inside. Fear?

Hardly.

Anticipation.

She peeked inside the casserole and saw the Walkman.

Her pulse shot way north of normal.

Once again she was off on an adventure. She was about to dash across the Brad Pitt line, again.

The family picture was a fiasco. Holly turned off the kitchen lights and herded everyone into the living room. Getting the ten children in place was like trying to get a bunch of houseflies to soar in formation.

Photos taken, Holly pulled the turkey from the oven, asked her oldest sister to remove the stuffing, and excused herself for a quick bath.

Instead of going into the bathroom, though, she scurried down the stairs, stopping halfway down to pull the headphones on and to hit the button on the Walkman marked "play."

Her voice, not his. The music in the background? Chant. Gregorian chant.

Nice.

"Bottom step? See the duct tape? Wrap a long strip around your head, covering your mouth. Good. Now do another. We're in the laundry room. Before you join us, take another strip of tape and bind your wrists. It's not easy to do, but I've done it. You can do it, too." Pause. "It's what he wants. What do you want?"

A few moments of silence, then:

"Are you ready, Holly? When you're ready, open the door to the laundry room. And come on in."

SEVENTY-ONE

SAM

I expected worse.

I was prepared for a whole mess of blood. I expected to find Holly's head bashed in—for some reason, that's how I thought she would be killed—but I was wrong. Holly's wrist and ankles were bound, and she was gagged. Duct tape. She was sitting on top of the washing machine, not the dryer, and her pose was absurdly proper, significantly less erotic than the laundry room loop that had been playing relentlessly in my brain.

A Walkman hung from the waistband of her skirt, earphones in place on her head.

Gibbs? She sat across the room in an alcove barely large enough for an orange plastic chair that would have been labeled for a buck at a yard sale and would probably have gone unsold at the end of the day. Her legs were crossed, left over right. She was gripping a kitchen knife with a five-inch blade—a good knife, she'd probably brought it from home—in her right hand. A cell phone rested on her lap.

She looked as lovely as she had the first time I met her. But that didn't matter to me at all this time. Not a lick.

Right.

"Let me go, Sam," she said. It was as though Carmen and Holly weren't even in the room.

Gibbs had two handguns pointed at her chest—mine and Carmen's—and yet she'd managed to make her request sound perfectly mundane, like she and I were out on a date and she was wondering if I'd mind getting her a beer.

"Drop the knife, Gibbs," I said. I'd like to say I barked the order. Or yelled it. But I didn't. I merely said it.

"If you don't let me go, Sam, I'll kill myself. I will. I'll plunge this right into my chest."

Where did my head go at that moment? For some reason I thought about those crazy people who destroyed art treasures in museums. Like the guy who took a hammer to Michelangelo's *Pietà*. I thought, *Gibbs, no! You can't!* But I also knew—instantly—that my silent protest wasn't about Gibbs, the person. It was about Gibbs, the lovely art.

Crazy.

"Drop the knife, Gibbs," I said.

She purred, "Come on, Sam. Hey . . ."

Carmen joined the discussion. She crowed, "Jesus H. Christ," took a little skip-step into the fray, and swatted the knife out of Gibbs's hand. The blade clanked against the wall and tumbled to the floor. "Cut herself? Shit! This princess? She wouldn't even use the wrong eyeliner on herself."

I kicked the knife even farther from Gibbs. I was feeling kind of stupid.

"So she gets to live," Gibbs said.

I assumed she meant Holly but didn't say anything at first. I thought it might be wise to leave the next move to Carmen.

Carmen immediately started the you're-under-arrest process with Gibbs, cuffing her and searching her and reciting Miranda to her like a bored schoolgirl spitting out the Gettysburg Address to a class full of kids who didn't really care.

I began the process of gingerly removing the tape from Holly's mouth. It wasn't coming off easily.

Miranda complete, I asked, "Why, Gibbs? Why does she get to live?" Part of me cared about the answer, part of me was trying to cover my embarrassment over the knife thing. All of me knew that whatever Gibbs said in reply would just be noise.

"Because you got here first. That's the only reason. If I had called you five minutes sooner, you would have rushed back to Colorado to save me. You know you would have, Sam. But you came in the house, you came down here . . . Timing. It was just a problem with timing." Her voice trailed away. "She wanted Sterling, you know? They all did. That wasn't the deal. One time only, that was the deal."

Suddenly I got it. I faced her. "Were you in the basilica that day, Gibbs? At Notre Dame? Up in the choir loft?"

Carmen stopped what she was doing.

I glanced at Holly. Above the duct tape, her eyes were wide.

Gibbs smiled. She actually smiled. "Of course I was." She looked right at Holly. "Chanel suit? Purple? You remember me? She wanted him to come back again. She e-mailed him *again*. That wasn't the deal. She knew the deal. She'd agreed to it."

I got it all. Every bit of it.

"The deal?"

"Yes. The deal."

That's what I meant about the noise. My phone rang.

I checked the caller ID. Alan.

"Yeah," I said.

Alan's voice was full of rookie-cop wonder. "I'm at my office with Sterling Storey, Sam. You're not going to believe this: He says he thinks Gibbs has been killing all those women."

"Just a sec." I turned to Gibbs. "Guess what? Your husband survived the Ochlockonee. He's in Boulder, and he just gave you up to your doctor. Is that romantic or what?"

An army of footsteps erupted above my head. The locals had arrived to take over.

SEVENTY-TWO

The question of which jurisdiction was going to get first dibs on Gibbs would keep a whole lot of county attorneys across the country busy for a while. Other than hoping that Boulder didn't win that particular lottery, I wasn't invested in the outcome.

I spent a couple of hours answering questions for the South Bend police, who seemed to have suffered amnesia about their decision not to keep an eye on Holly Malone, and then I prepared to leave Indiana.

First I kept my promise and called Lucy, letting her know what had transpired in South Bend. She was astonished at the developments. She had some news for me, too, though: The feds had finally tracked down Brian Miles. They'd found him in a big suite at a fancy hotel in the Bahamas where he was on vacation.

Not surprisingly, Carmen had learned more about what had really happened than I had.

When I found her after my interview, she told me that it had indeed been Gibbs, in disguise, who had delivered the Walkman and the duct tape to Holly in the covered dish on the front porch of the Craftsman bungalow. Gibbs's pitch? She had promised Holly a visit by Sterling, who was offering a carnal encounter in the basement while the turkey was resting on the kitchen counter upstairs. Gibbs instructed Holly to wear the Walkman and follow all the instructions she heard to the letter, which included directions on binding and gagging herself with the tape.

Wow.

I told Carmen I was leaving town and offered her a ride as far as O'Hare in Chicago. She declined. She was determined to stay in South Bend in case there were any loose ends to tie up. What else? She didn't say so, but I think she still wanted to find that South Bend detective who had called her "ma'am" and then blown her off about Holly's peril. She wanted to help Orange County win the Gibbs Storey lottery. And she made me promise to tell her what really happened that day between Gibbs and Sterling in the Basilica of the Sacred Heart at Notre Dame.

Carmen and I ended up saying good-bye on the sidewalk outside the South Bend PD in one of those poignant moments that I haven't had many of in my life since I left college. I admit it crossed my mind that had I lingered a little longer in South Bend, Carmen and I might have had only one room that night at the Days Inn, not two.

That was the main reason for staying.

It was also one of the two main reasons for leaving.

The other?

Simon.

I filled the tank in the Cherokee and pointed it toward Minnesota.

I napped away most of the next morning in Angus's den, and then Simon and I spent a wonderful Friday afternoon arguing whether having turkey and cranberry sandwiches while watching college football the day after Thanksgiving was almost as good as having turkey and stuffing while watching the Lions lose on Thanksgiving.

I lost the argument. I didn't care.

Sherry and I talked after Simon was in bed for the night. We said what we had to say to each other in about five minutes. I gave Angus a big hug, declined his offer of a bed, and headed south on Interstate 35. I ended up spending the night in a Super 8 in Mason City, Iowa.

Things were feeling a whole lot clearer.

SEVENTY-THREE

ALAN

It was my first trip to Omaha, ever. Given that it was the Sunday of Thanksgiving weekend and given that I was flying standby, I felt lucky to get there at all.

A taxi took me to Sam, who was flat on his back in the University of Nebraska Medical Center. A Puerto Rican nurse named Yashira was being much nicer to him than he deserved. She was refusing to even try to find his "lost" car keys unless he arranged for somebody to drive him back to Colorado.

The somebody was me.

"It felt just like the heart attack. Maybe worse."

"That's what I've heard."

The day before, around lunchtime, Sam had started passing a gallstone he didn't even know he possessed and had driven himself to the emergency room in Omaha thinking he was having another MI. Two hours of agony in the ER provided enough time for the stone to move on, a one-night stay in the hospital for observation convinced the docs that Sam's heart was stable, and my presence in Nebraska motivated Yashira to search a little bit harder for his missing car keys.

While I was still trying to find my way out of Omaha, I summed up the obvious. "Kidney stones, gallstones, and heart disease. You're a picture of health, my friend."

"Stress might have something to do with it," he said.

"You think?" I replied.

"That, and the fact I'm fat. Though I might have lost a few pounds. Can you tell?"

Before I found the westbound entrance to I-80, we'd talked a little about Sam's day-after-Thanksgiving trip up to Minnesota, and I'd answered all his questions about Lauren's health and the long-term efficacy of Emily's paw umbrella. The Gibbs and Sterling Storey saga was a little more complicated, though; covering that ground took us almost all the way to Lincoln.

Sterling's story didn't surprise Sam. I'd started, of course, at the river in Georgia with Sterling's contention that he was washed downstream maybe a quarter of a mile before he pulled himself out.

"The Ochlockonee," Sam had said. "Tell me something. Did he really go down there to help that woman in the minivan?"

"He says he did, but who knows? I don't think Sterling exactly found God over the past week, Sam. He's still the same guy he was when he was flying around the country having extramarital sex with strange women."

"Not just extramarital: recreational. Hell, not just recreational: extreme."

"Yeah?" I was curious but decided to proceed without the details. "Anyway, an old man with a semi full of chickens gave Sterling a ride as far as Montgomery. He had enough cash with him to make his way back to Colorado to talk to Gibbs."

"He knew she was setting him up?"

"By then, yes. She basically told him when he was in Tallahassee. He says Gibbs is smart, and he figured she'd done a great job of pinning the murders on him. He came back to Boulder to talk with her, try to straighten things out, see if he could get her to admit what she'd done before your colleagues found him. When he couldn't find her, he came by my office to give me his side of the story, hoping I could help influence her to give herself up. Then he was going to see a lawyer on Friday, turn himself in, and try to get her picked up. That was his plan, anyway. What a mess."

"Did he know?" Sam asked. "What she'd been doing?"

"He says he didn't. In fact, with the exception of Louise—the woman in California—he didn't even know that any of the women he'd . . . you know, had these things with . . . were dead. When the women recontacted him to arrange a follow-up sexual encounter, Gibbs took the message. She was always the liaison anyway. That was her role."

"Her role?"

"She set everything up for him with the other women. And then she watched. She liked to watch."

Sam sighed deeply, as though he were trying to get something toxic out of his lungs. "She watched? She told you this?"

"I can't tell you what she told me. What I'm able to talk about I got from Sterling."

"There's something I don't understand," Sam said. "After all these years, why did this bust open now?"

"After their move back to Boulder a few months ago, Sterling decided he didn't want to be married to Gibbs anymore."

"Ah," Sam said. "So she was going to lose him anyway. All her efforts at eliminating the competition were for naught."

"Exactly. She was determined to make sure she didn't lose him to another woman, though."

"What was your part?" Sam asked me. "Why'd she bring you in?"

"I've been wondering about that. Clinically, I can't comment. But criminally? I think she needed somebody to help her play the battered wife card. She figured I'd do it." I sighed. "She figured right. And she wanted someone she could tell things to, somebody who couldn't tell the cops. And let's face it, indirectly she used me to get you involved."

"She needed a channel to the police. I obliged. Gibbs fooled you about where she was the whole time, too, didn't she?"

"She fooled me about a lot of things, Sam. I was in a better position than anybody to figure out what she was up to, and I didn't see this coming. I thought she was the victim in that relationship. I was blind to it."

"Me too," he said. "She's good at smoke screens, Gibbs is. She's so pretty, that's part of it." From Sam that constituted quite a confession. I waited, but he didn't elaborate. He repeated his earlier question. "But she fooled you about where she was?"

"Yeah, I thought she was in Vail."

"That's what she told me. You know something? Before cell phones? She never could have pulled it off. Flying to the Midwest while we thought she was in the Colorado mountains? Used to be a phone number meant a place. Doesn't anymore. Doesn't mean shit."

Sam seemed to need a moment to lament some loss of societal innocence. After a mile or so of silence I filled him in on what had really happened with the listening device in my office.

"So it was the lawyer who did it?" was Sam's reply to my story, as though he'd known it all along.

"Yeah. With his bug in place he'd overheard this other patient of mine—he's a really vulnerable guy—and then he talked him into doing some of the dirty work, but it was the lawyer who planted the bug and set it all up. He wanted to get even with Lauren for something that happened in court last summer. Figured he had a foolproof scheme."

"You turn him in?"

"I gave it all to Lucy. She's been great. I have some fences to mend with my patients, but . . ."

"You won't tell me the lawyer's name, but I'll see it in the paper, right?"

"Something like that."

"Will I be surprised?"

I thought about that for a moment. "No, not really."

"The other guy, the vulnerable one—how's he?"

I'd visited Craig in the hospital the day before. I said, "He's not doing too well."

"I'm sorry."

He sounded sorry. It made me think about the waitress in Gold Hill, the one whose hand Sam had been holding since her sexual assault in the back of the van on the way to the frat house on the Hill. Maybe Sam was thinking about her, too.

We made it all the way across Nebraska—it's a wide state—and were paralleling the Platte River on the stretch of Interstate 76 between Ogallala, Nebraska, and Julesburg, Colorado, before we got around to talking about Sherry. The conversation was a little cryptic at first.

"You want to talk about Sherry?" I asked.

"No," Sam said. "Not really."

That was the first installment in its entirety.

A hundred and twenty-five miles or so later I cut off I-76 at Hudson for the final westward push into Boulder. I could've spent the whole drive beating my head against the wall of Sam's stubbornness, but all I would have learned is how good it felt when I stopped.

Sam said, "In case you're wondering, I don't believe that talking helps."

I hadn't been wondering. But I was eager to hear his thoughts on the matter. "Yeah?"

"Sherry thinks talking about things makes them better. Round and round we go. Me? I don't think so. Words don't heal. Time? Maybe. Words? No."

I thought he was making a veiled editorial comment on my chosen profession, but rather than taking the bait, I waited to see where he'd go next.

I had to wait a while—about twenty miles—until we crossed I-25 at Dacono. We were getting close to home.

Sam said, "Sherry and I are done. I'm moving out."

"You are?" I didn't have any trouble keeping the surprise out of my voice.

"Yeah. She's been seeing somebody."

"She has?" This time my voice was nothing but surprise.

"I've known about it. The affair. A guy came in to buy flowers for his wife, that's how she met him. He's a psych professor at the university. I followed him to work one day, that's how I know."

He'd emphasized the guy's profession, as though he wanted to spoil the air with the innuendo that the field of psychology had something to do with his problems. I wondered if I knew the man responsible for making Sam a cuckold. I hoped not.

"Did she know you knew?" I asked.

"No. I thought it was a thing. That it would pass. I still think it will pass. The affair's not the reason the marriage is over."

"What is?"

"Ask her? I'm a difficult guy. Ask me? I put up with a lot. Too much. She'd probably say the same, of course. That she put up with a lot from me. But I put up with a ton from her over the last few years. I did."

I recalled the tense visits I'd witnessed in the hospital. "What are you talking about? Criticism? What?"

His answer took a moment to compose. "There's a point where criticism stops and something else starts. Something more serious. More demeaning, damaging, you know? Somewhere near there was . . . us."

"Are you talking about . . . abuse, Sam? Sherry . . . did what?"

"Next topic, Alan. I said what I'm going to say."

Sometimes friendship means inquisitiveness, sometimes it means silent respect. I had a thousand questions. I asked none of them.

But Sam answered one that wasn't even on my list. "I almost had an affair, too. Over Thanksgiving."

I quickly catalogued the likely suspects. "Detective Reynoso?"

"Turns out we get along."

I glanced over at him. I was checking to see if he was joking. He wasn't. "Why didn't you?"

"Hadn't talked to Sherry yet. But . . . I've talked to her now, so who knows? California's not that far away. I like the beach."

I didn't know Sam had ever seen a beach.

"And you like Carmen?"

"Yeah, I do. Don't know how much that means. I loved Sherry. What good did it do?"

I hit the brakes to avoid running up on an old primer-covered Dodge truck that was pulling a long trailer piled high with hay.

"I'm sorry, Sam. About Sherry."

"Ever feel like you're playing the same music you were playing as a kid? When girls first became real? Where women are concerned, I don't know that I've progressed much in thirty years."

Sam's words transported me back to Teri Reginelli and *¡Dios mío, hay un hacha en mi cabeza!* I knew that the Gibbs Storeys of the world were still capable of capturing my feet in the quicksand of my

adolescence, but I desperately wanted to believe that I had developed
the maturity to pull myself back out. Before I had a chance to get lost
any further in that old swamp, Sam yanked me back to the present.

"You know what? Sherry and me? We had a good thing. And
then one day we didn't. It's been bad now almost as long as it was
good."

"Simon?"

"We'll do okay with him. We will. We're not idiots."

"You want to run anything by me about his reaction to all this,
I'm happy to listen."

"Yeah, thanks. If the phone doesn't ring, that's me."

I laughed.

"Marriage is a weird thing. Gibbs and Sterling—what was that?
All the screwing around they did. And Holly Malone? The good
Catholic girl from South Bend? Her and her husband? What were
they up to with their shenanigans? You and Lauren seem like you're
rock solid, but I know you're not. God only knows what sexual per-
versity the two of you are into."

I opened my mouth.

He held up his hand. "God knows, Alan—I don't want to."

The car lurched and hopped as we crossed two sets of railroad
tracks. "You're allowed to hit the brakes, you know, before you hit
the bumps," Sam said.

Metaphor? With Sam, I could never be quite sure. "I'll remember
that," I said.

"I know you're not," he repeated. "Rock solid, I mean."

"It's a challenge, Sam. For us, for everybody."

"I'm glad we agree on that. Because I don't really want to talk
about it after this."

I said I was sorry again about him and Sherry. He pretended to ignore it.

He said, "You see the papers? They found that woman who shut
down DIA. She's from Boulder. Figures. I wouldn't want to be her."

Thanks to a brilliant moon the mountains were looming large
against the night sky. The delta shapes of the Flatirons remained in-
distinct. It didn't matter. I could feel Boulder long before I could see it.

ACKNOWLEDGMENTS

Thanks to Jane Davis, Sharon Stein, Stan Galansky, Chuck Lepley, Elyse Morgan, Al Silverman, Patricia and Jeffrey Limerick, and Nancy Hall.

Enduring gratitude goes to my editor, Kate Miciak, and to my agent, Lynn Nesbit.

Rose, Xan, and my mother, Sara White Kellas—after a dozen of these I'm running out of ways to say thank you. You leave my heart full.